# Praise for Stuart Nadler's
# *The Inseparables*

"In this beguiling novel, three generations of articulate, self-aware women fall to pieces. Elderly Henrietta copes with the death of her husband and the hideous resurfacing of a famously filthy novel that she wrote years earlier. Her daughter, Oona, heads into a painful divorce. And Oona's teenage daughter, Lydia, is distraught when a nude picture of her goes viral. With a fine understanding of women and a delicate wit, Nadler shepherds all three through grief and humiliation and out the other side." —Kim Hubbard, *People*

"Simultaneously probing and hilarious."
—Kevin Nance, *Chicago Tribune*

"There is much to enjoy about this book. I laughed out loud.... But the most memorable moments examine the intricacies of familial love—the bonds between mothers and daughters, men and women, boys and girls.... Nadler's writing is carefully rendered, unpretentious, and always with the reader's satisfaction on the front burner."
—Ann Leary, *New York Times Book Review*

"Serious, empathetic, respectful.... This is a novel deeply concerned with how these women have been shaped by their relationships with men. But Nadler is also clearly interested in offering these women the opportunity to define themselves and their relationships anew.... *The Inseparables* is elegantly written and often funny and sharply insightful.... This story is ripe for thought and discussion." —Eleanor Brown, *Washington Post*

"Nadler writes with tenderness and empathy.... *The Inseparables* feels urgent, but without losing its warmth and humor."
—Daniel Johnson, *Paris Review*

"One of my favorite novels of the year.... Gentle and funny and cutting. We see how the family came together and eventually how it starts to fall apart, how these disasters both big and small befell these women and how they're going to find a way forward."
—Liberty Hardy, *Book Riot*

"The best fiction illuminates life's realities, and Stuart Nadler spotlights the fact that we all skate on a very thin edge between joy and sorrow, respectability and shame, life and death.... For all the serious topics this book tackles, Nadler takes a light tone. He doesn't preach; he reveals."
—Martha Sheridan, *Dallas Morning News*

"Incisive.... A sharply written exploration of feminism in the digital age."
—*Condé Nast Traveler*

"A comic, trenchant novel."
—Heller McAlpin, *Barnes & Noble Review*

"Nadler's work taps into a classic strain of literary fiction: one that picks apart the messiness of emotions and human connections and finds resonant drama within."
—Tobias Carroll, *Men's Journal*

"Nadler's female protagonists are so fully formed and relatable that readers may be surprised to realize the author is male. *The Inseparables* braids the stories of these generations, creating an emotional landscape that draws the reader into each character's world."
—Carla Jean Whitley, *BookPage*

"Stuart Nadler's savage wit and incendiary insights mix in this brilliant, funny, and deeply moving novel to give us a glimpse into the generational moment we're all living in. This is a novel about how our culture treats sex, and the lives—and rights—of women of any age."

—Alexander Chee, author of *The Queen of the Night*

"A droll, warm, and trenchantly observant comic novel.... Its generosity of spirit and its fascinating trio of women in crisis help make *The Inseparables* the smartest and most touching romantic comedy you won't find at a multiplex movie theater this summer."

—Gene Seymour, *Newsday*

"*The Inseparables* is funny and sad and so wise about so many things—sex in the modern age, feminism, food, ambition, animals, marriage, mothers and daughters. Fathers and daughters too, for that matter."

—J. Courtney Sullivan, author of *Saints for All Occasions*

"Nadler truly dazzles.... Love this writer. Love these characters."

—*Kirkus Reviews*

"By turns funny, thoughtful, and heart-wrenching, *The Inseparables* is a deeply satisfying saga of mothers and daughters, sure to be a hit with book clubs. Stuart Nadler writes with clear-eyed confidence, keen insight, and great empathy for his characters."

—Jonathan Evison, author of *The Revised Fundamentals of Caregiving*

"*The Inseparables* introduces you to three generations of totally complex and totally compelling women." —*Cosmopolitan*

ALSO BY STUART NADLER

*Wise Men*

*The Book of Life*

# The Inseparables

*A Novel*

## Stuart Nadler

BACK BAY BOOKS
Little, Brown and Company
*New York Boston London*

Copyright © 2016 by Stuart Nadler
Questions and topics for discussion copyright © 2017 by Stuart Nadler and Little, Brown and Company

Back Bay Books / Little, Brown and Company
Hachette Book Group
1290 Avenue of the Americas, New York, NY 10104
littlebrown.com

Originally published in hardcover by Little, Brown and Company, July 2016
First Back Bay trade paperback edition, July 2017

Back Bay Books is an imprint of Little, Brown and Company, a division of Hachette Book Group, Inc. The Back Bay Books name and logo are trademarks of Hachette Book Group, Inc.

The Hachette Speakers Bureau provides a wide range of authors for speaking events. To find out more, go to hachettespeakersbureau.com or call (866) 376-6591.

Library of Congress Cataloging-in-Publication Data
Nadler, Stuart.
    The inseparables : a novel / Stuart Nadler.—First edition.
      p. cm.
  ISBN 978-0-316-33525-6 (hc) / 978-0-316-33526-3 (pb)
1. Mothers and daughters—Fiction. 2. Domestic fiction. I. Title.
PS3614.A385I57 2016
813'.6—dc23                                   2015028889

10 9 8 7 6 5 4 3 2 1

LSC-C

Book design by Marie Mundaca

Printed in the United States of America

*For Shamis*

*They marry*
*and have a child.*

*The wind carries them off*
*in different directions.*

—Mark Strand, "The Marriage"

# *Part I*

# 1.

As usual, the book only made her problems worse.

The new editions arrived overnight from New York. One large box came, torn already at the corners. When the delivery-man knocked, Henrietta pretended she was not at home. From an upstairs window she watched him, obviously cold in his uniform, looking harmless, carefully holding the box as if it held something truly valuable. A storm was just beginning. Constant wind bent the stand of birches by the road. Snowdrifts gathered in steep, clean slopes beneath the casement windows. The best option, she decided, was to leave the box out in the weather. That way, mercifully, the snow and sleet might ruin everything.

Hours later, though, her daughter was digging in.

"Disaster averted," Oona announced, home from her shift at the hospital, snow and ice on the hood of her coat. "I've saved the books!"

Oona smiled fiendishly. This was the look that afflicted everyone who ever came in contact with this thing. She put down the box on the kitchen counter and expertly ran the sharp edge of her car key through the cardboard.

"Don't open it," Henrietta pleaded, reaching out to try to

stop what was about to happen. "Please. Let's just put it back outside and let them all get destroyed. That's the healthy, reasonable thing to do."

"You have to let me do this," Oona said. "I had the worst day. A guy came in from a car crash with his lower half in a zillion pieces." Oona held up some Styrofoam peanuts and crushed them in her hand until confetti poured through her fingers. She was an orthopedic trauma surgeon at a hospital in Boston. A good deal of her stories started like this. More confetti came down. "Like, a *zillion* pieces." Oona was the rare medical professional who somehow made surgical scrubs fashionable, a feat she accomplished by wearing all black, all the time, from scarf to clogs, as if she were a medical ninja. "The Styrofoam, so you know, is supposed to represent bones."

Oona had ended her marriage earlier this year, and ever since she had been living at home again, in her childhood bedroom. For Henrietta, this turned out to be good timing. Her husband, Harold, had passed eleven months ago, and it had helped to have her daughter back in the house, to have, however temporarily, another soul here, under the same roof, another person breathing and speaking. This sudden recurrence of mothering had become the perfect antidote to her widowhood.

Oona was tall, like her father, and had his same profile, his same wide-set eyes, his exact same laugh. Henrietta had never been more grateful for this than in this last year. At times it seemed inconceivable that they might have ever raised a doctor together. Especially in this house, with the occasional chicken running through, with its loud music, and with their gallons of artery-clogging homemade butter in the freezer. For years Harold was a successful chef with a French restaurant in downtown Boston, and it turned out that all their Sunday evenings here in the big open kitchen julienning carrots and butchering meat had at least left Oona comfortable with sharp knives.

Oona reached into the box and took out the first copy of the book, immediately pressing it against her chest and feigning devotional ecstasy. Henrietta looked away. After all this time, the familiar pink cover was back in her life.

"Oh my goodness," Oona cried out in mock surprise.

"Don't act like you weren't obsessively tracking this package," said Henrietta.

They had known, of course, that the box was on its way. People in New York had alerted Henrietta to this fact last night. *Let us know what you think,* they had implored her, deliriously excited, full of foolish optimism, as if she was inclined to think anything positive after all this time.

"This is so wonderful," Oona said. The box held eleven more copies. "Can I keep it?"

"You already have a copy, I'm sure," Henrietta said.

"I have a *collection* of copies. But none so pristine," said Oona.

The truth was that Henrietta was long in the habit of denying her book's existence, but this was difficult to do when it was there on her counter, and in her daughter's hands. This month her old publishers, Hubbard and Co., were set to release a new (still pink) edition, replete with, of all things, critical essays and appreciations. Henrietta had not known such things might apply to a book like hers. Her editors had asked her to write the introduction, something light but wistful, and she'd refused. They'd called after her for weeks. *Just write something,* they'd begged. *Anything! Don't you have any thoughts about your book?* She'd responded with an email that read,

```
For a very long time I have tried to ignore the
fact that I authored this book. You should un-
derstand that this is the work of someone very
young and supremely untalented. I know I am not
```

```
alone in that opinion. I say this with full
knowledge of how uncouth this sounds: I really
just need the money.

Enthusiastically yours,
Henrietta Olyphant
```

She had written the book here, during her first years in Massachusetts. Earlier in her life, she had taught in New York. Women's studies. The politics of the human body. The gendered dialectics of mass-market media. Harold had moved them here when she was pregnant. Without classes to teach, she thought she would try her hand at fiction. She was young and full of confidence. Mostly she wrote at night, in short fits while Oona slept. Her heroine was a twenty-five-year-old woman named Eugenia Davenport, a newspaper reporter tasked by her editors during the summer of 1967 with finding the most desirable man in New York City and then getting him to marry her. Henrietta had the idea to structure the book like a visitor's guide to the female body, designed to emulate the traveler's companion that tourists brought with them to Paris, replete with maps and photographs and historical anecdotes about the various cathedrals worth seeing. In every chapter, Eugenia Davenport had a new lover, and with every new lover there were discoveries to be made. Henrietta cringed even to hear the word "diagram" now: *The Inseparables* had in it the first in-depth diagram of the vagina that had ever appeared in a mainstream book, or, more accurately, a book that was being sold in the supermarket, and which any woman, or grandmother, or, for that matter, any nine-year-old boy, could pick up while waiting for the checkout clerk to finish bagging. This is to say nothing about the way she'd drawn this particular diagram—like an ironic treasure map to a mythic hidden colony.

If they spoke of it at all while Oona was growing up, they

called it *That Thing*. Or sometimes *That Motherfucking Thing*. Until a few months ago, Henrietta wondered if she was the only person who remembered what it really was, or what it had meant to that whole generation who'd professed to love it. But then Henrietta had needed the money, and this whole ordeal had started up in earnest once more. Her picture had appeared last week in the *Globe*, and then in *People*. Strangers had lately begun to recognize her again. Recently, whenever she was out in downtown Aveline, someone inevitably would stop her, someone about her age, squinting to see if she really was the same woman from the back of the book, the one holding that infernal silver teapot. The conversation was usually about the scene three chapters from the end, when Eugenia smashes her own teapot through the front window of the Cadillac belonging to Templeton Grace, the man she blames for ruining her impending marriage. The teapot was intended to be some ironic joke, some winking insult to the women she'd been trying to make a comment about, women like her own mother, for whom the teapot, or the serving spoon, or the watering can, had become the family coat of arms. That smashing of the window was supposed to symbolize some epochal generational shift. Women assuming some whiff of a man's primal violence.

The repudiation was endless. The book had been construed as something she hadn't intended. She'd been called out by smarter, better-educated feminists for having contributed to a caricature of women being shrill and unstable and willing to throw teapots through the windows of American luxury automobiles. The book was cheap, critics said, and irresponsibly witless. Its depiction of sex-crazed women would almost certainly prove counterproductive to the struggle. Henrietta had called the book *The Inseparables* because she was trying to make a point about monogamy and fidelity and about the unspoken hope of all newlyweds: that their marriage might go out into the world unbreakable, tough as steel. This, too, was criticized for being overly simplistic and sentimental and also too beholden to patriarchal norms. The people she'd set out to pillory had become the book's biggest champions. For a year, at every one of her public appearances, cheery housewives brought her silver teapots, hugged her, whispered loving encouragement into her ear. Finally someone had written a book for them! A breezy, fun, sexy book! And it had pictures, too! The men who Henrietta hoped might feel stung by this book—men who saw the advent of the Pill and the subsequent ushering in of the sexual revolution as an excuse just to fuck more and fuck everyone and fuck with impunity—wrote her letters suggesting that she very probably wanted to fuck them, too. These men also felt compelled to show up at her readings. Although she refused to admit it aloud then, she'd been crushed when her book was rejected by the erudite establishment she'd assumed she belonged to. If she chose to search them out, she found dozens of news articles attesting to this rejection, all with variations of a headline much like this: "Olyphant Insists Sex Book Is Actually Good for Women." She'd sought to make an asshole of people, and people had very rightly made an asshole of her.

She never wrote another book, or another article. There was just this. She had the original reviews packed away somewhere in a box, the collected array of her misery stored together with other similar artifacts that brought her shame: bills from her credit card company, the impossible-to-open case for the diaphragm her mother had ordered for her before her first semester at Barnard, her humiliating attempts at landscape painting.

Henrietta watched Oona flip through *The Inseparables* with something close to genuine enthusiasm, relishing, somehow, every page. It was one thing to have written a book like this; it was another thing entirely to have a daughter who enjoyed it so much.

"Oh!" Oona cried. "It has the diagrams. Still!"

"You're handling this all wrong," Henrietta said. "I need compassion from you. Or at least some genuine disapproval."

"You were a genius," Oona said, turning the book around so that Henrietta could see. "What kind of drugs were you smoking when you decided to do this?"

"Oona—"

"My favorite part?" Oona said, pointing to the most famous diagram. "Is the fact that you felt it necessary to include a label for pubic hair. As if we can't tell what this is."

"Okay," Henrietta said, turning away. "Now you're just being coarse."

Henrietta would not touch the book. The truth was that she had not physically handled a copy of *That Motherfucking Thing* for a decade. Perhaps two. This went beyond superstition. She detested it. The first sentence, the second sentence, the last sentence—every sentence. The cover. The back cover. The concept. The pictures. She had burned a few copies once, this having been the seventies, and a therapist of hers having advocated some combination of primal scream therapy and pyromania. Not surprisingly, it had not been very helpful to feel a kinship with Joseph Goebbels.

"You don't understand," Oona said. "It's a cult sensation now."

"Cults are not good things, Oona. Why should I feel good about this?"

Oona smiled. "Because it's wonderful and trashy and fantastic."

Henrietta took a deep breath.

"I know," Oona said. "You thought it was actually smart."

"That's not—"

"The trashiness was unintended, I know. But accidental trashiness can still be exquisite. The trash can age and ripen."

"I left the box out there to get ruined," Henrietta said. "*That* was intentional."

"What fun is that?"

"You were an infant when this was published. You don't remember."

"I've heard a million times about the cat on the porch," Oona said.

"Girls from Radcliffe brought a *dead* cat," said Henrietta.

"*Women* from Radcliffe, Mom."

"That's the wrong part of the sentence to be concerned with!"

"I know. You were an academic. A serious thinker."

Henrietta smirked.

"What was your lecture? The gendered economy of housework?"

This was true. She met Harold when he catered a lunch for her department at the university. Because there were empty seats, she invited him to sit and, surprisingly, he accepted the offer. There were charts, she remembered, registering the declining wage per hour of various domestic jobs before and after women began doing them. Days later, Harold invited her to the restaurant where he worked. He was slender, with long brown hair that he kept tied up above his head with kitchen twine. He worked at a small bistro in midtown, near the theaters. She went thinking that they would eat together in the dining room, that it was his day off, maybe, that he would, at best, politely disregard her lecture, or, at worst, confront her with the same tired invective she'd heard ever since she started teaching: *Why don't you talk about something more pleasant?* Or: *What's a pretty girl like you have to be upset about?* Instead, they ate out in the alley behind the kitchen. He had twenty minutes off, he told her. He had set up a makeshift table on the steps of the fire escape. He told her what he'd made. *Escargots à la bourguignonne. Fri-*

*cassée de poulet à l'ancienne*. She didn't know what any of the food was. She'd grown up poor, eating the cheapest cuts of meat, boiled potatoes. He had Sancerre in stemware that he'd carefully unwrapped from cloth napkins. It was fall. She wore a sweater. She had never drunk Sancerre before. He had lined up flowers and candles, she remembered, along the rusted steel staircase. Earlier that week she had lectured for forty minutes on the insipid mass-market depictions of men trying to woo women. He served the chicken in a shallow bowl. While she ate, he watched her, nervous that she would not like it. "You can tell me," he said. "You can tell me if it's awful."

For a small moment in time, she and Harold were both famous. Unlike for her, for him fame was local and fleeting and generally painless. His restaurant, the Feast, opened nine months before the publication of *The Inseparables*. Nestled in a wasteland of inedibility between Symphony Hall and the Christian Science Plaza, the Feast served real French cuisine: *boeuf au poivre* with a dollop of hand-churned butter adorning the meat like a piece of jewelry; a coq au vin that had made Julia Child weep in appreciation; a small but excellent cellar of Burgundy unrivaled in a city parched for good wine; and the Cabernet Franc glaze that Frank Sinatra, in town to sing at the Garden, had once said was the single greatest thing he ever put in his mouth—and that included Ava Gardner's tit. Nearly everything Harold could raise here he raised. Vegetables on the part of the land that abutted the river. Stone fruit in a small orchard that had only just begun to show maturity. And animals. So many of them that it was sometimes a shock to see it now, the hills bare, the grass snowed over, the stalls and pens empty except for ghosts. That first night together, in the alley behind his restaurant, she had asked him about her lecture. "What did you think about my class?" she asked. She remembered that she thought he was lying when he told her he thought it was fascinating.

Were there groups he could join? he asked her. What could he do to help? Were there any books he should read?

Oona flipped through the pages until she got to the back. "This is my favorite," she said, holding up the author photograph. "This picture of you is wonderful."

"Chocolate is wonderful. The ocean is wonderful. That picture of me is ludicrous."

"Come on. That's your problem with this thing. Embrace it!" Oona tried to get her to hold the book. "Embrace it! Embrace this woman!"

They had kept the same picture. Hubbard had wanted everything in this new edition to stay the same. Vintage typeface. Vintage sexual outrage. Vintage Henrietta. Since she was doing this for the cash, she had not put up a fight. It was the most contrived, most outrageously foolish photograph ever taken of her: the ecru turtleneck; the collection of dangling silver amulets; the white evening gloves up to her elbows; a tumbler of iced tea in her right hand; flared gray corduroys rising a foot above her navel; mustard-colored sunglasses; her old Himalayan pussycat, Albert Camew, asleep beside her. In her left hand, she held that stupid silver teapot. She had forgotten the photographer's name, but he was German, tall, delicate, blond, a little deaf. He loved the book (*all the hysterical women!*) and was thrilled when he saw the teapot across room. *Ooh. That is vonderful. I love it. Go! Now! Hold it up to the light!* They'd taken the picture here in the living room, in front of the mantel. She remembered Harold standing off to the side, holding Oona against his chest. She was nine months old then, maybe ten. Harold had always claimed to love the book, even amid the outrage, even as everyone wanted to know which of Eugenia's lovers was actually him.

Crossing the room, Oona gave off a small, quiet sigh at the mess the house had become. Boxes cluttered the whole first floor, as well as the barn and the garage. Now that Harold was gone, Henrietta needed to move. The intricacies of her financial distress were not complicated. The accounts were drained. The credit cards were at their limits. She had not saved enough. She was underinsured. She had come perilously close to bankruptcy. Death, it turned out, was very expensive. Because of this, she had packed everything these last few weeks, put forty years into boxes, watched as her husband's closets were emptied, his sock drawers discarded, his car sold, every trace of their life together dismantled and put away. So many rooms were crowded floor to ceiling with cardboard that the windows were blocked and the light could not get in. Bit by bit the house began to feel less like a home and more like a gloomy, light-starved storage locker. Oona wanted to help, to pay, to write checks, to rent her an apartment, and whether it was maternal pride or some deeper stubbornness, Henrietta cut off the discussion whenever it came up. With Oona it was more complicated. With your children it was always this way.

Coming back from the kitchen with a tall cup of coffee, Oona noticed a black suitcase wedged in between two large boxes.

"What is this?" Oona said, not as a question, but as an accusation. She put her hands on her hips. "I can't believe you still have this, Mom."

"Can we skip this part, please? Can we go back to when you were excited about my awful book? When you were spinning and talking about cults and pubic hair and bone dust?"

Oona flung the suitcase up onto the counter and began to unzip it.

"Please don't," Henrietta cried. "Please."

Before Harold died, they had a vacation to Barcelona planned. They were set to leave a week after he passed, and for some reason he had already packed, and put the suitcase by the back door, which, for the past eleven months, was where Henrietta had left it, despite Oona's constant protests. This kind of behavior, Oona kept telling her, was unhealthy and emotionally damaging, not to mention wholly atypical of the kind of woman Henrietta had always prided herself on being, which is to say not the kind of woman who kept her dead husband's packed suitcase still intact all this time.

"This is not okay," Oona said, which was probably the hundredth time that Henrietta had heard her say this.

"I'm aware, honey, that you don't consider this to be the most emotionally restorative thing to do," Henrietta said, using a phrase her daughter had popularized in the house these last eleven months.

"Oh, it's far from emotionally restorative," Oona said.

"As are most things in life," Henrietta said.

"Why don't you let me take you to therapy? We can go together," Oona said.

Henrietta smiled. "That sounds like a recipe for a delightful and productive afternoon."

"Or let me bring you some books to read," Oona said.

Her daughter was a surprisingly avid devotee of self-help literature. This had been a secret until Oona moved back in, and Henrietta had discovered the considerable library she'd amassed over the years. Books on so many varied subjects— on nutrition (*The Last Diet Ever, Part Two*), on leaving your husband (*A Workbook to Regain Dignity*), on grief and death (*Believing in Heaven but Not in God*). None of this should have stunned Henrietta as much as it did. Oona had always distrusted abstraction and gravitated instead toward the simple fix. This was what made orthopedics so attractive to her: you cut, you repair, you close the body. "I have my own books," Henrietta assured her.

"But your books are all probably about the depravity of mankind and the imminent cultural apocalypse."

"They are very good books."

Oona rested her hands on the suitcase. "I don't know what to do with you," Oona said.

"You shouldn't feel the need to do anything with me. It's just a suitcase, Oona. Eventually I will get around to opening it. And eventually, after that, I will get around to finding some restorative balance, or whatever you call it. I promise you."

Oona took a large breath with the same theatrical flair she'd used as a toddler, fuming over whatever was wildly unfair in her life at that time—going to sleep or bathing or being deprived of cake. The fact was that Henrietta had pretended months ago that she'd opened this suitcase, and had told Oona that she'd reckoned with the mundane things that were inside it before packing it all away. Afterward, they'd split two bottles of wine and had a wonderful and sad evening together in which they were united miserably in their grief. They had listened to an entire Leonard Cohen record. Oona had told her the next morning that she was proud of her, saying so without a trace of condescension or self-help sappiness.

"But you told me you opened it!" Oona said. "Remember?"

"I do remember."

"What happened?"

"What happened is that I lied to you."

Henrietta knew what was coming: Oona liked to console her by relaying some grievously awful story from the hospital, as a way to let her know that she was familiar with the trauma of death, and also with the loving family members of dead people whom she and her colleagues had to comfort in the waiting areas of their emergency room. As far as Henrietta could tell, this was either a woeful attempt at tough love or a terrible advertisement for Oona's hospital.

"Last week at the hospital—" Oona started.

"Please don't tell me something horrible."

"—we had a young woman in the emergency room. She had overdosed on cocaine and had done so, for some stupid reason, at the top of a staircase."

"I know you see death all the time," Henrietta said, her voice cracking.

Oona stopped. "You really don't want to hear the rest of it?"

"Let me guess," Henrietta said, her shoulders falling. "At the end of the story, she dies."

Oona nodded. "Yes," she said, sounding only a little disappointed. "She does die."

"See? This is not helpful. These stories of poor cocaine addicts are not helpful for me."

Oona had two hands on the suitcase. It was a small black thing, bought for thirty dollars at a discount store, nothing great. She had thought it was ridiculous that Harold would have packed so far ahead of their trip, especially considering that he was a famous procrastinator, always leaving these most crucial tasks for the last moment.

"I'm afraid to open it," Henrietta said. "That's why it's still here."

Henrietta thought she saw Oona readying a response, something typical for her. "Afraid? But why?" Oona might say. "What could possibly be inside that you would be afraid to find? It's probably just what's normally in a suitcase. With Dad, it's probably just, you know, an extra pair of underwear. Or, at best, a boring book about the history of butter."

Instead, Oona walked across the room and hugged her.

It wasn't what was probably inside, Henrietta felt like saying. It was what was *potentially* inside. This was an important distinction. All this time she had allowed herself to think that there was something special, or something surprising that had made Harold pack it up two weeks early. At first, after he was gone, she figured he did it because he was bored. With the restaurant closed he was home with nothing to do, so why not pack up early? But Harold did not do these kinds of things. Her Harold—the same Harold who that last year had grown a white beard, who had attempted to teach himself Ancient Greek, and had expressed an interest in learning how to play the banjo—this Harold simply was not practical enough to have done something like this. And so she'd begun to think that there must have been a different reason why he'd done it.

The coffeemaker chimed. Oona poured herself a cup, drank half of it, and then refilled it just as quickly.

Henrietta shook her head. "How long have you been awake straight?"

Oona looked at her wristwatch. Usually she worked nights. Now that she was in the middle of a divorce she worked days and nights. "Many, many hours," she said.

"How much caffeine have you had?"

"Tankards' worth," Oona said. "Gallons, probably."

"You need to sleep. It's not good for you to—" Henrietta stopped herself. She had fallen back into this recently. Motherhood for her had always been a conflict between proper concern and far too much worry. Widowhood had only made this worse.

Oona looked down at the suitcase. "Maybe we could open it together."

Henrietta took a deep breath.

"Just let me know, Mom. I can do it with you. Whenever you want. I can help."

Across the room, Oona's phone began to ring. She gave off an exhausted sigh. "One sec, Mom," she said. Over these last six months Henrietta had learned that the noise of her daughter's phone corresponded with another human's injury. This was how it went: someone's bones broke, the phone rang, and then Oona rushed off to repair the mess. Oona walked slowly toward her phone, which was on a table across the room. It was an old house and it loudly bore the weight of every step inside it. Henrietta used to be able to differentiate between her daughter's feet and her husband's. From the living room she watched Oona take the call. *Dr. Olyphant,* she said. She had turned forty years old this year, a number that was difficult for Henrietta to consider. For the occasion, Oona had allowed a white streak to emerge in her hair, running from the point of her widow's peak back across her head, like a skunk's tail. Henrietta wondered whether it was because of the death or the divorce or both. She sat on the sofa, waiting. The fact was that Henrietta did not want to move without her daughter. She had thought to suggest that they get a place together, like roommates, like friends, even, but found that she didn't have the courage to ask.

"Yes," Oona said.

Henrietta noticed the alarm in Oona's voice.

"Yes," Oona said again. "She's my daughter."

# 2.

It was Monday, not that it mattered, rain falling, weak light through the dead trees on Mount Thumb. Lydia sat in the back of a golf cart the color of persimmon, driven by a member of the school's disciplinary staff, a man in a faintly militant peacoat, his collar propped up. The iron arched gates of Hartwell Academy passed overhead, rusted and bearing a carved Latin inscription that meant either *Truth and Wisdom in Learning* or something like *Forget What You Thought: This Is the Place Where You Will Truly Actually Learn to Feel Deep Shame and Humiliation About Your Body*. This place. She took a very deep breath.

She had been here since September. A boarding school in southwestern Vermont advertised for gifted students, Hartwell Academy had looked vastly more promising in its brochures than the public school she'd attended at home in Crestview, with its legions of boys lingering near their lockers in expensive jeans and enough Abercrombie cologne to fumigate a basement. Or: those same boys in the parking lot after seventh period with their hundred-millimeter Kools and their cell-phone porn. She had found Hartwell online, after prompting Google with the phrase "Are there any normal schools anyplace where everyone isn't a pervert or a criminal?" If she had a sense of humor about this past week, it was possible she might find it amusing that she'd ended up here.

From the back of the cart, Lydia had to scream over the din of the motor to be heard.

"What about everyone else?" Lydia called out. They were passing the long line of brick dormitory houses where the boys lived, and as they went by she saw faces in the window peering back at her, pale and blond and aggressively well groomed and very likely sinister. For days it had been like this. "What about everyone else harassing me? Every other single human on this campus! Do they need to do this, too?"

The driver turned around. His name was Abernathy. Officially he worked as an assistant to the dean of students, but in reality he was a recent college graduate whose job it was to shuttle students around this large campus. "I don't know about anyone else," he said. "I only know about you."

Given everything, this was the single most unsettling thing he could have said. A week ago a nude picture of her had begun spreading around the school. At this point, it was difficult to say which was worse: the embarrassment or the ridicule. The fact was, everyone here had seen her naked, or was about to, and evidently at Hartwell being naked was cause enough to endure a hellacious torrent of harassment. Forget the strenuously constructed veneer of high culture this school prided itself on: the instant her nipples began popping up on people's phones all hell had broken loose for her.

Lydia slumped in her seat. She was dressed in layers, hoping that all the wool and cotton she had on—the long johns, the tightly wrapped scarf, the big parka zipped to the top—would create a kind of armor. All week she had suffered the urge to discover a way to vanish.

Abernathy offered her a kind smile. "If you want my advice, don't bring your phone in with you."

She looked up. She was exhausted. She had not slept. She was fifteen years old. Her makeup, she knew, probably could not cover her new, fledgling paranoia.

"Because they'll search you," he said, conspiratorially. "And if they find it, you'll get extra time. Especially with this. You don't have your phone on you, do you?"

Technically speaking, phones were not allowed on campus. Digital technology ran afoul of the school's stated ambition to create in its student body what it called a "linear brain," which was its term for a brain capable of reading the printed word, or negotiating around basic algebraic functions and maintaining the ability to do things like find Iraq on a map without losing one's train of thought. Cellular technology apparently interfered with this. Screens equaled distraction, as they put it, and distraction equaled a future of subpar earning potential and disappointing contributions to the alumni fund. Until this week, however, when everything blew up around her, the rule about the phones had gone largely unenforced. Or at least Lydia had thought.

"The phone's on my desk. Back at the dorm," Lydia lied. With everything happening, she was not about to leave her phone around for her roommates to scrutinize. There had already been far too much scrutiny.

Abernathy took a phone from his jacket pocket. "So you're saying if I call you right now, your phone won't ring?"

"I swear," Lydia said.

"I'm just saying: none of this happens without the phone. None of it. Am I right?" He pointed up ahead to the headmistress's office, which was where they were going. "That's what the headmistress is going to say. Trust me."

Thirty minutes ago she'd been pulled from her Intro to Cinema class, right from the middle of a group discussion about Leni Riefenstahl's influence on *Star Wars* and the commodification of fascist symbology. These kinds of discussions, she'd learned, were typical of a place like Hartwell, where everyone was mandated to wear the same gender-neutral uniform—blue slacks, white oxford, brown leather shoes—and where everyone had apparently digested the entire canon of Western civ prior to reaching puberty. For the first time in her life, Lydia fell to the bottom of the class. Abernathy had come to the door right at the soaring, demented crescendo of *Triumph of the Will*, interrupting the führer's speech, to announce her name.

Even before Abernathy ushered her into the school's spartan, cold disciplinary office, she knew she was being suspended. Walking behind him in the hallway outside her classroom, she saw in his hand the telltale pink file folder that signaled a suspension. At first she met with the dean of students, an older man who sat in front of a window that overlooked the chapel. Abernathy stood at the door, like a prison guard.

The dean began by telling her how alarmed everyone was. "I'm alarmed," he told her. "The headmistress is alarmed. We are all very, very alarmed at this." He paused to allow Lydia the impression that this meant he was serious. "Like I said, we're all alarmed."

She was given only a moment to offer a defense, which she stumbled through.

"This is not my fault," she managed. "None of this is my fault."

The dean leaned forward across his desk. "But it *is* you in the picture, isn't it?"

When she said, reluctantly, that it was, he opened the pink folder and wrote in it for a few moments. "Abernathy will drive you to talk to the headmistress," the dean said, looking up. "But before your parents take you home, we think it might benefit you to talk to some of our counselors on staff." He took off his eyeglasses. He rubbed at his eyes. "We have great people on staff who have experience with these situations."

Lydia felt momentarily grateful to hear this, thinking it was a subtle nod to the uproar of this last week—the endless catcalling and bullying. But she was wrong. School administrators, the dean told her, were so alarmed about the existence of her picture that they'd begun to worry that something else was at work aside from what Lydia had already explained was the simple fact that Charlie Perlmutter had asked her for a photograph of her topless, and then eventually a photograph of her topless began to spread around school. Lydia understood all of this to be code for their worry that she was being abused, or had been abused, or that something equally awful or unspeakable had happened to her. "We want to make sure you are okay," the dean told her. "Your well-being is the most important thing." Which was why she was here, in the back of what everyone on campus called the paddy wagon, a stout electrified vehicle used to ferry delinquent students up to the administration building.

"First off, I'm normal," she said as they drove. "Perfectly normal. And I never sent the picture. Not to him, not to anyone. He stole it from my phone. You were there. I told the dean this."

Abernathy turned. "I'm not in charge."

"But do you believe me?" she asked.

He shrugged, as if to say, *It doesn't matter what I think.*

"Why doesn't anyone believe me?" she cried. All of this was exactly what she'd wanted to say earlier, in the dean's office, but hadn't. As they went up the hill, she thought she detected a hint of a smirk on his face. This was how it had been these last few days. The onslaught of public shame. Someone's extended finger reaching out to mockingly tease the delicate skin of her earlobe. What did it matter whether this man, or any man, believed her? She had seen this elsewhere, at her old school in Crestview, certainly. The existence of a naked picture automatically worked to discount whatever academic or personal currency or dignity a person might have earned by, say, being alive. Every innocent gesture assumed a sexual intimation. Laughter followed her. She was branded now.

From the back pocket of her uniform-issue slacks, she felt her phone buzzing, and then, a moment later, heard it buzzing against the hard plastic seat.

Abernathy shook his head. "Look, I'm just trying to help you out. At least silence the thing."

The phone was nothing special. It was one of the three or four models of phones everyone else had. A present for her fifteenth birthday, it was titanium and white with a mirror-buffed screen. She was rarely without it. To her parents, it represented a digital lasso, a way to keep tabs on her. The embedded GPS showed as a blip on their computer screen a few hundred miles away. To her it reflected the absolute totality of her previously minuscule social life. She felt an appropriate love for it, or as much love as possible for something that could not love her back. The list of such things was short: her phone, her stuffed animals, Morrissey, the collected works of the Brontë sisters.

The phone was how Charlie had first come into her life. A tiny New Jersey kid with mild color blindness and Keanu Reeves's hair, he was preternaturally gifted with computers. On her second day of school he had somehow acquired her number from the school database and sent her a message halfway through a gruelingly bleak lecture on species extinction: Polar bears, blah blah blah: we haven't met. I'm the other beautiful person in the room.

The phone was how they always got in touch, how he, at midnight on a Thursday, for instance, would tell her that he was stoned across campus watching *Batman* on mute, or *Superman* on mute, or *Iron Man* on mute, and that he couldn't stop thinking about her. Come over, swim over, run over. Let's hang, get high, let's fuck around. Sometimes she would read these aloud to her roommates, but more often than not she simply stewed over them in silence. Turn on the fucking volume, she'd written back once. Or watch a better fucking movie. He was undeterred. Send me a picture of yourself, he had said. She took a picture of herself smiling. You know that's not what I meant. C'mon. This was the first week of school, and it did not stop until a week ago. A hundred and eighty mornings of predictable bullshit. His commitment to the cause, she was ashamed to admit, flattered her, but not enough to give him what he wanted. Months went on like this. In public, he made kissy faces at her, blew in her ear while they stood in line for food. In chapel, he passed her notes with plagiarized love poems by Petrarch. Still, he would not stop asking.

The universe of fifteen-year-old boys could be divided into two camps, she had decided: those who were, in their hearts, still boys, and those whose every impulse was sexually sociopathic. Tits, she had written to him once. That's all your mind can handle. Not even both tits. Just one.

He was relentless. Send me a picture of yourself.

Mornings, his was the first message she'd wake to. Send me something, make me happy. It sickened her to remember that for the briefest moment in time—October and November of this past year—she had found him charming. Something about his chin or his vulnerability. He grew flushed in the cheeks while he spoke. She felt something for him that was either pity or sexual attraction. She had not yet learned the difference. Walking between their Intro to Cinema and Intro to Oceanography classes, he took her hand delicately by the wrist and said, stupidly and probably falsely, *I think you're lovely.* Against her better judgment she felt alive.

She had never actually considered sending him the picture, because she knew what would happen. She had no doubt that he would send it around. She sometimes thought she could see the perversion floating through his head, like cumulus clouds passing by a window. Still, she had allowed herself into his bed for some entry-level crap—stolen wine, R. Kelly, some unerotic biting on his part—but the moment he tried to take her top off, she cut it short. His response—*Oh, I see how it is*—was typical for the boy Charlie Perlmutter turned out to be, which was the boy who, later that night, succeeded in sneaking onto her phone and extracting a picture she'd taken of herself in the shower house at Rosewater, an awful, green, wet photograph. She'd taken it because she felt flattered by him, or at least by the attention, and because she wanted to see what it was he saw. Am I sexy? Am I good to look at? A simple set of questions that had backfired spectacularly. This was a week ago. By now the picture was everywhere.

She'd tried to fight back, telling people some of the things he'd told her in confidence. He was riddled with phobias. Salt water. Butterflies. He had an inexplicable fear of being touched on his Adam's apple. For days she and her friends let loose near his bed butterflies that they'd stolen from the science lab, or they came up behind him in the line for the showers to gently touch his throat, saying things like, *Hi, Charlie, what a nice Adam's apple you have.* It all went on until this morning, when her roommates were caught depositing even more butterflies into his dorm. In this way, school administrators caught wind of her picture.

As Abernathy wound the cart up the path, climbing a small hill, Lydia spied the parking lot down below.

"Did the dean call my parents?" she asked, trying to disguise what had become an obvious panic. She could not imagine what exactly their response would be, what mixture of horror and anger she'd be met by.

Abernathy nodded. "I think the headmistress called them."

"Both of them?" she asked. "Or just one? Because they're splitting up."

This was the first time she'd said it aloud. The sureness of the statement surprised her. Admitting it verbally felt like a test against its reality. She said it a second time. "They're divorcing. Or something. I don't even know. It's shitty. You know?" She saw Abernathy's head lowering in sympathy. Or maybe she was just imagining this.

He slowed the cart. They were outside the administration building, which was white and modern and sterile-looking in the bright sun. Abernathy cut the engine. Down below, class was out. Streams of navy and white poured from the library. She was supposed to be in science class. As she began to walk up the front step, she saw, out across the lot, Charlie Perlmutter standing in front of a line of suitcases, waiting to be picked up. Involuntarily, she gripped the folds of her coat together. When he noticed her, he cocked his head, smiled, and blew her a kiss.

# 3.

Oona and Spencer sat silent as their car cut a straight line through the white foothills south of Mount Thumb. This was February in Vermont and the sky was simultaneously white and sunless. They had left right away. She had not slept in almost two days. Every few miles they passed through a small town built against the hillsides. Or cows in a herd huddled at the nose to keep warm. Eventually the road narrowed to one lane and the pavement gave way to dirt. On the driver's dash the GPS reflected the way ahead as a red line against a blank white field. On and on they went, the blinking, the slow progress, the snow. The daylight moon strung up above the tree line. Woodsmoke in through the vents. Deer print in the snowdrift. Out in the gray thicket, bird's nests left in the oak tops.

"We're close," Oona said. It was the first thing she'd said in hours.

She always got these calls; the mother always did. Whole days at the hospital, or in surgery, and if something went wrong, she got the message. Never mind that her soon-to-be ex-husband was almost always stoned and had been jobless for the past fourteen years, and was, because of these facts, home and freely available for parental emergencies: Oona always got the call.

The headmistress at Lydia's school was a German woman with beautiful English, but even so, Oona had needed to ask her to repeat herself. She was, even now, turning the words over in her head. *Compromising photograph. Illicit nude photography.* The headmistress had said that the picture was circulating around campus. Like a flyer, or influenza. Across the line, something had cracked. Static. Exhaustion. Impatience.

It was a four-hour ride from Boston. They were in Spencer's car, an enormous blue Toyota. She'd bought it for him just before the split. It was a foolish car but at the time a wellspring of guilt had compelled her to do something nice for him. Apparently this was the way her marriage fell apart: misplaced guilt and an inappropriately timed automobile purchase. She'd had it delivered to the driveway with a big white bow on it, just as they did in the television commercials. He had thought this meant that their troubles were over, that their twice-a-week couples therapy had succeeded, or that their latest emergency weekend away in the Caribbean had done what they had hoped. She had thought of the car as the first piece of a nice severance package.

Snow was falling. They were in the mountains. Hawks began to glide overhead.

"Look, I need your opinion on this," Spencer said as they crossed beneath a rail truss. He had been a lawyer before Lydia was born, and thought they might need to argue their case with the headmistress, that there was still hope. "You haven't said anything. I have no idea what you think. You've just been silent."

"What I think," she said, speaking slowly.

"Yes: what you think. Do you think anything?"

"What else is there to think, Spencer? I'm horrified. I'm nauseated. I'm panicking. I'm very, very worried."

They were trying. This was the official story. Once, she had loved him. In the beginning he was strong and full of confidence and so well-read and so convinced of the purpose of his life that just to be around him, in his presence, on his sofa, was to experience the world the way a king must: endowed with clarity and certainty and optimism and convincing opinions on global affairs. Then graduate school ended.

"We'll be blamed for this," Spencer said. It was less of a question and more of a whining protest. "Just to prepare you."

"So this is our fault? Our daughter exposes herself and that's our fault? Somehow that's on you and me?"

"Absent parents. Too busy to check in. Too willing to out-source responsibility." He fluttered his fingers against the steering wheel. "If I had to guess."

"She's at boarding school," Oona said. "All the parents are absent."

Oona worked too much. This was one of Spencer's numerous complaints. Their couples therapy had devolved into an exchange of grievances. She was never home. She had abdicated too much of the parenting. Lydia missed her. Why else would their daughter beg to go to boarding school unless she felt that the family unit was already degraded? This was his opinion. She saw it a different way. Her daughter was brilliant and independent and sure of herself and had the smart idea to get the hell out of Crestview a few years early. And besides, wasn't medicine an important and noble calling, worthy enough of the long hours, the privation, the sleeplessness? Weren't people still drinking too much and then drunkenly driving their Jeeps across highway medians and destroying their bones? And if so, didn't she need to be there when they were wheeled into orthopedics so that she could hammer the titanium pins into their femurs? She had hoped the therapy would result in some divine solution—the Camp David accord of marital distress. Quickly, their hope proved futile. The woman he fell in love with didn't exist any longer. He said this after their last session. The Real

Oona was gone, he had told her. They were standing in the driveway of their house, beside this car, in full view of the neighbors.

"If the Real Oona is gone, then who the hell am I?" she demanded.

They'd met twenty years ago this month at a party in Tribeca, introduced by mutual friends who were so sure that they would find each other irresistible that a photograph actually existed of them shaking hands for the first time. In the picture they were both laughing. He was basically a boy then: twenty years old, gangly still, with a trace of acne on the bridge of his nose. On their first date, he told her that he had just broken up with his girlfriend. And by "just broken up," he meant to say that he had gone home after meeting Oona and told his girlfriend that they were finished. Hearing this, Oona blushed. They were eating at Veselka on 2nd Avenue. Steamed pierogies. Black coffee. The place where, in the future, they would come to plot out their most important decisions. New York or not New York. Children or no children. A membership to a secular humanistic synagogue or yoga classes. She remembered that at the end of dinner he paid with his mother's credit card. For the longest time they each carried a copy of this picture in their wallets. His young face, his full head of hair, his long-forgotten pierced ear; her stonewashed denim, her Hillary Clinton headband, the Real Oona. Neither of them could remember what they were laughing at in the picture.

Oona dug her cell from her purse. Lydia occasionally sent short emails updating her on school. Dissected a cow's heart today. Equal parts fascinating and vomitous. She swiped hopefully at the screen. This action, this small press and swipe, had become a neuromuscular reflex, as indispensable to her biorhythms as blinking or breathing. Because the hospital could call at any time, and because bones were always breaking, the phone accompanied her when she slept. It was like a faithful pet in this way, or an unshakable case of night terrors. Mostly, though, the phone served to convey how badly she missed her daughter. On the home screen was a picture of Lydia when she was three, when her favorite thing to do was perform the entirety of "So Long, Farewell" from *The Sound of Music,* complete with move-for-move choreography and admirably fine pitch and, generally, just a heaping shitload of cuteness. These last few weeks Oona had started to transfer all the old pictures onto her phone so that she could do what she was doing now, which was to flip randomly, at light speed, through the first thirty-six months of Lydia's life. This—three years old, singing, obsessed with Julie Andrews—was as far as Oona had gotten. She thought it was crucial to remember that such a deliriously optimistic time had ever existed. *The oblivious years,* she called them. Often Oona tried to summon every important fact of that era. Lydia's first piece of solid food was carrot. Her first tooth came in February. Her first movie was *Singin' in the Rain.* Oona marveled at her infant daughter's enviable fascination with all the things that Oona, to be honest, did not pay attention to anymore. With dogs, with the moon, with grass, with wind, with eyelashes, and with dandelions and with little insects with wings! Her baby had reminded her that the world really was a wonderful and glorious place. This was a welcome revelation. They had very little furniture then. Because who really cares about furniture when you have each other? She and Spencer actually used to say this to each other, she remembered. *The oblivious years.* In couples therapy, they had agreed that it was the best time of their lives.

"Nothing?" Spencer asked. "No word from her?"

Oona put the phone down.

Spencer grimaced. "You hot?" he asked. "I'm hot." He reached to fiddle with the mess of buttons on the car's dash.

The car was a toy. There were buttons everywhere. The only people who drove this car were seventeen-year-olds and people who wanted to be seventeen again.

They'd been apart the past six months. He lived in the house they'd built together in Crestview. Four bedrooms, wall-to-wall walnut flooring imported from China, more than one chandelier—an undeniable McMansion. She had moved in with her mother so that she could look after her, although with Henrietta Olyphant, you couldn't just say something like that aloud. *I worry about you being alone.* Or: *Your sadness scares the shit out of me.* Or even: *I love you.* Even the most innocent acts of generosity were liable to be misunderstood by her mother as a political statement. They were the sort of family that kept their declarations of affection silent, or at least repressed them and disguised them as the typical ingredients of mother-daughter-granddaughter dysfunction: guilt, conflict, shame, cookies. All of these, you were to understand if you were an Olyphant, were an acceptable stand-in for love.

"This is all my fault," Oona said.

Spencer looked over. "That's just something to say. You don't mean that."

"I got her the phone. The phone has the camera. It seems pretty obvious that it's my fault."

"We don't even know if any of this is true," he said, in a perfectly lawyerly tone. It was always like this with him—his need to see proof and evidence.

"All of this seems fairly obvious to me," she said. "We begin to crack, you and me, and then she begins to crack. It's textbook."

He put a cool hand on the back of her neck. "Just breathe, okay? Close your eyes. Breathe." Then he seemed to remember that they were no longer touching. He took back his hand. This was the first time they'd seen each other since she'd left. She'd done it on a Tuesday morning, with what was likely the least amount of pyrotechnics ever managed in a separation. "I'm going," she had said, two suitcases with her, and he merely nodded and said, "I see that." They'd already exhausted themselves arguing. It was not a coincidence, Oona thought, that they had been separated exactly as long as Lydia had been away at school. Once Lydia was gone, they had no purpose as a "unit." This was the term he preferred. He used it frequently. They had discovered this, too, in couples therapy.

Signs on the roadside signaled them to a slow crawl. The Hartwell colors were navy and white, and as they drove, small pennants strung up on telephone wires flapped in the mountain wind. Oona flipped down the mirror to look at herself. She had tried with makeup to make something pop that would never pop. She hadn't known what to wear to retrieve her suspended, exhibitionist daughter, and so she'd gone with the only nice clothes she had in her closet. She was in scrubs every day of the week, but there was this: the same black dress she'd worn at her father's funeral eleven months ago.

"Do I look too severe?" she asked. "I think I look too severe."

He turned. "You look like you."

"I mean, what are you supposed to look like in this situation?"

He sighed. "Pissed, I think."

They passed through the gates. Blond students in cable-knit lounged in Adirondack chairs smoking smuggled cigarettes. From here the campus at Hartwell was shaped like a human eye: land on the top and on the bottom, with lashes ringing the perimeter in the form of old-growth oak, and in the middle a small, dark island of grass and granite and untended maple. Everywhere else there was the opaline water of Lake Rose. The boys lived on the south of the eye in two stone houses. On the north stood the girls' campus, everything in ridiculous shades of purple and yellow, like a cupcake shop. The headmistress had the top western corner of the administration building.

Oona and Spencer parked in the lot. They lingered a moment, girding themselves.

"I want to sue," he said.

"Sue who?"

"The school. Every person who forwarded the picture. The headmistress."

"Litigation isn't a substitute for genuine concern," she said.

He tried repeatedly to button his cuff, over and over, fiddling and fiddling.

"What are you doing?" she asked. "You look crazy. We need to project normalcy."

"I'm really worried," he said. "This isn't good, right? Normal people don't do things like this."

"No," Oona said.

"You send your kid to a school for gifted people, that means this doesn't happen, right?"

"Obviously it does," Oona said.

He scoffed. A familiar sound. The sound track of their last year together. "She's probably on drugs," Spencer said. "I mean, that would explain it, right? The picture, for one. Lydia would never take a picture of herself naked. Ever. And then all this business with the butterflies? It's drugs."

"Drugs? That's rich, coming from you."

This was her biggest reason for leaving. She detested everything about his smoking so much pot: having to smell the weed on his coat, or on his breath; having to worry about his being arrested in the parking lot of Crestview's Methodist church for buying from a nineteen-year-old; and, most of all, having to endure how dull he became once the THC reached his bloodstream. Because he remained under the adolescent impression that marijuana was not addictive, Spencer hesitated to think he was chemically dependent. She'd expected him to quit when they were engaged, and then, definitely, after they were married. When that didn't happen, she thought he'd certainly quit when he graduated from law school, and then when he started work at Bigelow. When he kept on getting high, she thought he'd quit when they moved out to Crestview, and then, again definitely, when Lydia arrived. Or when all the weed finally rendered his dick useless without the help of some pharmaceutical hardening product. Nothing, however, had made him stop.

"I'm not high right now," he said. He widened his eyes to show off the whites. "That's a fact."

She started to clap. "Good for you."

"I haven't been high in two months." He looked at his watch. "Three, almost."

He was supposed to have been a great lawyer. People used to tell her this all the time: his former coworkers, his various underlings, even the men who'd been his rivals, their voices choked with the appropriate reverence. She took their word for it sometimes; how could she ever know the truth? It was not unusual to find him parked in their garage, weeping at the wheel. He missed her, he used to say. Stuck at his desk nights on end, ironing out obscure legal disagreements between huge multinational corporations, he wanted more than anything to be at home with his family. For months he talked about this openly. What did she think of him staying home full-time with the baby? This marked the end of *the oblivious years*.

"How do you feel?" she asked. "Now that you're sober? Is it good?"

"I feel like you're mocking me."

"I'm being serious," she said. "Do you feel better? I bet you do. Clearer. Smarter, probably. Healthier, certainly."

He shrugged and cracked his knuckles. "I feel less high," he said. "Generally speaking."

"That's it?"

"Less high," he said. "Which doesn't exactly mean better. Or clearer."

A bell chimed. Far off down the hill the students rushed out of the library in a big blue wave. All this time without her daughter, Oona felt consumed with worry for her, and then, alternately, ashamed for worrying. She didn't want to become the kind of mother who was sure that everywhere her daughter went danger lurked, even if she was positive that danger was indeed lurking everywhere. She worked in a city hospital, after all. On a weekly basis she saw things that made it impossible to view the world as a kind and benevolent place. She sat up in her seat. Boys in neckties crossed a footbridge over a stream, bouncing on it viciously, trying, probably, to wreck it. She had not exactly been excited about Lydia studying here. Her daughter had begged, had left the brochures everywhere in the house, had deluged Oona's inbox with Hartwell-related propaganda. There was something in the air, Oona thought, or in the exacting side parts in the boys' hair that had felt threatening—as had the idea that she wouldn't be here to protect her daughter.

She turned to Spencer. He could not button his cuffs. She reached out. He was like a boy when it came to this. His skin was cold. Quickly she fastened the buttons.

"I've missed you," he said quietly.

She knew. He had written her painfully embarrassing love letters after she moved out. They were the most outrageous things. *What is a heart, anyway?* he'd asked in one of them. *Every day without you I am being buried by the world.* She had all of them hidden away in a low dresser drawer. She had not known what to do with his feelings.

"Have you been okay, at least?" she asked.

Spencer had on the cologne she liked. A French brand she could not pronounce. She had given it to him for their last Christmas. Every tiny choice of his was a small volley in his attempt to ingratiate himself to her.

"Lonely," he said. "Especially in the house. It's too big for one person. It misses you."

"The house misses me?"

"You know what I mean, Oona."

She had no idea what she was doing. She had no clue how to act, what tone to take, whether they would be friendly in the future, whether he would become a stranger. The morning she left for good she made it only to the end of her block before she wanted to turn back. It had rained that day. The town school bus was on the street, picking up the children, and all the parents were out, all her neighbors, the whole collected good cheer of their community. She started to back up her car then. She may or may not have been weeping. She had the picture— the original picture of their meeting, Day 1, Moment 1—folded away in her glove box, positioned conveniently beside a pack of tissues. The Real Oona. She had not anticipated feeling this doubt. She had planned on leaving for weeks. She had already forwarded her mail to her mother's. Backing up, she figured she would just go back in and pretend it had not happened, but then the school bus was in her way, the lights flashing, the horn honking. It was a narrow road, room enough for only a single lane of traffic. "What are you doing?" one of her neighbors said, knocking at her car window. "You can't back up. You can't. There's no space for you."

# 4.

Widowhood had made sleep impossible. At first it was the obvious things. Plainly put, the bed felt strange. She would reach out and feel nothing, and when she felt nothing, the horror returned. She had, at least, expected this, even as she had difficulty remembering to speak in the past tense. She *had* known him. He *was* here. We *were* in love.

Then the worry set in. Worry was the great constant of her life. She had worried as a girl, over the simplest things. Would they have enough food to eat? Would the landlord raise the rent too high? Would her mother hurt herself in the factory where she worked? When she became a mother herself the worry grew exponentially: Oona breathing, Oona swallowing, Oona on the school bus, Oona encountering cruelty in the world, or strange men, or violence, or encountering the simplest disappointments. Lately Henrietta worried about the elemental things: money and shelter. Her anxiety at this point was another limb. At the airport in New York recently, flying home to Boston after days of prepublication business for *The Inseparables,* she had half expected to see physical evidence of this when she crossed through the X-ray machine. Some hidden weight, some new stealth growth, a uniformed man stopping her with his hands up. *You don't expect to fly with that thing, do you?* Nothing worked to alleviate the sensation. At night she had counted in her head everything one was told to count to help get to sleep, every species of adorable farm creature, but she had lived all these years on this farm, and had seen Harold break down these animals into meat, and when she made the attempt, for example, to count rabbits, she saw them becoming dismembered, bone by bone, breast after breast, just before everything was dropped into a sizzling sauté pan and then smothered in white wine and butter. She was told to rub her feet together, that it would work to calm her. She was told to take long deep breaths, to time her respiration, to fool her own body into thinking it was already asleep. She tried the simple homeopathic remedies—warm milk, chamomile, New Age music, Scotch whisky—but she had always believed homeopathic remedies were bullshit. A pair of foam earplugs jammed in deep only made her heartbeat that much louder. She could feel and hear the path her blood took, in through each ventricle and chamber and then out and then in again, but the simple noise of her being alive proved too distracting.

Sleeping pills did the trick, but often getting to sleep only brought more trouble. She had two types of dreams. In one, he was dead already, and the task of burying him, of actually, physically shoveling the dirt onto his casket, had fallen to her. She had this dream most nights. If she was lucky enough to not have this dream, she dreamed instead that he was alive, here with her, that she was reliving their last minutes together, and that she knew what was about to happen to him, knew the exact time, even, but could not get the words out to warn him. *What is it?* he kept asking. *What is it?* When she woke, the misery was compounded. She was sure that she could feel the sensation of his hand on her hand. Her own cheek felt brushed by the stubble on his beard, a beard that did not exist, because he was not alive. Often, she'd discover that in a fit of dream-induced mourning she'd torn off all the sheets and blankets and sometimes the pillows as well. Which was what she had done last night. She thought of this shortly after Oona had left. She was in the bedroom cleaning because a visitor was coming from Sotheby's, of all places, and because Henrietta needed at least to try to make the house look presentable. This was a matter of making money.

Money had dictated so much of the eleven months. Money was why she had become an expert at all the substandard condominium complexes in the Greater Boston area, why she had lately taken to playing the lottery so often, and money, her absolute lack of it, her distressing need for more of it, was why she was selling the house and moving, and money was the reason why she had finally allowed *The Inseparables* to be republished. The editors at Hubbard had wanted to do this for the twenty-fifth anniversary, and then for the thirtieth, but she had refused, arming herself with attorneys, protesting even the slightest movement that might allow *That Motherfucking Thing* back into the world. She imagined the book sometimes as a hot-pink swarm of bees, trapped inside and banging against a windowpane, dying to get out. Now she had no choice.

All of this started a few weeks ago. Potential buyers were making their way through Henrietta's house on a tour when a young man had stopped at her mantel. He stared intently at a small copper statue of a woman in a hat and skirt holding the American flag in one hand and looking out with purpose and dignity at something impressive and far off in the distance. It had been part of the weathervane on the house when Henrietta and Harold first moved here, but after a storm knocked it off the roof one of the first winters, she had kept it on the ledge, damaged and dinged, a tiny chip missing from the top of the flagpole. The young man put on a pair of gloves and then asked if he could hold the statue. "Do you mind?" He turned it over in his hand. Then: "Do you know what this is?" he asked.

Henrietta had laughed. "I'm pretty sure it's part of my roof that blew off."

The man worked not far from Aveline, he explained, and taught Early American art history at one of the local universities. His specialty was things like this, he said. She felt an instant kinship: Henrietta had a particular affection for academic disciplines with no market value.

"I used to teach women's studies," she explained, to no real response. This was why she liked the statue. Something about the expression on the woman's face. An early symbol of dignity and power. Evidence of the continuing struggle. She was trying to make conversation.

The man offered two thousand for it. He took out his wallet. "We can drive to an ATM right now."

As much as she could have used $2,000, Henrietta refused. The next day she spent the morning emailing photographs of the weathervane to the various auction houses and specialists in Boston. Right away, a woman from Sotheby's named Juliet Lippincourt wrote to say that she was interested. "Depending on the condition," Juliet had answered, "these can be surprisingly valuable."

Henrietta had written back immediately. "What exactly do you mean by 'surprisingly'?"

To which Juliet had responded, "I mean that you could do much, much better than two thousand."

In preparation for Juliet Lippincourt's visit this afternoon, Henrietta had gathered a half dozen other items from the house that she thought might also be worth money. Suddenly, she wondered if there was more here that was surprisingly valuable. Perhaps her whole house contained valuable surprises. She had arranged everything on the dining room table.

A tiny cedar box, carried over on the passage from the family house in Odessa, inscribed with the first name of her grandfather. Jewelry inherited from her aunt Essie. A pistol given to Harold alleged to have once belonged to John Dillinger. The autographed picture of Frank Sinatra that Frank had given Harold the last time he ate at the restaurant. Also, the silver teapot from the back of her book.

It was important to note that these were things she could bear to lose. There were other things, valuable things, holy and crucial things that she had considered selling, that she had arranged here on the table alongside the cedar box and the picture of Frank Sinatra and Dillinger's pistol, and for the past three nights she had lingered over the whole collection, trying to decide. Sell or keep? Junk or save? All night she had been adding to and subtracting from the collection. One of Harold's wristwatches. His favorite chef's knife. This was all a part of death, she knew. The packing away, the discarding, the irrational sentimentalizing of inanimate objects. Or, in Henrietta's case, the realization that maybe she had nothing here worth anything at all. It was a cheap watch. A normal chef's knife. Room after room of clutter and tchotchkes. Drawers full of things that were once probably indispensable to her husband: a dog's leash, a candy thermometer, cartridges of super 8 film on which they were young and their daughter was young and everyone was alive and vital and ignorant of the future. Could she realistically envision herself selling Harold's watch? Or his knives? In the event that there was an afterlife, wouldn't he expect her to come bounding into heaven carrying these things?

Alone among all these packed boxes these last few nights, she felt sometimes as if she were present at her own death. Artifacts of Harold's life were also artifacts of her life. She had done this for her mother and father in their apartment on Orchard Street. They had lived in the same small place all of their adult lives.

Henrietta was born in the bigger of the two bedrooms, a room outfitted with an oak furniture set, the same room in which both her mother (heart attack) and her father (stroke) died, a few weeks apart. She had spent ten days there after her dad's funeral. They were ten days when she'd done exactly what she was doing now: alternating between labeling everything as waste and feeling the pressing urge to inspect every last item. This, she had reasoned, was how one bears witness to a life. By physically holding each thing: keys to forgotten locks; a hairbrush with her mother's hair left in it; letters from her grandmother to her grandfather dated 1906, when they were both teenagers, sent after they had left one of the innumerable pogroms they had survived. *Are you alive out there, Franz?* one began. When Henrietta finished, she had to turn over the key to the landlord, who was the son of the original landlord, a man she had known when he was a boy. He lived still in the same apartment where he had lived in 1954, two floors down from her parents. He was a larger, grayer version of the boy she'd known, and for an instant in his kitchen, which was a mirror of her own former kitchen, she had thought about whether or not it would be a comforting thing to stay in one place for a lifetime. Maybe everything would be easier here in these same hot rooms, in this same squalid building. She had the key in her hand and she thought to herself, *I could do this. I could just stay here. Another Horowitz woman in this same tiny apartment.* She cried when she turned it over. She was sixty years old then. She had always had a key to this door.

Juliet arrived shortly after Oona left. Henrietta watched from her bedroom window. A picket-thin woman about her age, with an impressively hard shell of immaculately white hair, Juliet tottered quickly up the snowy walkway. Greeting her by the front door, Henrietta suffered a moment of panicked anxiety. This happened whenever she met a person who appeared older than fifty and who looked vaguely bookish. Did Juliet know who she was? Had she gotten off the phone last month and then immediately Googled Henrietta's name to discover all the miserable reviews and all the countless pornographic diagrams she'd drawn? This was the old story, the old worry, which receded every year as more people forgot about her and her book and the scandal and those diagrams, leaving her here on her own. Everything, so quickly, was changing.

They shook hands. Juliet had come dressed all in black aside from a pair of white gloves, which Henrietta guessed she wore because she anticipated handling something precious and valuable. This made Henrietta smile. For years the weathervane had sat here above the fireplace, periodically encased in creosote, occasionally festooned with tiny Christmas garlands or, worse, used as a toy for the dogs to chew. If this thing held any intrinsic value after all this time, it was because she had used the image of the woman as an inspiration for the heroine in her book. Her family knew this, but no one else. It had not turned out to be the sort of book that elicited obvious allusions to Early American folk art. She'd settled on the name Eugenia because Oona, when she was very young, had rubbed her hand against the woman's belly as if she were a magic genie. This was how Genie became Eugenia.

"Excuse the mess," Henrietta said preemptively. "I'm moving."

"I see that," Juliet said, with a noticeable look of concern on her face.

"I take it from your expression that you don't often collect works of art in places as messy as this," Henrietta said.

"Not frequently," Juliet said. "No."

"It's safe here," Henrietta said. "The weathervane, I meant. Not you. Although you are also safe here. I assure you."

Juliet offered a nervous smile. "That's good."

Henrietta took her into the living room. She felt keenly aware of the mess, the dirt, the general disorder. The old house-wifely instincts rose up—instincts she detested, but instincts nonetheless hammered into her by her mother and grand-mother. She felt herself on the verge of apologies—a subject she had lectured on years ago: the gendered propensity for needless justification—when she remembered, *This is a business transaction. I need money.*

They had spoken earlier in the week by phone. Juliet wanted Henrietta to send pictures so that she could generate a general ballpark figure. Henrietta had managed inexpertly, using the camera on her phone. "If the market is right, there's no telling what one of these can fetch," Juliet told her.

This surprised Henrietta. "Is there really a market for weath-ervanes?"

"There's a market for everything," Juliet had told her, before emailing Henrietta photographs of weathervanes that looked vaguely similar to hers, and which had fetched nearly a half mil-lion dollars at auction.

The numbers astonished her. "You're sure we're talking about the same thing? Those things on your house that go round and round in the wind? I thought they were junk."

"Those very same things," Juliet said. "They're not junk. They're considered works of art." Instantly Henrietta did the math in her head. A half million dollars, even with the penalty for tax and commission, could sustain her for at least fifteen more years if she lived frugally. That would get her to age eighty-five. A good age. A full life. A life extended miraculously by the discovery of a weathervane. Then Juliet issued a caveat after looking over the images Henrietta had sent: "Mind you, the examples I emailed over, those were in terrific condition. Far more so than yours looks to be."

In the living room, Juliet stood expectantly, adjusting her

white gloves. Juliet's preliminary ballpark figure had come in at $10,000, which, Henrietta knew, would not change her life. But then again, $10,000 was ten thousand she did not have.

"Before we do the exchange," Henrietta said, "I have a few other things I was hoping you might look at."

Juliet said nothing. Impatiently, she stretched her neck, and then her gloved fingers.

"See, I've been packing the place up," Henrietta said, already feeling a queasy sense of humiliation and dread. "And I've found some things I think might also be worth something."

Juliet shrugged. "Well, I'm certainly happy to look," she said, although she did not seem it.

Henrietta moved toward the table, waving her hand across everything she'd gathered as if she were a game show host. Juliet paused a moment to regard the table and everything on it. There may never have been a more uninterested moment. And this, Henrietta thought, this was the best stuff she could find in her house.

Juliet took a pair of eyeglasses from her purse. They were thick and outfitted with magnifying lenses. First, she took the cedar box, inspecting it, shining a flashlight onto it.

Henrietta had tried to have someone do this in her parents' apartment. She'd brought in a man from one of the neighborhood antique shops, and he'd spent all of five minutes perusing her mother's gold jewelry, her furniture, her collection of Russian poetry, before deeming it all worthless. "The gold is fake," the man had told her. "The furniture is junk. Also, nobody cares about Russian poetry."

Henrietta fared only slightly better this time. Juliet turned the pistol over in her hand and then moved on to the cedar box. This was all that was left of Henrietta's grandfather's house, the story went. The village had burned, children were killed, but this box remained. Juliet put it down.

She inspected the jewelry impassively, glanced at the picture of Sinatra, and then held the teapot in her hand for an incurious moment before she turned away from everything and smiled blankly at Henrietta.

"Maybe it's best if I just see the weathervane," Juliet said.

"Nothing?" Henrietta asked. "You don't want any of it?"

Juliet took off her eyeglasses slowly. "I'm more interested in the weathervane, is all."

Henrietta picked up the box. She told the story of her grandfather returning to his house after the village was stormed and burned by men on horseback. Juliet listened politely. Henrietta emphasized once more the village storming and the horses and the fire.

"It's a very nice box," Juliet said.

"It's a relic!" Henrietta said. "It's history!"

Juliet nodded.

"What about the gun?" Henrietta picked it up clumsily and pointed it at the floor. "John Dillinger owned this gun. Dillinger the gangster."

"I can give you the name of someone who—"

"Or this? This is Frank Sinatra."

"I know that's Frank Sinatra," Juliet said.

"Frank's not worth anything?"

"I'm sure he is," Juliet said. "But you contacted me about the weathervane, which is potentially worth far more than Frank Sinatra."

Henrietta put the picture down beside the gun and the teapot. On the counter, only steps away, was the new box full of *The Inseparables*. She could, she knew, pick up the teapot and a copy of the book, and try, at least for a moment, to curry some favor with her own odd, shameful celebrity. Instead, she took Juliet into the formal dining room. This was one of the few rooms in the house not yet totally overwhelmed by boxes, which was why, after discovering that the statue might be worth something, she had stored it here, cocooned in protective Bubble Wrap and placed inside a shoe box for safekeeping. But when she went there now to retrieve it, she couldn't find it. The box was gone.

Henrietta stood, confused, turning. "It's not here," she said. Juliet took a deep breath.

"I put it in a box," Henrietta said, her voice rising. "A blue box. All month it's been here, stored away and safe."

Juliet turned in a circle. "The whole house is full of boxes. You sure you didn't pack it up?"

"You told me it was worth ten thousand dollars. I'm sure I'd remember."

"Maybe you forgot."

Henrietta closed her eyes. She had turned seventy this year and was growing used to these kinds of conversations. It had started with her last birthday. The doubting, the yelling, the endless repetition of easy questions, the slow speaking, the here-let-me-help-you-with-this. Seventy was, she knew, unmistakably unyoung, but out in town, at the store, people had begun to talk to her as if she were an infant. *This is a computer. This is a cell phone. Have you heard of email?*

Juliet sat down. "Let's think," she said, suddenly friendly. "Have you had a lot of people in the house?"

All this month Henrietta had had so many real estate agents coming and going from her house. The very notion of having to surrender a key to someone other than Oona or Harold terrified her. As had the indignity of so many people trampling in and out, casting their quiet but unmistakable pity onto her old house and, worse, onto all the last things Harold had touched, which were, by the transitive logic of death, the most sacred objects in her world. It was not a stretch to say that the place, set back against acres of lush dogwood and sumac and uncut switchgrass, was failing. Buyers today wanted something that looked old but felt new. Henrietta's house looked old and felt older. Her real estate firm tried to find a positive angle for the sale. They cut the price lower than she wanted. They brought in fashion-forward furniture for "staging." Everything was low-slung. Couches so low you practically needed a crane to lower yourself into place, or else you had to trust-fall into the cushions. Furniture like this reinforced the idea that you, as the human, were powerful and huge and could accomplish anything. Someone had told her this. The tinier the sofas, the bigger the cash. Someone had said this also. Everything would need to be white, because whiteness in the world of buying and selling was synonymous with optimism, and optimism here was necessary, because this place, this big old spooky place, had something about it that reeked of darkness. Someone, incredibly, had said this, too.

They moved into the kitchen, where Henrietta opened random boxes, looking for the weathervane. Juliet took a seat and waited. It was a big and open room, Harold's favorite, with three windows that looked out to the field and the river. They had eaten Sunday dinners here, every week, right from the very beginning, a secular tradition that went unbroken until his death. It was the one night Harold did not work, but still he would spend most of the day preparing the meal — rolling fresh pasta, or spit-roasting meat, or waiting for dough to rise in the hottest corner, by the sunlit glass. The very first night they were in this house together, they had slept here because their beds had not yet arrived, and she could remember waking that first morning, her husband asleep on the floor, warm light in through the windows, the sky clear, the river fast and dark.

Juliet stood up and began to walk. "When you find it," she said, "just call me. I'll come back."

"But it's here," Henrietta said, standing up, the box cutter in her hand. "It's here somewhere."

Juliet found Harold's suitcase. "Maybe you put it in here," she said, crouching, her hand on the zipper.

Henrietta felt herself lunging before she could open her mouth to speak. "No! Please! Don't!"

# 5.

At first Lydia met with an Internet specialist. She did not know such a person existed on campus. He was a young man, maybe twenty-two, with rimless eyeglasses. Did she understand that as she aged her notions of privacy and the privacy of her body would shift? She assured him that she did. He repeated the question, word for word, this time slowly, as if some not-so-subtle condescension might help her understand better. This picture, he told her, would exist on the Internet for all eternity. Did she understand exactly what that meant? Did she realize that the Internet forgot nothing? She had thought the question was open-ended and at first did not say anything. The man opened up the calendar on his desktop and started scrolling through the years: 2017, 2057, 2117. "This is the future going by," the man explained. Did she understand that this picture would still be floating around in the year 2117?

Next she met with the head of discipline. Evidently Hartwell employed a three-strikes policy when it came to matters like this. This was news to Lydia. *Distribution of forbidden imagery,* they called it, which was a perfect summation of Hartwell's approach to difficult problems. Needlessly arcane, bureaucratically heartless, and institutionally reluctant to call it what it was. She could, it turned out, have sex with a classmate if she so chose, but she could not send a picture of herself to that same classmate. A stern woman with a local accent, the head of discipline told Lydia that Charlie was gone for good and that because this was her first infraction she would be suspended for only a week. In her opinion, Lydia had gotten off lightly. *I give up with kids like you. This isn't a video game. You don't get to reset and erase your mistakes.*

Lydia sat up at this. "He had two other strikes before this?" she asked, her voice rising. "He's done this before? With other girls? And you let him stay?"

The woman closed her notebook. "I can't discuss the disciplinary files of other students. There are privacy issues involved."

"What about the privacy of my body?" she asked.

The woman nodded eagerly. "Exactly."

Then Abernathy took her to the therapist's office. Cinnamon candles sat flickering on the windowsill. On the side of a writing desk, there was a bust of someone who might have been Carl Jung or who might simply have been a younger version of the therapist himself. He said nothing at first, and Lydia felt a gnawing, queasy sense of unease. A pair of paper folders sat on the table between them. One was the pink folder, which had in it, she assumed, her disciplinary sentence. The other was black. Staring at it, she felt convinced that it held a copy of her picture. She felt ill again. Had this man—in tweed, caramel loafers, and a soul patch—seen what everyone else had seen?

"We can talk," the therapist said, finally.

Lydia folded her arms across her chest.

"About anything," he told her.

Down below, on campus, the school bell rang. She kept eyeing the black folder.

"But you don't need to talk," he said. "We can sit here."

She felt her phone buzzing.

"You know, it's a violation," he said, and for a moment she thought he was talking about the phone. "We recognize that. An alarming violation. It's a humiliation. An invasion."

A minute passed.

"Maybe we can talk about why you took the picture in the first place."

"I thought I didn't need to talk," she said.

He wrote down this sentence in a notebook. Then he picked up the black folder.

"You know," she said, looking around, "is there another therapist I can talk to? Maybe a woman?"

Now she waited.

She'd begun to think of it as a storm. Monday to Monday. A week, basically, of public nudity. On the walkway between buildings, she was nude. In chapel, beneath the looming stained glass image of the risen Christ, she was nude. During discussions on Napoleon's foray into Russia, or on the family structure of beluga whales, or on differential equations: nude. So often she had awoken at night having had a dream that she was naked in class and everyone could see. What did it mean when something like this actually came true?

The general socially accepted rule about nude selfies was that you were not supposed to keep them on your phone. If they were just on your phone, saved like any other picture, like a particularly adorable picture of a golden retriever, or like a picture of a really delicious plate of cinnamon pancakes you ate two weekends ago in Manhattan, then anyone could steal those pictures and distribute them wholesale to anyone interested in naked bodies. Which was what had happened to Lydia. If you wanted to send a picture of yourself topless, or topless and bottomless, to someone you were interested in, as a way to flirt, or simply as an innocent substitute for actual, genuine sex, then you did it in such a way that the pictures vanished the moment someone got them. This made the picture temporary and ephemeral, and most of all, it made it thrilling. "I can't believe you were this stupid. It's like you're the only one who doesn't know how to do this," one of her roommates had said. Everyone pretended that her having kept this picture was a sign of some burgeoning sexual dysfunction, when instead it was simply a result of how deeply she wanted to see herself the way some fucking idiot boy did, or a symptom of her own curiosity. Or maybe just an illustration of how deep her own vanity ran. She had no idea anymore.

Abernathy left her in a long corridor lined with photographs of the graduated students who had gone on to become things like Navy SEALs or television hosts. Electric fragrance fountains dispensed fake spruce into the air, and the whole place smelled like a shopping mall at Christmas. The tiny leather chair she occupied was clearly meant for a small child. Hartwell took students as young as six, taught them Mandarin, Shakespeare, and computer coding, and spat them back out into the world as currency traders or diplomats or white-collar criminals. Lydia was the rare thing here: a recent exile from a normal public education.

She snuck her phone from her back pocket, expecting the usual torrent of misery. This was how it had been this last week. They came every hour at least, a few dozen in total, all from anonymous addresses, nearly everyone with an obnoxious retort. Fuck girl, why aren't you in my shower? Or: Please let me fuck you. Or else photos of their dicks. In the outside world this wouldn't have been a blip. Pictures like this multiplied every hour, she knew, but at Hartwell, even the most timid prurience earned the biggest scandal. Some of the messages were surprisingly earnest. I think you're really pretty. Or: I love natural breasts. She had tried, in those first panicked hours, to stanch the bleeding, writing every single person back. `Please stop sharing this. Please delete this.` The moment she realized that there wasn't a soul at Hartwell who had not seen her topless, she was sick all over her bed.

At the end of the corridor a set of doors swung open, and Lydia saw her mother coming down the hallway. Beside her was the headmistress. Lydia's first instinct was to run to her mother. It surprised her to feel this. Boarding school was supposed to inculcate independence. Accelerate her becoming an adult. Separate her from her mother as painlessly as possible. She had pleaded to be allowed to come here. In Crestview, sending your child to boarding school was tantamount to admitting that you had stopped loving her enough to keep her around. It was not something you could readily confess at a dinner party. Lydia had lobbied hard, bombarded her mother with brochures. Look! The happy-looking people! The cavernous library! The grand-looking buildings! Appealing to her mother's vanity, Lydia had shown off the statistic claiming that Hartwell produced an inordinate number of physicians. I could be just like you! As her mother got closer, Lydia fought to keep herself from crying. She had her phone hidden against the waistline of her pants. She worried about it buzzing, because every buzz, she knew, corresponded with another message from someone here. She began to shake. *Mom,* she managed. *Mommy.*

The headmistress went directly past Lydia and toward her office without making eye contact. For a brief moment they were in the hallway together, Lydia and her mother, looking at each other, waiting for the office door at the end of the hall to close so that they could hug. The last time they'd seen each other was a month ago, on a visitors' weekend. Lydia had taken the bus to Aveline and they'd eaten takeout Korean food by the fireplace. For the first time, Lydia had a vision of her future—a future in which she and her mother were adults together, something almost close to friends. After dinner her mother had tried to explain the status of her marriage, speaking in euphemisms about the difficulty of marital togetherness and about spousal cooperation and about the myth of matrimonial compromise and about Gwyneth Paltrow. Before Lydia left for school, they'd agreed to talk every night. Then, when that hadn't worked out, they agreed on every third day, and then every weekend. She wasn't sure why they had stopped talking. She wondered sometimes whether a daughter's innate desire to admire her mother was like a kind of addiction you needed to break eventually. Or whether you got to a certain age and began simply to replace your mother with a regrettable string of people like Charlie Perlmutter, people who were readily willing to say that they loved you, or at least steal a picture of your nude body and deliver it to every inbox they could find.

When they were finally alone, her mother grabbed hold of her so tightly that Lydia let out a small gasp.

"Are you all right?" her mother said.

Lydia took a breath. "You just squeezed me hard, is all."

"That's not what I meant, Lydia."

Lydia looked up. "I don't know what to say. No. Clearly, I'm not fucking okay."

Her mother held her at arm's length, as if inspecting her for visible wounds.

"Did you send it?" her mother asked her.

"No," Lydia managed.

"People here seem fairly sure that you sent it."

"Because Charlie said I did. And because there's a picture of me floating around. So obviously they'd believe him over me," she said. "And do you really think I'd do that?"

"I didn't think you'd take a picture of yourself like that in the first place."

"Wait," Lydia said. "They *showed* you?"

Her mother let go of Lydia. "No, of course they didn't show us. They're not criminals."

She let out a long breath. She had assumed everyone had seen it. Her mother, realizing this, hugged her to her chest and held on, as if Lydia were about to fall off the edge of a building.

"Everyone's very worried about this," her mother said. "I'm worried about this."

"If they're so worried, why are they suspending me? Like *I'm* the one who did something wrong. Someone did something to me. This is fucked. Everyone's seen it. Every person here."

"Relax," her mother said. "Breathe."

"Impossible," Lydia said.

In her ear, her mother whispered, "And who the hell is this Charlie person? You never said anything about him."

Lydia closed her eyes. "He's nobody," she said.

"Your father will probably want to kill him," her mother said. "I want to kill him."

"Where is Dad?"

"He's downstairs. Fighting with the dean. Or one of the deans. There's too many deans at this weird school."

"Fighting?"

"He's a lawyer. He fights." Her mother reached out and put her hand in Lydia's hand. "He's good at fighting."

"Fighting about what?"

"I don't know. He started yelling. I got up and left. It's a reflex of mine at this point."

The headmistress came out into the hall, holding both the pink and the black folders. She was Gerta Schiller from Berlin, a supposed expert in educational theory. A celebrated author on the biological tendencies for risk-taking in the teenage brain. Readily armed with statistics about adolescent dopamine levels. So far Lydia had had exactly one interaction with Schiller prior to this, and it was about her grandmother's novel. Did she know about it? Had she read it? Did she have an opinion on the fact that some Hartwell parents were trying to ban it? Had she been deluded, because of this book, with any outmoded ideas about sex and smut and vice and the human female body? All were questions that seemed at the moment to be especially prescient.

"I want to go home," Lydia said. "I don't want to go in there."

Her mother nodded. "I'll go see what I can do."

"Instead of listening to why she should suspend me, maybe you should show her this." She held up her phone. "Look. Show her what people are writing. Look at the pictures people are sending me."

Her mother took the phone and allowed herself the first few messages in Lydia's inbox. Lydia stood, watching. Her mother's finger touched the screen gingerly, and then, with every comment or attached picture, her expression fell. Outside, the sky dimmed. Through a small window Lydia could see the roads leading in and out of campus, and far off, beyond that, the thrilling gray snake of the freeway, which signaled escape and freedom and anonymity.

She heard her mother, beside her, suck for air, out of shock or maybe out of disgust. She'd shut off the phone.

Again, she reached out for Lydia, clutching her by the arms, not letting go.

# 6.

The first thing Henrietta ever saw of the house was the big field, with the grass long and uncut and heavy in the summer humidity. This was August 1975. They had come up together from the city in a borrowed green Volkswagen, leaving after her morning lecture. Acres of fence line, white and chipped, gave way to fieldstone and the stumps of chopped birch. Harold was thrilled, and because this was how it went when she was with him, Henrietta felt thrilled as well. From the road, the house looked better than she had thought. She had seen pictures, and in the pictures everything looked old. Out in the grass, a tractor rusted. They parked and there were butterflies in the oaks and there were deer out grazing. She had never seen a live deer before. Just Teddy Roosevelt's deer, stuffed and behind glass on 81st and Columbus. Harold got out first and bent down to rub his hands in the dirt, and then turned with a boyish smile to show her his covered black palms. He knew things about soil and nitrogen levels and about how to change things to make vegetables sweeter. She had grown up Henrietta Horowitz, on the fourth floor of a tenement flat on Orchard Street. Her father collected junk for money. Her mother worked a steam press in a garment factory. She had shared a bedroom with her sister and her aunt until she was sixteen years old. The idea of personal space always seemed theoretical to her. She turned in a full circle, taking everything in—all the good acres and the wind in the trees.

They were moving because Harold was set to open a restaurant in Boston. Before this, she had always planned to keep teaching after the baby. She had a detailed ten-year plan that included scholarly research, academic appointments in Rome, social agitation. This was the town where he had grown up. It would be good for the baby, he told her. Inexplicably, she felt something close to excitement at the idea.

The house sat perched at the top of a steep hill. Spreading out, west to east, there were nearly two hundred acres. On the front porch, flowerpots hung from wooden stanchions, and rubber boots caked in mud were lined up near the steps. On the roof, wind spun the weathervane to a blur. It was true that a part of her cried out *treason!* at the notion of doing this. Or acquiescence. At the prospect of planting watercress and wax beans in the earth, she felt the sting of conformity. It came, deafening and endless, like an invisible chorus. Not you! A woman like her, a professor, almost a scholar, with dirt beneath her fingernails, assuming the retrograde position, a baby on her back, planting and digging and running a wet mop across the hardwood, or a vacuum up the runner on the big staircase. Farming? Gardening? This was not the same Henrietta lecturing most Tuesday afternoons on the political history of reproduction. Or on embedded structural oppression. Before this, she had never considered leaving her life in the city, or following any man anywhere, but here, all of a sudden, was Harold Olyphant, talking about the country, talking about babies running around in the high grass, talking about Henrietta transforming from an urban Poindexter into Laura Ingalls Wilder. This was where they would milk the cows. This was where they would let the chickens run. At any other moment in her life, his asking her to come here would have wrought such a simple answer. In the car up through New England, though, she knew already something elemental had changed. She wanted this because she wanted to make him happy and because, privately, secretly, half shamefully, she thought he was right: that being here, with a life like this, with some goddamned fresh wax beans, might be better for the baby. A month ago, a week ago, twelve hours ago, even, a sentence like this would have bordered on political heresy. Love had unexpectedly rearranged her.

She walked off into the dirt. She felt the word "fraud" ringing in her ears. The land sloped to the water, wild with goldenrod. Moss carpeted the fieldstone. He told her he would plant apple trees for her. She liked this. Birds passed overhead. She turned. "I like this," she said.

"You sound surprised."

"I am surprised," she said. "I'm very surprised. But I like this. I do."

He smiled. "Remember this," he said.

"Remember what?"

"I want you to remember that you just said that out loud."

She laughed.

"It's temporary," he said, reminding her of their plan. "I open the restaurant, it does well, then we get a place in the city in a few years."

"But maybe I'll like being a farmer," she said, smiling. "Maybe I'll write a book about farming. A social history of agriculture."

"I could definitely see it," he said. "Overalls. Cucumber harvest. Raspberries on the bush. Sure."

"You know I tried to grow tomatoes on my windowsill last year. They died. The ones that didn't die were covered in this weird, grotesque blue mold. I'm guessing they were practically poisonous. People at the university thought I was actually trying to kill my students."

"Fine. Maybe I grow the vegetables and you take care of the farm animals," he said.

She laughed. "I'm guessing that if I killed the tomatoes, the farm animals won't fare much better."

They walked from the porch down the steep hill. He caught her closing her eyes against the warm sun and the wind. A cow stood out in the yard, staring at her, at both of them, grass in its mouth.

Harold stood beside her, laughing. "Remember this," he said again. "You told me you like it. You actually said the words."

"I promise," she said. "I'll remember."

Over Harold's shoulder the river was full, and she could hear the rush of the current slamming against the stones on the bed. A true city girl, Henrietta did not have a driver's license. She would need lessons. She watched him. He had the hands of a cook. Burns on his fingers. Knife scars on his knuckles. She did like this. He picked up a long blade of grass, twirled it between his fingers, and put it in his mouth.

"It doesn't taste that bad," he said. "You want to try?"

Three months later, Henrietta gave birth to Oona in the small aquamarine bedroom on the second floor of the new house. She had not wanted an institutional birth, the antisepsis of a hospital, the divvying up by sex so that the men were in the waiting room with the cigars, and so they did it here, with a midwife, in this small room with music playing and with the windows open to the big field. A hanging pendant light swung in the breeze, and she focused on this as she breathed through the pain. At some point there was the smell of grass through the windows, and dried leaves, and flowers, maybe, all of this, she knew, a hallucinatory sensation caused by pain. Harold pressed a cold wet

washcloth to her forehead. "I'm here," he told her, in a soothing voice, standing off to the side. "You sure as hell better be
here," she told him. Her baby came at noon on the last warm
day of fall. Yet another Horowitz woman giving birth at home.

In the beginning it was good here. They threw parties in the
barn. Friends drove up from New York, armed with samizdat
and smoked fish and with toys for Oona, all the while regaling
Henrietta with stories about their rallies and marches and about
their late-night meetings in the basement of the Judson Church.
Henrietta did not miss the old life, she said, and when her
friends took her for a walk on the river and said out of earshot
of Harold that they did not believe her, said that they were in
fact *worried* for her, she said it once again, as convincingly as
she could manage. "Life is good here," she said, picking grass
between her fingers and putting it in her mouth. "Really. It's
good. Honestly."

During the first spring, they bought baby goats and chicks.
Their cows gave birth in the new barn and there was fresh
milk. Harold made his own butter. In the summer the restaurant opened and she named it the Feast. On opening night, the
line to get in snaked around the block. Afterward, at one in the
morning, she sat alone with him at a table in the corner, eating
a fresh roasted chicken that they had raised together. Beyond
their table, lantern light flickered on the cobblestones and they
felt, both of them, as if they were at the start of something honest and good and real.

She began her book after the Fourth of July, in the cramped
office she made for herself off the bedroom. She had painted the
room a pale yellow because she had read somewhere that pale
yellow inspired creativity. She hung pictures of New York above
her desk, not the obvious stuff, not the Brooklyn Bridge at sun-
set or the cloying postcard view of Central Park, but pictures of
her mother in her steam presser uniform, and her aunt Essie on

the front steps of the old tenement the day Essie had buried her husband. She wrote longhand, at night, in the creaking quiet, lukewarm coffee in a cup at her elbow, another hanging light-bulb swinging above her, her husband asleep a few feet away, with the baby on his chest, the two of them, more often than not, breathing in time with each other: Harold breathing, then Oona breathing; him breathing, then her.

Routines emerged. Each morning, Harold went out into the yard before leaving for the restaurant, heading across the meadow to the edge of the woods, where he'd built a pen for the animals and a small hut to keep stacks of firewood. In the cold months, when they needed it, he brought in the wood. In the warm months, he checked on the animals, or else he went to the barn to fetch wine for the house to replace what they'd finished the night before. When he was home at night, meat smoke on his skin, he made the same loop, checking the hut, the river, the oak, checking the animals. This was at two in the morning, usually. Sometimes later. He kept the worst hours. She watched him do this long circuit, morning and night. In the beginning she did this because at first life in Aveline was slow and boring. Then watching him became habit. Mostly it was because he was gone all day, and she stayed at home by herself with the baby for such long hours. Motherhood, in the beginning, was a form of loneliness.

Their second winter in the house, Henrietta was home with Oona when storms cut the power. Weathermen had been making noise for days about the arctic temperatures. This was Canadian weather, they said. Days of snow. Ice clogged the storm drains, exploded the pipes, flooded the basement. Dispatches on the radio warned of hail and thundersnow. An oak upturned in the yard while Henrietta watched, the huge root-tear of the earth rising up from the lawn like an embankment. She stood in the living room with Oona, eighteen months old by then and hysterical. Henrietta called for Harold at the restaurant but he was busy. The dining room, even in a storm like this, was full. She put music on the battery-powered radio, hoping it might calm the baby. She played her mother's music, Duke Ellington doing "Blue Goose." Eventually she needed the batteries for the flashlights. Then the only sound was the uneasy boat-creak of the walls in the wind. She put the stove on for heat. The baby wore two coats and two blankets. Outside: waves of sleet. Pink light above the tree line.

This was when the roof was hit. When she told the story afterward, she made it more dramatic. She had watched it flutter off, paper in the breeze. She saw it peel away, shingle by shingle. She blinked and then the whole thing vanished. In fact, it had happened over hours. A tiny hole made bigger, gust after gust. Water came in, soaked the second floor, and then eventually the first. She and Oona went to wait in the car, the engine running, warm finally. In the early morning, when Harold came home from the Feast, he sat with them in the car, watching the trees bend, the river whipped up, the barn listing against the blitz. When the weathervane blew off into the meadow, he went and brought it to her and Oona, resting it on the dash, sopping wet, green from the years. "She took a big fall," Henrietta said, joking. Then Harold went back out to pick up more of the debris from the lawn as the storm passed overhead.

This was the image she had of him still. Twenty-eight years old. Younger than she was. Burn marks on his hands. Knife scars on his knuckles. Rushing out, laughing, to pick up a meaningless piece of metal. Harold Olyphant amid lightning and hailstorms and Canada wind. Strong and fit and standing on the flagstone. This was the same spot where, eleven months ago, carrying firewood to the front door, he fell.

She was used to telling the story. It was the slightest thing, she would say. He was coming up the walkway with firewood. It was six in the morning. Not even that much firewood, really, and I watched the whole thing happen. I was standing right there. Where I always stood. It looked like the most minor thing, really. The fall looked so slight. Perhaps if she'd been behind him she might have seen his head smack the flagstone. The door, when she rushed outside after him, had locked behind her. There were marks still on the handle and the edges of the windows from where she'd tried so furiously to break her way back inside. For five minutes he was conscious, talking, woozy. He took her hand while she sat by him. *Isn't it nice here?* he asked. *Don't you like it?*

She thought he would get up. Simple as that. I thought he would get up.

For weeks afterward she found herself at the door in the morning and then again at night. The big field, empty, white in winter, yellow with goldenrod in spring. I'm waiting, she had told Oona when she was found out. This happened the first week Oona was back living with her. It turned out her daughter kept the same hours as her husband. Henrietta hadn't thought to hide anything. The mawkishness of her answer didn't embarrass her, mostly because it was true, and because death unmoored you and altered your gravity and because afterward the quiet of being by yourself goes blood-deep. She missed Harold. After that, Henrietta began to go out into the yard to do the circuit herself. First to the stack of wood by the trees and then down the waterline to the empty animal pens. The first time she did this, she found a spot near the river where the grass had been worn down to dirt. Turning here, she saw what he would have seen from this place, which was the window where she'd stood watching, a small square of glass. They were always waving like idiots. She rubbed her feet in the dirt. Then she got down and rubbed her hands, too, until they were filthy, and her fingernails were rimmed black. Marriage is habit, maybe. She liked to think of it as rhythm. A drumbeat going and going and then stopping.

# 7.

After his fall, Harold lived for days. His room at Mass General overlooked the cloverleaf of the Longfellow Bridge, and beyond that the gray crawling stripe of the Charles. Friends from his boyhood came. A chaplain sat with her. Suddenly the boundary between his body and his soul became necessary to negotiate. Her godlessness never felt so inconvenient. Where exactly were the boundaries, she wanted to know? Flowers arrived, and she measured his progress by the amount of blooms he outlasted. On the last morning, light over the river found its way through the scuffed glass to his forehead, a warm glimmering, maybe meaningless. The river moved outside. Then it froze.

His oldest friend was Jerry Stern. For weeks after the burial, he came to see her, brought her food, swept her porch. He arranged the funeral. She hadn't been able to clean out Harold's things, and he came and did it for her. When the house needed to be sold, he met the real estate agents with her, negotiated a lower commission. For decades he had sold aluminum siding and windows, and he talked down the price on everything with a huckster's ease. He was small and loud and he wore a necktie every time he came to see her. He and Harold had been boys together in West Aveline, on a street Henrietta could see from her back porch if the weather was clear. A whole life in the same spot.

In the afternoon, when the snow had let up and Juliet had gone, Jerry came in his black Mercedes. She watched from the window. He went to the barn, found the shovel, and after a few minutes had dug her out in his overcoat and leather gloves and his wool derby. He hadn't been here since she'd filled the front room with moving boxes, and, opening the door to find them, he stopped. Her leaving bothered him. He'd helped Harold replace the roof when it blew off. He loved this house. He wanted to give her the money to stay.

"Put the figure on a scrap of paper," Jerry said from the doorway, banging snow from the soles of his boots. "You don't even need to say it out loud." Since Jerry and Harold were both only children, they had considered themselves brothers, and Jerry saw it as his responsibility to take care of Henrietta. "Money embarrasses you. You're just like Harold. That's your problem. You're hung up on it."

"I'm not hung up on money," said Henrietta. "I just don't have enough to live here."

"Sacrifice just a fraction of your pride," he said.

"The chances of me taking money from you are nonexistent," she said.

"You take my shoveling ability. My wonderful good humor. My sheer brute strength," he said, trying and failing not to smile. "But not my dough. I don't get it."

"Since when are you so loaded, Jerry? That's what *I* don't get."

"I keep a low overhead."

"Strippers only twice a week?"

He shook his head. "Sex work is a patriarchal tool of oppression and violence, Henrietta."

"Look at you, learning from my old lectures," she said. "How gratifying."

Cleaning out a filing cabinet last month, they had come across a stack of her old class notes. For a few half-serious minutes he had read aloud from a lecture she'd given during her last year in Manhattan, notes on the violent, capitalistic, and patriarchal oppression of sex workers, and he'd pretended to regard her as if she had just admitted she'd come to earth atop a meteorite. "What are you?" he'd joked. "Some kind of left-wing wacko?" This was an old game Henrietta had played with Jerry and his wife, Shirley, who had been dead for a decade. Henrietta had loved her. The Sterns had lived together in a small apartment in Beacon Hill. Shirley Stern was the first real friend Henrietta had in Boston, the person who helped her weather the worst of the storm caused by *The Inseparables*. She was the first white woman Henrietta knew who made her own hummus. The first person she knew to use the phrase marriage equality. On her back terrace, she had grown adzuki beans. Henrietta often felt, searching Shirley's bookshelves, as if she had lived the life Henrietta would have if she'd stayed in New York. While Henrietta had the country and her chicken feed and her goats, Shirley possessed all the things that had gone extinct in the suburbs. Patience. Cultural literacy. Russian novels. Whole milk. She died from a fast-moving blood virus. On a Monday, she had a headache; by Friday, she was gone.

Jerry went across the room to the countertop stereo. He needed music playing. Or a pen to fiddle with. Or tobacco to put in his pipe. In a man like him, restlessness passed for personality. Not only did Jerry remind her of Harold—they talked with the same accent, used the same slang, shared the same childhood memories—but he also reminded her of the men she'd grown up with, men like her father, for whom every conversation was an argument, men with gruff Yiddish street smarts and unshakable superstitions. Jerry spun the radio dial until a rising wash of strings filled the kitchen. Out of nowhere these past few years he had discovered a love of the symphony. Harold had found this hilarious. Henrietta understood: Shirley had loved the symphony, and the music, quite simply, brought her back. He closed his eyes against a swell of violas.

"Mozart," he said. Then: "You know, I think everything is Mozart. I honestly have no idea."

Already this morning she'd told him about Juliet Lippincourt coming and about the missing weathervane. They talked daily. He had become her confidant. She showed him a copy of one of the more valuable examples Juliet had emailed over. He needed to squint to see the paper clearly. His eyes were bad but he refused glasses out of pride and vanity and some admitted stupidity. The downside to possibly getting his eyes fixed, he had always joked to Harold, was that with good vision he'd finally get a decent look at himself in the mirror.

"Is this the thing Harry risked his life for?" Jerry asked.

She smiled, both at the implicit exaggeration of her husband's storytelling and at hearing his old nickname.

"Rain and wind," she said. "That's all. It wasn't exactly the end of the world."

"The way he put it, it was the invasion of Normandy."

"I'm sure he made it sound heroic."

"He sprinted out amid lightning and hailstones."

She nodded. "Well, that *is* true, actually."

When Jerry saw how much the thing had sold for, he smacked the paper. "You're kidding me," he said.

"I had the exact same reaction," said Henrietta. "Believe me."

"This is a weathervane you're talking about?" he asked. "Like, those Waspy metal things on your roof that go round and round in the wind?"

"Harold liked Waspy things," she said.

"Except for you and me," he said.

This made her laugh. On the stereo the song changed. More strings. Jerry took out his phone and dialed out for Chinese. Wind buffeted the living room windows. The casements had gone bad a decade ago and the cold air blew through. Downstairs the furnace struggled and vibrated the house. Henrietta pulled her sweater's collar up to her neck. Jerry had offered Harold new windows every winter, but Harold could never do with free things, or discounted things, especially from his friends. This was only part of the reason why the Feast had closed. And why the house needed to be sold.

"Why's this thing worth so much money, anyway?" Jerry asked. "Is it made of diamonds or something?"

"It's art, evidently."

"Weathervanes are art now?" He put the report down.

"There are people who really care about weathervanes," she said. "Who care about them a great deal." She brightened. "I learned this."

The last month had been a miniature education in folk art. This statue that had sat all this time on Henrietta's mantel was the Goddess of Liberty, a maudlin name for a token of nineteenth-century patriotic fervor. After the War of 1812, she became a very popular figure, so popular that craftsmen eventually started fashioning weathervanes in her image. Jerry's response to all this information was the same as Henrietta's when Juliet Lippincourt initially shared it with her: he offered a genuinely appreciative hum of approval.

Jerry took his pipe from his inside jacket pocket. He and Henrietta went to the living room. She had a fire on. Out in the yard, wind blew the snow sideways across the river. This was when Jerry saw the box of *The Inseparables* across the room.

"That what I think it is?"

"Change the subject, Jerry."

He picked up a copy from the carton and flipped through it before looking up at her. "Can I ask about the diagrams? Harold never let me ask."

"Can I ask you not to say the word diagram?"

"They're the best part, though."

"I'm glad the book finally allowed you to see a vagina."

This was the way they bantered these days. It did not escape Henrietta that she sounded just like her husband, which did not exactly feel awful.

"You must be making dough on that."

"Not enough," she said.

A week ago the people from Hubbard had sent along a proposal for a book tour. Who thought such things existed any longer? Fifteen cities, radio interviews, speeches at women's colleges. Her first reaction was to ask why they would send her to all these places if no one would come and see her. Just wait, they told her. You'll be surprised. They were trying to pass her off as some looked-over doyenne of sexual health. A soothsayer of a new collectively libidinous generation. Yes, the diagrams were still funny, and yes, the story itself was not exactly the work of a great master, and yes, certainly it was true that the new generations were generally sophisticated enough to accept the concept of female pleasure as something obvious and real and not at all worthy of scorn. Yet she felt like one of those ancient golden cities they discovered in the jungle by way of helicopter and thermodynamic imaging: *Look! These old people here liked to screw each other, too!* It was a shoehorn job, as far as she saw it. They were doing to her book what people had always done to her book, which was to see whatever they wanted to see. The way her editor and her publicist talked about *The Inseparables*, it occurred to Henrietta that they truly believed a reputation like hers could be amended retroactively. Then came Hubbard's other requests.

*Cosmo* wanted the young Henrietta to interview the old Henrietta. To this she had merely said, *Now where do you suppose we get access to the young Henrietta?* More ideas: Would she do an interview with Chelsea Handler from the back of a hansom cab in Central Park? She did not know who Chelsea Handler was. Would she let Morley Safer interview her in a hot-air balloon? This, Henrietta needn't be reminded, was a nod to a regrettable sexual escapade in chapter 6 in which Eugenia is fulfilled by a balloon captain. Would she let Nigella Lawson cook the recipe—Harold's recipe—for *boeuf à l'orange* included in chapter 2? Again: Who exactly was Nigella Lawson? The list of requests felt endless, and at a certain point Henrietta found herself agreeing to it all. Yes, she found herself saying. Yes, yes, yes. Yes to the interview, yes to the hot-air balloon, yes to the teapot *and* the QVC special where she'd be hawking teapots. Yes to everything! Perhaps time had aged the book and everything would be better in the new century. Time had aged for the better many of the things Henrietta loved most in the world, like red wine and cheese and photographs of Paul Newman. She could, if she tried, imagine charming Morley Safer. She would wear a yellow chiffon scarf. She would be her most charming self. She could, if she wanted. Couldn't she?

Jerry dragged on his pipe. He preferred vanilla tobacco. She liked the smell better than the taste.

"You go to the grave lately?" he asked.

"Let's not talk about this. Pick another subject."

"Death is the only good subject, Henrietta. As a writer, you should know that."

She cringed. "I was never a real writer."

"I was there last week while some guy was getting buried."

"Jerry, please no burial talk."

"This guy was a big baseball fan, I have to assume. His whole grave was filled with these little Red Sox pennants. I figured it was a little boy. Who else has that kind of enthusiasm for base-ball? But it turns out the guy was ninety. It was charming the first day. Wind in the pennants and all. Two days later, there's a fucking million of these dumb flags everywhere." He fiddled with his pipe. "And that stuff isn't biodegradable."

"And this is coming from a guy who sold aluminum siding."

"I took them off Harry," he said, his voice dropping. "That way you don't have to."

Harold's grave was a pedestrian thing. She wished she could have built a mausoleum for him. A big monument some future citizenry would need to contend with. She went daily at first. Swept the stone, talked to the stone, felt his insistent deadness. She repeated the words alone to her moving boxes. Widowing. Widowhood. Widow's walk. The inscription on his gravestone had felt so wholly insufficient the moment she saw it. Just a name and dates, carved by machine. Just the inadequate and impersonal *Loving father and husband,* like every other headstone there, whether it was true or not. This was the tasteful way to do it, she knew, even though it showed none of the true shape of the man. Nothing of his loyalty, his talent, his temper, his obsessions. None of the treacly stuff: his cooking breakfast for her every day for almost forty years, his dancing with her in the kitchen every Sunday after dinner. This was the stuff nobody ever really wanted to hear about anyway, she knew. Nor did anyone need to know the truly personal things: that when they were together he always held her; that he would trace out messages to her on her skin, slowly; that in a movie theater he would invariably want to kiss like a teenager or put his hand up her skirt; or that they had fucked on the same park bench in the Luxembourg Gardens forty years apart. These facts, she understood, would die with her. But his grave had no mention of the real stuff either. She had envisioned a list, like a recipe he might use.

## The Ingredients of Harold Olyphant

Sang aloud daily.

Laughed constantly.

Drove poorly.

Spent wildly.

Snuck cigarettes.

Refused exercise.

Believed in God.

Never saw Rome.

Was a certifiable wizard with butter and chocolate and eggs and flour and sugar.

Was never once in a fistfight.

Cried over animals.

Cried at weddings.

Implored other men to cry more openly.

His last meal was honey on toast. I made it. Poor man.

Jerry was the only person who she talked to about this. He knew, for instance, that at the end she had dressed Harold's body for the burial. Had put him in his favorite socks. His favorite shoes. These were the most impossible things to consider. Why did he need shoes? Where was he walking to? They had left her alone in the mortuary to do this because she'd begged. She had stood there, in the frigid room, and she had held his foot in her hand for the longest time. They made her wear gloves. She took the sheet off his face so she could see him, and touch his cheek, even though it was horrible.

Outside, the grass was white and covered from the porch to the road and from the road to the river. A yellow birdhouse remained low in the crook of an alder that went blood orange in October. It was here when she'd arrived, a craft project made by the children of a previous owner. She had no plans to take it with her. The speed of life felt cruel and unreal.

"I remember the first time I ever saw Harry," Jerry said. "Seven years old. He was wearing a sweatshirt with his name on it. We were at baseball practice."

He did this often lately. Talked like this. Repacked her husband's life. At first it had bothered her. The grief of others only made the absence worse, she had thought. But now she was not so sure.

"He was awful at it. Maybe the worst in town."

She laughed. "How did I not know he played baseball?"

"Probably because he managed to get himself hurt every game. It was incredible. The ball always got him right in the mouth."

She laughed harder. "In the mouth?"

"It's how he lost his baby teeth," he said. "I swear. Baseballs to the mouth. How many baby teeth do you have? Twenty? That's how many baseballs he took to the face."

She squeezed her hands together into a fist, both to warm them and as a matter of self-preservation. She didn't know about his teeth. He had all these stories she did not know.

After the restaurant closed, Harold had written her letters, mostly love letters, but not all of them. He hid them around the house. It was a kind of game. It took her a year to find them all. They were often the simplest things, folded pieces of plain paper. *To you,* they read, *from me.* She continued to find them after he died. She had told Jerry this, which was a mistake, because every time she saw him he asked if any more had turned up.

"Nothing?"

"I've found them all," she said.

"You checked in his suitcase?" he asked.

"It's just a suitcase," she said, nodding and lying. "Now

what do I do about this thing?" she asked, meaning the weathervane.

"I'm guessing you're not going to let it go."

"I don't want to say that I really need that money."

"But you really need the money."

She wanted to explain more, but he very likely knew already. Jerry always asked how she was. Not *How have you been?* but *How are you now?* He knew the language of grief. The delusions involved, the imagined visitation of spirits. The density of loss. He knew about the urgent importance of having something, anything, to do. She was terrified, was usually the answer. Everything now is so goddamned different. Companionship, partnership, stability, money, family, shelter. She was trying to make that list shorter by one.

"The funny thing," she said, "is that I would have thrown it out. It wasn't worth anything to me. It was junk. Rusted metal. But if it's worth something to someone else, I'll gladly profit."

"You check all the boxes in there?"

She felt herself smiling involuntarily. "Yes I did."

"Well, you could call the police, but they won't find it. Not in this town. Those guys are basically professional traffic supervisors."

"I don't want to call the police," she said.

Jerry looked around the room. "This whole place is so rickety. I don't imagine it's hard to get in."

"Don't creep me out," she said.

"One of those realty guys probably took it," he said.

"I had that thought, too."

"You had so many of them in here."

"So assuming somebody took it, where do people go to sell stolen things?"

"You're asking me?" he said, laughing. "I'm a gentleman! Why would I know these places?"

"Because deep inside you're an unscrupulous schmuck and you know these things."

He let out a big loud laugh. "Harold told you this?"

"You're saying you're not? I've known you forty years."

He shrugged. "Give me a day to think on it."

Mendelssohn's Third Symphony played on the stereo while he refilled his pipe. The music made her feel like she was at the end of a very dramatic World War II movie. He loosened his necktie. On the coffee table was her lease for the new apartment. He'd come with her to sign it. All this time she had figured she'd go back to the city. But she could not go too far afield, it turned out. Four decades and she had become stuck in orbit here. Aveline with its wide boulevards, its brick downtown, its Chinese food. Harold's town had become her town.

They were quiet awhile and then finally he turned to her.

"Are the new people keeping *any* part of the house?" he asked.

She shook her head.

"They're going to bulldoze the whole thing," she said. "Every inch of the place. All of it."

She had sold the house to a development company that wanted the land and nothing else. Jerry was the only person who knew this. The money was barely enough to clear the debts and keep her afloat for a year. After that, she had no idea what she would do.

She sat quietly. The house was warm.

Outside, wind tore over the small hills near the river.

# 8.

Lydia brought all of her belongings out to the car. Having been given only a few minutes to pack for the week, she'd made the quick decision, standing over her tiny dormitory-issue mattress, that she would not come back. Why stay and endure the humiliation? Why allow herself the torment? It would only get worse. She put her phone on the nightstand. She worried that every buzz signaled a new anonymous burst of harassment. `Lydia, baby, come suck me off. Hey slut, where you at? Why aren't you on my dick? Lydia, baby, why don't you___?` (Any sex act could do here; she'd received every possible permutation.)

Thankfully it was lunch hour and the building was empty and she could pack in private. The dormitories for girls— never women—were named for things perfectly anodyne and sweet. Periwinkle. Kansas. Rosewater. In the brochure pictures, a group of girls had lingered on the beds here, perfectly made up, with salon-diffused hair and luscious-looking mohair shawls, every one of them holding hardcover editions of *Learn How to Speak Mandarin for Business*. Surely these were Danish catalog models, she assumed, brought in by a PR firm to reinforce some idea of what boarding school was supposed to be like—namely, full of tall blond girls, excellent on the field hockey pitch, fluent in French, and destined for Harvard or Oxford. When she arrived, she was shocked to find that they were real—all of them, every girl, and all of it: the conversational-grade Mandarin, the mohair, the diffusers, the blondness. Just yesterday, she'd mistakenly been on the receiving end of a mass message in which these same girls amended a version of her naked torso with their own diagrammatic commentary. Crude arrows pointed to blemishes on her chest: acne or crabs? Arrows to her nipples: ew, just ew.

Her parents had parked on the lawn. Her dad waited outside, leaning against the car door in his favorite camel hair overcoat, looking stunned, maybe nauseated, possibly mortified, while her mother waited inside, the engine running and the radio on. They were, it was obvious, unwilling to share space with each other for any longer than they needed to. Her father wore a sweater the color of moss. It was too large for him. Heartbreak had shrunken him, maybe.

Her dad, seeing the amount of luggage, knew immediately. "You're just going to quit? Just like that? Give up?"

"Looks that way," Lydia said.

Her mother got out. There were dark rings beneath her eyes. She was famous in the hospital for her capacity to go without sleep.

"What's happening?" her mother asked.

"Lydia's dropping out," her dad said. "She brought all of her luggage. Look. She's just giving up."

Lydia dropped the bags. "Call it whatever you want. I just can't come back to this place," she said. She held up her phone. "If you're interested in why, maybe you can read the wonderful, gentle tributes my classmates are writing me."

"But you got a scholarship," he said. "Think about that. Think about what that means."

"It means that I applied for a scholarship and they accepted me."

"Think harder," he said.

She was used to this routine. It was her father's way of dispensing with his guilt, which was considerable and legendary. White guilt, male guilt, househusband guilt, ex–corporate attorney guilt, owner of a sports utility guilt, soon-to-be recipient of alimony guilt.

"You took the spot from some poor kid somewhere who's dying to come study whatever it is you're studying."

"*Star Wars* and fascism?"

"Yes!"

"Good news for that poor kid! There's an open spot in my Leni Riefenstahl seminar!"

"You're just going to let them bully you?" he asked.

She swiped at the phone. The screen brightened. She selected at random. `This ho Lydia has the tits of a ten-year-old boy with a peanut allergy.`

Her father threw up his hands. "What does that even mean? That's nonsense. Peanuts? You can't let that bother you."

"You want me to read you more?"

Her mother stepped in. "Let the girl take her goddamn bags home with her if that's what she wants." She hoisted the biggest of the suitcases and tossed it into the back of the Toyota. Slamming the door shut, she looked at him. "Get in the car." Then at her. "Put your phone away. Don't torture yourself."

Her parents had told her they were living apart by way of a letter—two sheets of paper in the same envelope, one from her mother, one from her father. Not that it came as a surprise. She had tracked the progress of their various therapies and last-ditch attempts at love with the same energy that children in the forties expended to track the progress of the Allies against the Axis. When she'd received the letters, she had no idea how to react to such an old-fashioned touch. Her father's handwriting was bold and careful. Her mother's was quick, and she had used red ink, which must have meant something. Lydia had tried to divine some larger psychic meaning or hurt or honesty in the differences of penmanship. They were the first actual letters Lydia had ever received. She didn't know what to do with them afterward. Do I keep them? she asked her roommates. What do you do with real letters?

It was a fact that she had taken her mother's side in the split. Maybe her father knew it. Not that she knew anything about relationships or cohabitation or intimacy. She had kissed one boy in her life, a distressing statistic for a twenty-first-century fifteen-year-old, and that boy was Charlie Perlmutter. They had done something that was maybe almost dating for a little less than two months, a period of time in which she had confided in him, in which she had deigned to touch her tongue to his, and had experienced something that she was loath to admit was almost fun. And then, the moment he tried to take off her top, it had ended. All week she had wanted to confront him. Through intermediaries, they'd arranged to meet by Lake Rose last night at midnight, and dutifully, she'd snuck out of her dorm and skulked her way down to the water. Her willingness to do these things for him felt troubling. She had no idea what she would say to him aside from *Why, why would you, what's wrong with you, I trusted you, that's why I kissed you, what's your fucking malfunction?* These, she guessed, were not questions he would be able to answer. Nor would he ever be likely to tell her why it was that she had momentarily found him attractive when it was so clear now that he belonged to that certain species of teenage assholes whose one clear goal was to sexually coerce her. She waited for an hour. She contemplated the relative advantages of violence versus diplomacy. It didn't matter: he never showed.

The family drove in silence. Soon they were on the highway.

Her father drove with both hands on the wheel. The car was cool. The windows fogged. Lydia sat in the middle of the back three seats, equidistant from her parents, each of them leaning as far from the other as possible. "If I don't go back, do you think I could just finish high school online?" she asked at one point, and no one answered. "Or should I just reenroll back at home?" She tried to relax into the seats. They were leather or fake leather. She couldn't get comfortable. This was the first time Lydia had ever been in this car. Its size instantly miniaturized her. It was basically a small military vehicle, she thought, large enough to topple a village, with enough room in the back to stash two or three kidnap victims. "Is anyone going to talk to me?" she called out, sometime before they crossed from Vermont into Massachusetts. "Hello? Anyone there?" She leaned forward so that she was in between them. Her mother and father. "Whose house am I going to live at?"

It was clear they didn't know.

Her mother tapped listlessly against the glass. Her father occasionally cracked his neck. The sleet changed to rain and then to snow. Fantastically large kid-scissor snowflakes dive-bombed the windshield. Frozen icicles hung from the rock formations by the road, and they looked to her like gigantic teeth. Every few miles a hand-painted road sign advertised maple syrup. Six months in Vermont, and all she knew about the place was syrup.

"So are you guys not talking at all?" she asked, after an hour on the road. "Or is this just a show for my benefit?"

"We're talking," her father said, after a minute of silence.

"Yes, we're talking," said her mother.

"Right now, in fact," her father said.

Up front, her mother nodded. "This sounds like talking."

"Oh good," said Lydia. "Because I was worried the divorce would turn you two against each other."

Two hours later, they were pulling into Aveline. She recognized the stretch of forest and the river near her grandmother's house. Lydia had surprised her mother last month with the trip home. An hour before the train reached Boston, she'd texted, I had to get out. I just had to. Want to meet up for dinner? During the weekends at Hartwell, you were gently urged to enroll in one of its optional seminars: Van Gogh's Ear: Madness or Sword Fight? or Mathematics as an Art Form. She had gone away to school believing that homesickness was endemic only among weak people with perfect families. She'd felt bad about ditching school until she saw how excited her mother was for the visit. The problem, though, was that she hadn't told her father. When her mother drove her back to school that night, she'd begged Lydia not to say anything. *This will really hurt his feelings,* or something like that, which indicated that she had continued to maintain an unhealthy balance between her own freedom and his sadness.

Lydia wondered whether her mother had issued the same warning to her grandmother. As the car climbed the long drive to the house, passing the rows of dead birch, the animal pens, the swollen river, Lydia grew worried. Her grandmother stood waiting out on the front porch.

"Oh this is going to be great," Spencer said.

Her grandmother was walking out to meet them. The car's engine cut. Up front, her mother turned. "It's probably better that you go back home," she said.

Lydia looked at her father by way of the rearview. "Home?"

"Your actual house," her mother said.

"But you're not there."

"That is true, Lydia."

"There's no room for me here?"

She looked up at the house. The lack of paint. The old roof. The shutters. The sagging porch. Her grandmother's house had been in undeniably bad shape a few weeks ago, but it looked as though in the past few weeks everything, every part of the house, had gotten worse. The real estate agents, she knew, had tried to gussy it up, but the new furniture felt vulgar, all of it unseemly and too bright. It surprised her how much it bothered her to see the moving boxes in her grandfather's old study, books already packed, his collection of hats given away to charity.

Her grandmother knocked at the window, waving.

"Don't say anything to her," her mother said.

"Don't talk to her?" Lydia asked.

"No. Obviously, talk to her. Just, you know, don't tell the truth."

"Lie to Grandma. I get it."

"Don't lie. Just don't talk, or explain, or admit anything," her mother said.

"She'd probably understand," Lydia said.

"*I* understand," her mother said.

"As do I," said her father.

"Your grandmother will probably want to deluge you with all her theories about, you know, the fucking ontology of masculine depravity."

"That actually sounds fascinating," Lydia said. "And probably instructive."

She was used to this. Her mother harbored a protective urge to shield Lydia from her grandmother's reputation, and sometimes her intellect, and lately even from the fact that if you were to Google "Henrietta Olyphant," you might find photographs of her beside some genuinely famous people and/or some wildly hilarious india-ink diagrams. Her grandmother, Lydia was to understand, was the ultimate corrupting influence.

They got out of the car. Her grandmother smiled at her widely and yelped with joy before throwing her arms around her. "I was hoping it was you!"

Her grandmother smelled like rose water and talcum. Lydia wanted right then to whisper into her ear, *Don't tell him. Don't tell my dad I was here.* Kissing her wetly on both cheeks and a good portion of her mouth, her grandmother pointed her up to the house. "Come in! Come!"

Behind her, her mother explained, "She's just home for vacation. Spencer was going to get her and take her home. But then we went together."

Lydia could already see that her grandmother believed none of this. A vacation? In the middle of the week? Lydia wished that at some point in her future she would inherit a bit of her grandmother's shrewdness, or at least her pitch-perfect aversion to bullshit. Henrietta Olyphant, it was certain, had never been the kind of woman who would fall for someone like Charlie Perlmutter.

"I can't see her for dinner?" her grandmother asked. "Or you? Or all of you?"

Her parents looked at each other. Her father fiddled nervously with the buttons on his collar. "I can sit in the car," he said. "I don't mind. I have snacks."

"Sit in the car?" her grandmother cried. "You're not an animal."

He smiled. "I've actually been told the opposite a few times," he said.

A moment passed in which her parents exchanged between them a half dozen grievously awkward facial expressions. Theirs had become a language of despair that no therapy could cure. Lydia had known this months ago. Her mother looked as if she were chewing off the inside of her lips. Her father appeared as if he had suddenly inhaled poison. Mercifully, her grandmother burst out laughing. "Look at my beautiful, happy family! Look at the joy!"

Inside the house felt warm. It surprised Lydia to see that the amount of boxes and the filth and dust surpassed the amount of boxes and filth and dust of a few weeks before. She made her way into the kitchen, following her grandmother, who was talking about food—the lack of it in the house, the importance of always having *something* at hand, the need to call out for Korean or Thai or *something good and Asian and salty*. Her parents lingered behind. She could hear the low rumbling of a fight brewing. She knew the timbre. Silently these last months she had girded herself for the new reality, the impending shift in personal identity, the transformation from the only child of unhappily wed parents to the only child of estranged divorcés. Because of the hyphen in her name—Lydia Olyphant-Klein—everyone already assumed her parents were divorced. She knew what was coming. The split holidays. The systematic war-waging and guilt-seeking. Her mother's inevitable bout of workaholism. Her father's likely recommittal to his very lapsed Judaism. Pilates classes, intermittent veganism, aspirational attempts at watercoloring. One of them would probably try to write a memoir. She would need to meet their new lovers. She would need to expressly forbid the use of the word "lover."

Her grandmother went to the pantry in search of cocoa. On the counter Lydia saw the big box.

"Oh no," her grandmother said, clearly having heard the flaps open.

Lydia reached down and took out a new, pristine pink edition. "Look at this!"

If Hartwell had taught her anything, aside from reinforcing the notion that she was not, like her classmates, bound for the U.S. diplomatic corps or for NASA, it was that she knew exactly what it meant to have a grandmother who'd written such a spectacularly trashy book. Naturally, everything in the book that might have ever seemed scintillating had become, over time, passé. What was a mere allusion to a blow job when you could, if you wanted, take a few minutes during a dull lecture on differential equations and find countless examples on your phone? But there was something special about her grandmother's trash that gave it such a long life. Maybe it was all the creative sex positions. Or the people fucking in the hot-air balloon. Or the diagrams, which she had heard about incessantly from the first week of school, and which were evidently ebulliently hirsute. Apparently a pen-and-ink rendition of a vagina was a better, more fulfilling vagina than any of the millions of photographs floating out there in the ether, available to download.

Occasionally someone at Lydia's old school in Crestview would connect the dots between her and her grandmother. Boys would arrive at her desk with a printed article from Wikipedia, caught up in some dizzying, hormonal spell, and would stutter in caveman-speak, pointing at her, and then at a picture of her grandma. *You? Her? Sex? Family?* Usually she would feign ignorance: *I have no idea who this Henrietta Olyphant is. I don't know this book. What diagrams?*

At Hartwell, where the students were better, and smarter, and richer, she could not lie herself out of it. Everyone had it figured out quickly enough. Because of it, most everyone assumed she had grown up in some deranged sexual den full of vibrators and leather chaps and whips. Or else that every family dinner ended with some in-depth discussion of Caligula's exploits. Girls in the dorm came to her for advice or diagnostic help for possible infections. Or assumed that she held a liberal attitude toward the occasional three-way or four-way, or a deep affinity for porn.

This had happened with her roommate, Nisha Chakrabarti. A calculus whiz and a cellist of the first order, Nisha's love for *The Inseparables* bordered on obsession. She'd let Lydia hold her copy, but for only a moment. It had belonged to Nisha's own grandmother, a paperback edition from the eighties with a black cover. This, Nisha explained, was so that you could read it on the subway without feeling shame. Most of its pages were dog-eared, and some passages, such as the one in which Eugenia has her first orgasm (*"a sharp swan dive out of the Gotham air into the steamy, salty, skin-tingling tropical ocean"*), were underlined furiously in blue ink. Lydia had pretended not to be interested. She had consciously resisted reading it all this time. Surely there were other books, maybe books just as embarrassingly bad, written by other people who were not her grandma. Within the family, the book had become a talisman of anxiety and guilt and humiliation for her grandmother. Everyone knew this. Despite her mother's occasional joking about its pink cover or its trashiness, you were not supposed to speak of it. You did not bring it up. If a man at the bank saw your last name and somehow made the connection and then proceeded to say something hideous, you did not then report it back to her. Her grandmother worried most about this: that her book, which had already caused her so much trouble, would cause trouble for them.

Lydia started to open a copy, and then her grandmother knocked it out of her hands with a wooden spoon. It was a well-known fact that she refused to touch the book with her bare hands.

"I'd rather you didn't look at that," she said.

"But why? It's right here! And it's so new and pretty!"

"It's not a good book. That's why. It's awful."

Lydia picked up another copy and read off the cover. *"This much is certain: Henrietta Olyphant has written a wonderful book!"*

"A dirty book is different than a good book."

"Maybe I want to read a dirty book," Lydia said.

"You're young."

"I'm fifteen," she said.

"Fifteen is impossibly young. And besides, this is garbage and you shouldn't put garbage in your head."

"I've almost definitely seen worse online, you know."

Instantly she saw her grandmother's eyebrows rise.

The first weekend at Hartwell, she'd walked in on Nisha Chakrabarti midway through what was apparently an hour-long porn binge. This was typical behavior for the boys she knew, but not for the girls, not for the cadre of Danish catalog models and their friends, who were off interning at The Hague, and certainly not for someone like Nisha—gliding effortlessly through her quantum mechanics seminar and playing Bach in the Hartwell traveling orchestra. Perhaps owing to Nisha's tastes, what Lydia saw horrified her. Men choking women, throwing them into vans, teaming up with other men, sometimes lots of other men, screwing them in the backseat of those same vans, in airplane bathrooms, in motel rooms, in a pool, by a pool, on a table near a pool. None of it looked in any way pleasurable despite Nisha's entirely too-focused attention and the gaping hangdog grin that might have implied pleasure. And nothing Lydia saw on the dozens of videos she watched that night, or on the one other occasion they did this, made her want a boy to touch her, ever. The oily, hairless horror of porn filled her with anxiety. How could she ever be expected to do these things? Or act this way? And why was everyone so excited about it? Nisha had realized Lydia's distaste at about the same moment that Lydia realized that she never ever wanted to see Nisha again. "What?" Nisha complained. "You don't like this? You think it's all like your grandma's book, don't you? All sweet and romantic. With candles every time a guy whips his dick out?"

Lydia found the dedication page, inscribed *To My Darling Baby Oona*. She wasn't expecting to find something like this, something this sweet, in a book full of such ridiculous and explicit pictures.

"So what do I say," Lydia asked, "when people come up to me and want to talk about it then? When people ask me stupid questions about the diagrams?"

Her grandmother flinched. "Do people do that? Really? Still? To *you?*"

"Weekly. Which is why I should have my own copy to read. To arm myself."

"Just put it down," her grandmother said.

"Don't be so prudish about it," said Lydia.

"I *wrote* the damn book, honey. And drew the fucking *pictures.* I think history has already come down with its opinion on my lack of prudence."

"Well," Lydia said. "I guess we have something in common."

Her grandmother didn't miss this. Lydia noticed another tiny rise of her eyebrow.

"So what vacation is this you're on? It's a Monday in February. Don't vacations start on Friday? And didn't you just have a vacation?"

Lydia tried to come up with a quick lie.

"What happened?" her grandmother asked.

"I got in trouble," Lydia said.

"I figured so much. For what, exactly?"

"I don't want to say."

This, Lydia thought, may have been the single most substantial conversation she'd ever had with her grandmother. It was not as if she hadn't been a good grandmother when Lydia was young—with candy bars, and ghost stories, and Marilyn Monroe movies—but then some inability to communicate settled over them. Lydia supposed it was the generation gap. Too much time had passed between them. Years equaled difficulty. Her grandmother had grown up in a Yiddish-speaking world, in a tiny hot apartment, around old men who had fled pogroms and village burnings and marauding Cossacks. Her grandmother could not understand the umbilical connection to gadgetry that Lydia insisted on. And it had not helped matters that Lydia was indifferent to the things her grandmother liked so much: Henri Matisse, Clark Gable, Peking duck. Once, over dinner, her grandmother had said something in passing about wanting to take Lydia to Paris with her. A grandmother-granddaughter vacation! A bona fide cultural expedition! Lydia was maybe nine. She had, for reasons still mysterious to her, burst into tears at the idea. "With you?" she'd cried out. *Macarons* and *pain au chocolat* somehow provoked a miniature panic attack. After that, conversation between them had never been easy.

Lydia wondered if their more recent difficulty wasn't just a simple case of intimidation. Lydia had not escaped her grandmother's notoriety, or whatever it was you called the legions of senior citizens who gawked at her. Her grandmother was more or less invisible to younger people, but to a certain generation, she was suspended in time as an advocate for reckless sexual joy. How else to explain a man coming to their table at Sally Ling's, just a year ago, maybe a little drunk on dragon bowls, merely to ask, "So you're saying I should use my tongue?"

But there was something else. Beneath the kitchen lights, Lydia couldn't help but see her grandmother's wry smile and easy obvious magnetism as proof of the exact kind of coolness that Lydia herself lacked. The books, the ready glass of wine, the Pat Nixon stories, the obvious fearlessness, the ready command of Marxist-feminist-sociopolitical dialectics, the religious distaste for regurgitated political idiocy—it made sense why Lydia felt so cowed. What would her grandmother care about stupid stories of boarding school? Or about tiny boys afraid of butterflies?

Her grandmother reached out and touched her cold hand to Lydia's wrist, just exactly as Charlie had done. "Seems to me you have things to get off your chest," her grandmother said.

Lydia looked down. "I have the opposite problem, actually."
Her grandmother knew somehow. Her face shifted. Instantly
she understood. Lydia was not sure how, but immediately she
felt relieved not to have to go into detail. Her grandmother
stepped forward and hugged her close to her chest, close
enough that Lydia could hear her grandmother's heart beating,
a sensation that for the first time struck Lydia as terrifying: this
heart, going and going, and maybe, eventually, possibly stopping.

"What's your general advice on things like this?" Lydia
asked. "Shame. Humiliation. Nonstop harassment."

"Tell me," her grandmother said. "How bad is it?"

Lydia put up her hands. "On your scale?"

"On your scale, honey. My scale is the professional's scale."

"On my scale? Somewhere between nightmare and really
fucking bad nightmare."

"Would it help if I told you that society is addicted to sexual
shame? And that you can choose not to accept it?"

"Not very much," Lydia said.

Her grandmother nodded. "In that case, usually I tell people
to drink."

Lydia smiled. "It's just a picture," she said. "That's all. One
picture."

"Your mother knows about this?" Henrietta asked.

"She does."

Her grandmother offered the most minute and defeated
shrug. "I should probably defer to your mother. But there are
actual things to tell you. There's a substantial literature on the
matter, if I understand what it is you're telling me."

Lydia felt as if suddenly her grandmother had become part
X-ray machine.

"And by your posture and by the way you're crossing your
arms across your chest and by the fact that your mother was

looking at you earlier like she'd just had her own bones operated on without anesthesia, I'd say I understand you perfectly."

Lydia managed a tiny nod. "You do?"

Her grandmother hugged her again. "Unfortunately I do, dear."

"Maybe there's a way to just put everything in your brain into my brain very quickly?"

Her grandmother laughed. "You don't want my brain," she said. "It's filled with wickedness and memories of the nineteen seventies."

"I'd settle for half of your brain, then. The good stuff."

"I tried that with your mother, unfortunately. Wholesale transplantation. It didn't take."

The fighting in the other room stopped. The atmosphere shifted. Lydia's mother came into the room, her sleeplessness radiating off her.

"Someone needs to invent a cure for idiocy in middle-aged men," she said, not realizing that Lydia was there. Right away, she put her hand to her mouth. "I shouldn't do that," she said to Lydia. "That's bad form."

"It's fine," Lydia said.

"No. It's not good. All the books say that's destructive. He's not an idiot."

"Really, Mom. I can hold two ideas in my head at once. Father and idiot."

Her mother rested her hip against the countertop, closed her eyes, and let out a series of long deep breaths. When Lydia was young, she'd seen her mother go days without sleeping. Her hospital shifts were long and punishing and then, at home, she wanted so badly to be present. Lydia knew this because frequently there were books stashed in the house on the subject—workbooks, manuals, self-published meditation guides with embarrassing astral-inspired cover art. Across the room, her mother appeared to fall asleep on her feet for a second. Lydia saw her grandmother move to her. A tiny instinct. Correspondingly, her mother moved away. Her mother hadn't even needed to have her eyes open to feel the gravity change. Apparently, you can always sense your mother coming close.

"I'm fine, really," her mother said.

"You're comatose," said her grandmother.

"I'm conscious," she said, blinking slowly. "Isn't that enough for you?"

"Let me take you up to bed," her grandmother said.

Her mother smiled. Such a simple, lovely sentence. Lydia needed to be reminded of this occasionally. That her mother was a daughter. That there was, between the generations, a permanent, if not occasionally begrudging, sense of responsibility, even in middle age, and even for the basic things: food, shelter, sleep.

"Honestly, Lydia," her mother said. "I don't want you to think that I'm here saying these sorts of things behind your father's back. He's a good man." She recalibrated. "Or decent. He's trying. He's trying to try. Okay? He's failing most of the time. But he's attempting, at least, not to fail, which is progress. Kind of. I think. Right?"

He came through the back door then, snow on the shoulders of his camel hair. The room fell quiet.

"Talking about me?" he said, not really joking.

Her mother took a few steps, perhaps involuntarily, away, across the room, toward the hallway.

Against the wall, in boxes, there were stacks of napkins from her parents' wedding reception. Pink, square, embossed with flowers and roses and something that looked like a dancing teddy bear, they might as well have been artifacts from an alien visitation. Her dad peeked in and saw them.

"Look at this," he said sweetly, holding one up, first to

Lydia, and then to her mother, who turned away. "Remember this?"

For a long moment no one spoke or moved much and the discomfort grew so thick that Lydia began absently to flip through her grandmother's book until she got to a diagram of a long-haired man, spittle on his lips, bearing fangs and claws. *Illustration of the hungry gentleman in need of women or property,* it read. She looked up at her dad.

# 9.

Weeks ago, when the real estate agents came, Henrietta stored most everything in the garage. At first it had not bothered her so much to do this. The new furniture and decorations arrived by truck. Bright colors. Fresh tulips. So much white. She had thought the house would sell quickly, but the paint was too dull, she was told. The creak of the floorboards sounded too much like an effect in a horror movie. And there was an unmistakable smell of mold, one of the agents said. Likely something in the walls. Water gets in, day after day for years. It has no place to go. Can't you smell it? Henrietta walked around for days, inhaling vigorously. Apparently this meant the house would not sell as quickly as she hoped. Apparently all the water in the house and all the mold meant that the bones of the place had all this time been vanishing bit by bit without her knowing. Someone suggested that Henrietta simply advertise the land. People do this all the time, they told her. Sell the acreage. Accentuate the timber alone. Forget the house. Make it easy, they told her, for someone to come in and bulldoze the hell out of the place and build something new and clean and better.

"*People do it all the time?* That's never a good reason for anything," she said to Spencer, leading him out through the back door and down the small slope behind the house to the garage. On the off chance that she had mistakenly packed away this surprisingly valuable weathervane, she needed to look through all her boxes, or at least have her son-in-law do it for her. He was strong enough, barely, to lift the heaviest ones, compliant enough to deal with the filthiest, and also, he was the easiest member of the family to extract information from.

"You know what else people do all the time?" Henrietta asked. "People also murder other people all the time. Like their real estate agents."

"You didn't say that out loud, I hope," Spencer said.

She laughed. "Surprisingly, I do have some impulse control left."

"They really said it smelled like mold? It's a house! It's not a showroom! Stuff breaks in a house. People actually live here!"

"Apparently we people smell like mold."

Spencer lifted the garage door. Light snow breathed in across the threshold, mixing with dust and probably toxic mold. She had some of her furniture here, and her crates of books, and her old lecture notes, everything in boxes and draped beneath layers of plastic. This was where she'd packed all of the things she had decided not to show Juliet. The most vital things: Harold's wallet as it was the day he died, the menu from opening night at the Feast. Spencer flipped on the lights. Two incandescent bulbs hung on loose strings that lurched in the wind. "I know they were just trying to be helpful," she said. "It's an old house. It's practically falling apart. I'm not dumb. I get it."

"'Helpful' is probably the wrong word. They're just trying to make money," said Spencer.

"We're all trying to make money," she said.

Every few moments, Spencer looked over his shoulder. Henrietta was not naive enough to think that this was exactly kosher, his being here with her and her being friendly and pleasant to him and not otherwise cruel or cold. The separation was new, but still, divorce meant factions. Walls were about to go up. Guidelines for diplomatic contact and official kindnesses had yet to be negotiated. Just last week, Oona had asked, "Do I acknowledge his birthday this year? And if yes, with what? A note? What do you get a man you're divorcing? A savings bond?"

Henrietta had always liked him. Perhaps this was the first sign that he was not right for Oona. It was a good rule that the mother should never like the boyfriend more than the daughter does. The first time they met was at the Feast, at the good table by the window that looked out at the fountains behind the Christian Science Plaza. As a pair he and Oona looked as though they'd been matched by way of a color wheel. Tall, sun-kissed, they looked distressingly good in camel hair. Spencer had come an hour early. He was tall and prematurely gray and full in the shoulders. Over peasant bread and several glasses of good wine he was also speechlessly nervous, until, finally, looking out at the plaza and the church dome, he had turned to her and said, "Christ the scientist? Who knew he had such broad interests?"

In the garage he took out his rolling papers.

"May I?" he asked.

This was the big thing about Spencer. This habit. It was long-standing, as far as she understood it, something Oona had tolerated at first and then, over the years, had stopped tolerating. Henrietta, up until this point, had never seen him get high. His doing it here was maybe a product of the separation, or perhaps an indication of his level of despair. Or, more precisely, his deep desire to get high. She watched as he flicked at a tarnished lighter. The flame momentarily brightened the garage. She had heard Oona these last few months detailing how agonizing it had been to find her husband as stoned as she often found him. Here she was, coming home from the hospital, having just operated on fractured femurs and hips for ten hours, and she needed to contend with whatever Spencer thought was worth talking about: electric-era Miles Davis, theoretical explanations of dark matter. "As you can imagine, this makes having sex almost impossible, physically and emotionally," Oona said to her recently. Henrietta simultaneously felt embarrassed at hearing too much about her daughter's sex life and also a surge of maternal happiness at hearing too much about her daughter's sex life.

Spencer's hands moved quickly, the small, mindless dance of a habit. She watched to see if anything in him changed when he inhaled, some small shift in character, some silent accumulation of peace or calm, but there was nothing. He inhaled and he exhaled and he was exactly the same.

"What does it feel like?" Henrietta wanted to know.

"Come on," Spencer said with his eyes closed. "Let's not do this."

"You're avoiding the question. Tell me," she said.

"It's nothing." He shook his head. "At first it's nothing. It's like—" He smiled. "It's like nothing at all."

"Clouds?"

He laughed. "Clouds?"

"I don't know! It has to be something. If you keep doing it all this time, it must have some sensation."

"You never did it?" He looked straight at her. One of his eyes was open wider than the other, and she had to look away.

"Nope," she said. She used to like to drink. For a little while she had really liked to drink. Right after the publication she'd arguably gone a little too deep into the stuff, although she felt embarrassed to connect the two, the scandal of her book and the onset of a temporarily disabling attraction to alcohol.

"How's it possible you never tried it? All that awful music.

The bad hair. Everyone looked like a werewolf, or like they were auditioning to be the long lost Allman brother. Everybody had to be on it."

"Everybody was not on it!" She held a finger in the air, victorious. "Misconception!"

"Honestly?" he said. "I haven't smoked in two months."

"Until this moment?"

"I was on a streak."

"Spencer! That's not a streak. That's being sober."

She had not seen Spencer since the funeral. She wanted to know exactly what and who was responsible for the separation. She was accustomed to the divorces of her friends, Reagan-era splits, in which everything was either about fucking or spending. Who was fucking who? Who was mad about the money? But Oona was vague. They'd grown apart. People drift. Love goes. Oona was, Henrietta saw now, being kind.

"It was the big topic in couples therapy," he said. "Me being zonked."

"I feel like I should take it from you and throw it away."

He looked at the end of the joint. "I don't really feel guilty. I like it. It makes me happy and calm. Do I look zonked?"

"Let's not involve me in couples therapy."

"It doesn't really even feel like anything anymore. It's just nice." He looked up at the swinging lightbulbs, momentarily enraptured by them, like a cat with a telephone cord. "You know?"

"So it's a present," she said. "Is that how you think of it? A nice present to yourself?"

He took a second to think. "It's like a friend," he said finally. "Is that an odd thing to say?"

She narrowed her eyes. "Yes. I would say that's a problematic way to think of it, Spencer."

He took another drag from his joint.

"I feel like I need to tell Oona about the fact that you're high," she said.

"Why would you possibly feel that? She's free of me now. She doesn't care."

"Oona would—"

"Oona would what?"

"She'd want to know. She loves you."

He closed his eyes.

"I've had her here all this time. We talk."

"You do?"

His optimism was extreme and because it was so extreme it was heartbreaking. She hedged. "We sometimes talk. Yes. Occasionally. We have moments."

"She's made it very clear to me that love is not one of the things that occurs to her when she takes inventory of her feelings."

Henrietta shook her head. "I don't believe you."

"What has she told you? Has she said she loves me still?"

Henrietta said nothing.

"See?" he said. "In couples therapy we did this exercise. A free association. Typical Freudian nonsense. When it came to me her list was not positive. It was all, like, 'pizza,' 'rolling papers,' 'body hair.' Not good things."

"Nothing about Lydia? Nothing about being a father?"

He shrugged. "There was that, too," Spencer said. "But you know, buried at the end of a long list."

"She worries about you. That's love."

"Loving someone and worrying after them are not the same thing."

"You have a kid. You know how it goes. It's basically the same thing."

"Are you appealing to me Jewish person to Jewish person?"

She laughed. "Perhaps!"

"She wanted me in rehab. I heard it all the time. *We'll say that you're going to Canyon Ranch to do some tai chi. The guys in the office won't care. You've got eons of sick time. Tell them you're going away to find your inner jungle cat. Roger and Madeline will appreciate that.* Every week I heard this."

Henrietta nodded. This must have been an old argument. He had not been at the firm with Roger and Madeline for a decade at least.

"Tai chi is good for you," she said.

He raised his eyebrows.

"In the seventies, everyone was doing it," she said.

Snowplows passed on the main road, the blades scraping the street.

"I suppose we need to check all of these boxes," she said. "And then, once we're inside, we need to check all the boxes in there, too."

"What does this thing look like, exactly?" he asked.

She described it. The flag. The expression. The blue box she had packed it in. She held her hands apart to approximate the length. "It was on the mantel in the house."

"It was?"

"All this time. Every time you ever came here."

He shook his head.

"You're high," she said. "This is a waste."

"I'm fine."

"Please. You're as high as Louis Armstrong right now."

He shook his head. "That's not exactly a reference I totally understand."

"The statue was actually on the back cover of my book. Behind my shoulder in the picture," she said. "And unfortunately, it's both missing and worth a lot of money."

"Oh." He went red. "That little lady."

"Please don't," Henrietta said. Oona had confessed to her

that as a teenage boy Spencer had kept his copy of *The Insepara-bles* hidden under his mattress. "I don't want to know what role I played in corrupting your youth."

"A very large role," he said.

She hung her head. "You shouldn't have said that."

"It's the truth."

"Well, I'm glad for you. And your mattress."

He took down the first box and ran a razor across the top. He looked up. "I'm glad, too. But to be honest, the fact that you became my mother-in-law? Kind of complicated, actually."

She moved a pair of boxes with her feet. He leaned back against the cement wall, one eye larger than the other, smiling. "I'm surprised you're being like this to me," Spencer said.

"Like what?"

"Not awkward. Decent. Nice."

She smiled. "It's strategic, honestly."

"How so?"

"You have something I want," she said.

He knew.

"When this is all done," she said, "and you're a stranger, I want you to bring my granddaughter by, or make her come by and see me. Force her, if you need to. Entice her. Corral her. Bribe her if you must."

He nodded. "I understand."

"Especially with all this trouble she's into."

He blinked. "What trouble?"

"She told me."

"She told you?"

"I actually know things about this," she said. "*Especially* about this."

"I understand."

"She's terrified of me," Henrietta said.

"That's not the case."

"I'll rephrase: I terrify her. I know. I had a grandmother once. She was a tiny Russian woman. She spoke nine languages and none of them were English. I barely ever understood anything she said to me. She was always yelling about something. Every person she ever loved as a child was either murdered or kidnapped or died of something ridiculous—like diphtheria. She terrified me. Unfortunately, I think at some point I turned into my grandmother."

"I'll bring her by," he said. "Whenever you want."

"Like the last time she was here," Henrietta said. "Whenever that was. A few weeks ago. The girl barely spoke to me. She just sat on the couch with her mother, yapping away, all night long. I was just a spectator."

Spencer's eyes shot open in surprise.

She tried to save the moment. "Not weeks. Did I say weeks? I meant months. She came at Christmas. Right? Months."

His shoulders fell. "She came home a few weeks ago and she didn't tell me?"

# *10.*

When they were alone together finally, Oona pantomimed a picture frame with her hands. "We'll probably need to address the elephant in the room at some point," she said.

Outside, snow peeled off the roof. Wind made the lights flicker. They were in the bathroom on the third floor. It was a large room with a claw-foot tub and a window that looked out on the icy driveway. Above the faucet hung a tiny red print of her child-size hand, preserved all this time like the cave paintings at Lascaux.

"I think calling them elephants is probably a bit generous, Mom."

"Not funny, Lydia."

"Baby elephants, then."

"Still not humorous. Not even remotely."

This thing with the picture was among her worst fears. Had Oona enumerated the things she worried most about as a mother, she would have put it near the top of the list. A fatal car accident. An abduction. A swift-moving tumor. Then this. At night lately she had found herself bargaining with God about Lydia's safety. She did this even though she was fairly sure she did not believe that anyone or anything was listening. "I will gladly suffer a car accident," she thought some nights, "or a terrifying abduction or a tumor if you just keep her safe." Alone in the bathroom, she watched her daughter. It was a simple thing, yet she could not say it aloud anymore: All I want to do is keep you safe. When Lydia was younger, Oona could say this without risk of earning her daughter's disdain. *Stay with me. Come hold my hand. Be where I can see you. Stay close to Mommy.* So often lately, Oona felt actual fear about what she could and could not say around Lydia. Nothing obliterated her confidence as a mother or, moreover, as a human as much as her daughter's withering contempt. Lydia's new teenage intellect operated like a heat-seeking gas, filling every available space with its energy. Out of nowhere, she had a full, facile command of ridicule. And it had happened so fast! Five years ago Lydia was a child! A girl in the fourth grade, learning about frogs, sleeping with a stuffed hippopotamus, crawling into bed with her on Sunday mornings to say the most preposterously kind things. *You are the best person that has ever lived.* Now Oona worried that anything she said would be the wrong thing to say. *Do you need help? Because I will help you. Here's a thought: how about you just stay here with me, every second, all the time, forever?* Oona had read so much about this—about being a mother to a teenager—and she had found nothing in her books to give her any optimism. Instead, she had found that parenting a fifteen-year-old daughter was not so different than the way her colleagues at the hospital treated cancer. By the end, every cell in your body will be destroyed. You may or may not live. Above all else, you will need a positive attitude, you will need resilience, but prepare yourself for failure.

"I can't talk about it," Lydia said. "I can't. That's not ideal, I know. You like to talk things out."

"I do," Oona said. "Talking is healthy. Talking is therapeutic."

"But therapy is so bourgeois, Mom."

At first Oona wanted to let the comment go. This was the sort of thing she struggled with. Your child says ridiculous things and you need to answer. For fifteen years this was how it had gone, but not anymore. What Oona wanted to say was, "Bourgeois? That's actually genuinely very funny, since, you know, you chose to go to a boarding school that offers a class on the history of the BMW sedan." But what Oona actually said to Lydia was, "I'm here if you want to talk. I'm here right now."

"I already spoke to a therapist today," Lydia said. "Several, actually. Sorry to say, it was not therapeutic."

While Lydia sat on the bathroom vanity, Oona sat on the rim of the bathtub. Lydia avoided eye contact. At this, she was inordinately gifted.

"Are you okay, at least?" Oona asked.

"Am I okay?"

"Yes!" Oona cried. "Are you? Because I'm not. Not at all."

"I'm sorry, Mom."

"Can I hug you?" Oona asked.

Oona suspected that Lydia was readying something caustic, but she merely offered a shy, almost childish nod of her head. "Sure," she said, walking across the room and grabbing on to her.

"I'm worried about you," Oona said, trying out the words tentatively. "I know this is hard for you to talk about. But this is worrying. All of this." She let go but then, changing her mind, hugged Lydia once more, even though Lydia began to squirm in her arms. This, too, was something that had been easier when Lydia was younger: the permission to hold her child. Lydia used to allow herself to be hugged close for the longest time. In a crowded aisle at the Natick Mall, Oona could scoop Lydia into her arms, hold her for hours. At Fenway Park, when Lydia was five or six, she would gladly sit in Oona's lap for the entire game. Lately, though, Oona had found herself growing nervous about whether she could still do this—hug her daughter—or whether she needed to ask ahead of time.

"I'm trying to keep perspective," Lydia said. "I don't have tuberculosis. I'm not starving. My village hasn't just been fire-bombed. I'm just humiliated. I realize that is a very low bar."

"People have been awful at school?" Oona said. "I thought these were the best students in America."

"I showed you the phone," Lydia said. "They're all princes and gentlemen."

"How many of those messages have you gotten?"

"Enough," said Lydia, crossing the room. "We're talking about it. I told you I didn't want to talk about it."

"But why would you even take the picture in the first place?" Oona asked. "Did somebody make you? Or was it your idea?"

"This sounds suspiciously like you're about to say it's my fault," Lydia said.

Oona felt her shoulders tightening. She hadn't seen the picture, but she imagined it as best as she could: the dingy bathroom tile, lime scale on the hot-water knob, evidence of blond hair dye on her daughter's roots, probably a string of pimples across her chest, even more probably a knowing glare on her face borrowed from a porn actress. At the least she hoped for a terrifying lack of life in her daughter's eyes. Those eyes, which were her own eyes, and her father's eyes. Those eyes— she needed to imagine that there was nothing in the expression. She needed to think that there was a deep vacancy of the soul evident in the photograph, because that was the only way Oona could understand its existence to be true.

"Listen," Lydia said. "It's cool. I talked with Grandma earlier."

"You talked to my mother?" Oona asked. "You talked to her and not me?"

"I know you told me not to. But she asked. She knew something was wrong. It's her superpower. She just looked at me and *knew*."

Oona could guess what her mother had to say. Growing up in this house, she'd been subsumed in all of her mother's various theories on sex and the body: the intersection between female desire and male hegemony; the social origins of even the most innocent assumptions about beauty. When Linda Lovelace died, she heard for weeks about the deranged and implicit power structures of pornography—this even though, at the time, Oona was twenty-seven years old. As much as she joked with her mother about the book and its diagrams and its pink cover, this was the crucial thing about her mother: no matter how much social opprobrium she faced because of *The Inseparables,* no matter how many men approached her armed with something menacing to say, she had never backed away from her ideals. Second wave begat third wave and here, all the time, was Henrietta Olyphant, preaching the same sermon. Despite all of this, Oona had ignored most everything. This was the instinct, even if it wasn't wise. The things your mother tells you about sex are not the things you want to hear or accept as gospel, even if those things are good and true and generally helpful.

"I think we probably need to have a frank talk," Oona said, suddenly energized. "That's what we should do."

"A frank talk about what?" Lydia asked.

"Intercourse," Oona said.

"Oh that's a terrible idea."

"Are you having intercourse? Were you? Is this Charlie person someone you loved? Were you being pressured or manipulated into intercourse when you didn't want it?"

"Why suddenly do I feel like I'm on trial?"

"I know this is really uncomfortable. And probably very weird to have your mother asking you this stuff. But they're important questions."

"It's been a long day already," Lydia said. "I just don't know if I have it in me to talk about intercourse with my mother. Or really even say the word 'intercourse' anymore."

The urge to devolve the conversation into clinical terms was the doctor's habit, surely. Oona had taken this tack all through Lydia's early adolescence, eschewing the books and manuals and the low-grade banality of women's magazines to explain sex and menstruation and the very basics of puberty. This was very likely her mother's fault. With her mother, everything was frank. *This is what happens when people fuck.* Oona was eight, nine, maybe. There were French movies involved. By fourteen, she was well versed in all the various opinions about female orgasm bestowed upon the world by esteemed male sexologists. Having grown up amid the sharp fallout from *The Insepara-bles,* it was not a mystery why the cold language of medicine appealed to her so. Her childhood had caused in her not only a reflexively regressive idea of sex and an innate loathing of the libertine lifestyle, but a magnetic attraction to the clarity of science.

"I'm fine," Lydia said. "Really. I can see that you're worried. But I'm fine."

Oona wanted to grab her. *All I want to do is keep you safe.*

"The picture was stupid," Lydia said. "I accept that. One stupid thing. One part curiosity. One part vanity."

"Vanity?"

"I'm a human," Lydia said. "So, yes: vanity."

"Maybe one part sexual peer pressure?"

Lydia shook her head. "I'm not sleeping with anyone," she said. "Or making love. Or screwing. Or endeavoring to perform intercourse with other humans, or however you want to put it, Dr. Olyphant."

"Do we need to talk about diseases or the best practices for contraception?"

"Certainly not any more than we are right this second," said Lydia.

"I'm perfectly willing," Oona said. "I'm always willing."

"I think I remember the lectures and pamphlets," Lydia said. "All the many dozens of them."

"You can joke if you want, but I wanted to prepare you! For this!" Oona paced for a moment in the bathroom. "You have to understand, Lydia: you're mine! I made you! Whatever happens to you happens to me! When you suffer, I suffer! Even when you don't suffer, I suffer! Every moment you're away from me, I suffer! There is always suffering!"

"I understand," Lydia said quietly.

Oona said nothing. She could see Lydia testing the words, trying to see if they were true, or at least true enough. Oona could remember this. At fifteen, she was so flooded by doubt and vulnerability that she felt for the longest time as if confidence itself was a rare element, like lithium or radium, buried deep in some far-flung corner of the earth, available to only a lucky few.

"This boy," Lydia said softly. "He's the only boy I've kissed. Not at school, not this year—ever. In history." Lydia put up her hand and begged for mercy. "Which I feel really terrific admitting. Not because having kissed a lot of boys means anything important, but maybe because there are boys I've wanted to kiss that I haven't. And maybe because the only boy I've kissed is the same boy who stole a picture of my body and sent it around to all his buddies. Can we discuss something else? Anything more comfortable? Like cancer? Or the Middle East peace process? Or nuclear warfare?"

Oona hugged her. Lydia let her. What else was there to do but try to hold on?

Out on the meadow, there were tire grooves in the frozen mud. This was the fault of the moving trucks, but it may as well have been the ambulance. When she was young, her father had her memorize every species of plant here. Great Solomon's Seal. Hooker's Orchid. River Beauty. They were the only plants she knew. Beyond the water, church steeples decorated the valley in Aveline. In the spring, you could see the red roof on the house where her father had been a boy. Down below, directly below, on the hill, the walkway lay bare. She had helped her mother dispose of the flagstone.

"This house creeps me out," Lydia said, stepping away from the window. "I mean, he fell and died right there." She pointed. "Every time I come here, I just stare at that spot."

After the funeral, Oona put the flagstone in the back of her car and took it to the house in Crestview. Her mother needed it gone, and Oona obliged. Blood was not supposed to bother her. She was around it every day. Blood was a companion of her workday. She knew the feel of blood on her fingers, kept up to date on the recent hematological research, knew what the whizzing circuitry of blood looked like beneath a microscope. Even so, she'd needed to ask Spencer to clean her father's blood from the stone. He'd found her in the backyard with the garden hose, shaking. Death in her profession so often was a clinical state. She had been present in the emergency room for enough death that she had become numb to the holiness of the act. Even now, the reality of her father being gone had not settled in. How could it be? And to go the way he had? Hitting his head? Her sweet dad? Her dad out in the barn, nursing a calf with a bottle; her dad in the kitchen, whipping egg whites into meringue; her dad here, dancing with her mother to the worst music, to Billy Joel and Elton John? Her strong father falling and dying at home? How was that ever going to make any sense?

"Do you think he knew?" Lydia asked. "Like, when he fell. Do you think he knew that it was the end? I would hope that I knew. If it was happening to me, I would want to know."

Although Oona had not been there to see it, she knew exactly what would have happened. In the hospital she had seen it with others. The last moments of lucidity. The slow loss of consciousness. The gradual leak of life. She lied to Lydia.

"I don't know if he knew or not," she said.

Lydia looked unexpectedly close to tears. Oona put her arm around her and kissed the top of her head. This simple thing brought her back, one kiss to her daughter's hairline, something she'd done so many thousands of times when Lydia was a baby, on the futon in their apartment on 103rd Street. She and Spencer would take turns holding her, passing her back and forth so that one of them could sleep, and this was what they did, over and over, delirious with amazement. At the funeral, she'd done this, too, holding Lydia's hand, keeping her near her at all times. Lydia had never known anybody who'd died before, and at the cemetery, she was viscerally bothered by the actualities of burying someone: the turned-up earth, the dirt, the shovels. Lydia had not been close to her grandfather, which was something Oona blamed herself for. It was the old story. She was too busy. There were too many surgeries. She was always away.

"The last time I was here it was the same thing," Lydia said. "It just feels awful in this house. How can you be here all the time?"

Oona wanted to make her daughter think of something else. "Did you know that I was born in the room right next to us?" she asked, knocking on the door to the adjoining bedroom.

Lydia looked at the door in disbelief. "Did I know that?"

"I don't know," Oona said, smiling. "You know a lot of things now."

"You were born there? Like, right here, in this house? In that room?"

Oona nodded. "In the bed."

"Same bed?"

"The same bed."

"That's nuts," Lydia said.

Oona watched as Lydia opened the door to the bedroom and peered inside.

"It's like you're a woman from olden times," Lydia said. "Being born at home. It's so ancient. Had electricity even been invented then? Or antibiotics?"

"Hilarious," Oona said. She enjoyed the fleeting moment of victory as Lydia laughed.

So much had changed in her daughter these past six months. In half a year, something like the first evidence of her adult identity had begun to show itself. Even since the last time she'd seen her, for that quick stopover last month, things felt different. An increasing slyness in the way she smiled. Evidence of an expanding cynicism. A vanishing of her early teenage gawkiness. The new sharp refinement of her clavicle. The things that had reminded Oona of Spencer when Lydia was young—the lips, the subtle Hebraic profile—had shifted just enough for Oona to see the beginnings of something Spencer did not possess: a hatching elegance, cool grace in the slow way she ran her hands through her hair. The color in her cheeks gave the impression of good humor. Oona reached to hug her again and felt something hard against the waistline of her pants.

"It's nothing," Lydia said, protesting.

"I hope it's something," Oona said. "And that you're not suffering from some sort of awful rectangular growth."

"Mom," Lydia whined.

"Give it over."

Lydia handed over one of the new pristine copies of *The Inseparables*. Oona still could not believe it was being republished. Sitting on the edge of the tub, she flipped through the pages, smiling, pausing to linger over her favorite diagrams.

Lydia started to say, "The combination of my grandmother having written this and my picture floating around at school—"

"You do know you can't talk to her about this book," Oona said. "Right?"

"I don't understand," Lydia said. "You get to talk with her about it."

"I can joke with her about it. That's about it. I can't talk to her seriously about it. I've never really been able to. Not with any substance, at least. It took me a long time even to get to the point where I could joke. That's a very recent development."

"How recent?"

Oona shrugged. "Six months ago."

Lydia leaned over to look at the page Oona had open, which had on it an illustration of two centaurs fornicating in a jungle. "Yikes," Lydia said.

"Exactly," Oona said.

"My favorite is the photograph of Grandma on the back," Lydia said, pointing.

Oona turned the book over. "Magnificent, right?"

"That can't be the same person," Lydia said. "Pushing butterscotch on me. Cooking microwavable pizzas. How is this the same woman?"

Her mother was younger in this picture than Oona was now. With all her jewelry and her big overfed cat and the jodhpurs, it was easy to laugh at the picture, which was exactly what Oona had done when she was Lydia's age. To see it now, however, reminded her of what those first years must have been like here in Aveline, exiled from Manhattan, striving for a fashionable or intellectual existence in a cow town, and ending up looking less like a rustic Gloria Steinem and more like an extra in a Sergio Leone movie.

Lydia took the book back. Fifteen was probably the right age to read a book like her mother's, even if Oona had read it earlier, far too early, had devoured it, really, had taken it to bed with her and pored over the diagrams with a flashlight. She had, just like Lydia, suffered the indignity of having boys taunt her about it in the hallways of her junior high school. *Do you know what your mom thinks about manual stimulation?* Every boy she met, everywhere, had the same quip about hot-air balloons. *Been in any balloons lately?* Oona found it outrageous that her mother even knew this stuff, let alone that she had deigned to tell everyone about it. For years afterward, Oona had detested her mother for the book, for its scandalousness, its awfulness, for the terrible drawings of hairy men that her classmates would sketch on her notebooks during school. Every time she read the book, though, she was startled by how tame it was, how prim and modest the urges were, how simple the hunger was that existed at the center of the characters. In reality, the book's premise was simple—women, too, should enjoy sex—which made the public shame her mother had suffered even more heartbreaking. The truth of it was that the sex in *The Inseparables* was boring. Getting fucked in a hot-air balloon didn't mean exactly the same thing as being fucked well in a hot-air balloon. This was the thing about sex: it took a great amount of skill to make it interesting. If Lydia wanted to keep reading the book, at least she should know this.

"She's wearing so much jewelry," Lydia said.

"Nobody wore a half dozen amulets quite like my mother. It's like she's the female Mr. T."

"I know!" Lydia cried out before stopping to ask, "Wait. Who is Mr. T?"

"Oh," Oona said, laughing. "He's an African American actor who liked to wear a lot of necklaces."

Oona liked this: joking with her daughter. Motherhood—the real job of motherhood—had never made her feel competent the way the parenting books had claimed it would. Instead, she'd constantly found herself at a distance, wondering at times whether the experience for her might not just turn out to be one long stretch of anticipated estrangement. Mothers and daughters: she saw them fighting in shopping malls, in the waiting rooms of her hospital wing, a daughter in a restaurant throwing a grape soda at her mother's blouse. Those incremental separations that thrilled other mothers—walking, talking, swimming without flotation devices—were just evidence of what she was afraid would come eventually: she and Lydia seeing each other only at holidays, flanked by stepparents or poorly chosen spouses. It had been like this with her own mother until six months ago. Now the simplest thing made her mother so unreasonably happy. Just the two of them drinking coffee side by side on a Saturday morning, on the white sofas in the front room, Van Morrison playing, neither of them talking. *This is nice,* her mother would say. *You being here. Us being here.* The message felt clear to Oona. Stop trying too hard. It's not all that hard to be happy. Your misery, your cantankerous attitude, your anxiety—it's all a choice. But life interfered, she had thought to argue all this time. It was not a deficit of love or appreciation that had kept Oona away or made her unhappy. It was everything else. Marriage, motherhood, credit card debt, fucking up in surgery, having a husband who couldn't stop getting high—life.

While they talked, Oona ran a bath.

"You're going to be a divorcée," Lydia said.

"I don't like the sound of that. It's haggardly."

"Is it? I think it's hot. The word 'divorcée' sounds alluring to me."

"Unless you're a geriatric man, or an adulterer, I don't think anyone would possibly agree."

Lydia stood in front of the big magnifying mirror, inspecting her skin. "Maybe we should have a frank discussion about intercourse and proper contraception practices."

Oona allowed herself to laugh.

"Look at you, though," Lydia said. "You're fit. You're sexy. You'll be the most popular divorcée in the suburbs."

"Being almost a divorcée is many things," Oona said. "It's a legal headache. It's depressing. It's surprisingly expensive. And it's a mark against my ability to, you know, grow and age alongside someone I love."

"I guess I was thinking of what happens after this part," Lydia said. "You know: when you reemerge into the world all reborn and carefree."

"Is that what happens next? My anxieties vanish? I become a beautiful butterfly? That sounds wonderful."

"Maybe that's just what I hope happens next," Lydia said. "That would be good, right? After all of this?"

They'd been trying for so long now. This was the official story. She and Spencer: trying. The animating verb of their last few years. Everyone had urged this of them—their friends, their neighbors in Crestview, the butchers at their local Whole Foods who'd had to endure their vicious arguments over whether to purchase lamb chops or pork chops. Before they split, Oona had booked them a prescriptive vacation to Jamaica. The idea was to force each other out of the darkness and into the glorious lemony sunshine. They could spend whole afternoons on the beach, or out at sea, snorkeling and diving and parasailing. They could hike up into the hills and look for rare birds and treat themselves to some trust-building exercises: a rope course, a fall from a ludicrous height where each would catch the other. She really believed all of this. One day in, the trip collapsed under the weight of all these expectations, or else because of all the freely available drugs. In retrospect, Jamaica, in particular, had been a poor choice. For days Spencer languished, sunburned and stoned, on the white sand, or else he lay in the bathtub of their $600-a-night hotel room, listening to Ornette Coleman, leafing catatonically through the same issue of *Scientific American* that he'd been reading and rereading for days. At dinner the last night, over rum punch and conch fritters, she had warned, *This is not my future. This bullshit. Your fucking weed. Your fucking bullshit avant-garde jazz. Your magazines about space.*

Divorce had opened up some new darkness in her. She said this exact sentence in therapy. At night, she dreamed she was drowning, burning, falling, choking, tripping, dying. She wrote these words on index cards and brought them in during her last session with Spencer, spreading them across a coffee table, shocking him. This was an exercise their therapist had suggested. She didn't get to see his cards. He picked up hers, looking stricken. "What? Really? *Choking?* Is this a joke?" This was the end of therapy.

Her therapist's name was Paul Pomerantz. Once couples counseling was over, Paul became hers alone. This had felt like a victory of sorts. He chose her! A garden-variety talk therapist proud of his PhD, he had unmet aspirations of becoming a bona fide intellectual. His office was downtown, in a sleek mirrored-glass tower overlooking the harbor. From the waiting room you could see the whale watch boats hauling tourists out to sea. At first she went twice a week, confusing therapy with exercise. Surely double the effort might mean a better result, twice as fast. She hadn't gone in a month, though. During her last session, Paul had lost his concentration and looked up from his leather notebook to confess that he couldn't do this anymore, that her necklace was beautiful, and, more than that, her neck was kind of beautiful, too, and if she wasn't uncomfortable hearing it, her eyes were really beautiful.

She had sat, silent. He, also, had sat, silent. Beside her, on the carpet, a noise machine simulated the sound of rain on a window screen. She felt very conscious of her necklace, her neck, and her eyes. Then the session ended.

Apparently you could not simply date your patient. There were laws and professional codes of ethics. Time, she learned, needed to pass in order for Paul not to lose his license or, worse, be considered a sexual predator. Alone in her office at the hospital that night, she spent hours Googling. Most of her search terms were along the lines of: *How does transference really work?;* or, *Did Freud know what he was talking about or was he high all the time?;* or, *Is this really about my dead dad?;* or, *How bad is it to fuck your therapist?* Seeming to understand the gravity of what he'd suggested, Paul left her a message the next morning: What I suggest is us taking a month to see whether our feelings remain. She had found his use of the plural humorous. After all, she hadn't said a thing. He had merely begun rhapsodizing about her neck, and she'd received the information the same way she'd received all the variously vague things he'd been telling her these past few months. That the codependency of her marriage mirrored the equally codependent relationship she'd had with her mother. Or that the rigidly controlled life of a surgeon was a reflection of the loss of control she felt over how wayward and stoned a husband she had. It was clear now that Paul was not an especially astute therapist. A good deal of what came out of Paul's mouth during counseling struck her in retrospect as a canny way to finish off what was already dying. Lately there had been hints of what was to come. A small glance of his hand on hers as she was leaving his office. A Christmas card with a flirtatious salutation sent to her office. Small things that when put together added up to his gently putting down his notebook and talking about her neck.

For a month she sat with the possibility, turning it over in her head. At night, driving home along the Charles River, she could see the spire of his office building receding in the window behind her. She knew almost nothing about him. He adhered closely to the analyst's maxim of total opacity. Did his trim physique mean that he enjoyed the outdoors? Was he one of those fools who cycled around the city dressed up as though he was in the Tour de France? Did the piles of aggressively left-wing reading material in his waiting room mean that dating him would be like her freshman year at Columbia, when her boyfriend grew Vladimir Lenin's goatee in admiration? She only knew that Paul was divorced because his secretary had said something. Mysteriously, Oona could not remember what he looked like. An Internet search produced younger versions of Paul, versions in which he had hair. She hoped to find a profile of his somewhere, articulating a list of interests. At some point in the midst of all this curiosity she decided, why the hell not see what my therapist is like over dinner? Finally, she struck first. There was a Clive Owen retrospective at the Brattle. Some irresistible British accents. This seemed innocent enough. Paul's curt refusal came by way of an email: I don't think I would like that. But who didn't like Clive Owen? She was confused. What about her neck? Her necklace? Her pretty eyes? It was a confusing situation, she knew. So confusing, she told a coworker, that she thought she should probably see a therapist about it.

Then, a week ago, she found Paul waiting in her office when she returned from surgery. Enough time had passed, he told her. He was ready. He was in a suit and tie. She was in her black surgical scrubs, having just repaired a compact fracture to a man's arm. They were both standing around, smiling like fools. He kissed her gently on her cheek, and then on her mouth. They were the strangest two kisses of her life. He smelled of sandalwood and chewing gum. "Let me take you out," he said. "Would you like that?" She did not remember what she said in response, but she remembered, there in her mother's bathroom, that tonight was the night they'd agreed that he would come and take her to dinner. She remembered giving him her address, writing it on the flip side of a page from an Rx pad.

At that moment she heard the sound of a car's engine in the driveway. Lydia went to the window.

"Who is it?" Oona asked.

"A bald man," Lydia said.

She thought to tell Lydia everything. Wasn't this what mothers and daughters did? Erase, as they aged, the boundary between parent and child and become something close to friends? Or was this the exact opposite of what to do? Weren't there manuals to explain this next part of the parenting process? Craning to peek through the window, Oona saw a white Audi parked behind the house with its lights on. A moment later, Paul Pomerantz got out of the car and stepped onto the pebbled driveway.

"Who is that guy?" Lydia asked.

A second look out through the window revealed Paul coming up the walkway, moonlight bouncing off his scalp. Some men, it seemed to Oona, were able to achieve a more immaculate level of baldness, free of any wispy reminders of whatever glory their scalp may have once experienced, everything shiny, clean, and gleaming. Paul Pomerantz was one of these men: his baldness was exquisite and utterly complete.

"Mom?" Lydia said. "Mom, you're freaking."

"I am not freaking," Oona said, straightening herself, performing a quick diagnostic triage in the bathroom mirror. "I am definitely not freaking. I am normal. And not freaking."

After Paul came to her office last week, they went for a short walk around the hospital. With the rehabbing, arthritic patients struggling to walk in the hallways and the convalescing cancer patients slowly managing their way to the hospital's art gallery, it had not been a romantic twenty minutes. They met the following day for another walk, this time outside the hospital, around the frozen serenity gardens, again for twenty minutes—all that she had between patients. A third walk, a day later, left her feeling thrilled. If she was being utterly blunt about it, she had been very thrilled. This was stupid, she had told herself, feeling excitement at the idea of a new man looking at her, even if it was only because that new man appeared to regard her less-than-perfect body with more enthusiasm than Spencer had managed in two decades. Maybe Paul lacked all the judgment and scorn and jealousy of her husband. Or maybe this was going to be entirely carnal. Who ever ended up married to her couples counselor, anyway? And why, really, was she thinking of marriage at a time like this, reaching out to hold Paul's hand in the foyer of the otolaryngology department? Of everyone who might have been able to answer this for her, it was Paul.

Outside, Paul had his telephone in his hand. Instantly she looked to her own phone. Lydia caught all of this.

"Oh," Lydia said, seeing the phone light up. "He's here for you."

Oona watched the snow alight on Paul's shoulders. What on earth was it that she felt for him? This warmth in her, this desire to be close to him, to know everything about him. What was this? And what was it, then, that she felt for Spencer if it wasn't revulsion? Weren't these the facts? Wasn't this the truth?

Lydia, meanwhile, was studying her face. "He's your boyfriend," she said. "Isn't he?"

"No," Oona said, which was not a lie.

"Your flushed face is reading to me like this guy is your boyfriend."

"I have a date with him," she said. "That's all I'll admit."

Lydia smiled widely. "Him?"

Lydia came up beside her. They both peered out. He was in a beige overcoat and black slacks. He had on leather gloves.

"The leather gloves are creepy," Lydia said. "He looks like a hit man."

"Where's your father?" Oona realized, perhaps too late, that her husband might think it confusing to see his marriage counselor knocking on the front door of his mother-in-law's house.

"Oh, does he not know?" Lydia asked.

Downstairs the doorbell rang.

"He doesn't know, does he?" Lydia asked.

"I think your dad is in the garage," Oona said. "I'm going to go tell Paul to get lost. Can you just go down to the kitchen and make sure, if he starts to come out, that he doesn't?"

Lydia smiled too widely. "Paul?"

Oona took the steps down to the driveway two at a time, passing, as she hurried, her husband's car keys, hanging on the hook by the back door. In her hand, her phone kept buzzing. I'm excited, the first message read. Where are you? This kind of joyful, albeit childish, display of affection—nobody had ever done this for her. Her father had done it for her mother, she knew. Right up until the end, he did it. All the love letters in the house. The constant cooking for her, the dancing with her, the incessant, almost magnetic need to be touching her at all times. When Spencer had been wooing Oona, he'd done it with the reserved nonchalance of someone waiting to see if a store clerk had his size of chinos somewhere in a back stockroom; if she hadn't been interested, he'd have probably shrugged it off and kept on shopping.

Outside, she found Paul at the door. Again, he smelled like sandalwood.

"Hey you," she whispered.

Paul clutched both of her wrists. "I was *calling you*."

"I'm sorry."

Still holding on to her, he looked her up and down. "Do I have the wrong night?"

She looked out beyond Paul's shoulder at the slope of the

meadow, which was frozen, and at the place where the flagstone had been, and at the barn, lit now by floodlights.

"I can't do it tonight," she said. She pointed her chin toward the barn. "Spencer's here," she whispered.

"Oh," Paul said. His smile vanished. He let go. "I didn't know you two were speaking."

"We went together to get Lydia from school," she said.

"Lydia," he repeated.

"Our daughter," she reminded him.

On their first short walk through the hospital, she had learned only a few things about him. He was childless. He was from Texas. He had a fancy apartment. His ex-wife was a catalog model. He was a self-described Jew-Bu: some Jewish, some Buddhist. Also, he adored Stevie Wonder. This, aside from his choice of office reading material and, because it was there in the driveway, the make of his car, constituted every single thing she knew about him.

"So I should go?" he asked quietly.

"Let's reschedule," she said. "Next week, maybe."

"You're having second thoughts," he said. "I can see it."

"I'm not."

She looked back at the barn. She could hear her mother laughing, and then Spencer laughing. It had always been this way: her husband worked to be so much more charming in her mother's presence than in hers.

"It's unconventional," he said. "But not unheard of for this kind of thing to happen."

"Paul," she said. "Listen—"

"Your being nervous is perfectly relatable. In fact, I'm nervous!"

"I'm not having any second thoughts. I just—" She drew him close and spoke directly into his ear, her lips brushing his skin. "I can't be seen with you here."

From behind the barn, in the direction of the kitchen, Oona heard footsteps on the frozen snow, and instantly she looked frantically for someplace to stash Paul. Could the promise of love or sex ever not make you feel young? This urge to keep it a secret—she'd felt like this when she was a girl, hiding her boyfriends from her parents, stuffing Alexander Closker in a broom closet, his erection covered up by the pink hat from her favorite porcelain doll. Paul, however, wanted to talk. He had that particularly expressive look of pain across his brow that always prefigured him saying something serious. She knew it from therapy. As the footsteps got louder, she turned to see Lydia coming up from behind the barn, dressed in her parka and her hunter-green Wellies, *The Inseparables* tucked under her arm. Oona knew that Lydia was only trying to get a closer look at this man who'd come to see her. As she passed by, Oona met her eyes and tried wordlessly to convey a plea for mercy. When Lydia was back inside the house, Oona turned back to Paul. The yard and the big field were silent. Snow continued to fall around them.

"Is that her?" he asked. "That's Lydia?"

"That's her," Oona said, smiling.

"She's fifteen," Paul said. "Isn't that right?"

Oona felt flattered that he remembered this. "Such an easy age," she said, trying to joke.

"I can't imagine," he said. "Sometimes I think I really missed out by not being a father." He paused and looked around the dark, snowy fields, appearing to think deeply. "It's something I spend a lot of time wondering about."

She didn't know what to say to this. Her therapist, opening up about his regrets and doubts, sounding very much the way she probably sounded in her sessions. "That's something we can talk about next week," Oona said. She looked out nervously behind him, hoping that the next person who walked by was not Spencer. "Call me. We can reschedule. Same time?"

As he went to hug her, he stretched out his arms in a sign of innocence and forgiveness while trying to say something about how excited he'd been to see her, about how terribly nervous he'd been. Then, turning to go, Paul took a step toward the driveway and lost his footing. Oona saw it happening. He slid for a moment. Both feet in the snow and ice. He swung his arms out. Across the driveway, she saw Lydia in the kitchen watching through the window. When Paul's head smacked the hard frozen walkway, Oona yelped. She saw his head bounce. Instantly, she ran, and from the kitchen so did Lydia.

"I'm fine," he said, already on his feet. He rubbed at his head. "Don't worry. I'm fine."

She reached out to touch his head. "You're cut," she said. "You're bleeding."

He took off his gloves right when Lydia got there. "It's a small thing," he said.

Already, Oona was replaying it in her head. The bounce. The blood on the ground. She turned, hoping her mother was not nearby. "This is the same goddamn spot, almost," she said.

Lydia looked down at the ground. A tiny droplet of blood marked the snow. She smeared her boot into the drift, vanishing it. "You're right," she said.

"Oh," Paul said, blinking fast. "I see. This is where your dad—"

"We need to get you inside and sitting down."

"I'm fine," Paul said. "Really. It's just a cut."

"No," Oona said. She heard her voice catching. "After a skull fracture there's the lucid interval. You don't even know you're hurt. With my dad, he was fine for five minutes. Then, *boom*, everything changed."

"You're overreacting," he said.

After her father died, she had wondered so many times about what had happened here on the hill, about whether it would have made a difference if she had been the one who'd rushed out after him instead of her mother. After all, maybe she would have registered an uneven dilation of his pupils. Maybe she would have sensed evidence of intercranial bleeding. Or a quickening of his blood pressure. She wanted to ask her mother about whether she'd noticed any of this, but she knew this was an impossibility. These were the questions she could never ask, especially of someone who had expected, clearly, for her husband just to get up off the ground.

She took Paul's chin in her hand and moved his face up into the beam of house light. "I can't get a good look at your pupils."

"I know you're having flashbacks. I can see it. Flashbacks are just manifestations—"

"Don't analyze me," she said.

"This isn't what happened to your dad," he said. "Even if it's the same spot."

"I saw it. Your head bounced." She touched his small cut. The bleeding had stopped.

"See? I'm fine! Really. I played football in high school. I'm used to banging my head. I have a hard skull."

She stopped. She realized that she knew nothing important about him. "Football?" she said. "You?"

He shook his head, as if trying to lose water from his ears.

From across the meadow she heard her mother's laughter. The floodlight on the barn switched off.

# *11.*

For a long while, Lydia had tried to decide which of her parents' letters was better. At night, in bed at Hartwell, she reread them by flashlight. She figured it was distasteful to do this, but each had included its own rationales and arguments, both in the same envelope, as if begging for her to intercede. Her mother's letter was typical of the woman she was, which is to say typical of a doctor well practiced in the art of diagnosis and remedy. Here is the problem: love has vanished. This is the solution: I'm moving out, we are divorcing, the future for me is wide open. Her father had written longer—two sides of yellow legal paper, in big, blocky black ink, everything disjointed, sentences running into one another, sentiments disguised by complaints. Lydia was conditioned to mistake the intensity of emotions for importance, and in this way, for days, she had reserved a small glimmer of hope that he was right when he'd written, *I don't think this is the end for us, I really don't. I'm positive your mother still loves me.*

Lydia thought of this as her mother issued her two discreet instructions, both of them in the dim stairway that led to the attic, family photographs still hanging on the walls around them, pictures in which everyone was young and thin and happy.

The instructions were these:

1. Do not let Paul leave
2. Do not let him fall asleep

A moment earlier, they had successfully deposited Paul on a tuft of pillows in the attic. Downstairs, her grandmother and her father were calling for her mother. In light of the last few minutes, her father's letter seemed to have been written in another, earlier, even prehistoric era in which hope had not yet gone extinct from the earth.

"I need to go," her mother told her. "Just make sure he doesn't try to leave."

"You absolutely cannot go."

"I'll be back in a half hour."

"A half hour with this guy?" she whispered. "He still has the leather gloves on."

"He's not a hit man, Lydia. I promise."

"So keep him prisoner, you're saying."

"Just keep him here."

"Here. Imprisoned."

"Lydia, just stay with him here for thirty minutes. That's all. Then I can figure out a way to get him out of here."

A moment ago, she had watched her mom quickly clean Paul's moderately small head wound and then put him through a concussion test, having him follow the beam of a penlight while she inspected the dilation of his pupils. Sometimes she forgot about her mother's considerable medical talents. The fact that she could slice open a person's leg and drill titanium rods through that person's shattered femur had always struck Lydia as a kind of superpower: the ability to endure gore, but also the exact knowledge of how brittle the human body really was.

"Look, he's going to want to slip out and go home," her

mom said. "I know it. And I can't have your dad see him. That, I promise, would be awful."

"He's clearly not hurt," Lydia said. "He passed all your tests."

"We don't know that yet. Brain trauma can arrive—"

"There's not even that much blood."

"If the injury is in the brain"—her mother put her hands on her head—"then the brain will swell, and if the brain swells, and pushes against the lining of the skull—" She stopped. She looked down at Paul, and saw, probably, exactly what Lydia saw, which was that he was fine. "Like I said. I can't have your father see him."

"Have Paul just say he's a friend of Grandma's. Dad won't know the difference."

Her mother winced.

"Oh," Lydia said. "He knows this guy, doesn't he?"

"Kind of."

"Kind of?"

"Maybe he was our couples counselor," her mother said, nearly at a whisper.

Lydia took a moment. She repeated the words aloud to make sense of them. "*Maybe* he was your couples counselor?"

Her mother took a deep breath. She spoke slowly. "This is really not the proudest moment of my life, Lydia."

The revelation that her mother had a new man, or a secret life, or just something other than the monotonous grind of the hospital felt exciting at first. *Go, Mom!* But whatever misplaced enthusiasm she'd maintained for this new future in which her mother was single and fabulous, and poised to meet an equally single and fabulous new partner, had quickly vanished, erased by the fact that she had a tiny droplet of blood from her mother's boyfriend/therapist on the sleeve of her sweater. Perhaps Lydia should have known when her parents separated that her future might involve moments like this. You were inseparable and then you were separated and then there was blood. This was the side effect of insisting on your burgeoning maturity and adulthood and of your being admitted to a school for gifted psychopaths: you discovered information that you could not entirely process. How exactly did one go, really, from sitting beside one's spouse in a downtown office tower while a therapist yammered on and on to having that therapist here, readied for a date, smelling especially woody, bloodied in the head, and hiding in the attic?

"Don't worry, Mom," Lydia said, not entirely convincingly. "I can handle this."

When her mother left, Lydia sat alone in the attic with Paul, both of them wrapped in old Pendleton blankets. Quickly she doubted herself. She had her copy of *The Inseparables,* and she'd also brought up a stack of some of her grandparents' old reading material: ancient issues of *Cuisine Gourmande,* copies of *Redbook* dating back to when Julia Roberts left Kiefer Sutherland at the altar. For a while she and Paul both read. The windows here were bad, and the wind came through the cracks with a whistle. This was the oldest part of the house, and the creepiest. Old trunks full of clothing, marked with stickers from long-extinct railways, formed a partial buffer against the breeze.

Every few moments he looked over and grinned and she had to ask if he was okay and if he felt as though he was going to fall asleep. And by "fall asleep," she knew that he knew that she meant, *Do you think you might die on me here?* Because she could not handle death. Or anything close to a death. After the funeral, she had found her grandmother weeping alone upstairs in front of her grandfather's closet, and when her grandmother saw Lydia, all she wanted to do was tell her about how it had felt standing over him after he fell, watching him breathe and his head swell and swell some more, and it had all felt a little too precarious to Lydia—being alive, being able to walk and talk and kiss the people you love, and then to so quickly lose that ability. It was no wonder her mother had reacted the way she had when Paul fell.

Eventually she took out her phone. Since the last time she'd looked, she'd received a half dozen more messages. She kept accounts on every social media network. Her phone pinged whenever anything came through. Even on a normal day—a day during which her naked body was not multiplying across the Internet—the pinging was endless. The comments she got were a combination of the ludicrous and the abusive. She'd thought about showing them to everyone at Hartwell who was in a position to do something about them or help her. The headmistress, the assistant headmistress, the various deans and assistant deans of student ethics and student behavior. But every message was either anonymous and untraceable or linked to a dummy account with a fake name. She knew nothing would be done. Too bad she's gone, someone had written in a mass post that she was, for some cruel reason, attached to. What? someone had posted. She's gone? She scrolled. Don't worry, another comment read. There's always more where this came from. She felt herself close to shaking. She scrolled more, searching for another picture, something else, some other discrete invasion of herself. What else could that mean? More where this came from. Were there more pictures? She scrolled and then saw more photographs in the post, more tor-sos that were not hers, torsos borrowed and pasted from the Internet's general trash bin of nudity. More anonymous taunt-ing. More passionately happy comments. Yes! I love the sluts at this school!

She got up. "Are you okay?" she asked Paul.

"You keep asking. Are *you* okay?"

"I'm fine."

"You're shaking," he said.

She looked down at her free hand, which, indeed, was shaking. "It's cold up here," she said. Then: "I have to make a call. I'm going to be right outside the door."

Paul nodded.

Lydia turned back. "I guess I meant to say, you can't leave. So don't leave."

She went to the edge of the stairs that went down to the living room and found Charlie's entry in her contact list. She tried to imagine him at home in New Jersey, lounging on his bed. She had gone back to his dorm that night because he had told her, in full voice, that he wanted her to. His explicit desire felt romantic. *I want to kiss you,* he told her as they walked by the reeds and the ducks on Lake Rose. He was short, maybe five five, smaller than she was, small enough that she could almost wrap the entirety of her hand around his thigh, which she did while they kissed. He claimed that his small stature had something to do with his kidneys not working the right way, or his thyroid not functioning correctly. Which, knowing him, was probably bullshit. He'd been the head of his own group of students, a bandleader. His lack of height forced him to accrue an outsized combination of charisma and magnetism. Everyone called him Chucky, but she called him Bonaparte, which he loved maybe a little too much. At the end, with his cold hand on her stomach, and then under her skirt, on her chest, he bit down on her lip too hard. She wanted to go slow because she had the odd idea that she might want to remember this—forever.

His voice came across the line. "Is this who I think it is?" he asked. He had the same accent everyone at Hartwell had if they were there long enough: a broad Continental thing, half New England, half London, entirely fake.

"It's Lydia," she said, knowing that he'd entered her into his phone as Basic Boston Bitch. "You know it's Lydia."

"I didn't expect this," he said. He laughed, and behind him, in the background, other people laughed. She did not know what kind of town he came from. What his people were like. Everyone at Hartwell was wealthier than she was, and had gone to grammar school in places like Dubai or Davos, and had parents who knew Madeleine Albright and Boutros Boutros-Ghali. Charlie was high, she knew. She could tell by the languid oafishness in his voice. It was something different every month at school. Pills, synthetics, powders. Whatever came up through New York by way of Shanghai or Bogotá. Most people used the drugs to study longer, better, and then, after they were finished studying, mixed those same drugs with better drugs to get higher.

"Yeah," she heard him say. "It's that girl I was telling you about." More laughter and static and a snippet of that awful hip-hop song everyone was obsessed with. It sounded as if the phone was being passed around.

"What do you want, Lydia?" he said, his voice far away.

"Do you have any other fucking pictures of me?" she asked. She was trying to keep her voice down.

"I can't hear you," he said, although she was sure he could.

"I asked, do you have other fucking pictures of me, you creep?"

He laughed more. "I don't know. Do I? Have you taken any other pictures of yourself?"

"I was on some fucking sick message chain and I saw some cryptic comment about how there are more pictures."

"Reading Internet comments about yourself is not a good idea, Lydia," he said.

She turned back and looked to the attic door, hoping Paul was not listening.

"The fact that you took that picture got me expelled," he said. "I shouldn't even be talking to you."

"You deserved it. You stole that picture."

"Yeah," he said. "She's still on. This is hilarious. I don't know how to put it on speaker. Which button? This button?"

"Don't you put me on speaker," Lydia said. "Don't put me on speaker, you little fuck."

She hung up then. The phone felt hot against her skin, a not-so-subtle reminder that these things were radiating energy and waves that probably weren't all that great for you. She looked down at it, the glassy eye of the camera glaring back at her. There were ways, she remembered him telling her, to turn on a person's camera remotely, without the person knowing. "Assume that someone's watching you all the time," he'd said. This was at the beginning, before she realized that these kinds of things were not jokes, but were something like the confessions of someone who couldn't help himself. She vacillated between wanting to vomit and trying not to vomit. She dialed him back. She couldn't help herself. His voice mail picked up. *This is Charlie Company,* the message went, something she'd begged him to change the first time she heard it. He thought it was funny. "You're a real motherfucker," she said at the prompt. "Fucking speakerphone? Are you fucking kidding me? You're the worst motherfucker, Charlie Perlmutter." Her breath exploded into the receiver. "Are you fucking watching me, you creep? Are you?" she yelled. "Listen to me," she said, dropping her voice. "I hope everything for you in the future is awful. Everything."

For a while she sat at the top of the stairs, trying not to weep or scream, and when she went back into the attic she tried to bury herself in the copy of her grandmother's book, hoping that if she did in fact burst out sobbing, she might be able to hide behind the hardcover flaps.

After a minute, Paul cleared his throat. "Is it a man?" he asked.

He'd startled her. "What did you say?"

"Are you upset over a man?"

She wiped at her eyes. "A boy," she said. "Just a boy."

He grinned. "Don't let a boy—"

She waved her hands. "I know the speech. Thank you, but I've heard it."

"It's a good speech," he said.

"I just got it from my mom earlier today. So I'm all caught up on the motivational rhetoric."

"Well, she knows what she's talking about, then, your mom."

Lydia rolled her eyes.

"I was the same way with girls when I was that age," he said.

"A sociopathic voyeur?" she asked.

He laughed. "Not exactly."

"Weeping in an attic with your mother's boyfriend?"

He didn't smile. "I'd like a girl and then they'd find out and then I'd be merciless and cruel to them."

She screwed up her mouth. "So you're a mind reader now? What makes you think that's what it is?"

He shrugged. "Other than the fact that I heard you talking, and that you were three feet away, you need to know that this is a kind of ritualistic male impulse to tear the female down."

"Is it a ritualistic male impulse to invade a woman's privacy?"

"All I'm saying is that he'll work through it. The impulse, that is. Or most of us do."

"So you're saying that all I need to do is wait until middle age, and then maybe I'll figure out which tiny fraction of men are decent and which are sex criminals."

"I forgot," he said. "You were at that school for very smart people, weren't you?"

"This is not important," she said.

"Kids who are very intelligent often suffer from stunted emotional lives."

"That's a very obvious thing to say," she said. "People pay you money for this?"

He put the magazine down on his lap. "Love is always complicated."

"Who said anything about love?" she said.

"What word do you want to use, then?"

"I have the sinking feeling that we're therapizing," she said. "Do I need to have made an appointment with you?"

He smiled. "Okay. I can shut up and take a hint and mind my own business. It's okay. I just figured that if we were going to be prisoners together, you and me, we could talk."

"We can talk about your problems," she said. "I bet they're more fascinating than mine."

"Who said I had problems?"

Lydia's eyes widened. "This situation we're in at the moment does seem kind of problematic for you."

He offered a reluctant smile.

"I would say that my father would kick your ass—"

"Oh, I don't think that's true," Paul said. "I highly, highly doubt that would happen."

"Don't do that," Lydia said. "Don't smirk. He's nice. He's good. He's a good person."

"You're just like her," he said. "It's uncanny."

Lydia shook her head. "Since you're dating her, you should probably not say that to me unless you want me to think you're a potential predator."

"It's true. It's really quite something. Pardon my saying this, but it's almost creepy."

"*Creepy?* She's my mother! I'd hope we were alike. *This* is creepy," she said. "Me being here in this attic. Wrapped up in blankets together."

"Come on," he said. "It's not that bad."

"You're reading a twenty-two-year-old *Redbook*. And you have blood all over you."

He looked down at his shirt. Before her mother clotted the cut, a steady stream had trickled down the back of his head to his neckline. "It was a cheap shirt anyway," he said.

For a moment she worried he would take it off, but he merely unbuttoned a few buttons and craned his neck back and forth. Earlier, she'd had to back up his car onto the main road by the river so that her dad wouldn't see and figure it out. Inside, his Audi was beautiful and leathery and heavy with cologne, a bottle of which she found in his glove box, along with a prescription for Klonopin, an aerosol spray can of breath freshener, and a notepad onto which he'd written,

#1 Be Yourself!
#2 Be Kind! (AKA Don't Be a Dick!)
#3 Don't Talk About Ex-Wife!

"We don't know each other, really," Paul said. "Your mother and I."

"Except for therapy."

"Well, I know *about* her, I suppose."

"But she doesn't know you," Lydia said.

"Not much."

"Well, that doesn't sound creepy at all."

"Excuse me?"

"I meant, isn't that why this is unethical?" she asked.

He took a moment to think about this. "We've waited the appropriate length of time to avoid scrutiny."

Lydia smirked.

"I had a date planned," he said. "A first date. That's all. It's innocent."

"I'm guessing your date didn't involve a head wound?"

"Italian food. Italian movie. Then, for dessert, gelato in the North End."

"No matching brown shirts to complete the theme?" she asked.

"You know," he said, "sometimes joking is a form of panic."

"Oh, you're ruining the fun of me keeping you prisoner," she said. "And besides, I dozed off during the lecture on *The Joke and Its Relation to the Unconscious*."

Her phone buzzed. Although she didn't want to, she looked down. This was far worse than a habitual tic or a magnetic attraction to abuse. For days she had promised herself she wouldn't read any more of the messages, and then, because she could not help it, she dove back in for more. She found the chain. Even more people had chimed in. She closed her eyes.

"You should know," Paul said, "that humiliation is a by-product of high school."

She looked up.

"I heard you yelling through the walls. You want to tell me what happened?"

"Not even remotely." She felt her phone buzz and her eyes well simultaneously.

Footsteps came up the landing. For a moment Paul looked genuinely worried it might be her father. Her mother opened the door.

She pointed at Lydia. "Dinnertime," she said. To Paul, she held up a finger. "I want you to wait thirty minutes. Then I want you to go down the stairs, take a left, and go out the back door. Don't close it. Just run. Wait an hour and I'll call and come meet you."

# *12.*

In the dining room, Oona found the table already set and her husband, with his hair freshly slicked, pouring wine into paper cups. Evening had fallen. Burning applewood made the house sweet. Outside, on the road, the city plows scraped against the pavement, making high parapets out of the snowdrift. She had come down from the attic behind Lydia, and they both stopped at the foot of the stairs to witness this: her mother lighting a pair of paraffin candles, takeout Chinese containers arrayed in a circle, wooden chopsticks at every place setting. Spencer stood upright when they came into the room, smiling as if they had just caught him and her mother in the middle of some private joke. Perhaps Lydia was thinking the same thing she was thinking, which was, at once, that this felt delightfully familiar and that this was an inopportune time to feel a pang of nostalgia for better days.

"The glassware is in boxes," Spencer explained, holding up a paper cup full of Chablis, candlelight warming his face. "So it'll be like when we were in graduate school."

At the end, right before she left, he'd done this. He'd tried to appeal to her memory, conjuring up those first months in 1996 when they were first together, when the future seemed gloriously sunny. Accordingly, he was always playing Pearl Jam for her on the car stereo after counseling, or else dialing up Bridget Fonda movies on the flat screen at night, thinking, perhaps optimistically, perhaps witlessly, that she would regain some lost passion for their marriage in the middle of listening to an Eddie Vedder ballad.

"What do we do?" Lydia whispered.

"Say nothing," said Oona. "Do nothing. Be normal."

"He's going to get caught running out."

"He will not."

"Do you want my opinion on him?" Lydia said, continuing to whisper.

Oona shook her head. "Not really."

"Here it is anyway: you can do much better."

The food was from the Palace, her mother said, a tiny take-out hovel in town with a picture-on-the-wall menu. Her mother had shed most everything of the old world that had made her Henrietta Horowitz. The Yiddish: forgotten. The answers to the Four Questions: unknown. But this—the fervor for Chinese food, the favorite cuisine of every lapsed, secular, North American Jew of a certain age—this remained. Something about the heaping saltiness of the food clearly summoned ghosts. Her mother could hold a wonton on her tongue, and suddenly the whole long line of Horowitz aunts and uncles, dead for eons, would flood her. Like her dad, Oona couldn't stomach the stuff—unlike Spencer, whose Jewishness was equally lapsed and who, if she was being honest, had some of her mother's humor and panicky inclination to dread. This had never been lost on her, however odd it was to consider that she'd married and slept with and made a home with a man who reminded her so much of her mother.

Paul had found these particular facts predictably fascinating. She thought of this as they sat down to eat. With every creak overhead she looked to Lydia, who promptly met her eyes with a wry smile, as if to say, *Look at what you got us into.* Or: *Isn't this fun?* Or: *Really? Him?*

Dinner was mostly quiet. She did not know how to do this: eat with your soon-to-be ex, your rapidly maturing whiz kid daughter, and your mother, flanked by moving boxes and dozens of pristinely pink copies of her book, and also with your maybe boyfriend stashed away upstairs in the same spot where you had stashed away your priapic adolescent boyfriends. Thankfully, everyone else seemed equally at a loss. They emptied greasy noodle-filled cartons in silence. They reduced to bones a box of deep-fried wings, with a salinity content that rivaled the Atlantic's. Her mother tried to start a conversation by mentioning how they had drunk vodka out of paper cups when they'd first moved here. Tonight she'd finished a few such cups of wine. Lydia, ever shrewd, had countered, "Weren't you pregnant when you moved here? If so, that totally explains my mom in so many ways."

Fortunes were dispensed joylessly but not, for each of the family, without a foolish moment of optimism. Spencer held his in his hand, smiling. *"Your family is one of nature's great masterpieces,"* he read. "How about that!"

When they finished dinner, her mother took Lydia into the kitchen to do the dishes, leaving Oona alone with Spencer. The setup was obvious. She was used to the meddling in her separation. When people discovered that your marriage was failing, or about to fail, every odd stranger wanted to impart advice to you, some of it foolishly New Age (learn to find contentment in every moment), some of it indecently sexual (learn to fuck more often), and only some of it useful (get a separate bank account). She sat by the big window. Spencer sat just beside her. He'd refreshed his cologne, she noticed, and his watch face looked newly polished. She'd bought him the cologne, just as she'd bought him the wristwatch, the hair products, the dye for his temples, the golf clubs in the back of the Toyota, the pajamas he slept in, even the Viagra for his cock. All of her money had slowly, year by year, driven him mad. He had assured her it was not the case, had insisted that he was still the same congenial liberal kid from Chevy Chase who was fine with a woman earning all the money—better than fine—but she knew the truth.

He quit the law firm their first year in Massachusetts. He showed up that day at the hospital in his suit, weed smoke on his skin and hair, having just done it. "I told them I was out," he said, taking her, kissing her, patients watching, orderlies rushing by, cardiac monitors beeping. He laughed and smiled and jumped for joy. "Now I'm free!" They had talked about this happening, but only briefly. Leaving his job was a theoretical possibility in the same way that it was also theoretically possible that Oona might win the Nobel Prize in Medicine. Put simply, they needed his money. Without it, she would have to take on more patients, work endlessly, never see her child. For all of that year he'd been in a cubicle forty stories up, litigating a dispute between two petro giants, while Lydia languished at a day care miles away, in Crestview. This was how he imagined it, at least—his baby wasting away, *Midnight Express*-style, in a nursery as gloomy as a Turkish prison—when in reality the Crestview Child Care Center was plush and fine and run by a team of lovely women who read to the babies and put on fantastic puppet shows. Nightly, Oona would stop by the firm to rouse Spencer with banana and peanut butter sandwiches, or with chickens roasted the way her father had taught her: simply, with lemons and salt. Or better yet, she would visit him on weekends, toting Lydia, and inevitably he would become convinced that Lydia didn't recognize him anymore. "I've been gone so much," she remembered him saying. "She thinks every guy in a suit is me." He dreamed up impossible fantasies. He wanted to run away to a cheap town in the Midwest. Let's be poor, he told her. How much do we really need, anyway? Isn't the point of all this—love and family and fucking togetherness—isn't the point that we occasionally see each other?

Behind him ice froze over the holes in the window screen. For a few minutes they were silent. She kept trying to look past him to see a trace of Paul as he ran out. She tried to think of what exactly she would say if Spencer found out. Was there ever a real reason to have your therapist visiting you at home, late at night? Then she tried to imagine the two of them fighting it out, maybe here in the dining room.

When she tried again to look past him to the walkway, he smiled.

"I like this," he said.

"Which part?" she asked.

"All of it. Eating a family meal. Being here. You and me. Talking. Like humans."

She sank a little in her seat. Instinctively, she looked up at the ceiling. "I really didn't think the next time I saw you would be for something like this," she said.

"You look nice," he said.

She picked up a spoon, greasy with duck sauce, and searched out her reflection. "I do? How is that possible?"

"The white streak in the hair," he said, pointing, almost touching her head. "I like it. It's elegant."

"I was hoping it was more intimidating than elegant."

This made him laugh. He finished more wine. He began to say something, then stopped.

"What is it?" she asked.

"I don't want to ruin the night. I should be quiet."

She waited for him to talk.

"It's just that it's been bad without you," he said. "Very bad. Real fucking bad."

"I know," she said. Which she did. For the longest time she had been almost biologically attuned to his emotions. After leaving the law firm, he grew bored. He missed her even more. He yearned desperately to have conversations with other adults. She tried to rectify this. She called, video-chatted; she flooded the house with consumer goods, with enormous televisions; she rushed out on her short breaks to meet him for coffee in the hospital cafeteria; she blamed herself; she lost sleep; she grew her hair out; she bought ridiculous crotchless lingerie. None of it was enough.

"I meant what I said in the letters," he said.

"Which letter?" she said.

"All the letters. Every one. The ones you read and the ones you didn't."

"I have all the letters," she said, which was different, she knew, than saying she had read all of the letters.

"I'm a single man in my forties living in the suburbs. That's almost certainly a very specific circle of hell, I think."

"But you can move anywhere you want," she told him, knowing already that he had stayed in Crestview, in the house they had built, because he was convinced that their separation would end, and that she would come home.

"Would it be awful if I said out loud that you were my best friend?"

Before the separation, she had regarded his open sentimentality with suspicion. It was his big character flaw, she contended, the idea that emotions became more potent the more dramatically you conveyed them. But her concern for him was hardwired into her. Six months apart and she still felt the urge to do something about this—his sadness, his misery, his loneliness, his every daily problem. Immediately she reached to touch his wrist. Touching Spencer like this was habit. With her fingers on him she could feel his heart beating. Was there ever a way, she wondered, to do this, to express concern for a person, a man, without it constituting crossed signals?

"Did you help my mother in the garage?" she asked, trying to find a different subject, something, anything, less troublesome. "Did you help her find whatever it is that's gone missing?"

"I just took it too far, didn't I?" he asked. "With the best friend thing? Was that too much? I've been rehearsing things to say to you. I do it in the car, driving around town. All day, sometimes. Imaginary conversations, in which I am usually very funny and charming, and in which you remember what it is you originally liked about me."

She thought, if I smile, it will be a cruel smile, a lying smile, especially with Paul upstairs, especially in light of Spencer talking about how she looked nice, and how much he appreciated the new white streak in her hair. She also thought, if I pout at him or express any kind of pity toward his emotions, which are real emotions, surely it will be just as bad.

She drank.

In the beginning they told each other everything. Openness was healthy, they assumed. Secrets were stifling. Better to know what you're up against than to let unaired grievances fester and turn malignant. Not long after they moved to Crestview, she and Spencer began to keep a record of their secrets. They did this by habitually filling an empty drawer in their kitchen with small scraps of paper onto which they'd written the things they were most afraid to tell each other. Their friends found this charming, or at least obnoxious enough to lie about: *You two. Holy Lord, you're so adorable. A drawer of secrets! Who does a thing like that?* Surely by committing to paper their most deeply held secrets and wishes they would ensure a bulwark against repression. Mostly they believed this. In moments of weakness, when they no longer believed, they read books on believing. This was something they shared: an unhealthy faith in the written word, or at least a preference for the self-help section of their local bookstore. No other couple they knew could boast of having digested more self-help than she and Spencer. The sheer surplus of words buoyed them. We will make mistakes, they told each other. We will take each other for granted. We will at some point find each other repellent. We know these things and we are stronger because of them. The experiment was short-lived. The first wishes were typical and often lovely. *A week with just you in Venice and no babysitter or baby monitor or grand-parents.* By the next year, they had begun to startle each other. *Cocaine.* It was clear the spirit of the plan had quickly soured. She thought of this now. The drawer in the kitchen had long since been taken over by knives. Surely this meant something.

He smiled. Lydia came in and out of the room, clearing more food. He watched her.

"She got even smarter," he said.

"She'll be fine," Oona said hopefully.

"She's better than both of us," he said.

"That's not a very difficult thing to accomplish," she said.

Spencer turned to her. "You should come home with me when I take her back."

"See? That doesn't sound smart," she said.

"We could get the team back together. Have a movie night. Watch something scary."

He always did this—substituted the word "team" for "family," as if the whole business of cohabitation and occasionally fucking and more than occasionally feuding with each other was equal to the dynamic one finds on a football squad.

"You don't want to come home at all?" he asked.

"I do sometimes," she admitted, and it was true.

She had driven by the house, more than once, in the dead of morning, and parked outside in the dirt beneath the pin oak while the lawn sprinklers soaked the yellow siding. She thought that if she regarded the house the way a spy might, she could gain some perspective on what she had given up. This felt like a revoltingly sappy thing to do, to say nothing of how unwise or misleading it would be if Spencer discovered her. By the third time she'd done it, she had to reckon with the facts. Separating had confused her. She missed the place. It was a big ugly house, built in a period of outsized ambition and youthful recklessness. She had poured untoward amounts of energy into each decorative choice. The siding, for instance—she had deliberated over so many dozen shades of yellow before picking this one. Canary yellow. Hay bale yellow. Hawthorne yellow. The same went for the lawn sprinkler and the type and strain of grass it watered. The sheer pomposity of the neighborhood implied that everyone had the same hopes she and Spencer had: domestic bliss, suburban perfection, passable color coordination.

As much as her mother had wanted her to become a firebrand or an artist, or at least somewhat competent during a dinner conversation about, say, Susan Sontag's "Notes on Camp," Oona had become resolutely bourgeois. The luxury skin care, the occasional macrobiotic diet, the spin classes, the opinions on which brand of leather-ensconced turbo-dieseled German sedan was best. Not long ago she had installed a $5,000 bathtub. Environmentally disastrous, it required 242 gallons to fill, but when the bubbles were going, the effect was not unlike being pleasantly awash in the ocean. She bathed at the end of every workday, six times a week, no matter how long a day she'd worked. She researched the best luxury bubble baths. She did the research while soaking in other luxury bubble baths. It was important to note, however, that she harbored doubts about the ethics of all of this. On the Internet she'd found some statistics:

242 gallons of water would last the average horrendously impoverished African family forty days.

Dutifully she tacked a reminder note to her vanity.

6 baths @ 242 gallons per = 1,452 gallons a week
1,452 gallons a week for a year = 75,500+ gallons for the
year = 41+ years' worth of water for the average
horrendously impoverished African family
***Start volunteering more/bathing less***

What did it mean that this was what she thought of when she thought of home? To lie with just her eyes above the water, and everywhere around her the white splash-and-bounce of the jets! Was this so bad?

Spencer leaned forward. His good cologne wafted off him. This felt like a crude way of weakening her conviction. He knew that she loved this smell.

"Then come," he said, smiling, more good cologne wafting. "Come home and just be there in the house with us. Give it a week. Stay there while Lydia is home."

The real question was whether or not she missed him, which she did, periodically, at night, mostly, lying here in her childhood bed or, more mysteriously, alone sometimes in her car on the part of Route 9 full of shopping malls and fast-food restaurants and auto dealerships. He had terrifically bad taste in music, and more than once she had found herself listening to some abstruse forty-minute vibraphone solo with something like longing in her. He thought the Real Oona was gone, but the same could be said for him as well. Maybe she had left him in New York, in the apartment where they had lived when Lydia was an infant. Or maybe it went back further, to the restaurant on 2nd Avenue where he had first charmed her, to Veselka, to that first plate of pierogies. The whole project of marriage, she thought sometimes, was a constant labor to indulge the evolution. You met your husband at a party in Tribeca when he was twenty and you were twenty-one and you found his knowledge of books appealing and his apparent ability to accurately label on a map every country in Europe mildly impressive, and then, somehow, you were living three hundred miles north in a stucco split-level with zoned heating and central air-conditioning and a three-car garage, and his daily life consisted mostly of getting high and listening to Ornette Coleman. These last six months she had practically disallowed this kind of thinking. Who really gave a shit whether anyone ever missed anything? She said this to herself sometimes while running a scalpel through a patient's leg. Spencer's evolution was a downward trajectory. It seemed to her that if you made the decision to leave a man, then you left a man. Equivocation only worsened things. She knew what he wanted her to say. To Spencer, missing someone meant loving someone, in the same way that, to her mother, worrying about someone meant love.

Just then she saw a flash of white in the yard. Paul sprinted out past the garage. Moonlight bounced back off his precious bare head. She watched as he awkwardly hurdled the split rail and booked it for the road. When she looked back at Spencer, she saw that his right eye was dilated. She leaned in close enough to smell his clothing. Only now did she realize that he was high.

"Of course," she said.

"Of course what?"

"When? When could you have possibly gotten high?"

"I'm not high," he said.

She took out her penlight and flashed it in his eyes, watching the slow response of his pupils. "Spencer," she said. "Why would you ask me to come back with you when you were like this? I thought you were clean and sober. I thought you had almost three months."

"Clean and sober implies some deeper problem. Which, as you know, I refuse—"

Overhead, the ceiling creaked. He reached out and touched her hair, swinging a loose strand behind her ear, something he had done hundreds of times before.

"I think you probably shouldn't be touching me," she said.

"Oona—"

"It's just important for us to erect boundaries."

"*Erect boundaries,*" he said. "You sound like Dr. Paul."

She felt warm. In the other room, she heard Lydia laughing.

# *13.*

Some restaurants die quickly. Interest wanes. The food becomes underwhelming. Reviews are poor. For Harold, the end was slow and grueling. The Feast closed at the end of the Great Recession. By then it was a curiosity, a stopover for drunk students flush with their parents' money. It had become a museum of butter. People wanted to eat like birds and Harold didn't know what the fuck to do with people like that. Vegans? Pescatarians? People who wanted to see the nutritional information for foie gras? People who asked if he could prepare a quiche without butter or eggs or salt? Who were these people? Diners suddenly spoke like chefs. Meat was not meat anymore. Meat was "protein." Vegetables were "product." Your average eighteen-year-old Boston University student came in full of uncompromising ideas about what French food ought to taste like. People watched five episodes of a televised cooking competition or read a book about the dangers of monoculture and thought they knew what they were talking about, or worse, they came in wanting to loudly proclaim their most entrenched convictions: the country's belief in food as art was evidence of a civilization in decline; the French domination of culinary culture was outdated and overly Eurocentric. Can I see the chef? Harold heard night after night. Henrietta knew this because after Oona went away to college she had worked with him, mostly at the front of the house, seating people, or sometimes upstairs in the office, ordering linens or sundries. An early life spent lecturing on Germaine Greer and Shulamith Firestone, and now she endured the questions of food-obsessed cultists. Who are your vendors? Were there pesticides involved? Could you explain how the body digests gluten? Could you make a heart-healthy version of this madeleine? What did she think about the emotional life of geese raised for foie gras? Were these eggs laid in happy circumstances, did she know? Harold had tried, in those last weeks, to explain that what he did was no different than what all these new celebrity chefs were doing: "I was doing farm to fucking table before Dan Barber learned to chew." He said this to a customer one night when it became clear that the Feast was doomed, and when for weeks it had been empty, when every night they poured down the drain masterpieces of béchamel and velouté. The customer turned out to be a food blogger, and the outburst went out into their tiny world as evidence that the formerly great (or at least good) Harold Olyphant had turned into the currently bitter Harold Olyphant. The Feast closed a week later.

Henrietta thought of this as she went out for firewood down across the yard. It was late, near midnight. The house was empty, the yard moonlit. For a moment earlier, with everyone inside, with food being served, it felt normal again. She crossed the meadow and went through the rows of apple trees. He had planted these the first winter. One to the left of the house, one to the right. At the fence line, she undid the latch on the hut. She was down to the last dozen logs. Just after the Feast closed, this was what he did, dark to light, out here with an ax—not exactly the most subtle display of aggression. She would watch him all day with that dumb ax, over and over. He had nothing left to do and so he chopped wood. They were hurting for money. She handled the bills and saw the accounts dwindling. They went without insurance. They mortgaged the house, and then, so quickly, fell behind on the loan.

What had bothered Harold most was that he had to get rid of his animals. All the chickens, the goats, the dairy cows—they sold everything to a farmer in southern Vermont who had the land and the money. All that was left was Dougie. Henrietta usually went to feed him twice a day, on Harold's old circuit, first thing in the morning and then again after midnight, but today, with everything going on, she had not yet come to see him. Dougie had been a gift from his sous chef years before the restaurant began to slow—another bird to add to the collection. A few years ago, Lydia had painted Dougie's name on the wood of his pen, and this, this yellow paint, this delightful child-scrawl, was the first thing Henrietta saw as she came up over the hill toward the pen. The last night Harold was a living, breathing person, he'd been prepping to use Dougie for his coq au vin. Usually he'd starve the bird before slaughter in order to use the organs, and in order for those organs to remain unsullied by food and grain and shit, and Harold had done this, but not without some twinge of guilt. Henrietta watched this happen. He had hedged at the gate. He'd done it hundreds of times, a simple thing. Here, though, he couldn't go through with it.

"What?" she asked. "Harold, what?"

He turned to her and tried to talk.

"You don't want to cook him?" she asked.

He shook his head. "No, I do."

She waited for him to make a move. "We don't need to cook Dougie."

"Don't call him by his name."

"Let's just go to Whole Foods," she said. "Get an anonymous chicken. A dead chicken."

"Fuck Whole Foods."

The thing was, Dougie didn't run. Harold had his hatchet with him, blood on the blade. When animals sensed this they always ran, or else tried to run, but not Dougie, who had never struck Henrietta as an especially bright bird, or really a bird possessed of any of the anthropomorphics people affixed to roosters: cranky, mean, bullyish. Dougie merely looked up at Harold, his eyes fixed on him, a disapproving look of judgment on his tiny, red face.

"Come on, Dougie," Harold said, girding himself. "Time's up, little guy."

Another minute passed. Harold didn't move.

"Do you want me to grab him?" she asked, knowing the answer already.

"I'll grab him."

"You don't want to do it. I can see it."

"Hi, Dougie," he said, crouching. "C'mere, Dougie."

Yet another few minutes went by. He loosed his grip on the hatchet.

They'd had dogs and then the dogs died, and then they'd had cats and the cats died. All that was left was Dougie, and this was the problem: the bird was his pet. Harold loved him, and Henrietta was fairly sure that Dougie loved him back. There was no way to prove this, to quantify their shared affection, or whatever it was: respect for making a go of it here, in the cold, on this tough earth, this farm, with its sweet, subtle rolling slopes and its goldenrod and, more than anything, its silence.

Henrietta stood at the gate to the pen, watching Dougie as he searched desperately for food. He was a big red bird, with white around the face, and something like a hint of a smile in the feathers around his beak. She did not know whether he registered Harold's absence at all. In the mornings they had a routine in which she would hold the feed and he would run and sing, and it was true that this goddamned bird had a brain and a personality, and he had feelings, and at this very moment the bird looked at her with an expression that could not be construed as anything but affection.

They would completely rearrange this place, surely. Subdivide it. Pack it full of condos. A multiplex. Put up a Starbucks. She rubbed her boot in the dirt. Her dirt. There were only two real options for Dougie. She could kill him for food, for the coq au vin that she knew at this point how to make exactly the way Harold would have. Or she could sell him to the same farmer to whom she had sold everything else. That farmer would then, naturally, turn Dougie into food. It was fair to say that the development company that bought this place was not interested in birds, and she did not legitimately think she could take Dougie with her to her new apartment. Roosters did not fare well on wall-to-wall carpeting.

Dougie, for what it was worth, gave the impression that he knew all of this before Henrietta did. He began singing, chirping, yelling, running.

If you kill me, Dougie seemed to say, then you will be the last bird left here. Not me: you.

# Part
# II

# *14.*

The road back home from her grandmother's was empty this late. Polluted moonlight fell through the thicket of sycamores. Signs on the curbside warned against jumping deer or deaf children. Lydia was at the wheel because her dad was high. It had happened at some point before dinner. When they pulled away from the house in Aveline, she wasn't sure, but maybe her dad was weeping silently to himself. They made it to the intersection of the main road, where the traffic was fast and steady, before he admitted that it was best that he not drive.

"Are you fucked up?" she asked.

"Generally?" he asked. "Or actually?"

Although she'd had lessons at Hartwell, her dad gave her pointers as they went. He put his hands on her hands, making an already dangerous situation more dangerous. Don't be nervous, he said. Go slow, he said. Both hands, he said, and still she went faster than he wanted. The towns close to the city blended together into a long stretch of Catholic churches and chain bakeries, rotted siding and concrete wrecked by a season of winter salt. The city this late was a flood of students. Boston could be best understood this way, as a collection of campuses masquerading as neighborhoods. It made sense to her now. From the direction she was traveling, northeast to southwest, the students she saw were, according to the school rankings, incrementally less intelligent and promising than the students she had just passed. "This is nice," he said, his voice low and flat and far away. They passed a forest. "Just don't hit the trees," he told her. She turned then and saw that he was laughing to himself. "I just told you not to hit the trees. God, I'm father of the year."

Because her hometown was perfectly situated between two interstate highways, Lydia had always thought of it as a luxurious truck stop. Everywhere, from every lawn, a distant, invisible humming rush of traffic buzzed. She blamed herself sometimes for the fact that they had moved here. You had a child, you forsook your curated urban exploration, and then you moved to the suburbs. This was the natural order of white middle-class life. The idea that they all might have stayed together on the Upper West Side, in their delightfully sunlit apartment where she'd been a baby, with their cats and their Jacques Pépin cookbooks, had never been a real possibility. Cosmopolitan children were eerie, her parents had decided: overly adjusted to the adult world, too familiar with crime statistics and contemporary art installations, and indecently suspicious of open spaces. But secretly, her parents adored the parceled order of the suburbs. Their shared fondness for the smell of cut grass was a dead giveaway. Whatever urbane dreams they had for themselves they'd gladly traded for what Crestview had to offer. High oaks. Native grass. Salamanders. Laws against unsustainable species of wood, bottled water, tobacco products, plastic grocery bags, and public displays of religious affiliation. Pulling into the driveway, the electric garage door rising promptly, Lydia suspected that her parents had probably made a poor choice.

Once inside, her dad helped her bring her big suitcase to the second floor, where she noticed that the guest room door was open and the bed unmade. She stopped.

"Are you not sleeping in your old room?" she asked.

He put down the suitcase. "I can't sleep in there," he said, pointing up the hall.

"It's just a room, Dad," she said. "Just because she's not in the bed—"

"No," he said, opening the door to the master suite, revealing a big blank space. "I literally can't sleep in there anymore."

She turned on the light. The room was basically empty. "Where's the bed?"

"I may have gone a little overboard when your mom left," he said.

She walked into the room. Her parents' wedding photos were still aligned on the dressers. Everything was serenely beige. "You junked the bed?"

"At the time," he said, "I thought I was making an intelligent choice."

"How is that possible?"

"I thought sleeping on the floor would be a healthy way to punish myself."

She turned and looked at him and he leaned against the doorframe with his hands in his pockets.

"Please don't tell your mother," he said.

Lydia found sleep impossible. Her old bed felt uninviting. The linen chafed her. She changed the sheets, discovering in her closet the same cartoon-covered *Sleeping Beauty* bed kit that her father had picked out for her when she was younger, despite her grandmother's constant protests about admiring princesses. These are not the ideals you should value, her grandmother had told her. Dynastic power, jewel worship, the reanimating capacities of Prince Charming's lips—none of this will help you. Lydia was four years old. Alone with them now in the darkness, her stuffed animals seemed to regard her with some new scrutiny, as if they, too, had seen the picture and could not believe she'd done it.

In the morning she woke to the smell of her father's smoke, a trail of it snaking its way up through the vents. She found him in the garage, with the door open to the neighborhood.

"Did I wake you?"

"Doesn't matter," she said.

"Did you sleep?"

"Not well," she said. "You?"

"Not at all, really."

"Upset?" she asked.

He pinched the end of his joint between his fingers until the cherry went out. "Your mother's in love with our couples therapist," he said.

Lydia nodded. "You know?"

"I know."

"I don't think 'love' is the right word," she said.

He winced. "How long have you known?"

She shrugged. "Not long."

"I don't know what to do."

"I don't know either," she said.

# 15.

Paul Pomerantz's ex-wife left him during the middle of a vacation to Mount Everest. Oona heard this early the next morning, nude in his sheets. Her name was Deirdre, but she was DeeDee to him, always DeeDee, even at their wedding. DeeDee: the redheaded daughter of a particle physicist and a middle school gym teacher. DeeDee: she'd proposed to Paul outside a sidewalk café in Trieste, a crowd having gathered, thinking it was street theater. DeeDee: she'd planned the trip to Everest for a decade. DeeDee apparently had wanted to go so very badly to Everest: *Please, Paulie, let's do it, we need to do this, I need to do this, we both really need to do this.* She wasn't a climber. Or a mystic. Or a nature photographer. Or particularly interested in mountains. What she wanted to do was meet the Sherpas, the men who climbed the mountains for a living and whose names never made the newspapers. Their selflessness attracted her. Their untold stories. The grit of their devotion. Something about coming into contact with people who had so little fear in their lives, who did what they did without any trace of ego. For Paul the trip had always felt impossible, given the constraints of his schedule and his devotion to his patients and the long flight from Boston to Nepal, which promised to trigger within him a long-held phobia about air disasters, confined spaces, and deep-veined thrombosis. To DeeDee, though, the trip became a pilgrimage that she needed to make. She begged Paul to commit to it while they were on far less exciting vacations in places like Lake Winnipesaukee or Las Vegas. *When we get to Everest.* This was the mantra in their marriage near the end, a cure-all for their problems. Stuck in traffic on the expressway outside the city, DeeDee would say that after Everest, everything would be better. A bad meal at a restaurant, and DeeDee would invoke Everest. *After the mountains we will both be changed,* she uttered in line at a sporting goods store, in the grandstand at a Bruce Springsteen concert, on the lawn at Tanglewood, sipping steely Muscadet and listening to Mahler's No. 2. "I believed it," Paul told Oona, a cold hand on her bare stomach. "I really did. She was so sure. She evangelized me."

Eventually Paul surprised her with the trip, for her fiftieth birthday, the distance between them having become so great that the only thing that might fix it, he thought, was a visit to the biggest mountain on earth. He canceled a month's worth of appointments. They flew to Kathmandu first class, making connections in DC and Doha; drank champagne forty thousand feet above the English Channel; watched five Julia Roberts movies back-to-back. They hired a driver to take them into the Himalayas. The roads were poor. In the villages, children came to the car windows begging for change or candy whenever Paul and DeeDee stopped. All the while, she held his hand. She'd dressed in a white Nehru and a cluster of jade necklaces. He thought she had never been more beautiful. Something about the Nehru or the jade necklaces. Oona listened carefully to this particular detail. The air, Paul said, was pure, a different air than the air in North America. He rolled down the window, took big gulps, and felt, out of either a sense of adventure or oxygen depletion, as if this indeed was the greatest decision of his life, to come here, to the top of the world. As they drew closer to the first camp, the roads became worse. Signs began to appear on the roadside. Prayer flags in every color were strung up above and across the gravel. Then the peaks. The moment she saw Everest she began sobbing hysterically.

"What is it?" he kept asking. "Tell me."

She kept sobbing. The driver ignored them.

"Tell me what it is," he begged her.

They drove on. The mountains became bigger. DeeDee cried harder. Out the window wild poppies swayed. Plant species for which he had no name astonished him. He put a hand on her knee. She shrugged it off. Her crying was something elemental. An animal's noise. They kept going up a narrow road. She tugged at her jade. The peaks were occluded by mist and clouds and weather. He whispered to her the whole time.

"It's just that it's so beautiful," he told her. "That's the reaction you're having."

Long-haired Europeans stood on the roadside selling prayer books and beaded bracelets.

"It's so pretty," he said. "It's okay to cry. I want to cry. You're right. It's so damn pretty."

Finally they stopped. The driver parked and got out, leaving them alone. For a half hour DeeDee buried her face in her hands. While she wept, he expounded on the reasons for her outburst. It was the sudden confrontation with a larger force, he told her. A force capable of making mountains. Evidence of God. The fingerprints of the universe. When she refused this— *Fingerprints of the universe?*—he tried a different tack. It was the realization that she'd been right. That Everest was the cure. That she and he had been saved. It was not this either, however. DeeDee took off the jade necklaces. She was sweating. Maybe, he tried, it was the airplane food. You know, the food just sits in the holding bays gathering microbes, and it's so much more heavily salted than normal food, and it's no surprise that you're not feeling well. Then, finally, she came out with it.

"I have something I need to confess to you," she said.

Paul claimed that he smiled. To Oona he said, "I honestly believed she was going to say something beautiful."

She never wanted to go to Everest at all, she told him. She just didn't want to be married to him anymore. They sat inside the car, parked on the side of the road in the shadow of Mount Everest, and she said this to him, with the tears gone, the sweat dried, mountain light on her skin, all trace of nerves vanished. She smiled because she was free of him. She'd realized just after they left Boston that she wanted this, the plane barely a thousand feet over land. Everest had turned out not to be the huge metaphor in her life that she'd imagined, the biggest, most unscalable mountain not the symbol of an egoless existence or a higher state of being that she'd expected, or even a symbol of the unattainable. Everest was just a long-held distraction from her marriage to an overly talkative Texas-born post-Freudian she didn't want to sleep with any longer. She had the hired car turn around, leaving him there.

When he told Oona this, near dawn, ylang-ylang essence breathing from a countertop dispenser, a microfiber blanket positioned just so over his groin, she asked him what he did then. "I stayed at Everest for a month," he said. "I lived in a monastery near the base camp. I learned the constellations. I ate yak butter soup. I read *Beowulf*. I made friends with a group of Belgian climbers. I wore her jade necklaces. And I met the Sherpas, these people who lived with so little fear in their lives, who did what they did without any trace of ego. DeeDee was right. I was on the mountain. I let go of things. I touched something different and new. Something opened in me. It was life-changing. DeeDee was right. She was always right."

"Was she, now?" Oona said. Out the window the sun was rising. She sat up. "Tell me more about this wise, sage DeeDee."

They were in his bed, the windows open clear to the channel islands. He grew indignant.

"I'm not kidding," he told her.

She felt the need to cover her breasts. "Yak soup," she said.

He stood up. "I'm still not kidding."

It did not help to hear this story right after she'd slept with him.

After Spencer and Lydia left last night, she'd met up with Paul at a bar in Aveline, where she had three quick bourbons, and where he had none, and where they talked—she struggled to remember—about head wounds, and the physics of intercranial swelling, and her father's passing, and the infinite permanence of death, and about how long blood can remain on a piece of flagstone. Afterward, she left her car in the lot there and they came here together. At one point, perhaps on the road to his apartment, or in the lobby of his building, or maybe even in his bed, Oona hoped that she could love Paul. That was all she would allow herself. The hope of love, the promise, or at least the seeds. In retrospect, these were the wrong goals. She did not believe in love at first sight, or in love that emerged solely through sex. Either because of a childhood full of bad television or because of her mother's book, these were concepts that she had grown up believing were possible, just as she had once been led to believe that a woman could realistically reach orgasm in less than three minutes. The ideas were childish, she knew, and it infuriated her to encounter adults who held fast to the idea that sex, the physical activity of intercourse, was something sacred, something capable of replenishing the soul, when for her it was just a reflex. An urge. An itch to scratch. How shocking it had been to discover that Paul was one of these people.

They had become nearly nude in the elevator up to his apartment. Admittedly she was drunk, and the prospect of a peering voyeuristic surveillance camera or a sudden passenger did not deter her. She was excited. It was important to remember this. Here was a new person. A new body. Something that might help her feel good about herself. They tumbled in through his front door. He wore a bandage on his head. She took a moment to collect herself, to ask, amid her drunkenness, *Do I want to do this? Do I really, truly, actually want to go through with this? Is casual sex acceptable? Maybe I should recheck him for concussion symptoms. Am I substituting sex for self-esteem? Is this person going to murder me? Can't I get someone better? Am I clean enough? Am I washed? Is casual sex with your therapist even legal?* He interpreted her thinking as some kind of foreplay. Or a sign of her needing to be ravished. She backed up unwittingly into the doorway to the bedroom. "Stop," he said, taking off his underpants, exposing his cock to her. "I want to do it on the floor."

To be sure, this was not the most uplifting moment of her life. But there was something in his animal desperation that she found compelling enough to make her willing to do what he asked. He'd cribbed the whole thing, she knew, note for note, from chapter 8 of *The Inseparables,* wherein Eugenia Davenport tells Templeton Grace, "I want to do it on the floor of the solarium." She could only guess that he had read her mother's book and loved it, and she could assume that fucking the daughter of the woman who wrote one of America's most famously trashy books could only inspire something like this: the floor of his apartment, overlooking the whole of Boston Harbor, any number of hundreds of people looking in through the glass. A few minutes later, she was on her back on the cold slate of his kitchen floor, with her therapist on top of her as he issued instructions, telling her, in the same soft voice that he used in their sessions, what he wanted her to do.

"Put your fingers in my chest hair," he told her.

Which she did.

Then: "Pull on my chest hair."

She did this also.

Then: "Pull harder on my chest hair."

And there she was, tugging, pulling away, on her therapist's chest hair.

Some thoughts had occurred to her during the ordeal. One: It was not pleasant to rip a man's chest hair from his skin. Two: She thought of her mother. For someone like Oona, tutored early on in the inherent power structures of sex—men asking, men demanding, men taking—and in the necessity of emotional consent, there was the sinking suspicion that she should have at least asked for a bed. Sex demanded dignity. Her mother had hammered this into her from the start. Make it your mission to feel good, she had told Oona. Refuse shame. Disregard the cacophony of catcalls, the ogling, the vacuousness of vanity. Fuck with the lights on. Possess your own body. Reject conformist ideas of beauty. Make others reckon with your body on your terms. Oona found the advice, like everything her mother had ever told her, at once impossible to disagree with and impossible to heed. There was a new hand on her body, after all. A hand that was not Spencer's. For a very quick moment, this felt pleasant. Here, she thought, is someone new. With her hand on Paul's back, she thought, this is a new back, a new piece of skin. Then the sensation passed. He squeezed her thigh so hard that she wondered whether he was trying to tear a piece of her off to keep for later. The light overhead felt indecent on her bare stomach. He made animal noises. Here, she thought, is a new hand. These, she thought, are new noises.

Which brought her to the third thought: Paul was in terrible shape. She felt only moderately guilty registering this. Weren't people supposed to ignore the failures of other people's bodies? Wasn't this the polite, decent thing to do? Wasn't this the way to build a society free of degradation? In light of everything that had happened with her daughter recently, shouldn't she at least feel a bit ashamed of judging his body? The truth, sadly, was that she didn't. Sex for Paul looked so incredibly arduous. She thought of this now—the short, stubborn slope of his neck as he struggled for breath. The disconcerting flush of his skin. The way his eyes showed his exhaustion. Capillaries everywhere engorged and oxygen-starved. The whole time he was working so goddamned hard. He lowered his head because he was having such a difficult time of it, and she ended up just staring back at a reflection of herself. His head and scalp were so immaculately bald that she suffered the sensation that she was being fucked by a full-length wardrobe mirror.

In his bed, she fought to keep herself from weeping. She had been afraid of the feeling she sensed growing—that particular breed of remorse and indignity that affixed itself to poor sexual decisions. She searched for her clothing. "Why would you tell me that story?" she asked.

"What do you mean?"

"About your ex-wife? Right after we slept together?" She stood up. A hint of latex hovered. She noticed that across the carpet, on the credenza, he had folded her underwear and jeans and her black bra into a perfect square.

"It's important to know this about me," he said. "I know so much about you."

"*This* is the most important thing about you? Your ex-wife? Fucking Mount Everest?"

Across the room, an alarm clock read an ungodly early hour. She had not slept in three days.

"This was obviously a mistake," she said.

"I don't think it was," he said.

"Well, thankfully, we don't need to agree on this for it to be true," she said.

"Maybe I can make some coffee and we can hash it out."

He lived on the penthouse floor of the Intercontinental, in a corner unit with a view of the harbor. The collective mania and marital troubles of the city had clearly provided Paul with a luxurious life. The inside of the apartment was generous and sleek, and there were books everywhere: in lines, on shelves, in stacks, by the toilet, on the big Persian rug, and in the kitchen by the bowl of decorative kiwis. Out the window the water was gray-green, flecked with birds and boats and tourists, the beached-whale glimmer on the silver hide of the Aquarium throwing light in spangles onto the boat hulls bobbing. Paul had bought the place three years ago, after his own marriage had come apart. This was the way he talked about divorce in therapy, as if some couples were a poorly knit angora sweater that had fallen mistakenly into a washing machine. Initially Oona had thought that this was a profound metaphor for marriage, and she felt bonded to him over this fact. His sadness, her sadness: their conjoined loneliness and misery was like a mutually discovered taste for Lebanese food. Not entirely rare or special, but good enough for now. She mentioned this to Spencer at some point, having begun to think of their own marriage in these terms, the two of them a ball of yarn, raveling and unraveling.

"It's hard to get the yarn back into a ball," she told him. "It's just loose and messy. That's us. That's you and me. We're yarn."

At which Spencer scoffed. "It's not hard at all. You just roll the fucking yarn back up into a ball! It's easy. It makes a perfectly fine ball of yarn."

Out in the kitchen, Paul made coffee with a sleek Italian machine embedded in his cabinetry.

"Maybe this happened too soon," he said. "Maybe we needed to wait another month for the feelings to evolve."

She noticed a small file folder across the room on the kitchen table. "Is that my patient file?"

He flinched.

# 16.

Later that same morning, Lydia and her dad parked outside a sleek, black-glass high-rise near the harbor. She guessed at the building's significance without asking.

"This doesn't seem like a good idea," Lydia said.

"No, it does not," he agreed.

The city this early was bright and cheerless. It was Tuesday. He'd let her drive a second time, having punched the address into the GPS. They were close to the ocean, and from here the city unfurled behind them, hills of buildings, hills of houses, hills and hills. Gulls loitered. A water taxi with a shark's mouth painted on the hull carved out a path to the islands. Traffic helicopters hovered in the sky over the channel like robotic dragonflies.

"How long have you known?" she asked.

He collapsed deeper into his seat. "Six days," he said. He looked at his watch. "Or, I guess, now that it's morning, seven days."

"That's a fairly exact number."

"I have very little else to do but count," he said.

"How did you find out?"

"I wish I had a good story."

She turned and picked up a pair of binoculars on the back-seat. "You're stalking her, aren't you?"

"Is there a difference between following and stalking?"

She tossed the binoculars back. "You asking that question is probably not a good sign."

"Probably not, no."

"You must have seen signs, at least," she said. "Hints that this might happen. I mean, maybe not with your therapist. But you *are* divorced."

"We're separated."

"Which, by definition, means that you're not together."

"What's a sign, and what's a normal moment of your wife being annoyed with you?"

"The frequency of those moments, maybe," Lydia said.

"Fine," he said. "There were years of moments."

"So there were signs."

Her father lit a small, already burnt joint that he'd stashed in the change tray. He blew a stream of smoke that drifted and itched at her eyes. She tried not to show her disapproval, but this was not something she was particularly good at doing. His lack of shame about getting high right in front of her felt like a new low. He hadn't always been so hooked. Lydia knew full well that the escalation of his habit coincided exactly with her growing up and needing less of him. There were pictures in the living room in Crestview that attested to an earlier, opti-mistic, more motivated era of his life. Good hair, good shoes, cuff links, clarity behind the eyes. His present wounds were, she knew, largely self-inflicted. The narrative of his needing to quit working in order to raise her, which he sometimes cravenly pulled out during a fight with her mother, was easily debunked. Fatherhood fit him better than lawyering ever had. It struck her that her mother had probably loved him more then, de-spite his misery as an attorney. Occasionally she thought that the existence of these facts (miserable lawyer = love; happy house-husband = divorce) made her mother a bad person, but most of the time Lydia seconded the opinion that maybe it was not such a terrible thing to want your husband to be sober and have ambitions and maybe a place to go in the morning. She felt confused about it all. On one hand, her father was her best friend. This was undeniably true. On the other hand, it was not the most encouraging thing to realize about yourself—that your very best friend was a middle-aged unemployed stoner.

"I'm medicating," her father said when he saw her frowning. "It's medical."

"If it's medical, then what's the disease?" she asked.

He inhaled, held it in his lungs. "What's it called," he said, "when your wife starts going to bed with her therapist?"

"Professional malfeasance," she said. "Criminal misappropriation of power. Dereliction of psychological duty. Any of those things would do."

"You're smart, but I'm being serious," he said.

"Heartbreak," she said. "It's called heartbreak."

He shook his head. "Heartbreak. Isn't that convenient that a doctor would be the exact person you'd want to see in the event of your heart breaking."

"But that's a metaphor," Lydia said. "It's not real. And she doesn't cure heartbreak. She fixes bones. You're high. There's a difference. Actually *and* metaphorically."

"Look," he said. "I'm trying to express my feelings, given the circumstances."

"What are the circumstances, exactly?"

He raised his voice and was almost yelling. "That we're here, downtown, stalking her lover—"

"Oh God, please don't say 'lover.'"

"—and that I'm really high at the moment, as you said, like, very high, and you know, maybe I'm underestimating the difference between heartbreak and cardiac arrest, but to me, Lydia, they're kind of the same thing right now."

A yellow-footed gull landed on a curbstone ahead of the car and shook rain from its feathers. They were beautiful birds, she thought. Remarkably resilient. She had taken two weekend seminars on ornithology at Hartwell, if for no other reason than to have something to talk about with her grandmother, who liked birds. The gull spread its wings but did not take off. It was stretching, she guessed. It was looking right at them. Then it flew away. Her father ignored it.

"What are we doing here, exactly?" she asked. "What's the plan?"

"A confrontation," he said. "Obviously."

"You're stoned out of your mind. What kind of confrontation are you envisioning? A very slow confrontation?"

"Her going for a walk around the hospital garden with this creep is one thing. Her being here is another thing altogether. I'm going to tell him to back off. One man to another man."

"I don't think that happens in real life, Dad. I think that's just on television. I think in real life, when that happens, you know, someone ends up murdering someone else."

"Murder?" her father said, laughing. "I smoke pot. Pot smokers don't murder people."

"But that doesn't eliminate the possibility that *he* might murder *you*."

"Blah blah blah," her father said, frustrated, senseless. "That shrink stole my wife."

"You guys are getting divorced!"

Her father turned to her, his face a wreck of despair and pain. "It was supposed to be a *trial* separation! We were in couples therapy!"

"With who?" she asked, pointing up at the black face of the

Intercontinental. "With that guy? That guy up there with the nice view?"

"Fuck," her father said, leaning back against the seat. "This is depressing."

After a while she told him, "She's not a six-pack of beer. He can't steal her. She went willingly."

"Willingly," he repeated. "Willingly."

There was a seafood restaurant across the road from the Aquarium concourse. This fact seemed unnecessarily cruel to Lydia. Her father used to take her to eat there when she was young. The dining room was built into the underside of a series of fresh- and saltwater fish tanks, the whole place done up as an aquarium in miniature. They came here when her mother worked late, to this blue room with the fish swimming up above their table. The vastness of the place, the huge blueness, had thrilled her. Her dad liked to tell her that this place was actually under the sea, that they had, when they went through the front door, gone underground. She was five—six, maybe—and perhaps he thought he could fool her. But really, she knew: they were just eating inside a fish tank, waiting for the same person to get off work.

"You want me to take you across the street?" she said. "Cheer you up?"

"Funny, Lydia."

"I don't think I ever really connected the idea of seeing pretty fish and then going across the street and eating those same pretty fish."

"You always wanted to go," he said. "You were always very confident with your opinions. I was reading a lot of books on fatherhood back then. The books said that I should listen."

"See? That's where you went wrong," she said. "You should ignore me always."

"That was what the marriage counselor told me about your mother," he said.

Lydia fell silent. The separation was only half a year old, but the dissolution of her parents' marriage felt as substantial in her own small world as the disbanding of something enormous, like Europe. A breakup had always been possible, if not plainly obvious, but the reality of their being apart, her mom and dad, and in separate houses, and their occasionally falling in love with their therapists, and getting high pre-sunrise and smoking Cheech and Chong volumes of weed and freely stalking each other—it was too sudden and new for Lydia to laugh about.

"I shouldn't make a joke like that," her father said. "That's inappropriate."

"Of all the inappropriate things you've done today," she said.

He put his seat back all the way, until it lay flat, and he closed his eyes.

After a while she spoke up. "You read books on fatherhood?" she asked.

He smiled at her. His voice came out low. "Quite a few," he said.

"Did you learn anything?" she asked.

"I don't know," he said. "You tell me."

# 17.

It wasn't as if Oona went home with Paul without deliberation. Last night they'd been at the bar, talking about death, and he'd said it plainly enough, with no subterfuge involved, no mystery as to what they were agreeing to. "I think it would be nice if you came home with me to my condo," he said. She hadn't answered right away. Instead, she'd gotten up and walked to the back of the bar, pretending at first to wait in line for the restroom, and then she snuck off through the rear door, into the parking lot, where, through the thicket, she could see the rim of the lake that connected to the river that ran behind her house, and where, gathered in the shelter of the derelict bank of pay phones, there were young people, not much older than Lydia, all of them smoking cigarettes. She begged for one and smoked it alone by the side of the building, standing on a pile of soggy leaves, in full view of one of the bar's windows. She hadn't smoked a cigarette since the first George Bush was president, and she wanted to vomit. She spied on Paul inside. She didn't know what she was looking for. Maybe some kind of oracular divination. A hint as to what to do. He finished his diet soda. He checked his email. He made the bartender laugh. These were good things, weren't they? Did all people suffer these deliberations? The ancient questions rose up. To screw or not to screw? Go inside or flee? A woman passing behind Paul's barstool tripped slightly, or stumbled, and Paul caught her elbow and helped her upright and made her laugh as well, and while Oona watched, he got up from his seat and walked her to the door. This tiny act of kindness had done it. Twenty years of immaculate fidelity. She had not so much as kissed or touched or corresponded inappropriately with another man since her first date with Spencer. She walked inside.

Now, standing barefoot in Paul's kitchen, she noticed that there were fingernail marks across the skin of her belly. Also, her sweater lay in a humiliating pile by the oven door, just where she'd had it torn off her body.

Paul walked quickly to the file folder on the kitchen table, picking it up and stashing it on a bookcase.

"So before our first date you read up on me?" she asked.

"I wouldn't have done that," he said.

"Just so, what, you could remember more clearly what exactly makes me vulnerable?"

"You're putting the darkest possible spin on this," he said.

"Just so we could discuss…what was the phrase you used about my father dying? *The transfer of energy between the living and the dead?*"

"It was a nice conversation between two people. There was nothing creepy about it."

"What is this, then? The transfer of fluids between the pursuer and the pursued?"

"That, again, is a sinister way to think about what happened with us."

"There is something deeply creepy about this, Paul. First the long story about your wise, sage, gorgeous ex-wife with her red curls and her jade necklaces. Then this, the dossier to my emotional life?"

"I can't tell you whose file it is," he said. "You know that. You know the rules."

"It's clearly my file."

"I can't say."

"Then give it to me. Let me see."

"Doctor-patient confidentiality," he said.

"I'm a doctor. Maybe I need to consult on the patient's medical history."

"Oona, these are the rules."

"So now you like rules. Is that so? I'm in my underwear. Which is more than I was wearing ten minutes ago. How does that fit in with your rules?"

They passed into the living room. She stood alone at the window. Buoys in the harbor rocked, wave-thrown. Boats in the channel passed, horns blowing. For a few minutes, helium balloons brushed by the glass, a stream of them released by children or peace protesters or perhaps a balloon vendor with a very poor grip. His office was on the ground floor of the building across the way. She could see the revolving door that she and Spencer had passed through, twice a week for months, listening all that time to Paul as he urged them to practice patience, because, as he told them, this is a process, life and love and fidelity and marriage, all of it a long, tough process. She wondered now where in the process fucking her therapist fell.

"We waited the recommended length of time," Paul said.

"Who's doing the recommending here: the doctor or the patient?"

"Where is this aggression coming from? A half hour ago you were so lovely."

"Oh here we go. Unhinged woman acting so nuts and crazy! You tell me, doctor. Where is this aggression coming from? How long have I been in therapy with you? You must have the answer by now."

"You can't use my therapy against me as a weapon. DeeDee had the hardest time with that."

"DeeDee."

"Yes," he said, realizing perhaps that mentioning DeeDee was not a good thing to have done in this particular circumstance. "DeeDee had some difficulty with the rules."

Oona looked around. Pictures of DeeDee littered the place. Oona knew how it was. Leaving a marriage was like scraping plaque from a bad artery. You could never get rid of all of it. It was not as if she had not kept pictures of Spencer in her phone, or on the dresser in her bedroom in Aveline, but hers was a newer separation, everything still fresh. Apparently, in between catalog shoots DeeDee worked as a personal trainer at a gym in Concord not far from where the minutemen and the royalists began the Revolution. This was a fact that Paul believed was symbolic of some larger personal struggle within her. Oona had heard all of this in bed. Sovereignty rebelling against tyranny, or liberty overcoming the crush of imperialism, or some crap like that. DeeDee was the freedom fighter; he was the monarchic oppressor. None of this did anything to calm Oona's concerns. If Paul was a tyrant, then who had she just slept with? And if DeeDee was too good for Paul, then where did that leave her?

She said this to him. "Don't you get it? Don't you see? It's like a math equation."

He acted confused. "What is this? A test? If A is bigger than B? I was never good at this kind of thing."

Finally Paul slunk into the seat of a leather sofa.

"I thought we had a great time," he said.

"It was a decent time."

"In bed, I meant."

"Like I said."

He shook his head. "Earlier, you were so excited."

"I was excited for someone new," she said.

"But I *am* someone new."

# 18.

For a while they waited. This had become a stakeout. Her father
went across the street for sticky cinnamon donuts and scalding
coffee. If they were going to wait, he told her, they might as well
wait with some food, or at least something sweet and satisfying
and terrible for you. Alone in the Toyota, with its silent climate
system humming, Lydia surveyed the silver walls of the Aquarium, watching the streams of families coming off the MBTA and
lining up outside, everyone holding hands, whole masses of hu-
manity ready to see the fish in their fish tanks. The hand-holding
moved her. It was the exhaustion, or the proximity to heartbreak. Toddlers ambled uncertainly across Atlantic Avenue in
search of penguins or manatees or razor-nosed dolphins, oblivious to the hazards of traffic and urban life. Young couples,
old couples, tourist couples. She could remember reaching for
her father's hand. It was always her father, for the unavoidable
fact that her mother was always at work, too far away to reach.
Some future therapist, she knew, would delight at hearing it
put this way. She still suffered the instinct to reach for a hand
when crossing a street. She had reached for Charlie's hand in
this way, grabbing it once while sneaking out of Hartwell and
into the town center. This was at the beginning, when he was

kind. They were in the forest that separated the school from the town. He had taken her hand freely. A teenage boy, she had learned, will take whatever physical contact he is given, but Charlie had regarded it with some confusion. Her small hand gripping his as they ran out through the campus forest and out to the state highway—intimacy stripped bare of any sexual context had clearly mystified him.

She checked her phone and found, waiting for her on the screen, a fresh message from Charlie, delivered five minutes earlier.

```
Thanks for the new picture(s). I'll keep them
safe. I promise.
```

Then, a minute later:

```
But only if you come to New Jersey to see me.
```

The picture was a crime, she had decided. He had wanted to curry favor with his idiotic gang by scintillating them with her body. Her bare breasts were a form of currency that he had and wanted to trade for something like coolness or friendship. He wanted to shame her. That was the kind of boy he was. The boy who connects the nudity of his own body with shame, and who assumes that everyone else must feel the same way. This was the boy who had not been willing to take his own shirt off when they were together in his bed, while he played R. Kelly's "Ignition (Remix)" on repeat, afraid to show her that he had a divot in his chest, pectus excavatum, cobbler's chest, an indentation deep enough to hold half a cup of water. Here was the root cause of his sexual anxiety, this divot, the reason why he needed the lights off, why when she had deigned to rest her hand on his chest while she kissed him, something that she thought people did when they kissed, he had flinched beneath her.

She clicked around, checked all her accounts, her feeds. She looked for new pictures. She suffered competing impulses. She knew that there were no other pictures of her out there. Nothing else to leak or hack or steal. She had taken only the one. But then, looking at the glint of the glass on the lens, she remembered his warning: *Assume that someone's watching you all the time.*

She composed a message back, struggling for the exact right words. She settled on this:

```
You are a deeply sick human being.
```

The irony of her ever taking a picture like this was that she had been so reluctant to be naked in front of anyone, ever. Here was a fact of the kind of place like Hartwell: public nudity was endemic. Girls walking back from the shower, towels slipping. Roommates changing out in the open. The Danish catalog models slept nude in exorbitantly expensive Frette linen, or else they occasionally set up impromptu figure drawing classes in the common spaces, one of them posing, the rest sketching. They sent nude selfies preprogrammed to self-destruct with such a dizzying regularity that Lydia felt foolishly prim. Which was why people thought she was an alien—because she would not change in front of them. "What's the big deal?" one of her roommates had asked. This came directly following a dorm-wide meeting during which everyone in Rosewater agreed to ban the color pink. No pink clothing, toothbrushes, underwear; no salmon-colored phone cases, pink being the color of conformity, of Barbie, of a widespread assumption of girlish insipidity. It seemed ridiculous now to admit that she'd taken the picture because she was curious, or because she'd felt some vague invidious peer pressure to do what everyone else was doing, or even because of the simple fact that her body was relatively new and potentially beautiful and that she hoped to be able to age without the heaping shitloads of shame everyone else she knew felt.

The chime of Charlie's new message startled her.

```
Come to New Jersey
```

She was quick with a response, and already she could see him typing on the other end:

```
You're a criminal


        I'm wonderful


You're revolting


        I need you in my life, Lydia


You should be in jail you sick fuck


        I should be in your pants


You wouldn't know what to do in my pants if you
got there.


        Come to New Jersey. Let's make up. Make
        nice. Hang out. Get high.


Please leave me alone Charlie
```

In the car, she had to hold the phone against her knee, she was shaking so hard. She considered the photograph. She'd made it at three in the morning, alone in the shower. She'd gotten high for the first time that night. Not that it was an excuse. She had been out in the woods with Charlie, sneaking around on the lip of the ridge that looked out at the valley and Mount Thumb. Barn owls were hunting. He told her that they mated for life. Just like black vultures. Just like termites. He connected his phone to wireless headphones that they each wore, and as they went up through the underbrush he put on his kind of music for her. Ambient wind rushes of digital noise. Washes of color. He gave her a pill. She took it without thinking. They sat on a white rock and waited for it to hit. He knew the names of all the bugs in the mud, the Latin name for the tulip tree.

"Termites mate for life," he said, dazed. "Think about that shit."

Earlier they had sat through a lecture on the biology of thought. Images of the brain, adult and teenage, were broadcast to their laptops. *Notice,* the teacher had said, *how incompletely formed so much of the teenage brain is.* An animation of the prefrontal cortex lit up in indigo on their screens. The lack of development here indicated, among other things, an increased tendency toward risky behavior. She and Charlie had messaged through this. Fuck this, my brain is beautiful, she had written. Fuck this doctor and her stupid slide show of brains. The blinking indigo was supposed to explain everything about her teenage personality. The foolish impulsivity. The poor choice in hiking partners. The ingesting of unknown pills when your father was very clearly a drug addict. I want to fuck your dumb brain, Lydia, Charlie wrote. The answers to everything about herself were medical, physical, concretely real. How about you just give me a picture of your hot naked brain? This was the reason for all these end-time feelings. No invasion of privacy had ever been this bad. No betrayal of trust had ever been this severe. Her head was a wastebin filled with the stuff. The surfeit of dopamine. The equal measures of heartbreak and blood lust.

On the white rock he had put his hand in her hair and then kissed her, and this was her very first kiss.

One last chime: `Come to New Jersey. Your offer expires at the end of the day.`

Lydia remembered a lecture her mother had given her before her first day at Hartwell. They were in the car, waiting outside her dormitory, and all the girls were coming out and going in, everyone looking supremely confident and acne-free and blond. People make mistakes, her mother had said, out of the blue, anticipating, it was clear, everything that was about to happen, perhaps for both of them. People get lonely. People act foolish. People sometimes find other people attractive physically even if they don't find them particularly attractive personally. People are occasionally capable of extreme cruelty. This doesn't mean that people aren't capable of good deeds and trust and redemption. All of this had been a poorly articulated way to tell Lydia not to sleep around, and Lydia, ever shrewd, had leaned against the car door and said, When you say "people," you really just mean you, right? She hadn't meant anything by that at the time. It was just a way to fight back. One learned the language of insults before learning exactly what they meant. Looking back, her mother's speech, and the insistent don't-fuck-with-me look she had given Lydia, suddenly took on an entirely new dimension.

The face of the Intercontinental shimmered, the glass reflecting back the sky above the harbor, sun-white for the instant. She tried to imagine her mother up there, fifty stories high, having embarked on this sudden new life with this strange new man, months of therapy and weeping into aloe-infused tissues having evolved into this—whatever this was. A new coupling, a spate of self-sabotage, a needlessly cruel way to sever a marriage. It was a fine building, Lydia could see, a combined hotel and condominium complex, with doormen dressed like sentry, and bellhop carts loaded high with monogrammed Italian luggage. Outside the front doors, a stream of wealthy-looking people lingered without any obvious purpose—people smoking, people reading the *Financial Times,* people looking blankly out at the ocean.

She saw her father across the street, waiting to cross at a stoplight, wind bothering his hair, coffee and a bag of donuts and a newspaper balanced precariously in his hands. He wore his camel hair unbuttoned in the sea breeze, open to an untucked dress shirt and a pair of jeans torn at the knee. He looked up at the building with some mixture of distress and resolve and envy at its obvious sleekness, its imposition on the skyline, its militant blackness, as if the building itself had come and taken his wife away.

In the bright light he looked healthier and younger and, for an instant, unlike a father. Just a guy on the street balancing coffee, donuts, and a newspaper. Earlier they had argued about the picture. He needed to do his due diligence as a father, she knew. But still: "How am I supposed to react to this?"

"With compassion, maybe."

"I have compassion, I do, but I also have feelings. And anger. And worry. And anxiety. And enormous concern. And you're my kid. My little kid. You don't remember that person, but I do. You don't realize that. Ten minutes ago we were getting lunch in the restaurant across the street. You gave names and detailed family histories to all your stuffed animals. I still remember all of that stuff. How the hippo's best friend was the owl. How the owl's brother was somehow a lion. You get that, right? I will never not remember that stuff. The genealogy of your stuffed animals is imprinted in me. It was, like, ten minutes ago to me."

"You're high all the time," she had said. "That affects your sense of time passing."

He'd put his face in his hands. She was hurting him. "Please say something to reassure me," he said.

She touched his arm. "I'm fine."

"Say something else."

"Don't worry, Daddy."

Paul Pomerantz stepped out from the front revolving door of the Intercontinental. Watching her father watch this man, Lydia felt a stab of guilt for having helped hide Paul away in the attic last night, and a deeper stab of guilt, maybe a lifetime's worth of guilt, for everything she had ever done to him. Her poor dad. Her fucked-up stoner father. Paul wore a knee-length herringbone trench with a red scarf coiled tight around him like a fashionable neck brace. The valet had pulled around the same sleek, polished Audi that Lydia had sat in last night. For a moment they both watched him, she and her father, each probably thinking the same thing: nice coat, nice luxury condo tower, nice car. In a way, Lydia could see the appeal. He was not terrible-looking. He had a decent smile, a dignified nose. The kind of face you saw on a foreign coin. He made a joke with the valet and the valet laughed. The same yellow gull went by and Paul stopped to watch it. Look, Lydia wanted to say. He's alert to nature, he likes birds, he makes jokes with the valet, he's probably nice! Take some notes!

Her father had realized his chance. He headed toward Paul.

From inside the car Lydia cried out, "Dad, no."

Her father rushed forward with purpose. Foolish, idiotic purpose. Paul, meanwhile, had one foot inside his Audi. He kept talking to the valet. Maybe an impromptu therapy session. Lydia got out of the car. Family didn't let family do shit like this.

Her father began shouting something. Lydia was too far away to hear. This clearly was not the confrontation her dad had imagined. Paul nodded and smiled. His graciousness looked studied, entirely fake. She had seen this in Charlie Perlmutter after everything turned. Weaponized warmheartedness.

Her father became startled by something. Paul took a step toward him, his hands up, as if to say, *Let's talk it out, buddy. Let's you and me work it out, pal.* Lydia escaped back to the car. She had a preternatural sense for someone's inevitable embarrassment. She let out a small moan. *Come back,* she said aloud, inside the Toyota. *Come back, Dad. Let it go.*

Paul came closer. Her father stood on the corner of Atlantic Avenue. The ocean lay behind him. He looked dignified, she thought, in his camel hair. Snow fell lightly. This was when her mother appeared. She pushed through the revolving door, onto the sidewalk, her hand already up for a taxi. Lydia saw her a moment before her father did. Her mom's coat was open to the same clothes from last night. Even from across the street, Lydia could see her mother's exhaustion, the wear on her face. She had sunglasses on, crooked across her nose. When her dad saw her, he froze. From inside the car, Lydia thought she saw her father say the word *Honey?* or *Sweetie?* Right then, he dropped everything. The paper. The dozen sticky donuts. The cups of coffee. All of it ran down the front of his coat.

# 19.

From the outside, Witherspoon's did not seem like the kind of place that might accept stolen things or fence them or attract the kind of buyer interested in getting a deal on a pilfered piece of damaged folk art. Henrietta had expected a pawnshop. Instead, Witherspoon's gave off a kind of shabby Francophone glamour, with its gray-and-navy-striped awning and its window boxes planted with ice-hued cabbage. This was miles from home, in a shop on the edge of the city. In the window a Cézanne rip-off and a baroque brass candelabra shared space with a studded orange-sherbet-colored settee. Henrietta was no expert, but in her experience this was the exact store window of every antique store everywhere. She'd come here because Jerry Stern had told her to. His message was brief: *Try Witherspoon's. I can't promise anything.*

A big man, looking somewhat close to her in age, met her at the door wearing white suspenders and a huge untamed mustache.

"I'm wondering if you can help me," she said. She approximated the size of the weathervane with her mittens. "I'm looking for a little woman—"

Before she could finish, the man's mustache rose, a sly grin underneath. "That makes two of us."

"No," she said, laughing. "It's a statue. Sixteen inches. Made of copper."

He put a hand to his face, absently or nervously scratching. His mustache looked capable of swallowing his fingers up to the knuckle.

"It was part of a weathervane," she explained. "Not the whole thing. Just the top part. The ornament. It looks like a very small statue."

The man shook his head, which she expected. She did not know exactly how to go about doing this. Had someone in fact come to her house and taken this thing, and then sold it here, to this stuffy place, with its awning and its reams of dust and its mustachioed clerk? Would it just be on the shelves? Was there some secret patois that thieves used?

"We have a few roosters in the back," he said, smiling. "Maybe a lady got in without me noticing."

"Can I look?"

The air inside was musty: damp library books and potpourri and the latent hanging reminder of a morning cigarette. On a bar cart inlaid with cracked mirrored trays, a Lalique decanter needed to be washed. Overhead, a Neil Diamond song played in French. There were two rooms, Henrietta saw: one with rings and watches and gold earrings, and another with furniture and pastoral paintings, most of them pictures of fat peasant girls hoisting hay bales or milking goats on their knees. She paused for a long moment in front of the best one of these: a river scene, with a farmhand jamming his pitchfork deep into the earth while surveying, or admiring, or planning to sexually menace a young woman washing her laundry in the water. Henrietta would have lectured for ninety minutes on this picture back in New York. The pitchfork as a substitute for a cock. The artist's insistence on making the woman's skirt dirty and, by way of this choice, reinforcing the inherent filthiness of female sexual desire. Ideas like this came to her all the time. Some better than others. When the money finally evaporated, she'd tried to get a class or two. In Boston, she thought, this wouldn't be too hard to do. There were more places here to study than there were to get a decent chicken taco. But she'd been turned down everywhere. Her ideas might have become commonplace now, but the crucial fact remained that her book was still an embarrassment.

"Here are our weathervanes," the man said, opening a small cabinet to two roosters, one codfish, and a wooden racehorse with a crack through the middle. He quite obviously took great pleasure in this small menagerie. Finally, he took the codfish into his hands.

"They're charming little things," he said, petting the fish across its scales. "And valuable, too."

The fish's dead metal eye glared at her. "No women?"

"You sound just like my mother," he said.

"I had this on my house, you see," she said. "A storm blew it off."

"And so you've lost it," he said.

"In a sense."

"And then how would it end up here?" he asked.

She tried to keep herself from flushing with color. She used to be a skilled liar, but it was an old talent, rarely used now. "I moved houses," she said, trying. "And I've always liked that thing. And I've been searching all the antique stores in the city, hoping."

"Well, the codfish could work," he said, bouncing it in his hands. "This guy seems capable, don't you think?"

Against the back wall, a humidifier buzzed. A fat gray cat emerged, waddling through the room. On the shelves behind her were tiny wooden curios ready for sale. Birdhouses, walking canes, clockfaces, everything tagged.

"There's no back room?" she asked.

"No back room."

"No basement?"

"Not with anything good in it," he said.

She followed the man back to the front of the shop. The dust made her sneeze. More French Neil Diamond played. The cat ran out in front of both of them.

Up front, a small television balanced on a wooden stool. On the screen, Henrietta saw a family out in the sunshine flying kites as part of a pharmaceuticals ad. She always noticed families on television these days, families looking healthy and lovely and engaged moment to moment with the world and doing obsolete things like flying kites.

"I feel like I know you," the man said.

Henrietta was wearing a long winter coat, which was black and wool and old, and she had sunglasses pushed up through her hair like a headband. Oona called this her *look of intentional anonymity.*

"Do you live in the neighborhood?" he asked.

"Not really," she said.

"Are you famous, then?"

"Most definitely not."

"No, I've seen you. I'm sure. Maybe on the news?"

She shook her head. "My rule is that if I'm on the news then something horrible has happened."

This charade had always bothered her. As with all things related to that semipublic part of her, Henrietta maintained a gnawing ambivalence toward whatever remained of her fame. She always underestimated it, or overestimated it, or denied it. What was she supposed to say? *You may have heard of me: I'm the woman behind the diagram with the pubic hair.* Or: *Your mother read my book in the bathtub with the door locked.*

They walked to the front counter, which was a glass cabinet

full of engagement rings and pocket watches. She left her name in the event that something close to what she'd described came into the shop. Standing near the door, she could hear the electric hustle of the Green Line trolley as it ran up into the city and then back out toward the reservoir in Chestnut Hill. She took a moment to look. It was midday. This was the way she'd come, on the train from Aveline that ran aboveground for miles, through the white forests and the frozen school ball fields and into the city. During their first week living in Aveline, Harold had taken her on the train for the first time. She was eight months pregnant. He wanted to show her how easy it was to get into town. He wanted her to know that he had not marooned her. They went from their house all the way to the beach, she remembered. Think of that, he said: country, city, ocean. All of it is so close.

In the corner of the top shelf, Henrietta saw a black velvet box displaying two silver pens.

She did not need to look very closely to know that these had been Harold's. His name was printed on the front of the box in white lettering. She'd paid extra for this. She had bought them for his thirty-fifth birthday, thinking foolishly that he might use them to write recipes. Not just one overpriced pen, but two. It became a joke between them, these kinds of gifts. Monogramming, personalizing—the strident attempts at ascending social class. He claimed to love the pens but had never, not once, ever used them.

"Could I see those?" she asked.

He gave her the box happily. A white tag hung from the corner. Five hundred dollars, it read, which was four hundred more than she had paid for it.

She opened her purse to buy the pens, but she knew she could not. There were credit cards, but they were maxed, and there were checks, if anyone still took checks, but those would bounce. There was Oona's credit card, slipped in there a few weeks back, without mention, as a kind of prompt: *Quit being so proud and use me.* But she could not.

He always wanted something like knives for his birthday. Knives or trips to New York to eat at Jean-Georges, and she always did this instead—silver pens and tie clips and driving gloves.

"Can you tell me who brought this in?" she asked.

The man shook his head. "I don't keep names. I'm sorry."

"Could you tell me at least how long ago you got this?" She thought of Jerry, cleaning out everything in Harold's closet, in his office, in the series of shoe boxes he kept stacked in the basement and in which he stored all the letters his parents had sent him at summer camp, their postcards from Europe, their birth and death certificates. She hadn't checked over anything.

"Oh, well, I've had those for a while," he said.

"A while," she said. "Is that a month? A week?"

"Oh no," he said. "At least a year. Eighteen months, even. I know because they're right here where I sit. I see them every day. You're the first person who's ever even asked to see them."

# 20.

Lydia and her father drove home wordlessly. The same path, gunmetal-gray sky, the river black and mud-clogged, and the street white with road salt. His humiliation was a third person in the car. What could you say to anyone after this, let alone a man like your father, previously proud, maybe a little too addicted to weed, but still, generally mostly decent? Was there anything to say? Lydia drove too timidly, too slowly, traffic accumulating behind her, the car's weight and force and power increasingly threatening. Her father held a wad of napkins to the stain on his coat as if he were applying pressure to a bullet wound. She put *A Love Supreme* on the disc player. He preferred jazz, intricate rhythms, the kind of music that made no sense to her. She let it play, hoping it might rouse something in him. Also, it occupied the silence. A hockey game in town made the trip slow. At each stoplight she searched the faces that filled up the crosswalks. Every man, she guessed, was better than Charlie Perlmutter or Paul Pomerantz. Each of them. All of them. Dozens of them moving in packs across Commonwealth, Beacon, Huntington, Congress, Atlantic. Why did men move in such huge groups?

Back home, her father put on his black apron and cooked them lunch. Linguine and clams. Her grandfather had given him lessons and he had become over time a very good cook. She watched him, hoping for inspiration about how she might fix this, what she might say to make it better. All the typical words of consolation felt hackneyed and worthless. *Forget that guy. Visualize happiness. Maybe think about not being stoned all the time.* The noise of his knife against the cutting board was immense and angry. Bowls appeared, stuffed with parsley he had savaged. Lemons were juiced. Clams shucked. More Coltrane on the in-home wireless. They ate in silence with a soccer game on in the background. Some Spanish team full of beautiful men sprinting around in the honeyed sunshine of Valencia. He ate with his mouth ajar, a continuous open passageway for his fork. He finished a bottle of Pouilly-Fuissé. Sports consumed him so deeply and so hypnotically that she felt, watching him watch these men run, a deep jealousy of his capacity to disappear into something meaningless. He roused only when the action commanded him to. On the screen a tiny, beautiful, black-haired Spaniard scored a goal and then took off his shirt to reveal an abdomen cleaved into so many tiny squares. Accordingly, her dad, in his drowsiness, lifted his own shirt. "I've become convinced that I don't have those things," he said, looking at her, and then at his own belly. "The square things. Abs? Like, I think we could hire an archeological expedition to dig around there, and I don't think they'd come up with anything."

She blinked at him.

"It's okay to laugh at my jokes," he said.

It had been, by any measure, a bad day. Cuckoldry, disgrace, spilled coffee, ruined camel hair, indignation. And for her, the continued threat of more leaked pornography. How could she laugh?

Across the room, she found her reflection in a hanging bistro mirror. A cheesy decorative touch made by a neo-Georgian decorator her mother had hired, it hung as a divider between the culinary badlands of their kitchen and the trophy room of their library, filled even now with the self-help paperbacks her parents hoarded—books with titles like *Thinking: A Graphic Novel* and *Role-Playing Exercises to Cure Your Panic*. Years ago her mother had become convinced that the true path to happiness lay in creating a lovely home. Perhaps this was something she'd read about, maybe in an instructive guide to homemaking that promised a replenishment of the soul, or perhaps this was merely the predictable response to having grown up the way she had, alongside the pink shadow of her mother's book. But there was a problem: the home she'd made with her husband was a dump. The decorator had left their house full of velvet chaises, brass sconces, and a since-removed Rembrandt print that showed a fifteenth-century autopsy. The kitchen light against the mirror erased the contours of Lydia's face. It made her look like an old person trying to look young. She used to believe that a person looked different in each mirror she came across. Small variations, subtle changes, the shape of an eye. She wondered sometimes about the ancient people of the Bible, how in the desert there was no water or mirrors, and no way to see what it was you looked like exactly, except in the flickering, tiny reflection of another human's eye. You would need to really hold on to someone to truly see yourself.

She and her father both looked out to the backyard. The members of the Singh family were on their deck grilling octopus and slamming the hell out of a badminton birdie. Priya Singh, resplendent in azure Gore-Tex, equipped with a wicked forehand, the current Crestview High champion of being effortlessly good at shit, caught Lydia staring across the fence and waved. They had been best friends when they were young but had grown apart—Priya to boys, field hockey, and pop music, and Lydia to Hartwell.

"Wave back," her father said.

"Maybe first we should talk about what happened today," Lydia said.

"Just wave at your neighbor."

"We don't know what happened up there in his apartment, is all I'm saying. They could have been having coffee."

"Coffee? Is that a metaphor for sex? Or maybe a euphemism for some new illegal therapeutic technique in which psychologists sleep with their patients?"

Priya stood at the fence. Lydia's father turned to her.

"I'm waving with my mind," Lydia told him. "I assure you."

"She's being generous and nice. So wave with your hand so that you don't come off as an alien."

"Oh," Lydia said, waving with mock happiness. "Priya Singh believes me to be a hundred percent alien, I assure you."

"She's happy to see you. And she might turn out one day to be your best friend again," her father said. "And it all might hinge on this very moment. You waving at her."

"Explain to me a scenario in which that beautiful girl over there becomes my best friend."

"Is it so outrageous?"

"She's beautiful in that stupid, hideous coat. Nobody could be beautiful in a coat like that. Gore-Tex is a natural beauty reducer. So, yes, it is outrageous. In another context, with another person who is not me, it might not be."

"Do you have to go someplace to special-order teenage self-loathing like that? Or does it just happen that on your fifteenth birthday a stork appears in your window in the guise of Morrissey, and he touches his beak to you, and then gloomy clouds fill the sky and you're miserable until you're thirty?"

"That would make a great children's book," she said.

"You're just as pretty as she is," he said.

"Seriously, write that book. Make millions."

"She could be your maid of honor at your wedding. I could

see a version of the future in which it isn't so outrageous. People crop up places."

"With all this awesome marital happiness around me—I can't wait."

This hurt him, she knew. He'd kept the wedding photos up as well as the picture taken the moment they'd met each other at the party in Tribeca. While he'd ditched the bed, he'd kept the photos. At first this had seemed a sentimental touch, a reminder of happier times. Lydia wondered, though, whether this was simply a cruel way to remind him of his new reality.

"Don't let the present trouble sour you on love," her dad said.

She laughed. "My present trouble or your present trouble?"

He didn't want to answer. Outside, Priya Singh continued to wave. Lydia's father's eyes were bloodshot, his hair standing on end. *Please play along,* he appeared to be saying.

"Hypothetically speaking, where will I be living when Priya Singh happens to just crop up?"

"Let's say that in this version of the future, you're living in Chicago."

"Chicago? I've never heard you say anything about Chicago."

He screwed up his face. She wondered whether this was where he was planning to go when everything finally fell apart here. "I like Chicago. It's a good city. Not as showy as New York. Or as vapid as L.A."

"What am I doing in Chicago, then?"

He squinted at her. She knew this game. Occasionally she got a glimpse of the kind of life her parents had imagined for her. A slim, cheerful-looking fifteen-year-old waiting in line for a skim latte, having come from rehearsals for the school production of *Into the Woods,* the script under her arm—this urbane young woman, looking healthy, ruddy-cheeked, looking positively well-adjusted, this woman and all the young women like her, invariably elicited pangs of quasi-nostalgic longing from her parents.

"You're an actress," he said.

"Ooh. No. That won't happen."

"A fashion designer?"

"Again, no."

"I don't know what you want to do when you grow up."

"Do I have to choose right this instant?"

"Okay," he said, searching. "You own a hip little coffee shop. You know, cupcakes in the display case. And Stevie Nicks on the stereo."

"Do I serve alcohol?"

"Do you want to serve alcohol?"

"Knowing my childhood, probably."

He didn't find this funny. "Sure. Alcohol. Whatever."

"I'll agree to play along, then."

"But only really expensive alcohol," he said.

"So this is for rich people?" she asked.

"Unemployed former attorneys, mostly."

"This actually sounds like a good business model. You're full of ideas tonight."

"So, one day, this young woman comes to visit."

"Is she, perhaps, South Asian, and wearing a tight blue Gore-Tex coat, and is she maybe holding a plate of grilled octopus in one hand and a badminton racket in the other?"

"You're working the counter. It's been a tough day. Something's off."

"Money trouble?"

"Maybe illicit pictures of you have turned up online and derailed your fledgling congressional campaign."

Lydia threw up her hands.

"Okay," her father said. "Too soon to joke."

"You can never ever joke about this," she said. "Ever."

The moment stung. Her father waited at the table for her anger to pass, something she knew he was doing and which, in retrospect, she probably should have allowed. Instead, she leaned back and crossed her arms against her chest. He sighed and got up to wash dishes, leaving on the table his new phone—black, gleaming, and reflecting back the image of a happy, waving Priya Singh.

A few things occurred next.

One: Lydia reached immediately for her phone and found herself within moments scrolling frantically through all her accounts and feeds and inboxes. While doing this, she considered the fact that she had been, for the past two hours or so, at least, completely off-line, a stretch of time that was practically equal to the Victorian epoch. She scrolled her fingers across the smudged glass, past all the new crude messages and the come-ons.

Then she stopped.

Her father had the water on.

First, a short message delivered by email and text: New Jersey really is wonderful this time of year. Too bad you didn't show. I warned you.

Then, in her inbox and online: a pair of pictures from the night she had gone to Charlie's bed. In the first, they were together on his unmade, fetid mattress, as if to dispel any rumor on campus to the contrary. His hand rested on her bare thigh, her skirt pushed up. Behind them rain hung in fat beads on the window screen. He had, it was easy to see, taken this picture himself. His arm was outstretched. She had not noticed. She had, senselessly, been trying to enjoy herself.

The second picture was more simple. Just a photograph of her underwear, her pink underwear, taken, clearly, up her skirt.

The final thing that happened was that a horrible noise escaped her.

"You all right over there?" her father asked.

Priya Singh had jumped the fence and was on the deck, waving and smiling and at that very moment knocking on the window. He thought that was what the scream was about.

Lydia slid the phone back across the table. "I'm perfectly fine," she said.

# 21.

Henrietta went to see Jerry Stern at his club at Mount Pleasant. She knew what he would say. It always came back to money. Harold had none, spent too much, always needed more. The Feast had been the biggest drain. The rent had been exorbitant, the bills from the vendors excruciating. Harold refused to skimp on ingredients. Refused to move the restaurant to the suburbs. They kept the animals until there was no point. The day they were trucked off, Jerry had to come because Harold knew that if Jerry was there he would never allow himself to weep. Despite all of this, he'd kept on with the place. How the hell could she ever tell him not to? For months, it went on like this— dripping, then bleeding, then hemorrhaging money. The empty restaurant, the wasted food, the electric bills, the staff salaries— she kept the books and watched the debt grow. Eventually she stepped in to pay everything. It bought Harold another half a year and ruined their finances. She'd had to explain all of this to everyone lately—the lawyers, the creditors, the real estate agents, the motley collection of doomsayers analyzing her future prospects—because everyone assumed she was rich. Money from the book had been good in the beginning, it was true, and it was also true that there was a horrendously bad movie with

Loni Anderson, in which Anderson, or a body double, went topless in a hot-air balloon, but it was also true that this was 1977 money, Jimmy Carter–level currencies, stagnation dollars. But over twenty years, *The Inseparables* had slowly stopped selling and then had eventually gone out of print, its supposed pornography eclipsed by books far smarter and smuttier than hers and by the digital torrents of actual pornography. She loved Harold and so she gave him everything until she had nothing left. It always came back to money.

Jerry did not seem surprised. "Since he's dead, and since you loved him, I don't want to say exactly that he was an idiot."

"Seems like you just did."

"Just with money. That was all."

"Most people are idiots with money."

He pointed at himself.

"Not you, Jerry. I know. Mazel tov. You're the king of aluminum siding. You should be nominated to run the Federal Reserve. You win."

"Both of you were uninterested in money. That was the problem. Disinterest leads to ignorance. Then, before you know it, you're pouring all your money into some restaurant that nobody's eating in."

She shook her head. Every time she was with Jerry they talked about money, and every time she talked about money she felt the need to articulate the fear. Because this was what these last few months had meant. All at once, the shape of things had collapsed. Her husband, her house, all her money, her daughter's marriage, and then, week by week, the idea of her future.

"I always told Harry two things. I said don't ever borrow from someone you don't know. And don't start selling shit."

"It seems so desperate," she said. "Birthday gifts?"

"It's pathetic," he said.

"A pen is a bad birthday gift, I admit it. But—"

"At least he didn't sell his blood," he said. "Or his semen."

When she winced, he put up his hands.

"For the record, I'm positive he didn't do any of that."

Jerry had lived at Mount Pleasant for sixteen months, and for the past seven he'd been after Henrietta to move in. It wasn't as bad as it looked, he told her, which was almost certainly impossible. He could get her a deal. Skip the wait list. He could get her into the Ladies' Group, whatever that was. He told her about the greens fees, about the electric golf carts, about the carbon neutrality of the dining facilities, the performances that the local children's choruses put on this past weekend. A bunch of miniature Maria Callases, he claimed. Honestly! Voices like birdsong! She understood the attraction to the promise of an institutionalized decline. The opposite had the potential to be horrifying. Here, at least, there were things to look forward to. The structure of the place promised escalators on the way to death. And when the time did come, nurses would live in your spare bedroom, or wheel you across the ninth fairway to the on-site hospice. In the meantime, you could sit back and enjoy the mahjong tournaments or the piped-in sound track that somehow always played the hits from when you were seventeen.

Henrietta felt the men around her staring. If she needed any other reason to resist this place, here was one. The men here were the perfect age to have known of her when she first published *That Motherfucking Thing*, to have acted scandalized by her, to have written sanctimonious op-eds in the *Aveline Beacon* decrying the diseased state of her soul, and then to have gone home and devoured her book in private before fucking their wives with a new vigor. Jerry knew all of this, certainly, but he kept trying to sell her.

"Let me just show you around," he said.

"This again?"

"It'll be better than wherever you're moving, Henrietta.

Plus, you'd have all this land. Just like at the house. You could still see animals out your window. It's just like the wilderness."

"Do you hear yourself? Just like the 'wilderness'?"

"Look around. Picture this in summer. There are birds. We have buttercups in the grass."

"It's a golf course, Jerry. There'll be men in shorts swinging huge clubs at a tiny ball, breaking my living room window."

"That does happen," he said. "I can't lie."

"I don't see myself at home here," she said.

"You like birds, though!"

"I do," she said. "That's true. I really like birds. I especially like them with teriyaki sauce."

"You'd have a *community* of people here."

"Like I need a bunch of old codgers harassing me day in and day out," she said, looking back at a particular group of men in white Lacoste and plaid trousers, all of them smiling at her.

"It's all fun and games with that bunch," he said.

"They'd make lecherous comments to a mannequin, Jerry."

"Probably."

"So you're saying I should move here and have my beautiful granddaughter come to visit me? The girl's getting harassed already as it is. And that's at her fancy school."

"Is that true?" he asked with genuine concern. "That's awful."

"She barely talks to me as it is, Jerry. If I move here, and she has to contend with all these degenerates, she might never speak to me again."

He grimaced at this, knowing that she was right. She thought to mention to him everything about what had happened with Lydia and the picture, but what would a guy like Jerry know about something like this? A guy who, for an embarrassingly long time, believed that the Internet was a physical product you could buy in the store, like a television. Henrietta missed Jerry's wife at moments like this. Shirley made Aveline tolerable those first years away from Manhattan, especially after the book was out in the world and it became impossible for Henrietta to do the simplest things, like go to the grocery without being accosted by strangers. Shirley came every Saturday afternoon, did so for decades, bringing along her dogs, or bags of candy, or Bogart movies that they watched together.

It was late morning. A fire lit up the big stone hearth. Their table sat beside a window overlooking the tenth green, blue with ice, the sand traps like lunar craters. Men at the bar to her right were already onto their second cocktails. Jerry leaned back. He had on a red and white necktie, tied too short, resting on his belly. Henrietta remembered his wife's funeral. Afterward, they had gone back to the small apartment in the city. Henrietta had excused herself at a certain point and gone into the kitchen for wine or food or merely to escape the shivah. The back porch was crowded with wisteria. When she opened the refrigerator she saw that Shirley had packed it full of homemade food for him. As if she had been going away on a trip. *Spaghetti sauce,* she'd written on one small tub. *Reheat in microwave, two minutes, stir, reheat thirty seconds.* Or: *Chicken Kiev—bake on low temp.*

"Did you bother with the police?" he asked. "About the weathervane."

She shook her head.

"It's lost," he said.

"I appreciate your optimism."

"I'm a Jew. Fuck optimism. The world is bleak. It's gone."

"To be honest, I probably would have thrown it away anyway when I moved."

"Maybe you did and you just don't remember. When was the last time you even saw the thing?"

She closed her eyes.

"It's not an insult to suggest you forgot something," he said. "Even the great, brilliant Henrietta Olyphant could forget things."

"Who ever said I was great or brilliant?"

Jerry turned in his seat. Across the room, a table full of men were looking at Henrietta. "Your fan club here is thriving."

"Throbbing," she said.

He smiled. "That's exactly my point."

This year would mark forty-one years in Massachusetts, which was almost twice as long as she had ever lived in New York, which meant, more or less, that this idea of herself as some cosmopolitan émigré, imported here to the country without her books and her women's studies classes and her occasional pitch meetings with the editors of *Ms.* magazine—all of it was officially ancient and dead. She had begun her adult life writing about the female figure—about the shifting standards of acceptability, and about who exactly shifted those standards, and about which came first: the high heel making you feel sexy, or a man designing a high heel to make you appear sexy to him. And here she was, searching for a tiny little figure of a woman that someone in an auction house wanted to buy.

"How much do you think he got for the pens?" she asked.

Jerry took out his pipe and fiddled with the stem nervously.

"Oh," she said. "You know exactly how much he got."

"You should know I took him around to every bank. But nobody was loaning money then. Housing market collapsed. Commercial paper market collapsed. Fucking Bear Stearns. Fucking Lehman Brothers. Every one of these bankers told him the same thing I told him. Cut your losses, go home, retire, be with your wife, talk to your pet rooster, or whatever. He wouldn't listen. You go to sleep with dogs, you wake up with fleas. I told him that. He thought people would come back to the restaurant. He thought people were ready to eat good

French food again. Did I think he was right? No. Did I think, you know, people maybe want to eat less butter? Yes! Yes I did!"

"He didn't tell me any of this."

Jerry laughed. "Why would he?"

"Because we were married," she said.

"So?"

"And because we lived together."

"Like that's ever been an excuse for any other married person in the whole history of people."

"Because I paid for everything at the end," she said.

He pointed the end of his pipe at her. "There you go."

# 22.

The first night no one came for dinner—no one, from open to close, not one single person—Harold hid in the kitchen. He'd been fussing over a veal stock, skimming for hours, simmering and skimming, watching, skimming, timing, skimming. It was a task he usually assigned to a line cook, but Henrietta knew that he'd had a feeling about tonight. In the car on the ride from Aveline, he'd told her. All month, the dining room was thinning. A man's head in the final stages of balding. Two women would come in, fresh off the train from Philadelphia, eager to see the Boston Pops, with coupons, with traveler's checks, of all things, as if this were the 1980s, and they'd get the table by the window, just so the place didn't look so empty from the sidewalk. No drinks. No wine. No sparkling water. Nothing to start. Not even a Caesar salad. They'd send everything back. Henrietta handled this. The *boeuf au poivre:* too bloody, too spicy, too small. The duck: too fatty. The quiche: too rich. She was always the one who had to tell Harold. Customers would haggle over the check. That much? For this? It was six bites. Honestly. Six small bites. This, too, she needed to relay to him. Daily, the waiters would idle by the bar, obsessing over their phones, sharing the new online reviews. It used to be that you got one review every other year. Now a review came every day, sometimes more than one, and all of them were worse than any printed review Harold had ever received. She tried to hide them from him. Such venom. Such pointed cruelty. *Apparently this restaurant used to be famous but now it's just sad.* Or: *So much butter I probably needed an angiogram afterward.* Or: *We were the only people in the place.* Or: *The chef just lingered in the kitchen window, sulking. Don't go here. Such a creepy vibe.* Or: *Did we mention the butter?*

It was a Friday evening. The very beginning of spring. The city felt alive finally, after a long winter. Across the road at Symphony Hall, Beethoven's Ninth played all week. From the kitchen Henrietta could hear the afternoon rehearsal, the spots in the score where the conductor stopped the orchestra, the spots they ran through again. *Ode to Joy* a hundred times a day. A glorious week. She helped out, swept floors, changed broken lightbulbs. In the afternoon the young ballerinas from a local ballet lingered on the sidewalk after class, some of them still in their leotards, all of them smoking, making kissy faces at Harold's cooks, speaking bad French, smoking more cigarettes. These first few days of spring, the whole city had a collective libido to exercise. The streets buzzed with sex. Everyone's body reemerged from their winter layers. They'd always done the best business this week. People ate, drank, flirted, went home with people they shouldn't have been out with in the first place. She'd tried to get him to temper his expectations. She'd made him order less food. For tonight, they'd taken only six birds, less than the usual full dozen. One lamb instead of three. They got their veal from a farm in a town a half hour from Aveline. There were men there who could birth a breech calf and also, six months later, kill that calf. Hard men, all of them, free of any sentiment, they'd urged him not to kill the animals if he didn't need to. Henrietta had gone with him and tried to mediate. One of the farmers had read online that the Feast was empty most nights. A grizzled Mainer, he'd cocked his head toward the pens. "They're all doing just fine the way they are. No need to kill 'em dead if you're just gonna throw it away."

The stock took three days. A day for the first bit of flavor. A second day with the same bones. A third day to combine the two. This wasn't the classic preparation—the way Harold had learned, the way he loved, the way with the roasting and the good color. She'd been with him when he decided to change something up. As if this was the reason nobody came to eat here anymore: the fucking veal stock. He stole the new recipe from *The French Laundry Cookbook*. Something needed to give, and so he stole recipes. He bought Keller's book, the big white thing, fifty dollars, just like a home cook, and there was so much skimming. Skim, skim, skim, it said, and so he did.

Harold tried to get the staff to respect the animals. His staff was careless. They burned the meat. Or else they seasoned it wrong. Killed it with salt. He couldn't get the best people any longer, not even close, not with the competition, not with Thomas Keller and his beautiful clear veal stock, and so he got cooks who burned the meat. He gave a speech that day over the stock. This was my calf, he said. He knew this animal, saw it birthed, actually, had stroked its head, fed it with a bottle. If you had a gun to his temple, he'd admit that he had kissed it that first night, before he penned it. Have you ever seen how lively a young calf is? How they run and play, like dogs? He stood over the stockpot, skimming. Henrietta stood off to the side, watching. Now she had the marks of a chef on her arm. Burn marks. Knife nicks. I fed these calves by the bottle, he told them. They've sucked on my fingers. She wanted to step in then to stop this charade, to keep him from embarrassing himself, but something in her held her back.

The dining room sat empty. It was nine. Ten. He kept skimming. A good stock shouldn't overwhelm the senses, he told her. It was a fine balance. Ten thirty. He stopped, looked out. The waitstaff was at the bar, sitting, playing games on their phones. "The symphony will get out in five minutes," he called out. "Be ready. There'll be a rush."

Some of them believed him.

"Henrietta," he said, pointing to her. "Stand. On your feet. Be by the door." He pointed. The bartender. "Peter. Do you have your bases mixed? Do you? Be ready." Behind him, on the grill, Philippe. "Mark the pork. Mark the filet. Mark the chicken thigh." Others wouldn't move. Henrietta watched, grew nervous. The dishwashers, all of them Ecuadorian, sat playing cards. There'd been a time when he employed a huge kitchen staff. Teams for the meat. Teams for the vegetables. They'd prepare forty of everything on the menu, and then, before the night was through, they'd run out. Everyone had feared him. Men happy to be screamed at. He took young chefs straight from the Culinary Institute, trained them rough for eighteen months, traded them with chefs in New York or Paris. All that was gone. He had only ten people. Everyone had to do everything. Even Henrietta broke down meat. "Be ready," he yelled. But there was nothing to wash. Nothing to prep. The place was spotless. Everything was clean. To his right, a neat *mise en place*. Large mirepoix, small mirepoix, carrots turned, carrots in neat batons, carrots julienned. She waited for the jolt of energy. Watching her husband summon his kitchen into chaos was less like seeing a conductor striking up an orchestra and more like seeing a conductor commanding that orchestra to fight one another. At its best, this place had been loud and vulgar and filled with so many vats of boiling stock and fire, with everyone sweating for hours. She loved to see it then: he would raise his hands and people would rush to work. Later that night, he'd raise his hands and the kitchen would be gleaming.

He'd been in a kitchen since he was a boy. When they met, he told her that he had the typical biography of a chef. His grandmother's lobster shack in the summer. Old Orchard Beach. Feeding the fishermen, the bikers, children fresh from the water, sand everywhere, even in the food. He had a simple job. Reach in, grab the lobster when someone ordered one, drop it in the boiling water. He was the executioner. Even then, he told Henrietta, he'd been able to hold both thoughts in his head. One being that he loved these animals when they were living. Even a lobster. Even a bug. The other being that he had no problem killing them.

Ten forty-five. "Show's out," Henrietta announced. She had her face pressed against the glass of the front door. The doors opened at Symphony Hall. "Okay," she shouted. "A good crowd coming our way. Five couples." This last year she'd been on full-time. "Okay, four couples." Last week it had been a young Chinese pianist doing all of Chopin's nocturnes. Such beautiful afternoons listening to the rehearsals. Chopin fans loved to eat good French food, and they'd had a decent run this late in the evening. Some dedicated Francophiles, white-haired, scarves around their necks, ordering in Bronx-accented French, in Quebecois, ordering three bottles of Côtes du Rhône. "Okay," she called out. "Losing people." Through the reflection in the glass she could see Harold tightening the ties on his apron.

"How many?" he called out.

She turned back. "Waiting on one couple right now. They're standing outside. Discussing."

He tightened the ties even tighter.

"Should we go outside and invite them in?" she asked.

"No," he said. "They'll come."

This did not happen at a restaurant with the pedigree of the Feast. They'd had two stars, and then one star—a matter of bad service and a partially undercooked duck—and then no stars at all. By the door, they had the first reviews tacked to the wall. Just this, putting these up, violated certain rules of decorum. In a fine dining establishment, one simply did not hang one's press on the wall as if it was a pizzeria. Oona had suggested it. Let people know you mean business, she'd said. And here it was: October 1976, two stars. This had been the height. He could do no wrong. A young man cooking in the grand tradition, waiters in tuxedos, Vivaldi on the hi-fi. October 1979, one star. The business with the duck was a scandal. He had fired the entire kitchen, replaced it entirely with men from Paris and Lyon. This alone, this commitment, this evidence of the tyrannical artist-cook, kept people coming back. Farther down the hall, the photos of Sinatra were tacked up. The photos of Brando, Jackie Onassis, Cronkite, Katharine Hepburn, even Nixon. Again, this was Oona's idea. Never mind that every one of them was dead.

Behind her the cooks waited. A dozen filets, marked. A dozen chops, marked. A dozen chicken thighs, marked. The stock. The quiche. The custards. The *mousse au chocolat*. The madeleines. Hotel pans of canapés, tomato terrine, foie gras. The cold bourbon-vanilla glaze in a squeeze bottle. The duck. The duck fat. The quail. The quail eggs. The smaller saucepans, simmering. Pepper in the air. Butter softening. Olives Provençal at room temperature.

She peered. "Okay," Henrietta said, her voice falling.

She turned back.

"Okay what?" Harold asked.

"We lost them."

He tightened. "What? All of them? How?"

She stepped away, following him into the kitchen. "What do you want me to say, Harold? We lost them. They stood. They discussed. They left. Julius Caesar in reverse."

He shook his head. "Then go get them! Go!"

She frowned.

One of his line cooks stepped forward. "Chef, no."

He pointed at the kid. "If she won't go, you go!"

"We don't do that, chef."

Behind Harold stood another young line cook. A Jersey guy. A guy who showed up the first day thinking that a ball cap was an acceptable substitute for a hairnet. "I've never actually worked a shift where no one came."

Harold turned, fired him. "Anybody else?" he yelled.

Two line cooks took the opportunity to fire themselves. Aprons and hats on the clean, empty countertop.

Finally, from the corner, his grill man, Philippe. Long tenured, elegant in stature, Napoleon's nose, a true genius with fire. "What do I do with the meat, boss?"

On the grill were pieces of animals Harold had raised. Three pigs, three lambs, three of his own chickens he had seen hatch and who had buzzed around his feet in the mornings while he fed them. A sign hung near the freezer: No Protein Allowed. He would not freeze the meat. He had never done it. You could taste the difference, he told Henrietta. Anyone who ate here, he told her, would be able to taste the difference, too. And even if they couldn't, he would know, and he wouldn't allow it. Philippe pointed at the steak.

"This," he said, "this we can keep. Freeze. Serve it tomorrow. It's a great cut."

Harold untied his apron.

"Or, we can make a staff meal."

Harold shook his head. "You already ate."

Behind him one of the Ecuadorians spoke. "We can always eat. We're men."

From the front, Henrietta frowned. "We're not all men. But I can always eat, too."

Harold went back to skimming. She came over. The stock

looked intermittently clear and then murky. She knew what was in his head. Every night now they had some form of the same conversation. What do we owe? Who's waiting on payment? What kind of promotion can we do?

"No," he said. "Toss it."

Henrietta threw up her hands. "Don't toss it."

"Toss it," Harold yelled.

"Freeze it, at least."

"Have you not seen the sign?" he yelled. "We don't freeze!"

"Donate it, then."

He shook his head. "To who?"

"To homeless people." She held up a hand and started counting. "To battered women. To college students. To a culinary school. To the VA cafeteria." She lifted another hand. "The Hare Krishnas will take the veggies. I know that."

He threw his hat. "Fuck off." He threw up his hands. "Fucking Hare Krishnas? Are you kidding me?"

"Seriously. Everyone in the city does it. The food banks here offer better food than most of the restaurants."

Harold scoffed.

"Even Thomas Keller does it!"

"Do not mention Thomas fucking Keller!" He smacked the counter with an open palm. "I will not give this food away. Not this food. No. This is my food. This is great—"

"It's not great anymore," she said. "It'll be trash in a second."

She knew this was not what he did here. Throw away food. Freeze food. Donate food. He birthed the animal, raised it, fed it, watched it play, gave it medicine, and then had it packed humanely. She knew all of this. No gigantic killing floor. No overwhelming stench of blood that sent the animals into a crazed frenzy. After that, he treated the meat right. Treated it as though it was valuable. His meat, he said once, was like the color a painter had to extract from a berry that grew only on one bush, and bloomed for only one week. She had laughed at him. He sounded so pompous! But he meant it. His pomposity was genuine. He cooked slowly. He watched through the kitchen doors as people ate. He wanted to see the satisfaction. Wash their dish. Send them home happy.

She could not say aloud just how badly it wrecked her to see this. When she met him, he had dreams of this place, fledgling sketches, delirious visions of honey-glazed bread, place settings already imagined. He had never been a man who had desired anything else but to have his own shop. On weekend mornings, on his days off, he would wake early to cook in their tiny galley kitchen. He was in his twenties then, working in New York, already practicing recipes. She would wake to the smell of caramelized sugar, or roasted duck. Her young husband, sweat-stained in an undershirt, rolling out salted flour on their small square of countertop. She would come groggy to the breakfast nook, and he would feed her the most ridiculous treats first thing in the morning. Butter-poached oysters. Fried artichokes.

In the harsh kitchen light, he looked diminished.

"Tomorrow will be better," Henrietta said, overruling him, ordering the food cooked and bagged, some of it frozen. She took him into the back office, leading him by the arm, her wrist tight against him like a handcuff. She paused when they were alone, and then spoke slowly. "Look, either you change this place, cook something different, or it dies." They'd had this conversation before. They had no more money. *Let me get some money, then. Let me borrow some.* They'd needed more than money, though. A new menu. Better music. She'd gone, just recently, around town to see how others were doing it. Rock music in the dining room! People eating in rooms deafeningly loud with drums and guitars! Scallops and a light butter reduction and Bruce Springsteen groaning on about New Jersey! Foie gras and Keith Richards! Bone marrow and Cabernet Franc and David Bowie! Molecular gastronomy and electronic dance music! Less butter! The dining rooms were all bright and open. The Feast was dark, red and burgundy, the only brightness the white of the tablecloths, which were frayed, almost all of them, the dim lighting scheme hiding the worst of it.

Philippe came into the back room carrying the veal stock. "Chef?" He looked down at the big pot, the broth sloshing. "I'm sorry. There's soap in it."

"What?"

"Some of the boys," Philippe said. "They had a sponge fight."

Harold got up to see. Philippe lowered the pot. An oil slick atop his stock. Two white peaks. A hint of bleach. He took the pot from Philippe and went out into the kitchen. The cooks were lined up against the stove.

"Who did this?" He was losing his composure, she knew. Having an animal killed and then throwing it away—it was getting to him. "Who did this? I demand to know!"

"It's fine," someone said, a young cook, blond, possibly Swedish. He got his people from the most unlikely places these days. "Just boil it off."

"Leave," Harold said, pointing. "Don't come back."

The Swede left. Harold put the stock on the floor. "This was an animal," he said, beginning softly. "This was an animal. It was brown when it was a baby. Brown with white spots."

"Harold," Henrietta said, whispering, pulling on his sleeve. "Don't do this."

"It was a lovely animal, and the only reason this isn't an animal any longer is so that it could be food. Something to feed to someone. That was its purpose."

"Chef," Philippe whispered behind him, "you need to stop. No one will come back to the kitchen after this."

He turned, pointed. "You too. You're fired. Get out."

Philippe stood, indignant. "I refuse."

"Fine," he said. "You drink that, then."

"What?"

"Get down and drink it if you think I'm being crazy."

"You're joking."

"I'm not joking. Drink it."

"You're crazy."

"Get on the floor and drink the stock!"

"Stop." Henrietta put both of her hands on Harold's shoulders. "Let's get you to sit down. You're tired."

"No. Philippe! Get on your hands and knees."

"Fuck off, chef."

"Get on your fucking hands and knees and drink this fucking stock, Philippe! Do it! Drink it!"

He kept yelling and Henrietta picked him up off the ground as if he were a child and dragged him back into his office. "I'm just asking you all to respect this!" He wept. "This was an animal and now it's just liquid with soap on it. What is wrong with you people?"

# 23.

All night she worried that more pictures would come. Lydia sat up in the dark, sleepless, snow outside and plows circling, her phone flat on the comforter.

This was her girlhood bedroom. Stuffed animals lay piled up on top of her dresser. Had it always been so pink? Pink walls, pink sheets, pink curtains. Everyone's childhood bedroom was a museum while it lasted. In Lydia's mind, there should have been a chronology attached to the wall of hers in the form of a gallery plaque.

A history of a girl's personality by way of
her regrettable obsessions.

Twelve years old: She'd scrawled her favorite melodramatic song lyrics directly onto the walls. Her taste in music, she saw now, had evolved by hairstyle, from conservative to ecstatic: Morrissey to Robert Smith. Thirteen years old: Above the bed, pasted over the glow-in-the-dark constellations, were an array of shirtless male models advertising cargo shorts and body razors. So much hairless flexing. In the beginning, she had believed, of course, that grown men were supposed to be as sleek as a porpoise. Fourteen years old: Stevie Nicks records. And then, because of those Stevie Nicks records, there were horoscope clippings tacked to her dressers, all of them foretelling a good month/a good year/a spate of good romantic fortune. Fifteen years old: Preppy culture. Tennis sneakers. Julie Christie movies. The existence of the nation of France. Boarding school novels. Tripartite wool scarves. She locked the door.

She held the phone in her hand, refreshing every account and inbox, one after the other, hour after hour.

Finally, near morning, the videos came. There were two of them. The first arrived just after sunrise and in it she was walking, innocently enough at first, across the Hartwell quad beside Charlie, his voice faint in the background, Vermont in September, breeze-bothered maple trees at the edge of the frame, a shard of the navy collar of her uniform, but mostly just her ass as she walked on ahead of him, believing that he was behind her just fiddling with his phone. He zoomed in on her as she went across the field, getting close enough to trace the contour of her underwear as it pressed against her skirt.

In the second video, she was in his bed, lying down, his navy sheets ruffled beneath her, a few buttons undone on her blouse. She was reading something on her phone. R. Kelly played in the background. He zoomed in, this time between her legs.

She sensed that things would get worse, and they did.

She received a link from an anonymous address for a website where she found her original picture from the shower house at Rosewater, available to download for a fee. Now she was for sale.

Just then the garage door opened beneath her, shaking the house, and she rushed down from her bedroom to the carpeted landing, shouting uselessly for her father as his car pulled away. Just the word made her fill with helplessness: *Daddy!* A word she used only in distress. Lost in the department store.

Separated at Gloucester beach. Or standing as she was at this instant, in her empty garage. He had left a note on the kitchen counter. *I need to go out. I'm sure you'll enjoy the time alone.*

The train from downtown Aveline deposited her a block from the front door of the hospital. She wanted her mother. It was early enough for her shift not to have ended. Lydia knew her way. Up the glass elevator to orthopedics, the city emerged in parallel stripes of ice behind the pines and the reservoir and behind the white steeples of the Unitarian churches. No one ever liked the hospital. She understood. She realized that for most everyone, the hospital, with its chapels and rooms full of weeping relatives and its garbage bins full of wilted carnations and its basement morgue, was a miserable place. But the hospital had always calmed her. This was where her mother was.

Down another glass corridor, past the nurses' station, Lydia let herself into the empty office, a simple cluttered room full of family photos and plastic replicas of the hip joint. She waited. An hour passed. She found a lab coat hanging on a hook on the back of the door and put it on and felt glad that it smelled like her mom.

The reality of having an orthopedic surgeon for a mother, even if that mother was, according to a recent online survey of Boston-area physicians, the forty-second-best orthopedist in the city, was that her mom often needed to rush off somewhere to tend to someone else. This was not particularly interesting to anyone but Lydia, nor was it at all an original complaint to have a busy parent, especially in this new economy, and especially when you went somewhere like Hartwell, where everyone's parents had all but deposited them for safekeeping. But facts were facts. Her mother's ever-improving array of pagers and cell phones and homing devices became over time a fourth person in the family, a second child. Lydia, when she was young, probably worryingly young, affixed human qualities to her mother's phone, calling it Chimey after the way it dinged and beckoned for her mother's attention. During her first- and second-grade years, Lydia had full-on conversations with the phone. *Hi, Chimey, today I went to school. Hi, Chimey, today is Valentine's Day.* That sort of thing. It had brought her mother to tears more than once.

After an hour, Lydia left the office in search of her mother. It was a rule of hospitals, she had discovered, that the worse a potential malady was, the more serene and beautiful and full of glass their attending departments were, so that ophthalmology was drab and beige, and maxillofacial surgery was even more drab and even more beige, while pediatric oncology was a veritable forest of floor to ceiling windows and urban panoramas. Every available wall space that was not taken up by windows was filled with delightful murals of *Sesame Street* characters. She stopped for a while here to consider the juxtaposition of the wildly beautiful surroundings and the terribly ill children. She crossed several skybridges. Down below, ambulances idled. The city sky dimmed. A hulking potted indoor palm brushed the glass roofline between hematology and sports medicine. This was the centerpiece of the hospital's last renovation, completed when Lydia was a girl. Plaques and portraits hung in the anterooms attesting to civic largesse. At the time, this was evidence of the hospital's institutional optimism: the vestibule, the views, the new white paint, and the luxury of a palm tree here in Massachusetts. A doctor had put it to Lydia this way: *If we can grow a palm tree in this place, we can sure as heck keep people alive.* She'd come to the opening party, where her mother's boss had cut a ribbon with a comically huge pair of scissors. Doctors delivered speeches in which they claimed that this clinic would rise to the vanguard of American health. Diagnostic capabilities would exist under this roof that would not exist anywhere else. Boston was a city full of world-class hospitals, and they, that night, were supposedly witness to the newest member of the class. Also, they had refurbished the cafeteria! She remembered her mother, in a new yellow dress, clapping enthusiastically. To keep Lydia quiet, her mother had given her a real stethoscope to play with. All night, while the adults drank, she circled the room, listening to their hearts beating.

When she became afraid that her phone wouldn't stop buzzing, she turned it off, but then light from the windows caught the camera lens in a way that unsettled her, and so she went to a restroom and put the phone on the ground and stomped on it until it came apart beneath her boot, and then, when there was nothing but a pile of pieces and shards, she stepped on those pieces and shards until there were more pieces, and then, because Charlie Perlmutter had finally succeeded in terrorizing her, she threw everything into a toilet and flushed.

The first floor of the hospital was more or less a municipal triage unit. Gunshot victims, tractor-trailer jackknives, city bus crashes. In the big waiting room, the chaplain stood at reception. An orderly ran a wet mop over a streak of something that was either vomit or blood. At practically every moment, an alarm sounded, beckoning experts or forestalling death. A chorus of bleating chimes. Behind the hospital, cars gathered in the lot of a cathedral built against a hill. You could hear the bells through the heating ducts.

One thing about a hospital: you could cry in public here and no one looked at you twice.

At the nurses' station she introduced herself, her face probably red and wet, her hands shaking. "I've been waiting for quite a while. Can you tell me when my mother will be out of surgery?" she asked.

The nurse looked confused. She stood up, touched Lydia's

hand. "Honey," she said. "Your mom's not in surgery. She's not here today at all."

Lydia gripped the counter.

"Is there something we can help you with?"

"What do you mean?" Lydia asked. "She's always here. Where is she? I need her."

# 24.

Before everything with Spencer began to come apart, Oona did not believe that a mature, grown woman could ever be unsure about something so serious as falling out of love with someone. Falling in love seemed like something powerful enough and vaguely mystical enough to be confusing. But deciding one day that you needed not to sleep in the same bed as someone, or endure his whims or tempers, and that you needed to become effectively no better than a stranger to that person—this had always struck her as rather cut-and-dried. You decided, you left, you became for some period of time a villain. Answering to any doubt about these facts only meant that you were willing, still, to subordinate your happiness to someone else's. But after yesterday, with her husband standing in the middle of traffic, with his favorite coat ruined, and with Paul standing perhaps a little too proud in front of his luxury condominium tower and his luxury German sports car, she could maybe admit that being a villain did not suit her.

So there was this: overnight she had become full of tenderness for her husband. Or full of doubt. Or swelled with pity for him. Or maybe it was something simpler. She missed him. Awake at night in her girlhood bed, alone in the dark, in the room beside her dreaming mother, she took inventory of the past few hours. Making a diagnosis was easy. The experiment was over. The separation had failed. She had tried someone new and come away from the experience feeling disgusted. In the shower she'd scrubbed Paul off her skin as assiduously as if she was trying to sterilize herself for surgery. Afterward she tried to imagine her marriage as a bone she needed to repair. A knee or a hip or an elbow shattered in a crash. This was the only way it could make sense to her. Find the injury. Make a cut. Fix everything. The remedy felt obvious. She wanted to be home again, on their quiet street, in their yellow house, in bed, back beside Spencer, where she had been since she was twenty-one years old. She longed for normalcy, for the regular morning, for the routine of married life. She wanted to not feel Paul on top of her, or hear his bestial grunting in her ears. Spencer was right. It *had* been nice eating a family meal. She and him. Talking. Like humans. Perhaps nice was as good as you could bargain for after twenty years of marriage. Maybe this was the problem. Maybe she'd been bargaining for something better than nice, and maybe nice—something easy, something comfortable, something normal—maybe this was better than someone new.

In the morning, first thing, she called him, and he came straightaway from Crestview. They met at a restaurant near the river. As he snaked his way around the café tables in one of his old coats, she sensed some revitalized hint of purpose in the way he walked. He looked rested and cleanly shaven and sober. When he got to the table, she stood up and found that she didn't know what to do—kiss his cheek, hug him, or do what it was she ended up doing, which was shake his hand. The books on divorce and separation said nothing about the simple things.

"I've been thinking about what I want," she told him, "and what I want is to come home with you."

At first he didn't speak.

"This is exactly what you asked me to do the other day," she reminded him. "And every week before that for the last six months."

"I remember," he said quietly.

"You don't want me to come back?" she asked. It surprised her how desperate she sounded. "Did you suddenly change your mind?"

"You fucked our marriage counselor," he said flatly. "So yes, I changed my mind."

Suddenly Spencer seemed far away from her. She felt her skin turn hot. She thought to say, "You weren't supposed to know." Or: "You can't even imagine how much of a mistake this was." Or even: "It was on his floor. It was awful." But she saw that it was pointless. This revitalized fresh face of his—this was the face of someone who had already reckoned with the facts. The marriage was dead and she was the one who'd killed it. Her disappointment gave way to resentment. Wasn't this what her mother had been trying to tell her when she was young? Even Spencer, the good liberal Jewish boy from Chevy Chase, having read the right books, having marched against apartheid, having divested the family portfolio from fossil fuels, having genuinely wept over Djimon Hounsou in *Blood Diamond,* having never once made a creepy joke about *The Inseparables*—even Spencer believed that her body belonged to him. The issue was not one of forgiveness or sin or his attitude about the practicality of monogamy. The issue was property. This was the obvious truth. She saw it all over him.

"So this sounds to me distinctly like a punishment," she said.

He squirmed. "Is there another, softer word for 'punishment'?"

She sat back. Waiters circled. Bread in the kitchen burned in a toaster.

After they first met, at the party in Tribeca, she'd left without his number and was a block away, walking with friends north on Lafayette Street, when she realized. She turned back, alone, to return to the party, and found, before she even reached the building's stairwell, that he had done the same thing. These were the elemental things, these facts, their finding each other in the building's vestibule, by the elevator banks. This was the story they told at dinner parties. Every family has a creation myth and this was theirs. She had felt, running into him that night, as if it was the beginning of something. She even said it to him. "That sounds ridiculous, probably," she acknowledged, even though she was telling the truth.

She looked around. They were in a half-empty coffee shop in suburban Massachusetts. Did this feel like an ending?

"Yesterday was a disaster," she said. "I want you to know that I think it was a disaster."

"You have to admit," Spencer said, "it's a really good racket. Advising couples about how best to break up. Weakening the marriage. All the while preying on vulnerable women. In an immoral, psychopathic way, he's actually kind of brilliant."

"It's not like you were completely innocent yesterday yourself," she said. "Showing up there with our daughter! What were you thinking?"

"Honestly?"

"Yes, honestly."

"I was on drugs," he said. "So that's my excuse. I was on drugs in front of our kid. I'm basically the greatest father in the history of fatherhood. What's your excuse?"

"What do you want me to say? That I wanted to screw another person?"

"Do I want you to say that to my face? That you wanted to fuck our marriage counselor and eventually you did in fact fuck our marriage counselor? No. I don't think I need to hear that."

Slumping back in her chair, no longer hiding how dejected

this made her feel, Oona saw Spencer's expression change. He leaned forward. He reached out to touch the sleeve on her coat. She could see that his instinct was to help her. This had become his role in their marriage. He came when she called. Any bad experience, and he came running. This, she realized, was exactly why she had called him. Because their marriage had become a habit, a series of faithful patterns. She hadn't called because she wanted to come home, but because she needed him to make her feel better. He checked the time on his watch. She felt a new distance opening. What did she honestly expect him to say that she didn't know already? Yes, casual sex could be fantastically and distressingly weird. Even with a stranger, someone you met in a bar, someone who was not your therapist, it was almost always a bad experience. Yes, you could find yourself on your back on a cold kitchen floor, pulling out a man's chest hair with your fingers. Or hearing about that man's redheaded ex-wife having an epiphany in the Himalayas. It was not like in her mother's book, she knew. Dependency happens. Good sex was not enough. Guilt was inevitable and useless. Occasionally you needed someone to make you feel better. Across the table, Spencer wore a confused expression. Half pity, half anger. An expression that appeared to say, *I don't have anything good to tell you about this. In fact, I need someone to make* me *feel better about it.* She felt unreasonably close to weeping and hated herself for it. He was her person. What were you supposed to do when you lost that?

"This isn't how I thought this would go," she said finally.

"How did you imagine it?"

"Amicable."

"That I'd just welcome you back home?"

She shrugged. "More or less. I mean, that's what you asked for two days ago. And in the letters, right?"

"I thought you didn't read the letters."

She smiled. "I think I read most of them. Or at least half. There were a lot of letters. Like, many, many letters. Thousands of words."

"I had a lot of feelings, I guess," he said.

He laughed and then she laughed, and for a minute they let this moment exist between them, and when it was over there was silence. The coffee left in their cups rippled in the mugs. Her smile lasted longer than his. She felt as if they had just watched a lunar module fall into the sea. A rare occasion tinged with the possibility of impending doom or sadness.

"I won't write anymore," he said.

"You can write if you want," she said.

"I've clearly embarrassed myself."

"You're very good at it, though. It's one of your best skills."

"Or call. I won't call."

"You can call, too," she said.

"I just don't think that this is the part of the process that's amicable," he said.

"Then what part of the process are we in?"

"The part of the process where one of us starts sleeping with other people before the other one does."

She shredded a napkin. "I thought we were about to transition into the part of the process where we get along."

"Fine," he said. "This is the part of the process filled with bitterness and jealousy and maybe one of us standing on a city block with binoculars."

"So, madness, you mean."

"Fine. Madness," he agreed.

"When does the peaceful part of the process happen?"

He sighed. "After both of us find someone new."

"What if we don't find someone new?"

"I didn't finish reading all the divorce books," he said. "I don't know how it ends."

"I don't know either."

Outside, a hydroelectric waterfall sent mist into the air that froze into a slurry on the street. This was the ugly season, they had always called it. In Massachusetts they had football season, the color season, the drinking season, the Christmas season, and finally this. Mud everywhere, stubborn winter, forests of gray. Still, there were ducks. She watched them waddling from the river to the land and back to the river. Wood ducks, their green heads wet and shimmering, a magnificent line of them. This corner of wet earth, with its gentleman's farms, its resplendent waterfowl, its meticulous landscaping, the seat of the American Revolution with café parking lots full of luxury Bavarian engineering—maybe they should have never left New York. She said this to him.

"Don't you think the end would be the same, though?" he asked.

"I don't know."

"Geography doesn't affect fate."

"That sounds like stoner teenage talk," she said.

"Love is a teenage emotion," he said.

"Your pessimism is inspiring."

"All the songs on the radio, the love songs—they're for teenagers. They don't write love songs for actual adults. They would be too depressing."

"Songs about divorce attorneys and couples counseling. That sounds like a lost Merle Haggard record."

"If we had stayed," he said, "we'd just be arguing in a coffee shop in Manhattan."

"Maybe."

"A more expensive coffee shop."

"You were happier there, at least."

"I was twenty years old. My brain hadn't fully formed yet. I was happy and stupid. I didn't know anything about anything."

When they were finished, he walked with her out to her car, over the covered bridge that spanned the river, slick with ice, past the ducks, gulls from the sea overhead, and she remembered how, when they came to Aveline the first time, she had explained to Spencer that love was a chemical reaction, how a surfeit of hormones prompted a bond with another person, something as easy as a light switch flicking on and off. She had learned this in her endocrinology class. She remembered how angry this had made him. Such a cold, clinical explanation for something he considered vast and unknowable and beautiful.

At the end of the bridge she took his hand as they walked, and for a moment before they got to the cars he held on to her and squeezed very hard until her fingers went white, as if he was an injured man about to have a limb cut off without anesthesia, all the while saying nothing, looking out at the river, at the ducks and the ice. A part of her understood. She had felt this way about him when things were better, that she wanted to grab him so tight because she was afraid he would vanish. Before he unlocked his door and drove away, she said to him, "You know the picture of us at the party? The one where we met?"

"Sure," he said.

"Do you still have it?"

He nodded.

"I think I lost mine," she said.

"Oh."

"Maybe when I was packing up."

"Okay."

"I was looking for it," she said, not knowing whether this was something she could say anymore. "And I realized I must have misplaced it."

"I can make you a copy," he said. "If you want."

"Yeah," she said. "Maybe."

She had watched too much television and she expected then

that he would kiss her. A last moment. A parting thing. Fucking snow falling around them. Goddamned stupid waterfall nearby spraying up stupid sentimental mist. She waited for it, even. She would think of this later and cringe and make promises to herself not to expect unreasonable things from the people closest to her. Instead, they lingered in the parking lot in silence, not even really looking at each other, even though this was what she wanted to do. Another foolish impulse. To really look at his face. To remember it better.

"This is the end," she said. It came out wrong, her voice too deep, and Spencer laughed.

"The end of what?" he asked. "Is this the part where you kill me?"

For minutes after he left she stood in the lot, the exhaust of his car dissipating, the water rushing, snow everywhere, all this fucking snow, this admittedly pretty waterfall, and she could not stop looking at her phone, hoping he would call, change his mind, come back, wishing the screen would light up for her.

# 25.

Her mother was out in the snow when Oona pulled into the driveway. Across the meadow, wind shook the stand of elms. Up the hill her mother didn't look up. Instead, she was on her hands and knees with a garden spade and an ice pick, hacking away at the frozen ground.

"What are you doing?" Oona called out.

From the bottom of the hill, the house looked unsteady on its foundation. In the dim light she saw the missing shingles and the rot at the base of the chimney, and there was, she saw for the first time, a new spiderwebbing of broken glass that had formed in one of the attic windows. The word they kept using all this time was that it was "failing," which was another way to say that the house was ready to fall in on itself, one big gust of wind or big snowfall away from something caving and people dying inside. The real estate agents used this word. The lawyers, in their appeals to creditors, used this word. The county surveyors brought in to walk the property line had used this word, had put it in their notes: *The structure is in danger of failing.* To say that it was failing implied something worse, Oona couldn't help but think—that the house had suddenly ceased to do its job successfully, a house being a place to keep a family whole and intact.

"There's blood," her mother said, rising a little when Oona got up the hill. Her mother was out without a jacket, her hair untethered and sopping, mud on the knees of her slacks. She pierced at the ground with the point of the ice pick, trying to dig away at something.

"It can't be blood," Oona said. "It's been raining and snowing for days."

Her mother put down the ice pick and took a flashlight to the slope. "Look," she said. "See?"

Oona crouched.

"Is that not blood?" her mother asked.

"I don't know," Oona said.

"You're a doctor. You know what blood looks like. That's blood."

Oona followed the beam of light across the hill to the edge of the driveway and then back, in a loop, to the front steps of the crumbling porch. A snake of a half dozen droplets. All from Paul's head. Beside her mother, a bucket of soapy warm water gave off steam.

"This isn't what you think it is," Oona said.

Her mother stood. "I saw when I came home. Clear as day. It's blood."

Oona stood, watching her mother scrub.

"Someone fell," Oona said. "That's all that happened."

"I know someone fell," her mother cried. "I was here! I saw it!"

Oona blanched. "Someone else fell. Trust me, it's someone else."

Inside, Oona got the fire going. She put her mother on the couch. Beside the fireplace, in place of the kindling, Oona saw, all the remaining copies of *The Inseparables* were stacked up, one after another, in a line. Her mother wanted to burn them.

"We're almost out of firewood," her mother contended.

"A book burning? Really?"

"Somebody told me once that it might make me feel better," she said. "So I decided to give it another try."

Oona picked up a copy, flipped through the pages, and landed on the diagram of Eugenia Davenport throwing the teapot through the front window of Templeton Grace's car. *Just a woman preparing for afternoon tea,* it read. Sometimes Oona allowed herself to fixate on the version of her mother who had made this, who existed only in pictures, the version her father had fallen for, that first Henrietta Horowitz, who was brilliant and brilliantly energetic, and who her father claimed had occasioned in him an instantaneous political awakening during that first lecture. That woman, for the most part, was a ghost. What remained of her emerged in fractions, and Oona always thrilled to recognize a hint of her mother's old confidence, her incisive academic eye, the old radical's energy and outrage. Who she was now was a product of the shame the book had caused her. Oona looked over at her mother, small on the large couch, wrapped in a blanket, warming herself. The book had sent her behind walls here, on this big farm, with all the acres and the animals, and because of it, she had become too much like an indoor cat whose instincts for a hunt have no purpose in a carpeted living room.

"The blood outside," Oona said. "It's not Daddy's."

Her mother shook her head. Oona had seen this before, at the hospital. The shock of death made even the most rational people senseless. This was why doctors were trained to talk about it with such cold, clinical logic. The brain has stopped and so he is dead. The heart cannot function any longer and he will die tonight. She hated to see her mother like this again, after eleven months.

"I know it's not his blood," her mother said finally. "Most of me knows it's not his, anyway."

"Good," Oona said.

"But whose goddamned blood is it? It's not mine. Is it yours?"

Oona tried to explain everything about Paul as succinctly as possible. She did not want to say that Paul had fallen on the same spot as her father, or that he'd done so because it was icy, just like her dad, or that she'd seen his head bounce off the frozen ground in the same way that her mother must have seen her father's head crack. Instead, Oona just stated the facts. His name is Paul. At first he was our therapist, mine and Spencer's. Then he was only my therapist. Then we stopped therapy because he liked my necklace and my neck. Then we kissed in my office. Then we made a date. Then he came here, he cut himself, I put him in the attic, he escaped, we got drinks, we went to his house, we made out in his elevator, we fucked on his kitchen floor, I ripped out his chest hair, and I felt deep, deep personal shame. And now this is happening: I'm telling you about it.

Her mother took a moment to process this. "Wait a second," she said, smiling.

"We don't need to fixate on the details," said Oona.

"Yes, we certainly do need to fixate on the details," her mother said.

"Please," begged Oona.

"So you're saying this man was your therapist?"

Oona cringed.

"And that he came to this house the other night? When we were all here? When Lydia was here, even. When we were eating Chinese food? And that you hid him in the attic like you did with your old high school boyfriend?"

"You're enjoying this far too much," Oona said.

"And later you slept with this man?" her mother asked.

*"Mom,"* Oona protested. "This is actually worse than the sex."

Her mother appeared unmoved. "And you're saying the sex was bad?"

Oona flipped through a copy of *The Inseparables,* to one of the best diagrams, labeled *Fantasy of the Male Ravishing the Supplicating Female.* The drawing corresponded with the escapade in which Eugenia lures Templeton Grace onto the floor of her solarium. Her mother had drawn the man with wild eyes and wet hair and with fangs and the woman as happily compliant and hungry. A thought bubble rises up above the woman's head: *I'm so hungry for your prick.* This was the picture that her old friends and activists had been most bothered by. Her mother had claimed that everyone needed a better sense of humor. In retrospect, Oona thought it was outrageous that her mother might have assumed people wouldn't be angry with her. Oona held up the picture. "It was like this," she said. "But worse."

"How could it be worse than that?" her mother said, laughing loudly.

"If you really need to know, he had more body hair."

Her mother shrugged.

"And like I said: it was on his kitchen floor."

Her mother shook her head. "Not even the counter?"

"He wanted the floor."

"It wasn't one of those nice floors that are heated underneath, was it?"

"Cold kitchen floor."

"That's a good Freudian case study, right there. Why is it that the kitchen always summons some deep sexual desire in underconfident men?"

"This is not helping me."

"Do you need help?" her mother asked, prompting in Oona an old, somewhat repressed memory of her mother entertaining the idea of doing this for a living: penning a sex advice column.

"At worst," Oona said, "I thought, just jumping into bed with someone new might energize me."

Again, her mother shook her head. "Or onto the kitchen floor."

"At best, I thought, maybe this is someone new. And maybe someone new is something good. And maybe, miraculously, I would enjoy myself."

"Sex on the floor? Where the hell would you get a dumb idea like that?"

Oona tapped the edge of the book.

"I love this: you sleep with your psychologist and it's all your mother's fault! How convenient!"

Her mother was on record as thinking that Oona's quasi-religious adherence to her own talk therapy was a simple matter of being addicted to her own voice. Oona was not sure she was wrong. In the New York of her mother's youth, such things were not done. One simply worried with dignity. You lived down the hall from your aunt and your grandmother, and you listened to their stories about mass slaughter and poverty, and then you were alone with your problems. Making such a big deal out of your anxieties, her mother contended, was the most egregious of first-world luxuries. Like hiring a man to shower you. These complaints had not changed much over the last few months. Therapy exacerbated narcissism, or reinforced some upper-middle-class victim syndrome. After all, they weren't talking about Jacques Lacan. Oona wasn't involved in some deep intellectual reconfiguration of her psyche. Modern day, suburban psychotherapy was glorified adult day care. Twice a week for the past six months, Oona had heard her mother's line about hiring a man to shower you. They agreed to disagree, but it was not for nothing that Oona had not told her mother about Paul. How did one ever explain such a thing, anyway? It might have been easier for Oona to have said, *Remember the story I told you about the man whose knees I operated on last week? The man who was hit by the bus? Yes, well, when he woke up from the anesthesia we became lovers.*

"What did Spencer say about all of this?"

"Oh," Oona said, "he was super excited for me. It was a happy family moment for both of us."

Her mother looked genuinely concerned.

"I just came from asking him to take me back," Oona said.

Her mother cringed. "You did nothing of the sort, I hope."

"I thought it was the smart thing to do."

"How is that possible?"

"Fucking my therapist on his kitchen floor also seemed intelligent."

Her mother smiled. "Look, I'm not going to make you feel guilty about it," she said. "Any of it."

"What if I'm already feeling guilty?"

"I think I can dig out my lecture notes on the nexus between sex and social shame, if you want." She turned to a big wall of boxes. "It was fairly boring and obvious even in 1974. But there's probably something worthwhile in it."

"Please no," Oona said.

"I'll give you the same advice I gave your daughter about her nude picture. Which is that shame is a choice."

"She said you two talked."

"Briefly. It's always brief with me and Lydia."

"What else did you tell her?"

"I didn't tell her much," her mother said. "Mind you, I wanted to. There are things to tell a girl like that. Lots of things. But I didn't want to step on any toes."

"What did she tell you?" Oona asked. It occurred to her that perhaps Lydia might have confided in her grandmother, really confided, and this possibility stung Oona.

"She didn't have to tell me anything," her mother said. "It's fine, honey. Really. She's going to be fine. Everyone's going to be fine."

Oona was not sure she believed this. Optimism felt impossible. Had her mother still been writing or teaching, she would have likely agreed. This house, all this space, the privacy—all of it had caused her to lose touch. The world was happening far away from here. Oona imagined the fiery lecture she might have given had she been more engaged. The Internet: Radicalizing the Future Misogynists of America. Or: Stay the Fuck Away from My Granddaughter. Her mother, however, let out an exhausted breath.

"Come sit next to me," she said, and when Oona did, her mother let her head fall slightly onto Oona's shoulder. "There," her mother said. "This is so much better."

For a moment they were silent. The fire warmed the room. Overhead the ceiling sagged. Oona put her hand in her mother's hair, which was still wet from the snow. This was the best part of living here again. Being able to do this, to sit quietly with her mother. Outside, lights went by on the main road. Everything was packed already. The room was nothing but boxes. When she moved in here, Oona had imagined herself as a bulwark against her mother's grief. As if she were strong enough on her own.

She held on to her mother.

When the fire went out, Oona got up and went into the back room and looked for some actual firewood to burn in the fireplace. This was where she found the small folded piece of paper, wedged into the back of the cabinet. She knew the handwriting. *To you*, it read, *from me*. She looked in at her mother, on the sofa, wrapped in her father's old big sweater. Her mother had been finding these notes for the better part of the last two years, but Oona knew that her mother had not found one since her dad died. Oona had found her mother countless times opening drawers and emptying out cabinets, looking and looking. She hesitated, the paper in hand. Everything, everywhere, was packed.

Then, quietly, she took her father's suitcase and opened it just enough to slide the note inside.

# 26.

They went out that afternoon while the stores were still open. Oona drove. They went west at first, out of the suburbs and into the countryside, passing cow fields and Walden and then the high razored walls of the state prison. The sun set white and gray over the elms. In the first two stores they found nothing, which pleased Henrietta, and which allowed her—temporarily, at least—to believe that you could in fact live with a man and know that man and know in fact that man's secrets and the things that shamed him so that when he died, perhaps in your arms, perhaps with his blood on your flagstone walkway and your blue jeans, you did not find, as she did, in a third store, his overcoat hanging in a closet full of overcoats that had belonged to other men.

Objects, she used to teach, were inherently without value until a culture assigned that value. This was usually during a lesson about the female body as object, given typically to a group of college boys hostile to the idea, or in trouble for some sexual violation, all of them sitting sullenly in a lecture hall with their legs spread apart in subconscious defiance. She had a chart registering the price of an ounce of gold, the price of an ounce of marijuana, and the price of a woman on West 42nd Street.

While Oona watched, Henrietta enacted a new, silent debate: the brain says, this is a coat, it's worthless, fuck it. Everything else says, buy this coat, or steal it, or wreck it here, right on the rack, so no one else can wear it.

Back in the car, they went east toward the city, into the towns where Harold had felt comfortable. All of these small villages near Aveline had stores that sold antiques and collectibles and proffered their meager hauls from less-than-impressive estate sales. Henrietta and Oona went to each of them.

In the fourth and fifth stores, they found nothing.

In the sixth, Henrietta found a copy of her own book for sale, autographed to a woman named Cindy. *Be proud!* Henrietta had written, the handwriting bubbly. *Be bold!*

In the seventh store, they found leather belts and silver candlesticks and old kitchen knives. Were these his? Henrietta wasn't sure. Oona was. Henrietta held them in her hand. There were fingernail marks on the handle of the butcher blade. She put her fingernails into the grooves.

They went north along the shore. The weather warmed. Oona put down a window. Ocean salt and frozen ryegrass and clams frying in the grease huts. In Marblehead they waited at a red light, the languid sea tide lapping at the storm wall.

"I gave you my credit card," Oona said somewhere north of there. "In case you needed things."

"I saw," Henrietta said.

"You can use it," she said.

Henrietta nodded.

"Let me rephrase that," Oona said. "Use it. Please. Use it."

In Salem the witches were out taking pictures with the tourists.

In Ipswich they passed a waterway called Labor in Vain Creek.

In the eighth store, they found a watch. His thirty-seventh birthday gift.

Back into the city. Easter decorations, hung prematurely, swung frozen in the tide wind.

In Dedham she found, once more, her book for sale. *Dear Judy, Thank you for reading.*

In Dorchester she stood outside, in tears.

At the twenty-first store, she went next door to a liquor store for wine and drank it on the sidewalk.

Finally, at the last store, a pawnshop in Mission Hill, they found tennis trophies, stand mixers, electric guitars, two cameras, a film projector, a silver necklace (birthday thirty-nine), a gold money clip inscribed by her to him (birthday forty-two), and also, importantly, a record of Harold's signing over these items. Because Henrietta had gone to wait outside, Oona needed to walk out onto the sidewalk to show her the piece of paper bearing Harold's handwriting.

*Look*, she said. *Look.*

# Part III

# 27.

Lydia took the trolley back from Boston and walked the short route from downtown Crestview past the cemetery and the First Baptist Church and the flower nursery and the manmade lake with its buoyant and chlorinated fountain. Later in her life she would struggle to remember the way her town had felt to her this day, with its barren and treeless cul-de-sacs and its caravan of parked snow-slick SUVs and its chorus of snowblowers in place of wildlife or birds or children or joy. Her father was in the kitchen when she came home, the whole place heavy with meat smoke and bacon grease and messy with flour. All of this indicated to Lydia some low-level crisis happening with her dad, probably about her mother, probably about Dr. Paul, probably about the impending quiet doom of a divorced middle age. When he saw her he knew something was wrong. Maybe this was fatherly intuition. A genetic ability to sense distress. Or more probably this was because she looked so awful. On the train home she had watched the shape and condition of her reflection change in the mirror black of the trolley windows. In the city, on the bridge in Cambridge over the Charles, near Coolidge Corner, with the train full of college boys reading Kant, at Boston College, with two priests in front of her, she had fought to look composed, to feign an expression that read, *Yes, there are pictures of my naked fifteen-year-old body available for download in every corner of the earth that has an Internet connection,* but she did not wear this well. Anybody could download her. How did anyone ever wear this well?

She did not have a phone now and so she needed to take her father's. She swiped at the screen and found the site and then found the section of the site that advertised teenage girls, and then she found the section of the site with teenage girls where her picture was currently the advertised picture, beside a caption that she guessed was supposed to be alluring: *Dumb Teen Sluts.* She adjusted the screen so that it was just her face showing, not her body, her chest, stomach, legs, crotch, knees, toes. "This is me," she said, giving the phone to him. Her goddamned eyes in that picture.

He did not know what to do. She saw the thoughts happening. Tears welled. He turned away. He put reading glasses on. He squinted. He looked straight at her. He grabbed her and squeezed her and whispered in her ear, *I will beat the blood out of this kid's skull.*

This was not helpful. Charlie Perlmutter having the blood taken out of him, slaughtered like a kosher cow, did not eliminate the fact that in Ulaanbaatar, in Seoul, in Sydney, in Caracas, men in the open fields, in subway cars, on yachts, in football stadiums could and would look at her and masturbate.

For a while he made calls. She watched him pace. He went out on the deck. He didn't want her to hear. She could see him yelling but could not hear exactly what. He rolled up his sleeves. The hair on his arms was the thickest hair she'd ever seen on any arm. Something about this had always made her think that he was well suited to the job of being a dad, a superabundance of androgen being in some way directly proportional to his ability to parent, when instead he was just a guy, a failed lawyer in a cheaply built house in a blankly named American town, a guy with a daughter.

He made more calls. He paced more. He came inside and burst out sweating. He went back out into the cold, onto the deck, and did more calling and pacing and sweating.

When he came back inside, she allowed herself a moment of relief and optimism.

"I called the cops," he said.

"Good," she said, nodding. "Good." She took a breath. She held out her hand for her father's phone and began constantly refreshing the page. "So it must be down," she said. Then: "Is it down?" She refreshed. "It's not down." She turned to him. "It's not fucking down."

"No," he said. "Not yet."

A new surge of panic hit her. Everywhere her phone had gone, it was possible that Charlie had gone also. *Assume that someone's watching you all the time,* Charlie had told her. The reality of what exactly this meant hit her: her showering, her shitting, her idiotic dancing around in her room to illegally downloaded Nicki Minaj, drunk on Goldschläger and possibly high on caffeine pills. It was not just the pictures he had taken— her crotch, her chest, the fringe of her pubic hair beneath her skirt—but everything else. All of it. Her whole last six months.

"Can't we find someone who actually, really, genuinely knows what to do?"

Her father reached over and took the phone from her. "First, stop looking at this thing. That's step one."

Talking was difficult when you were hyperventilating. He put a hand on the back of her neck, soothing, calm.

"Second thing: breathe." She turned to him, dizzy, queasy, bloodless, mid–panic attack.

"What if there's more pictures?" she asked. "Why can't they shut it down? Let's call better cops. Surely there are better cops."

It was not as easy as it sounded to just flip a switch on the whole global architecture of the Internet, just for one picture, one body, one fifteen-year-old girl. His saying it this way, slowly, pedantically, explaining every tiny detail, did not help. Nor did it help when he told her that he had called around to friends of his at the old law firm, experts in cybersecurity, in domestic cyberassault, who told him that on quick glance the site that hosted her picture was located on a Southwestern Pacific island with no real government or law. This was where people went, evidently, to host their dark web, black-market narcotics superstores, or their specious digital currency exchanges, or their wholesale Hollywood bootlegging businesses. Hearing this, she felt hopeless.

Also, he told her, they simply couldn't prove definitively that Charlie had been the one to upload it. She made him repeat this. "There is no real proof," he said. She did not like this part of her father's personality. The trained equanimity of lawyers enraged her.

"What do you mean you can't prove it?" she asked. "Who else would upload this picture?"

They were at the kitchen table. The Singh family stood outside wearing matching lilac snowsuits.

"The picture went around the whole school," he said, simply, annoyingly. "Anybody could have done it."

"He did it."

"I believe you that he did it. But the police need actual evidence. Proof. Something that has his fingerprints on it. A chain of custody."

"I understand that fact. But he's the one. I have the messages from him," she said, realizing as she did that the phone was broken and the messages vanished.

What her father wanted to do, he told her, was go talk to Charlie Perlmutter's dad, man to man, father to father. If Charlie had really done it, and if the police were going to take their time *looking into it,* this was the best way to get the pictures gone. "I can get him to get Charlie to take it down," her dad said. "I know I can do that." Watching him as he said this, stubble on his chin, cheeks pink with anger, Lydia figured this to be some basic macho bullshit. A man needing to fight another man about a woman's body—which it may have been. Or some vestigial primal violence that needed occasionally to rise up and find an outlet. But then she saw his hand shaking as he put the phone down on the table. Skin was missing from the nail bed of his thumb. Blood had dried. He turned to her. "I'm going to fix this," he said.

For hours they drove in silence out from Crestview through the country, along the Aveline Trail, the fast river, the gray rocks, the slow river, the big white sky.

The snow line stopped in Connecticut along the Merritt, where the earth was dry and brown and the sky through the thicket of alders in the rich towns and the railway towns and the seaside towns was clear and cloudless.

Eventually they crossed over the George Washington Bridge. She turned to see Manhattan along the river, the whole ridged spine of the city.

Night loomed. The city lit up.

Over Hackensack, a child's toy of the moon hung. Bridges were suspended, car-cluttered, across soot-wrecked marsh. The sky was full with clouds. There were clouds at the window side, polluted clouds, striated and hot with light, shelf upon shelf and drifting.

Getting closer, they drove through a series of towns that could have been Crestview, full of red brick-laid sidewalks, handsome at dusk, cute and stately with Tudor storefronts. A standing clock in one of the town squares threw gold light into traffic. Municipal employees in reflective vests emptied parking meters in front of the antique shops. The layout of the American suburb was a uniform thing, multiplied across the country, like bacteria, one after the other, between rivers, amidst superhighways, obliterating landscapes, impervious to state borders. That this was not a new thought to anyone but her did not lessen the shock of realizing the eerie sameness of this town and her town. She sensed birds overhead. She closed her eyes. They had driven for hours and gone nowhere.

The whole way, he kept asking her, *Are you okay?*, and she had the same answer, which was, *I'm definitely not fucking okay.* Her father managed to look composed and confident, and this was enough that when they got to the Perlmutters' town, she said nothing, and as they got to Charlie's street, she still said nothing, and as they went past the houses close to his, and her father sat up, she finally felt as though maybe he knew what he was doing.

The Perlmutters' neighborhood eclipsed anything Lydia knew from home. Nine-foot privet; hand-laid Belgian block; serious, probably dynastic wealth. When they got to the house, she was not surprised to find that it was the largest on the street, nicer, bigger, less gaudy, less tacky, less spooky than she'd expected. It was white and stone and sprawling, the hedgerows out front better than the neighbors'. Twin ornamental lions bookmarked the end of the driveway. She had heard stories about Charlie's parents, about how each of them was a tycoon, his mother the CFO of a biotech company that manufactured experimental vaccines for pandemic-worthy pathogenic viruses, and his father a television executive, neither of them, by Charlie's own description, around very much. He told her this once, during the brief moment in which she thought he was charming. "My dad," he said. "He treats me like one of his underperforming stocks. Instead of selling, he just dumps me here, at this place." He sounded sincere and vulnerable and real. But then again he was trying to fuck her.

They stopped out front. In a small window above one of the many garage doors, a ceramic cat statue looked out onto the street.

"I'm not ready," she said.

"That's fine," he said.

"I'm not talking to him," Lydia said. "Or seeing him."

"He won't be there," her father said.

"How do you know?"

"I know because I called them."

This had not occurred to her. "You called his parents?"

"I called everyone," he said. "Every single person I could think of. Everybody."

They were out in the street. She had the paralytic sensation of her body moving independent of her brain. Neighborhood kids in thick winter jackets rode by on sleek bicycles. Juncos and waxwings perched on a cypress. She knew their names from her class.

Two people moved in the window of the house.

At the front gate, she stopped. "And what if he's there?"

"I made them promise he wouldn't be here," he said. "Especially if you were coming."

"But what if he is?"

Her dad put his hand on her shoulder. "If he's there, I'll beat him to death with my own fists," he said.

She did not know whether he was joking. The gates opened.

# 28.

At night sometimes, sleepless, dwarfed by Harold's absence, Henrietta tried to chart the progress of her grief. I'm no longer certain that his ghost is beside me in bed, she sometimes thought. Or, I no longer have nightmares about being buried alive. Or of caskets. Or of the Kaddish being chanted above my body. Or, I don't find myself lingering so much on the very last moments: light on his forehead in his hospital room, or the cracked-glass smack of his head on the flagstone. Lately, she was stuck on the brief moment before, when he was in the kitchen, and she was, too, and he was putting on his boots, that brief moment in which she could have said, No, stay, don't, wait until it's warmer, there's ice, be here.

Oona had asked. It was morning. The questions were always innocent and yet impossible to answer. *How are you?* They were in Oona's car, parked outside Witherspoon's. Icicles hung like fangs from the wrought iron joints holding up the shop's awning. Up on the avenue the trolley tracks were slick with ice. This morning the store had called to say that someone had come in offering to sell what she was looking for. The vagueness had not deterred her from coming right away. The shop was closed. They had come early.

"What do you think happened?" Oona asked.

They had not spoken on the ride home the night before. Oona had wanted to buy back everything, every item.

"Money makes people foolish," Henrietta said. "That's what happened."

Oona shook her head. "You did the bills, though. Wouldn't you know if Daddy owed people all this money?"

"You'd think I would, wouldn't you?" Henrietta was tired. None of this made sense. All of her husband's things, scattered. This new sudden deficit of trust and money. The whole narrative of her marriage felt skewed now. Apparently you could live with a man and sleep beside that man and still have no idea about that man's desperation.

She had dreamed last night that everywhere she walked she saw more of Harold's stuff—his clothes, his boots, knives from his chef's kit. She had followed the bread crumb trail by foot all the way to New York, two hundred miles south, to her mother's apartment door. She had knocked and knocked, calling out for her mother, dead for ten years, knocking and knocking, louder and louder, *Mom! Mom!*, until Henrietta finally woke up with her hands wringing. How good of her mother to stop in at a time like this.

"He was impossible at the end," Henrietta said. "The restaurant failing was so public. An empty dining room? A night's worth of meat? Even his friends wouldn't come. People were writing the worst things on the Internet. I told him not to look. But he looked. How can you help but look? His confidence vanished. It made him angry. I see now that it also made him stupid." Henrietta reached to turn on the car's heat. "He could have borrowed money from anybody, really. Any odd person he knew growing up here. Any Boston scumbag charging exorbitant interest rates in exchange for cash and free dinner. I did all the bills. I paid for everything. I always said that he couldn't have what he wanted. I was the bad cop. That's what I'm figuring out."

"I don't want to believe that. I think that's crap."

"It's the truth."

She had already spent the night trying to find out what it was exactly that he'd borrowed for. Another month of rent, right under her nose? A crate of fresh Maine lobster. Heritage turkeys that they had smoked together out behind the house and which were delicious and left her smelling like meat for days and which, also, no one, not one person, bothered to order. She had dug out from the garage the box containing the Feast's accounting records. She spread them across the kitchen table. She'd never been able to find any good answers, though, in a page of numbers.

"Are you mad at him?" Oona asked. Old snow blew off the shop's awning and onto the street.

Henrietta thought about it.

When their money troubles first became glaringly apparent, she figured she would try to write another book. By then she knew she would need cash. She kept phrases in a notebook. *The new quiet. The infinite quiet. The miserable quiet.* She strained to hear ghosts in the woodwork. She bought books on astrology and Kübler-Ross and the possibility of reincarnation. It had gone on like this for months.

"He's dead," Henrietta said. "If I'm mad at him for anything, it's for dying."

She saw out the window an intrepid cross-country skier cutting across Commonwealth Avenue and cresting the small berm to the frozen reservoir. He wore white superhero spandex. She watched as the man stopped at a traffic light. The car windows were closed and so she couldn't hear what he was yelling, only that he was doing so, his hands cupped to his mouth. He waved toward someone, and then, after a minute, another skier in a white suit came around the block, clearly exhausted. For the longest time she'd been noticing things like this. The mated species: swans, geese, skiers in spandex. One mate leading, the other failing. Considering the relative uselessness of astrology and Kübler-Ross and the possibility of reincarnation, she reasoned that there might need to be an entirely new set of stages of grief. The mate stage: seeing pairs of everything. The ghost stage: feeling the severed limb.

The skiers glided out across the ice.

"Twits," Oona said. "They're going to fall in."

"Oh, I would love to do that," Henrietta said, surprising herself.

"Fall through the ice?"

"Look at them," she said, watching their easy rhythm, the pushing wind. "Just being in the elements like that. It looks nice."

"It looks life-threatening."

Henrietta shook her head.

"I have a fear." Oona pointed. "The ice. You go down. It freezes up over you."

"Not here," she said. "When Harold first moved me here, he tried to keep me entertained because he thought I was so bored, and he brought me to these hockey games in town. As if that's what I wanted to do. Watch the police versus the fire department. Everyone would come, the whole town. And they'd park all the cars wherever they could fit on the ice. They'd even park the fire engine out on the ice."

"Ice isn't what it used to be," said Oona. "Think about it. Today it's snowing, and it's freezing. Three days from now, it'll be sixty."

Henrietta sighed. "Global warming is so boring."

Oona produced her phone, displaying the week's weather to come: a string of icons representing a sunny day or a windy day or a snow squall. It was weather the way a five-year-old thought of weather.

"See? Three days out, sixty."

Henrietta pointed to the lake. "I used to have this idea that we would get skis and you and I would go across Aveline from one corner to the other."

"When was this?"

"When you were young."

"Did you ever ask me?"

"All the time."

"I don't remember."

"You were small. And you said no to everything I ever asked you. Museums. Concerts. Sports. Everything. As soon as you could speak, you were disagreeing with me."

"Well, individuation is healthy," said Oona.

Across the street, the store clerk from Witherspoon's made a slow, lumbering effort down the block.

Oona pointed. "Is that him?"

Henrietta leaned forward. "That's the one."

On the phone that morning, the man had sounded delighted to be able to help. "So you have this?" she'd asked him, almost breathless. "I'm holding it," he told her. "Could you describe it for me, please?" "There's a woman," he said. "And a flag."

The lights in the shop flickered on. The security grate went up. Sunlight on the knockoff Cézanne.

"Does he think he's just going to sell this thing back to you?" Oona asked.

"Perhaps," said Henrietta.

"Even though it's stolen?"

"He doesn't know it's stolen."

"And you're going to buy it?"

"I'm completely broke. So, no. That's obviously not an option. I can't buy anything."

"So *I'm* going to buy it?"

They'd been through this already. Oona wanted police here. Someone had stolen this, they couldn't forget. Perhaps, having been married to a lawyer all this time, Oona was more predisposed to focus on what was legal and illegal, rather than leading with what Henrietta thought was important: do you have this thing I need or do you not?

"I don't even know if it's the right one. Why don't we just see?"

"I'm not buying stolen property," Oona said. "I'm not getting arrested."

Henrietta turned, smiling. "You're panicking. Let's cross that bridge when we come to it."

Oona laughed. "Listen to you! A lifetime of anxiety and Jewish worrying and psychic angst and now—*now!*—you're talking about crossing bridges and patience!"

Henrietta got out of the car. She had become less bothered with the winter as she aged, even as there was less of her, year by year. The thin air invigorated her. A big dry breath of courage. She went across the street with purpose. In another life—the life in which she did not hunt down possibly stolen artifacts— this would have been an impossibility. Oona was right. Surprisingly, though, Henrietta was not worried. Grief vanishes and then you are still here, breathing. She had learned this.

Out on the ice, the skiers were circling and laughing. The city from here flickered on the horizon, gray and large. Evergreens dotted northward.

"I want to come in with you," Oona called out.

This new protective urge of Oona's made Henrietta happy, but she tried not to show it. This, probably, was not healthy, or what other families did, this suppression of joy. Such a simple thing—your daughter doing this.

"Why do you want to come in?" she asked.

"To shadow you. Guard you."

"That's not necessary, Oona."

"Tell him I'm your bodyguard," Oona said. She yelled, "Tell him I'm watching your back."

Henrietta put up her hand.

# 29.

The first floor of the Perlmutters' house was spare and white and titanically, oceanically large. Lydia resisted the urge to be impressed. A man in a suit who may have been the family's butler asked them to remove their shoes. A faint whiff of chlorine hinted at an indoor pool somewhere. Maids or assistants scurried. The moment Lydia saw his parents, saw the hard, exhausted, pissed expressions on their faces, she knew this was a waste of time. How could it ever have been any different? They were dressed for business—his father in a gray suit, his mother in a black suit. Each clutched a telephone. The urgent noise of their heels on the tile in the hallway as they led her and her father into a sitting room indicated that they, too, considered this a waste.

For a moment, as she sat there, she was certain that they had already seen the pictures of her online. This feeling, she knew, would follow her for years, this initial sudden prick of distrust. A man's eyes on her in a certain way. A scolding narrowness in the expression of a bank clerk, an airline steward, a university professor. At job interviews later in life, she would worry over whether her secret was visible on her. *Olyphant humiliation,* she thought, an inherited disposition, easily accessible by way of any computer. She fought the urge to cover up. She would not wear a V-neck in public until she was fifty years old.

A buzz began somewhere in the room—a heating vent, a vacuum, a secret recorder.

They exchanged mindless pleasantries.

Yes, the weather. Yes, traffic. Yes, the Internet, it seemed, was a repository for bile and danger.

Lydia kept her coat zipped up to her neck. The room was brown with cowhide and hung mounted moose and decanted brandy.

His father's name was also Charlie, which meant that every infraction of the son reflected doubly on the father, and that when, in the future, Charlie's name found its way, as it would, into the crime blotter, his father would suffer twice. He turned to her. His eyes were closely set and his hair was inexpertly dyed. Even rich men felt shame about getting old.

"Lydia, would you mind if I spoke to your father outside for a minute or two?" he asked.

She looked at her father. He had warned her about this on the sidewalk before going in, the probability of their being separated by gender. Something about the gate out front or the neighborhood or perhaps the stern expressions on the stone lions had given him a hunch. For the first time she hoped the rumor of his courthouse acumen was real and not a myth.

She looked at Charlie's dad. "If that's what you feel you need to do," she said.

"We'll work this out, you and me," Charlie's father said to her father.

Charlie's mother's name was Evelyn. She wore a thin necklace with a letter *E* hanging and embossed with a blizzard of tiny diamonds. She was a small woman, which did not surprise Lydia, given Charlie's frame. She had some of his compacted energy, his wrists, his mouth when it was nervous. "We can talk. You and me. Woman to woman."

Lydia watched her father go. He turned as he left, looking back at her apologetically, mouthing, *Don't worry. I got this.*

The house smelled the way Charlie smelled. She had gotten close enough to him, to his skin, to know this. In the moment it had been thrilling. Her hand on the actual chest of a real human boy. Conversely, the hand of a real human boy on her actual chest. Thinking about Charlie this way, she wondered sometimes whether she'd had her first sexual experiences with Pinocchio. Even still, her heart had been going crazy and she had wondered whether he would notice, and then, to her credit, she realized that he wouldn't notice or care to notice anything except what her skin felt like to him.

Alone with his mother, she fell silent.

She searched the room for pictures, photographs of the family, evidence of a decent home life. Charlie's ever having been a child seemed impossible.

"Would you like me to put on the fire?" Evelyn asked.

"That's not necessary," Lydia said.

"I would like the fire," Evelyn said, picking up a remote control and pointing it at the fireplace. A false-looking and small fire appeared on command.

Lydia pretended to be enraptured by the flames.

"In the winter it gets cold and a good fire is nourishing for the body," Evelyn informed her.

Lydia had her father's phone between her palms. She could feel her sweat gathering on the glass. She had bought into her dad's risible notion that she would show the Perlmutters what their son had done and they would care and they would then make a phone call to Charlie, who would quickly wipe it from the Internet. She felt wildly embarrassed at having ever thought this might happen.

A painting over the mantel showed a woman cresting a ridge in the midst of hunting a black bear with a rifle. Evelyn saw Lydia looking and cleared her throat. "I find it an inspiring picture," she said.

Lydia nodded because, really, what else were you supposed to do in a situation like this?

"It's a metaphor, you see."

"Right," said Lydia.

"It's a tough world out there, basically, is what it says."

"Yes it is."

"Sometimes a lady just needs to kill the bear, also, is what it's saying."

In the other room she could hear her father's voice, low and insistent.

Charlie had told her stories about being a child in this place. Maids tucking him in at night. Late-night parties at which he wandered down in his pajamas after nightmares to find stereos blaring and stoned television executives and pharma-millionaires devouring shrimp cocktail. Personal assistants one year out of Princeton and hoping for professional connections, he told Lydia, drove him to playdates, cooked his meals. My parents, he had said, see me as an employee of theirs. And not even an especially important one.

Very quickly the fire made the room unbearably hot.

Evelyn leaned forward. "You should know something, Lydia."

Stupidly, Lydia answered. "What is that?"

"That I don't believe you," Evelyn said.

Lydia heard yelling in the other room.

"What don't you believe?" she asked.

"Any of it." Evelyn shrugged.

Lydia felt an upwelling in her chest.

Evelyn sat back. She shrugged again. "Charlie's a good boy."

Looking at the painting, Lydia saw another bear lingering in the brush, behind the woman, camouflaged, rendered in shadow, ready to pounce. Had Evelyn never noticed this before?

Her father's voice grew louder in the other room. Evelyn leaned forward and, with the remote control, extinguished the fire. A small gray snake of gas smoke lingered.

For a long moment they sat together like this, in the dark room, with the dead moose on the wall, with the remote-powered fireplace, and with this weird bear painting that Evelyn had misinterpreted as a metaphor for female empowerment and that was really just a picture of one bear getting ready to pounce on this woman in order to save another bear. Cars went past on the road. Headlights momentarily brightened the room. Evelyn adjusted the bracelets on her arm.

Finally she turned to Lydia. "You want my advice, dear?"

Lydia shook her head. "Not particularly."

Evelyn leaned forward to whisper. "Keep your clothes on. It will save you a lot of trouble. It's a fairly simple concept to understand."

Lydia stood and went across the room and sat right beside Evelyn, who looked momentarily startled about what Lydia might do. Lydia turned on the phone. He had made the videos into loops—twenty seconds, on a string, over and over, always playing, one moment made infinite, so that anyone, at any future moment, could drop in on this stolen instant to see, as she showed his mother, how it looked when she lay on Charlie's bed that night, rain on the window screen, her cardigan on his quilt, R. Kelly playing, how it looked as she talked to him, saying embarrassing things about certain people at the school who had otherwise been her friends, the whole of it conforming to some idea that Charlie had that she, as a woman, was petty and duplicitous and incapable of stable noncombative relationships. Slowly, he zoomed in on her crotch. Her underwear showed.

The camera held. If you were to listen to this with headphones, you could make out Charlie's rapid breathing. He kept zooming. Going and going.

Eventually the video tripped and the loop began again. Lydia watched his mother's face. A flickering at the corner of her eyes. Something tightened in her.

"You know," said Lydia, "I totally did this myself. You're so right. I forgot. Charlie's such a good boy."

Evelyn got up then, grimacing, and rushed out of the room, leaving Lydia alone. She stayed here for the next few minutes, thinking that her father would come. Eventually she heard a commotion in the hallway and got up, expecting to find the two men fighting—her father, his father, blood on the expensive tile. Instead, she found her father alone in the big foyer, chlorine hovering. The lights were off. He was looking out onto the gargantuan expanse of the Perlmutters' first floor. He had his back to her.

"Not successful?" she asked.

He said nothing.

She asked him a second time.

Still nothing.

"Daddy?"

Then she realized he was crying.

# 30.

Inside Witherspoon's the heat was off. Henrietta could see her breath leaving her in white, individual storm clouds. A bell had chimed as the door opened, but no one was at the front counter. For a moment she lingered. The shop cat emerged, stalking something. Dust hovered. On the phone he'd given his name as Turner, and she was not sure whether this was a first or a last name. At the counter, she saw Harold's pens for sale, in the same velvet clamshell case she'd picked out for him. Outside, Oona stood at the window with her arms crossed imperiously against her chest. There were moments when Henrietta saw her husband in Oona—moments like this: the stubborn, protective, pugilistic instinct. Maybe something in the chin. Or the cowlick in the right eyebrow. When this happened, Henrietta felt a surge of recognition, then a thrill, then the disappointing crush of her brain putting it all in place, organizing the thought into grief. The experience of missing someone involved a constant negotiation with greed. She wanted all of Harold back, walking the earth, his warm body, his heart going. Not this tiny fraction. The logical, smart, thankful woman in her said, here is a flickering image of the person you miss inside a person you love. Be grateful.

She heard his footsteps before she saw him. Turner came lumbering into the room dressed in black—sweater, trousers, loafers. His hair was slick. The cat followed behind him, thinking maybe he had food. "It's you!" Turner said cheerfully, a stubby arm raised up in salute.

"It's me," she said, trying to match the mood.

"How funny," he said. "Not even a few hours after you were gone, a man came in with exactly what you'd described. Right down to a T."

"You said on the phone."

He stood at the counter. She waited. She did not know how this was going to go.

"I got a good deal on it," he assured her.

She braced herself. She had seen the prices these things fetched. Outrageous sums that reminded her that people put value in the strangest stuff. Lately, everywhere she went she saw these foolish spinning things, on homes and schools. At James Hook and Co., on the channel in South Boston, a gilded, gorgeous lobster capped the roof. On the library in Aveline, a grasshopper, gleaming.

Turner put a canvas bag on the counter.

"Is that it?" she asked.

"The weathervane? No." He pulled the zipper on the bag. "Before we get down to business, I have something I'd like you to sign, if that's not too much trouble."

He arranged two books on the counter. That old shade of pink. Instinctively she turned to Oona, outside, who stood on her toes, peering. She had her hands up in disbelief.

"You found me out, I guess," Henrietta said.

"I said you looked familiar!" Turner said, laughing. "Didn't I?"

"You did."

"Although I can't claim to have remembered on my own." He brought out the small card onto which she'd written her name and number. "It certainly helped that you left your name with me to Google."

He put a pen on the counter.

The books on the counter were not the American version but the French. *Les Inséparables.* The cover was the most explicit of the foreign editions published, featuring only a nude woman staring at the camera with a look Henrietta had always taken for severe confusion. As in, why is my picture being taken? Why am I nude? She had detested this choice. She'd written letters in her pidgin French to her editor, claiming that the photograph exacerbated already sticky notions that female sexuality was brainless and supplicating and dumb. The French had loved the diagrams. *Les diagrammes sont incroyables!* The French loved anything that reaffirmed their belief that America was sexually regressive and mindlessly puritanical, and they especially loved that her book had outraged so many people.

She picked up the copy and looked closely at the picture. The model was a girl. A teenager, probably eighteen. Or, knowing the French, sixteen and coaxed into it. Why wouldn't the model look confused? The picture was supposed to be alluring, she knew. A young body. New skin. A darkly lit room. White curtains. A bed in the background, the sheets unmade, as if to invite you, the reader, to come and fuck this girl on this bed. Henrietta thought of Lydia and Lydia's academy full of supposed geniuses, none of them above ogling her picture, fetishizing her, and she thought that here, in this science-fiction century, nothing much had changed. A rite of passage disguised as a harmless prurience or, worse, beauty. The culture kept clamoring for the nipple.

"Do you sell books, too?" she asked.

He shook his head. "This is my mother's," he said. "She lives with me. Across the road a bit." He pointed. "She came from

France after the war. I remember that when I was younger, she loved this book."

"Oh did she," Henrietta said with a wide smile.

"She just thought it was the funniest thing. Every Christmas she reread it."

"That's a terrible tradition," Henrietta said.

"And we would always know. We could hear her laughter downstairs. She loved the hot-air balloon especially."

Henrietta flipped through the pages. Her own mother had never acted scandalized by her book, or ashamed of her. It was important to remember this. A tough woman, born in Odessa, carried to America in the arms of her own mother amid the sewage stink of steerage class, only to steam nurses' uniforms ten hours a day in a factory on West 38th Street as hot as a steel foundry, and her reaction was more pointed. "All the *shtupping* and all the allusions to male genitalia is one thing, hon," she'd said not long after the book was published and Henrietta was a wreck. "It's just not a very good book, is all." She was a tiny woman. Everyone was tiny then. A lack of food, of good nutrition, of sunlight. Her lack of height did nothing to reduce her fury, however, or her sense of righteousness, or her confidence. "Forget this happened," her mother told her, talking about her book. "Do something else with your life."

"Have you read this?" Henrietta asked Turner.

"This?" He grew instantly twitchy.

"So, yes. I know that look. That's usually the sign that someone has read it."

"I loved the hot-air balloon!"

"Everyone always did," she said.

"Because it's sexy *and* dangerous!"

"People say that to me, but I've always imagined it would be cold and cramped and difficult to balance yourself."

"Also," he said, a finger raised to make a point. "The diagrams are magnificent."

She put up her hand. "Please don't. I know."

"Funny. And vulgar. And occasionally disgusting. Magnificent."

"Please," she said, firmer. "I said I know."

He found this funny. "I assume you would know, wouldn't you!"

She signed the book with the same looping, ugly scrawl she'd used forty years ago. Right after it was published she'd gone to so many bookstores to read and sign. *Meet your happy readers,* her publishers had implored. The lines usually went out the door. They'd set her up at a small card table at the back of the store. Men in suits would file through, straight from the office, liquor on their breath. Buying the book for the wife, they'd say, smiling, lying, eyes on her tits, asking her not to sign at the front but, say, perhaps on one of her diagrams, on the ballast of the hot-air balloon, or on the treasure map trail to the clitoris. She'd needed to bring Harold with her at a certain point. The attention became too much, the brouhaha too ridiculous, and he would stand at the back of the room so that she could find his eyes, or his confident smile, while she signed and signed. Henrietta's usual banter about autographs had not deviated in all these years. *Autographs,* it usually went. *I've never understood them. Especially mine. It's just a scribble and a circle, anyhow. You could do it for yourself if I trained you.* It did not escape her that her shtick was a deflection. The fact was that she had never known how to react to her own notoriety, and so she'd chosen self-deprecation because she thought demeaning herself was charming. She had preached self-confidence to her students all those years ago, and still she kept up with this inane banter. Here was another lecture for her imaginary academic career: A Metaphysical Investigation of Female Self-Criticism: The Socialization of Despair.

Turner smiled when she handed the book back to him. "My mom, she's unwell," he told her. "And I think she would get a hoot out of knowing that I met you."

"That's very nice to hear," said Henrietta. "I hope she feels better soon."

For a while she listened to Turner talk of his mother, hearing of her terrific recipes for madeleines, her opinions on Parisian fashion, her frustration over Turner's lack of a wife, her disappointment with how ugly and staid and vapid America had turned out to be. In Henrietta's normal life, which is to say in the life she had before Harold died, she would never have stood for this. This man's odd stories, this strange store, his obese cat. Outside, Oona protested. Her arms were up. *What the hell are you doing? Where's the stupid statue? Did Mr. Mustache steal it?* Henrietta lingered, though, and for a moment she forgot why she was here. He was making her laugh. He told a joke about a customer of his—*A man asked if I had any Rodin. And I thought he had asked if I had any rodents*—admittedly an awful joke, the kind of joke that probably only worked in a place like this, both art- and rat-filled. She found herself accepting his offer to sit. He had a bag of fresh baked bread that he'd brought. His mother's bread. Small and buttered and warm with a trace of the oven. "This is my breakfast," he said. "A grown man and still, *ma mère* makes my meals for me." Harold used to have the best bread at the Feast, she found herself admitting. "Harold was my husband," she said. This, she had decided, was the worst sentence in the English language. Turner listened carefully. In the mornings, if you wandered past, you could smell everything baking, she told him. Harold had a window out to the street, where you could watch the pastry team working. This was when things were good. The pre-debt years. Mornings in the restaurant were the most wonderful times. She would come in by trolley some days, reading a book, and have coffee at the bar beside Harold, or a fried egg made on sourdough that he would grill for her.

"That sounds very nice," Turner said.

"It was very nice."

"When did he die?" he asked.

"Not long ago," she said. Then she caught herself. "Eleven months ago. Three hundred days. Is that long? Or short? I've lost track of how other people think of this."

He reached out to touch her hand. "It's short, I think," he said. "But what do I know? I'm here in this shop filled with all of this strange stuff."

"I used to have boxes of these in my house," she said, pointing to the book. "They came all the time. Every new edition. I used to hide them from the family. But someone always found them and left them places to embarrass me."

"Did you throw them away?"

She nodded. "Whenever I found them. But they're like locusts. They descend, often in groups, and they are very difficult to eradicate."

"You could have made money on them."

"No, I couldn't have."

"Especially you. With your fame. Look around," he said. "There's always money to be made selling your things."

She wondered what of hers he might want. Would Turner want her clothing? The outfit she wore when she first met Loni Anderson? Would he want her lovely but environmentally disastrous teak bedroom furniture? Her teenage journals, which were squirreled away in the garage and full of lusty paeans to Rock Hudson? How about the copy of the letter that her former colleague from the women's studies department Dr. Darlene McClaren sent to her, which began, *I just wish you'd asked me to read this beforehand. I could have saved you what will surely be an excoriating embarrassment. I could have told you to quit. To do something else.* Or a copy of the note that Henrietta had sent in return, pointing out that such a remark reeked of patriarchy. The note began, *You're telling me that you know what's good for me?* Would Turner want these?

Oona impatiently knocked on the front window.

"That's my daughter," she told Turner.

"Checking on you, I suppose."

"I think you may be right."

"Asking, who is this weird gentleman harassing my mother?"

Henrietta got up and went to the door, stepping over the cat. Oona, red from the cold, leaned in, shaking her head in disbelief.

"What on earth, Mom?"

"He's *nice.*"

"He's nice?"

"He fed me his mother's bread. He's being nice."

"The bread is poisoned, probably."

"Listen to you," she said.

"Arsenic. Strychnine. Who knows?"

"Who made you so suspicious?"

"You did!"

"Well," Henrietta said. "He's fine and nice and there's no need to worry."

Oona threw up her hands. "Does he have the dumb statue or not?"

Henrietta looked behind her. Turner was cleaning crumbs off the counter. "We can go get the dumb statue now," he said loudly.

"He heard you," Henrietta said.

"This is weird," Oona said.

"Also, the bread is not poisoned," he called out.

"See?" Henrietta said.

"I repeat, this is weird."

"This is *you* being weird," said Henrietta. "Arsenic! Strychnine! He's nice. His mother loves my book. He's a fan of mine."

"Did you say that he was a fan?"

"Of mine!" Henrietta said. "They do exist."

"But you hate your fans," said Oona. "They scare you."

Henrietta nodded. "Maybe I'd reevaluate that position if everyone brought me baked goods."

"If he's a fan, he's a creep."

"Not all of my fans are creeps."

"Your male fans?"

"Fine. Most of my male fans are creeps. I'll accept that as a fact. But he seems kind."

"What happened to you?" Oona laughed. "Where did my mother go?"

"It was refreshing in there, to be honest. He let me speak. And he didn't interrupt me. Do you know how rare it is for a woman my age to speak without being interrupted?"

Apparently Oona believed this to be a rhetorical question, and then, a moment too late, she offered up a response. "Rare?"

"Yes, Oona. Rare."

A set of keys jingled behind. Turner stood waiting in the hallway with his coat on.

"The weathervane is in my car. Do you mind walking? It's in the lot just behind us."

Henrietta turned back. Oona shook her head. "Don't you dare," Oona said.

Henrietta pulled up her coat's hood. "Wait five minutes," she said, smiling. "If I'm not back by then, call in the cavalry."

Turning around, she went slowly through the shop and out through the back door. Turner waddled on ahead of her. Snowplows had left enormous piles high against the brick tenement walls surrounding the parking lot. "It's right up here," Turner called out, pointing to an old Cadillac, painted purple, surely a collectible or antique or something uniquely rare.

The snow had turned to a freezing rain, and as Turner unlocked the car, Henrietta started to shiver. "We can do the exchange in the car," he said.

She watched him. Rain in his mustache. Squinting while the sleet hit his face. He shivered, too. She looked into the car, upholstered with brown leather. On the backseat he had a box roughly the right size to fit the weathervane.

"Is that it?" she asked.

He nodded.

"Fine," she said, opening the door. "Let's make this quick."

Inside, the car was stale with cigarette smoke. Turner started the engine so that he could run the heat. "Your daughter is very protective of you," he said. "That must be nice."

"She's suspicious in general," Henrietta said. "It's an inherited disposition. I suppose I have to accept responsibility for that."

Turner took the box from the backseat and put it on his lap. He'd wrapped it in blue paper and a yellow ribbon. A white tag stuck to the edge had her name on it.

"I didn't expect such a nice package," she said.

"Consider this a gift," he said, handing it over.

She shook her head. "A gift?"

"My mother insisted that I not charge you."

"That's ridiculous."

"She adores you. She says that it was a crime America did not treat you well."

"It sounds like I might get along very well with your mother," Henrietta said, smiling.

Turner laughed. "I got this for basically no money. And you seem like you really need it."

"It's that obvious?"

"Those are your husband's pens in the store, aren't they?" Turner asked.

"How did you know?"

"I could pretend that I'm incredibly astute. But his name is on the case."

"That's right," she said.

"Was he sick?" he asked. "Your husband?"

"No," she said quietly. "It was sudden. It happened suddenly."

Turner appeared to think about this. "I don't know if that's better or worse," he said.

"Neither do I."

They were parked against the back of a corner grocery. Through the shopwindows she could see what she guessed was a father and a mother and a son shopping. Maybe this was yet another stage of grief: refusing the urge to feel jealous of other families.

"Do you remember him?" she asked. "From when he brought the pens in?"

Turner frowned. "I wish I did."

"He was tall," she said. "He was always cleanly shaven. He had blue eyes. He would have had on a brown coat with big pockets. He was nice. He would have probably been very nice to talk to. And he had a good smile."

Turner shook his head. "I'm sorry."

"I don't know what month it would have been. But he always wore the same sneakers. They were blue Nikes with a white stripe. They're very distinctive shoes. They're hard not to notice."

Turner kept shaking his head. The longer she was away from her husband, the longer the list of essential facts about him became.

"He had white hair," she said. "Or maybe a red ball cap. He

sometimes wore the hat if the weather was bad. I bought it for him."

"I don't remember."

"Right," she said. Then she grew excited. "Maybe you have video surveillance? Cameras? Maybe we could go back in time and look and find the day? Is that something you could do?"

Even as she said it, she knew that he wouldn't have cameras, and that even if he did, she could not say for sure that she would want to see what Harold had looked like that day when he came in with his bag of belongings, looking for cash. She closed her eyes.

"I'm very sorry," Turner said.

The heat felt good against her bare hands.

"Can I ask you a question?"

She nodded.

"Is there any chance you're working on a sequel?" he asked.

"A sequel?" She laughed. "You're one of those."

"One of who?"

"Not enough screwing around in the first one? You needed more?"

He laughed. "Well..."

She waited.

He laughed. "It's not that. I just wonder." He chuckled. "Whatever happened to her? Whatever happened to Eugenia?"

"What do you mean, what happened to her?"

"Did she end up happy?"

"Happy? She wasn't real. I made her up. She's a character. What happened to her? The book ended. She ended. That's what happened to her."

"She's not you?" he asked.

Henrietta's shoulders fell. "Why would you think she was me?"

"Everybody thinks she was you."

She hesitated a long moment, long enough for him to laugh awkwardly.

"I see," he said. Then he turned off the car. "Here I am, ruining a perfectly fine morning between two nice people."

She smiled politely and then began to reach for the door handle. "Thank you for everything, Mr. Turner."

"What happens now?" he asked.

"What do you mean?" she said. "What happens now is that I leave. I go home."

"You're single, though?" he asked.

"I'm married," she said straightaway.

"I don't understand. You married again?"

"Turner," she said. "Thank you for the weathervane. And the bread."

"Maybe you would like to come with me to see the symphony?"

"Like I said, thank you—"

"Or maybe you would like to go see some poetry being read," he said.

"Goodbye, Mr. Turner."

Before she turned to the door one last time, he kissed her. He put his hand behind her neck, took her by the scruff, really, as if she were a kitten, and he pulled her to him. His face smelled like the cinnamon from his bread. All of this lasted only a few short moments. His tongue was all over her, against her clenched teeth, against her pursed lips. The push broom of his mustache mashed into her face. He moaned. As if this was supposed to be pleasurable. She had made a fortune once, pretending to know about this, about being this woman, this person who had casual sexual experiences with strange men in antique shops, or in the basket of hot-air balloons, but she had never been that woman. People had always made this mistake. She'd drawn the diagrams, inked the black lines of the pubic hair, the vulva, the hungry man, the supplicating woman, the comically long prick; she'd written the idiotic floor fucking scene, the balloon fucking scene, all the scenes in which her invented characters fucked each other dumb. And even though she was a seventy-year-old woman, this continued to happen.

Turner pulled away. He smiled at her. What am I doing here, she thought, in this purple Cadillac, with this man with this big mustache who had my husband's things in his shop?

"I like you very much, Henrietta Olyphant," he said. "Maybe you can come see me again." While her hand was on the door handle, he leaned forward and put his hand gently across her cheek, as if they had always been lovers, as Harold had done, as she'd written in her book.

Oona opened her door then, surprising Henrietta and making Turner jump and pull away. Henrietta got out quickly, wiping his saliva from her mouth, his spittle.

"What the hell is happening?" Oona shouted at him. "What were you fucking doing to my mother?"

"We're leaving," Henrietta said quietly to Oona. "We're getting out of here."

"Were you kissing my mother, you sick fucking animal?" Oona pushed past Henrietta.

"An animal? It was just one kiss!" Turner cried. "One little kiss! That's all!"

"She's seventy years old!"

"Oona!" Henrietta called out. "It's fine. Walk away. Leave."

"What's the big deal?" Turner said. "It was just kissing. We were having such a nice time. We were laughing. I thought she and I were—"

"What happened?" Oona asked, running after her. "Tell me what happened."

Henrietta shook her head. "Why did I go in his car?" she asked.

"Are you okay?" Oona asked.

"You were right," Henrietta said.

All this time Turner was yelling for her: *Come back, sweet-heart! This is getting out of hand.* Henrietta and Oona were in the middle of the parking lot. *Henrietta! Come on!* Henrietta had the blue box in her hand. She leaned against the back wall of the store to unwrap it. She removed the yellow ribbon and then pried open the top folds. Immediately she knew that it was not her weathervane. "This isn't it," she said. She repeated this over and over, louder each time, her anger growing, not simply about the weathervane, which was not hers, but about the whole of the past eleven months, the slow vanishing of her normal life, the sudden terrifying emptiness of the future. "This isn't it!" she cried out one last time. Beside her, Oona squinted down at the box.

"Are you sure, Mom?" Oona asked.

Meanwhile, standing across the parking lot, Turner had lost his patience. "You're crazy," he said. "You know that? You're just a crazy cocktease!"

Henrietta took it—this copper thing that was not even a woman, but a man in a golfing cap, the top of a trophy, perhaps, a man holding a nine iron—and walked deliberately across the parking lot, past Turner, and threw it through the window of his purple Cadillac.

# 31.

The night that Lydia ended up in Charlie's bed, they sat out first
on the lip of the ridge overlooking the valley in Mount Thumb.
This was a Thursday night, early in February. It was mild for
Vermont, which meant that it was still frigid. They wore thick
winter coats. A meteor shower was about to happen, he had
told her, which was a lie, just a way to get her to sneak out of
Rosewater and come see him and maybe afterward get her to
come up to his bed and take off her top and very likely do things
to his body. While they sat, he gave her wireless headphones,
and they listened together to someone talking about *Voyager 2,*
the space mission that left Earth in 1978 and reached Neptune
twelve years before she was born. "What is this?" she asked. "A
lecture?" Their legs dangled over the edge of the rock face. It
was hundreds of feet down. He had on yellow socks and blue
canvas sneakers caked in mud. He pretended that he was losing his balance, and she pulled him back and hugged him close
to her. "Stop," she said. "You're scaring me." He kept trying
to impress her, to show her that he occasionally did things like
contemplate the shape of the universe. "I'm not just a pretty
face," he said.

They had been out long enough that her eyes had adjusted

fully to the dark, and when he said this, she looked closely at him. "Not just a pretty face? Let me be the judge of that. Turn and let me look at you." She reached out and took the point of his chin. He mistook this for a chance to kiss her, which he did, unskillfully, when in reality she'd just wanted to look at him, to see exactly who it was she had attached herself to. All across Hartwell they were being discussed in tandem— Lydia and Charlie, Charlie and Lydia. He was her boyfriend now, whatever that meant. "Stay still," she said, holding him, both hands on his cheeks. He had a perfectly round face, oddly round, a complete and whole circle, in the middle of which was his small and subtly squashed nose. "What happened to it?" she said, touching it. "Did someone punch you?" She laughed. "Some people, you can just tell that someone punched them. You seem like you're one of those people."

He wore black knit mittens, and he took one off to touch his nose. "What do you mean?" he asked innocently. "What's wrong with my nose? Nobody punched me! Is my nose messed up?"

He wanted her to hear about the Golden Records scientists had put on board the Voyager missions. He turned up the volume. This was what the lecture was about. The Golden Records were a catalog of everything that humans had accomplished on Earth. On it, scientists had left recordings of the human voice, photographs of the Taj Mahal and the city of Boston, photographs of dolphins and chimpanzees and toads and airplanes, evidence of the languages that people had created, reproductions of great art, Senegalese percussion, Peruvian panpipes, Glenn Gould playing part of *The Well-Tempered Clavier,* Louis Armstrong playing "Melancholy Blues." There were examples of the mathematics that people had invented, and analog reproductions of the sound a dog makes and an airplane makes and of crickets and rain. Jimmy Carter left a greeting. Scientists hoped that wherever the Voyager missions ended up, in whatever corner of the universe, whichever gas-or-ice-filled star they eventually crashed onto, light-years from now, someone or something might excavate these records and see what people had made here. Charlie wanted Lydia to hear this. "This is some dope shit," he told her, which, in his way, was as deep as he got.

"I bet the aliens will be really psyched to hear from Jimmy Carter," Lydia said. While they listened, he tapped her knee or wrist and nodded gravely, as if to say, *Listen: this is important.* These were things she would not forget, beautiful things, essential things, maybe, experienced with a person she would not forget either, all of this becoming in the future inseparable for her—the endless sky and her new body and this person and the sense that she was always being watched.

Also, he wanted to sleep with her here. When the lecture ended, he told her this. "I think it would be really nice," he said, pausing, nervous, sweating in the freezing cold. "It would be nice to make love here." It would be his first time, which was news to her, since he bragged so much about how incredible he was in bed, how smooth he was, and yet how powerful, how he was, more than most boys, so carefully attuned to a woman's needs.

"Wait a second," she said. "You want to do it now?"

"You don't?"

"Here? On this rock?"

"It's private. It's the only private place on campus."

She banged her hand against the rocky edge. "You expect me to lie on this thing? It hurts just to sit on it."

"But it's cool. We're beneath the stars."

She threw a pebble over the edge. "It's also hundreds of feet down," she said. "Imagine the headlines if one of us fell over."

"Oh, I'd catch you, baby," he said.

She rubbed a finger across the top of the rock. Dirt and

pollen and probably cigarette ash came up on her skin. "It's su-per hygienic, also."

"What about on the ground, then?" he said. "Beneath the maple trees."

"I love that you just said 'beneath the maple trees.'"

"It's softer than the rock."

She put her hands in her pockets. "It's really cold here, Charlie."

"Well, let's go back to my room, then."

She laughed. "You thought this lecture about the *Voyager* would get me in the mood?"

He laughed also. "So what you're saying is that space is not a turn-on?"

He had pretended to know the names of the constellations that night as they walked back to his dorm. He kept looking up and tracing indeterminate shapes with the tip of his finger.

"That line out there, that's Cincinnatus," he said.

"No it's not," she said. "Cincinnatus is not a constellation."

"And that," he said, making an oval in the sky. "That—the princess's crown—that's Diana." Lydia had smiled.

"Wait. Do you think Princess Diana has her own constella-tion?"

Lydia thought of this as she left Charlie's house with her father. It was evening and the stars were out. It was warmer here, two hundred miles south, warm enough that she didn't need the gloves she'd stuffed into the pockets of her coat. They were her mother's. Lydia had found them at home in her mom's closet, which was mostly empty now that she'd gone. The only things left were things like this—forgotten gloves, worn-out black surgical scrubs, her wedding gown.

Her father walked off ahead of her, down the brick walkway that went from the Perlmutters' door to the sidewalk. He had his phone out.

"What are you doing?" she called out, rushing after him.

"I'm going to get this kid arrested," he said.

"We tried," she said. "It's over."

"We're *trying*," he said. "I have to keep trying."

"Enough is enough," she said.

"No it isn't," he said, trying to dial, failing, cursing himself. He looked red, irate; his hands shook.

When all of this was over, she'd learn that Charlie's father had apparently done nothing but ask her dad how much money it would take to make them go away. *How much for all of this? Two grand?* They had been in a room that sounded very much like the room Lydia had been in—leather and animal heads and oil paintings of animals about to be murdered. This was Mr. Perlmutter's opening figure: $2,000 for her body.

At the end of the pathway a line of huge oaks towered over the Perlmutters' house, which was lit up behind them in white, like a temple. The neighborhood had gone quiet. All the other mansions had their gates drawn. Her dad dialed the police. She could hear the ringing through her father's phone. He leaned against one of the trees, attempting to catch his breath. Tears had dried in a line running into the stubble of his beard. The moon hung low above the slack telephone wire. Black birds perched on top of the utility pole.

Someone came on the line. Her father stood up straight, and he began to cite offhand the whole litany of crimes against her: illicit photography of a minor, distribution of child pornography, cyberharassment, aggravated stalking.

Maybe she knew already that this wouldn't work. She thought of the government-free Pacific island where her body lived now, dispossessed, eternally fetchable, always fifteen. Her father paced, first in wide circles around his parked car, and then up and down the sidewalk along the fence that separated the Perlmutters' house from the road. This was his habit, the walking and talking, a relic from his old life, something that her mother had told her about in stories of their years in New York, this inability to stay put, to sit, to act normal. He was so skinny then, her mother said. He always looked nervous. He always wanted to argue with someone about the news or about politics. Lydia watched him now, his fist clenched, the white hair on his temples messy in the breeze. Motion-detecting lamplight fell aslant on the decorative stone lions. *I'm here,* her dad was saying, his voice bounding down the empty street. *I'm waiting for someone to come and do something.* She sat on the curbstone to wait.

In the opposite direction, she heard a bicycle on the street, and before she turned she knew already that it would be Charlie. He came to a small rise in the road and stopped there. To see him here, without his Hartwell uniform—his shawl collar, his necktie, his ever-present cigarette, his sneer, his phone, his camera—momentarily startled her. His bicycle was tiny, something built for a child, a relic, probably, from the last time he had lived here full-time.

"I heard you were coming," he called out.

She turned around to find her father, but he had walked down the street far enough that she could not see him.

Charlie got off his bike and walked with it. She put her hand up. "Don't get any closer."

"I was under strict orders to stay clear—"

"Stop fucking walking toward me."

He stopped. "—because I guess your dad's on some mission to have me strung up and hanged."

"Who says it's just my father's mission?" she said.

"I guess he wants me locked up."

"I want that, too."

Charlie moved forward a few steps.

"I told you, don't you fucking come any closer," she said.

He stood beneath a streetlamp. He brushed back his hair,

hooking it behind his tiny ears. This hair: the first hair of any boy she had touched or admired, and certainly the first hair she had ever deigned to tuck behind someone's ear. Acne had bloomed in an archipelago on the soft ridge of his chin, purple as a bruise, picked at already, proof of stress, maybe, or guilt. Evidence, perhaps, of a soul.

"So you met my parents?" he asked, turning to look at the house. "Pretty wonderful and kind people, right?"

She said nothing. She looked down the street, hoping for her father.

"Should explain why I am the way I am," he said.

Again she didn't answer. Behind her the motion-detecting lamp went off and then on, brightening one of the lions' hides and the pavement between her and Charlie.

"I don't know how to get it down," he said. "The picture. It's not like I didn't try."

"You're a liar," she said.

He kept getting closer.

"Stop walking," she said.

"Let's just talk," he said.

"Stop fucking walking."

He got closer. Light marked the dark spot of his pupils.

She turned. "Dad!" she called out.

"Are you okay, at least?" Charlie asked.

"Did you seriously just ask me that?" she said.

He took yet another step toward her. His face was calm, his eyes wide. The look, she knew, was a perfectly crafted replica of what a concerned person looked like. He took out a cigarette. "You want one?" he asked.

She took a step away.

"You never answered. I want to know if you're okay, Lydia," he said. He was trying to sound sweet. The effort from him appeared so obvious now. "Are you? I hope you're okay."

"Yes, I'm doing terrific, Charlie," she said. "Really fantastic."

Just then the brass gate to the Perlmutters' house closed, the lock clicking into place.

"I feel bad," he said. "You know what I'm saying? It got out of hand, I guess is what I'm trying to say."

Finally her father walked up the street. He had his head down and his car keys out. Years from now she would think of this moment—her father on the street, Charlie on the street, two stone lions watching them—when she heard, finally, that Charlie had been arrested, not for anything he'd done to her, but for something with a different woman altogether. Lydia looked for a sign from her father, some hopeful motion of his hand to say that, yes, he'd done it, and that, yes, someone was coming for Charlie. Her dad lifted his head and must have seen her standing in the middle of the road and Charlie standing behind her, because he stopped. She heard sirens then, and it wasn't a moment until she saw the blue lights of a police cruiser flickering behind her father on the tree bark and the houses. She turned back to Charlie, still in the middle of the road, smoking, his hair having fallen in his eyes. She allowed herself a smile. The sirens grew louder. She turned back just as the first police car came into view, speeding, its sirens deafeningly loud. Then the second car. Her father, she thought, had done it. She stood off to the side, expecting surely that they would come to a stop here, beside her.

When the police passed, the first car rushing, and then the second going even faster, she threw up her hands, confused.

"What's happening?" she cried out. "Come back!"

Behind her Charlie had changed his tone. "I don't know why it had to be this way," he said, but she had stopped listening. Why had the cops passed by? Why weren't they stopping?

"Why can't you just be cool like everybody else?" he asked. "It's like you're the first fucking girl this ever happened to."

He narrowed his eyes and tried to give her the impression that he could read her thoughts.

"You just think you're that special," he said. "That's it. This shit happens all the time. It's happening this second, probably. Like, who really cares?"

Charlie had his phone out. The lit screen glowed white on his face. She recognized it as the same phone, the same lens and camera. He flicked at the screen. She watched him.

She turned once more. Her father had begun to walk toward her and she put her hand up to stop him.

"Actually," she said, "do you have a cigarette for me?"

Charlie smiled. That smile. His perfect teeth. She thought of the years of orthodonture that smile must have necessitated, the countless trips back and forth to and from the dentist, ferried, so he claimed, by his parents' underlings. Everyone hoped for a perfect child. Sometimes you just got a boy with perfect teeth. He came to her. He took out the pack.

"You light it for me," she said, trying to sound sweet.

He fumbled for the lighter.

"Do it quick," she said, nodding her head in the direction of her father's car. "I have to go."

He was so close.

"My stupid dad," she said.

"Yeah," he said.

"This is so fucking stupid," she said. "He makes the biggest deal out of everything."

"I know," he said.

She could smell his breath.

"We should make up," she said.

"You serious?" He didn't move.

"So serious," she said. "Fucking ten thousand percent serious."

She saw his shoulders fall in relief. "Oh, that's so good to hear," he said. He cocked his head back toward his mansion. "So good. You have no idea."

"First, light the cigarette," she said.

Wind rushed down the street, and he had to flick at the lighter over and over. She watched him as he tried to get the cigarette lit, his breath quickening. She remembered that when he first explained his phobias to her—the butterflies, the salt water, the Adam's apple—she did not believe him. They were walking across the campus at Hartwell, and because it was raining she tried to fit underneath his umbrella. He kept telling her to get closer because she was getting drenched, which was true, but it was also probably true that he just wanted to touch her. *We can both fit,* he kept saying, pulling her in by the shoulder. Because Lydia was taller than him, she needed to crouch to fit beneath his umbrella entirely, and as he pulled her in, her cheek accidentally grazed his Adam's apple. She'd barely touched him, but even so, he'd flinched and shuddered so badly that he dropped the umbrella entirely.

"There we go," he said, finally getting the cigarette lit.

She took a drag. She had never smoked before. She forced herself not to cough.

"If we're made up, maybe you could call me sometime," he said. "You know? Or come visit."

"Definitely," she said. "New Jersey is so nice."

He had gained confidence, she could see. He stood up straighter. He let the cigarette dangle on his lip. "It's not like we didn't have fun together," he said.

She squinted. "C'mere," she said.

"What?" he said.

They were a foot apart.

"Just come."

She forced a smile. He was so close that his toes were touching hers.

"You have something on your face," she said.

She reached out and put her cold thumb square against Charlie's Adam's apple. Beneath her skin she could feel the pump-and-flow pulse of his blood and a terrified rush of air charging through his trachea. She had the thought then to try to remember the way he was looking at her, the cat-quick dilation of his eyes. Did he think she was going to hurt him? He dropped his cigarette first, and then his phone, both of them landing on the pavement. Immediately she bent down, picked up the phone, and walked off toward her father's car.

In the car, her father gunned the engine. "Let me run him over," he said, so quietly.

She shook her head. Charlie stood in the middle of the road, a streetlight on above him.

"Please let me run him over and kill him," her father said.

"Let's go home, Daddy."

# 32.

Oona held her hand as they drove. Beneath the engine, a faint clicking sound rattled the heater. Oona squeezed every few minutes. A wordless check on her condition. They went for miles this way, her daughter holding her. The taste of Turner's mouth in hers. Hair from his head or his mustache littered her coat, a shedding. Oona had the stereo on low. "I'm bleeding," Henrietta said, just realizing it. She held up her arm for Oona to see. After it was over, Oona had picked her up and carried her across the parking lot and in through the store and out to the street, but not before Henrietta had slammed the weathervane through the window of his car—*This is not it!* she had yelled; *This is not it.* Oona had lifted her so easily. Henrietta tried to remember the last time she had been carried like this. She must have cut herself on the glass. Oona found tissues and wet wipes and bandages in her glove box. The ready ingredients of motherhood.

They passed through all the quiet towns. The monotonous rhythm of these Yankee villages comforted her. Snow on the eaves of the Episcopalian churches. Fog in the window of a donut shop. Salt streaks on the road. Hockey nets on the frozen ponds.

"You all right?" Oona asked as they crossed into Aveline.

"No, not really," she said. She kept wiping at her mouth, hoping the feeling, the taste, would vanish.

"Try to relax," Oona said.

"What were you even doing there?" she asked. "One second he had his hand on my cheek like I was his long lost lover, and then—"

"I told you. I had a bad feeling."

"I shouldn't have been in the car," she said. "You were right. I just thought—"

"As soon as you followed him into the parking lot, I followed you."

Henrietta shook her head. "I figured at seventy I was done with this crap."

Oona looked over. "That creep."

They crossed through the center of Aveline, everything clean and gleaming and new, nothing remaining from the twentieth century aside from the telephone poles and the manhole covers. This had all happened fast. The keystone on the corner of the bank bore a wholly typical date—2006, it read. If Harold were to come back to earth, he would not recognize so much of this place. In a few months the same would be true of her house. Her real estate agent had offered her the chance to see the provisional plans the development company had for her land, whatever they were aiming to do—swimming pools, clubhouses, a golfing green, tract housing—and she'd refused. Looking around at what the town had turned into, she had an idea of what was coming.

The moon emerged in the daylight, branding the dim sky. A string of crows aligned themselves in a cluster on the peaked roof of a shuttered station house. Oona pulled off the main street and onto the thin, pocked road leading to the house. Near her, in the iced-up gullies, there were paw prints. She knew them by shape. She had gotten good at this. Coyote prints.

Deer prints. Raccoon prints. The prints from the neighbor's dogs. Not bad for Henrietta Horowitz of Orchard Street. The postman's prints. The county surveyor's prints. The paramedics. The priest. The mourners. The real estate people. The movers. The appraisers. Jerry Stern. Her daughter. Her granddaughter.

On they drove, down toward the house, looking worn in the bright light, and chipped, the shutters crooked, patches in the roof where storms had taken the shingles. They went past the dead birch, past the barn and the animal pen, the salt lick, the John Deere up on blocks, the hay holds, the tool-shed, the propane tanks, the empty pigsty, the chicken coop, Dougie's house, the septic tank.

Before they reached the driveway, they passed the curve of the river as it emptied into Lake Patricia, and Henrietta put her hand up.

"Stop," she said, pointing. "Park over there. By the lake."

The thermometer on the dash registered an ungodly temperature.

"I want to go out," Henrietta said.

"Into the weather?" Oona asked.

"Onto the ice."

"This again?"

"I won't fall through, Oona. Stop worrying."

"You're the one who taught me to worry."

Henrietta searched her handbag for gloves.

"It's not as firm out there as you think," Oona said. "We went over this. The earth is warming. And you could go under, and the ice could close up over your head—"

"My new place," Henrietta said, cutting her off. "It doesn't have a river or a lake nearby."

Oona said nothing.

"It has a tiny oval swimming pool. A wading pool for babies and elderly people. Three feet deep."

Henrietta still had Harold's car keys in her purse.

"And I do like this place, you know," she said. "This weird town. The water. The big open space." She pointed to the meadow and the water bank, mist rising. "I think it might be nice to enjoy it before it's gone."

"Gone?" Oona laughed. "Where is it going?"

"The house sold," Henrietta said.

Oona smiled. "I know this."

From here she saw only the top point on the roof. They had never put up another weathervane. Weathervanes were stuffy, Henrietta complained, and useless, and most of them, anyway, were ugly.

"They're going to knock it down," she said.

"Oh, you don't know that," said Oona.

"No," Henrietta said. "I do. A company bought it. They're knocking it down. It's what they do. They're house wreckers. It's probably the name of their company."

Oona was quiet for a while. The song changed.

"It's just a house," Henrietta said. "Just shelter. Wood and nails and glue and dust. I keep telling myself that these are just objects. A staircase, a living room, a toilet. They have a neutral value, I know. The house doesn't have a soul. It's not a person. There are no spirits here. All that dumb bullshit people say. All the correspondingly dumb bullshit that people believe. I don't know when I suddenly stopped being able to differentiate between these ideas. Between an actual understanding of objects and a sentimental understanding."

"You sound like a professor," Oona said.

"Good! That's good! Finally!"

"It's natural to think those things about your house."

"That's therapy-speak. And it's juvenile. Thinking that maybe my husband's ghost is in the house? You think that's natural? Or rational?"

"Absolutely. Natural. Human. Beautiful."

"It's what my mother used to think. It's old-world nonsense. She wouldn't touch her father's cigarette lighter after he died, because she thought his ghost was inside it."

Oona laughed. "Okay, that's foolish, I admit."

"Is it any different than a house?"

"It's a home," Oona said. "That's the difference."

"I'm not impressed by semantics," Henrietta said. "Tell me. Where do the dead linger? Where? In the bathroom? The kitchen?"

"Daddy? Yes. I would guess he's lingering in the kitchen."

Henrietta closed her eyes. She stayed quiet a minute. "The thought that he might be in the kitchen is very, very hard to bear," she said.

"Faith," Oona said, "requires a suspension of disbelief. Not all of it. But a little."

"If I were to believe it, Oona, it would be evidence, as if I ever needed it, that my intellect has finally vanished."

"Smart people think this way, you know," Oona said. "Doctors, even. In the hospital, in surgery, in *brain* surgery, you see doctors praying, you hear them say, *Oh God Oh God Oh God.* People speak openly of miracles. It's not a matter of intellect. It's the opposite of intellect."

"Exactly."

"But aren't you doing the same thing with the suitcase?" Oona said after a while. "You won't open it. It just sits there by the door. All this time. You won't even really go near it."

"*That* is different," she said.

"How is it different?"

"Because I don't actually think there's a ghost in the stupid suitcase, Oona," Henrietta said. "It's just that once I open it, and clean it out, that's it. It's over. That's the last thing left."

Oona sat back against her seat. Henrietta, too, leaned back. She had found herself spending all her time in the kitchen these last weeks, trying to summon if not a ghost then some phantom waft of his cooking, some remnant sensation of his presence. She had also found herself holding the handle of Harold's suitcase, standing by the door, just looking out at the path he used to take, up and down the hill. Her good sense, quite possibly, was dissipating.

In the beginning the land embarrassed her. Henrietta Horowitz, city girl, with all these acres. It was a fiefdom, she told her mother on the phone. Enough room for blocks and blocks of apartment towers and tenements. You could fit the whole neighborhood in the backyard, she told her mother. Now, she figured, it might just happen.

"The new place is very blank," Henrietta said. "That's the word that comes to mind. Everything is cream-colored. There's carpeting. I'm allowed to have a small dog. Under fifty pounds, they told me. I don't know—maybe there's a doggy scale they bring in to see if I'm following the rules."

"That doesn't sound awful."

Henrietta laughed. "Is that the standard now?"

"That is the standard now, yes. Modern American life means being able to afford someplace that isn't awful."

"I wanted to ask you to move in with me," Henrietta said. She had rehearsed this. Another thing that embarrassed her.

"With you?"

"Like roommates."

Oona laughed.

"Why is it funny?" Henrietta asked. "It's been nice to have you near me."

Oona nervously zipped her coat up to her neck. "It has been nice."

"It's hard for you to admit!"

"I'm emotionally underdeveloped," Oona said. "What do you want from me? It's genetic."

"You could have gone elsewhere, I know. You have the money."

"It's not like you never saw me before all of this."

"That's debatable."

"I came for holidays."

"People don't want to be around their mother. I understand. When you were the littlest girl, I knew that you would be that kind of woman. And that made me happy. But to see you every day. And to have you sleeping in my house. I've liked it. I've liked it very much."

"The novelty will wear off. Trust me. Ask my husband."

Henrietta said nothing. She knew the trickiness of time and language. Husband. Ex-husband. Late husband.

"So, what happens if I want to bring a man home to the apartment?" Oona asked.

"Sex? That's the first thing you think about? Are you sure you're my daughter? What happened to you, Oona?"

"Yes, that's what I think! You're my mother! You wrote the stupid book. Which I read far, far too early. Obviously sex is what I think about!"

"You misread the book, sweetie."

"Me and apparently everyone else."

Henrietta opened the door partway. The cold came in. "What I would like, at least, is for you to bring my granddaughter over. So I could, you know, potentially have a conversation with her before I'm senile."

Oona grinned. "You're ruining the fun with guilt," she said.

"I would like her to know me as a human. Especially since she'll probably read that stupid book."

"It's a delightful book."

Henrietta scoffed and opened her door. "Come with me," she said. "Come out. It's great this time of year. You can walk right on it. Right on the ice."

"How about I watch?" Oona said.

From the road to the shore was a hundred yards. Henrietta pushed through the weeds and bushes. Underfoot the leaves were frozen, which she loved, that sound your foot makes on frozen leaves. The original plan had been to give the house to Oona. Henrietta found Harold's will while she packed up the house. All his best laid plans. He had given Oona the Feast, too. *The quality of the establishment must be maintained at all costs,* he'd written. She kicked her way through a tangled mess of dead chestnuts and dogwoods. Overhead there were blackbirds. Behind her Oona approached slowly. There were patches where the tree cover stood so thick snow hadn't reached the ground yet, and autumn was visible, a few stray shards of green, October colors: red and yellow and the orange of a jack-o'-lantern.

At the water's edge, the ice looked purple. She stood there, tapped her foot against the sheet of it.

"Don't do it," Oona shouted.

She went out two steps, closed her eyes, pushed off, and glided. After a moment she started to bellow with laughter, and when her laughter echoed across the ice, bats sprung from the trees.

"Look," she called out. "Look."

Oona stood on the shore, her arms crossed, with Harold's face and eyes and nose and chin. Maybe this was where the spirits went.

Henrietta spun on her heels. She swung her arms in an arc, twirling. She whistled with joy. All this childish happiness surprised her. "This is the most fun I've had in ages," she said, pushing out, one step and then two, gliding and cutting the air and sliding while the snow brushed up over the toes of her shoes. The new construction in town threw lights up into the sky that deadened the stars, so that even very late at night you could not make out the belt of Orion in winter. She spun a second time, inexpertly, her feet leaving smooth loops on the surface of the ice.

She knew that all this talk of ghosts was just another way to talk about memories. If the dead lingered, then they were doing a poor job lingering around her. She needed help recalling her father's face. Her mother's voice and laugh were gone. Every Horowitz who had ever crowded into her mother's apartment on Orchard Street—all of them had vanished, and she could not, even when she wanted to, remember the way they were when they were living.

If she lived long enough, the same thing would happen with Harold. He, too, would go eventually.

She knew that she was losing not just her house, but the land Harold loved, the foot-beaten dirt paths to the chicken pens, his idea of the place, the spot where he fell. All of this was just something else to grieve, and she was exhausted by grief.

She went out far enough that she could see the whole house and the stripe of land that was hers. The pasture, the barn roof, the back meadow, the mess of it all. She kept going, almost to the center of the lake, because this was the only place where you could see, against the hill, far off and on either side of the porch, that the apple trees he had planted that first year were planted in the shape of two Hs, one for her, one for him. When the saplings came up the first or second winter—she could no longer remember which—he took her out here to see, and she had, because she was joyless and a crank, mocked him for the whole idea: this corny thing, this cheap attempt at romanticism. She had told him that it was the single most schmaltzy thing anyone had ever done for her.

She pushed out, her feet gathering slush. Behind her Oona stayed at the edge of the lake, full with worry.

"I swear to Christ if you fall through the ice and drown I will kill you," Oona called out.

Henrietta kept going out, five feet, ten feet, and the whole of the place began to come into view. Eventually she stopped and gaped at the hill and the house. Oona finally came out onto the ice, managing slowly.

"What are you looking at?" Oona said when she reached the center of the lake. "What's so damn important in the middle of this stupid lake?"

Henrietta pointed.

# 33.

Before Lydia went away to Hartwell, her parents had been talking a good deal about the old days. This made sense now that they were separate from each other. Before everything falls apart one goes back to the crucial decisions. Babies or no babies. City or country. New York or not New York. They had decided on everything, she knew, over pierogies at a Ukrainian restaurant in the East Village. Marriage, motherhood, Massachusetts.

She thought of this on the way home, as her father insisted on taking her through Manhattan in order to show her the place where she was born, the room, the window that was her first window. It was late and the city was full. They drove uptown to the west side, passing the big avenues, light-drenched and looking, each of them, like parted seas. He changed the disc to something different, more jazz, and he said, whispering, forced awe in his voice, *This is something you'll love. I'm sure of it.* The blocks were thickset with shadow. Wind careened off the sycamore branches. Horse piss from the hansom cabs wafted from the street and in through the vents.

All of her parents' friends had babies the same year. Lydia had seen the home videos. Small Brooklyn apartments full of young-looking people and outdated technology, and all these babies drool-splattered in their oversize strollers, looking so life-affirmingly adorable. This was the beginning of the new century, and all the baby names were the names of sitcom characters. Niles. Monica. Carlton. Lydia knew all these children vaguely. They were tangentially related, she liked to think. Manhattanites in exile, each of them born in a hospital one block from Central Park, and then whisked away to places like Crestview. Because of this, she was supposed to feel a deep connection to this city, some spiritual kinship with the skyline. But she regarded this place with none of the regret and sentiment of her parents, whose zest for the city grew every year they were absent from it, and who tortured her with stories of their brief foray into metropolitan glamour. She had all their stories memorized. How her father knew a man who knew a man who groomed Jacqueline Kennedy's dogs. Or how her father read poetry earnestly and for entertainment and was not embarrassed by either of these facts. She knew that her mother had tried to inhabit the spirit of Bridget Fonda. And that she'd momentarily had Jennifer Aniston's hair, two years after it was fashionable. All of it needed to be recited yearly, like the Passover story.

She watched her father as he drove along Central Park. His face brightened. Time, he had told her, began to feel so strange the moment they moved away from here. The body ages fast, but the spirit lags. He narrated as they went, a finger raised to point out buildings black against the bruised sky, to show her the homes of their old friends, or of other babies she had played with, of roommates and old girlfriends and places where there were parties and restaurants in which they had plotted their future and whole city blocks—unchanged, he claimed, brick for brick. This city, she was supposed to understand, was full of ghosts.

"You miss this," she said. "It's obvious."

"Only a little," he said.

"If this is you missing something only a little," Lydia said, "I can't imagine how my mother feels."

He allowed only a small smile at this. The Toyota glided uptown on a string of successive green lights.

"You were only twenty-five when I was born," she said. "That's young."

"Very young," he agreed.

"What were you thinking?" she asked.

"I think I was too terrified to be thinking anything," he said.

"I have a hard time picturing you as a young person," she said.

"I was very charming," he said.

"Doubtful."

"Before you were born I had all these convictions that child-bearing was a political act, incompatible with certain notions I had about social privilege and global overpopulation and food shortages. I just thought, does the world really need another person?"

"I don't think I'm the one you tell this story to," she said.

"Another person just gobbling up fuel and creating more garbage."

"Like I said, this is really doing wonders for my self-confidence," she told him, her voice nearly lost in the city noise through the open windows.

"Naturally, you would think, this person sounds like a person who should definitely go to law school. That sounds wise, right?"

She shrugged. "Lawyers make money."

"I borrowed every cent. We were in debt for so long. Your grandmother supported us financially."

Lydia smiled.

"Which occasioned all sorts of guilt about inherited wealth and entitlement and the scourge of first-world capitalism."

"The twenty-five-year-old version of you sounds like a real catch."

"I kept a very, very serious journal on the matter," he told her.

"Oh Lord."

"There's a possibility that some of the entries may have been written in iambic pentameter."

"You did not just utter those words."

"One day, when I lose my capacity for shame, I'll let you read it. You'll get a kick out of it."

She smiled. "Please don't do that. Please burn these journals before you die."

They stopped. Red light from a traffic signal glowed in the puddles on the avenue. Up ahead the clouds over Manhattan cloaked the island like a fire blanket; midtown stopped at the fortieth story, all the skyscrapers with their tops smothered by the weather.

"You were the first baby I ever held," he said. "I knew nothing about babies. I'd never been around them."

"You told me. You read books on fatherhood."

"I read books on everything," he said. "Cooking for your baby. The songs to sing to your baby. I read every book I could find on being a father."

"You thought you would drop me?"

"Or do something wrong. Everybody wants to show you how," he said, cradling an imaginary infant. "You hold the head. Make sure it's safe."

"Seems obvious enough," Lydia said.

"Except I didn't know. It wasn't obvious to me. I was sure I had no idea."

"You were also stoned all the time."

"It was like someone handing you a table saw for the first time and telling you to go to work."

"Are you saying that you read baby books to learn how to hold me?" she asked.

They went north along the river into the West Nineties. "Do you remember this?" he kept asking, at everything, at bakeries, at high trees, at the flight of pigeons gathered on church steps. She remembered none of it, and if she said she did, it was only because he wanted her to remember it so badly. His best years, he kept saying, his happiest years, his most important, most formative years, pointing at subway station staircases and sidewalk cafés.

She rooted around in the glove box for tissues and found a picture of her parents that he used to hang from the rearview mirror. It was from the early days, taken outside the apartment on 103rd Street. In it they were clutching each other. It looked less like an embrace than a way to keep the other person from floating away. All the pictures from that era were like this. The hair. The evidence of leftover adolescent acne. All the rapturous smiling. Eager for proof that these were in fact the people who had spawned her, she had always inspected pictures like this for clues. Who were these happy smiling people? What exactly were their customs? Whatever happened to this society of gleeful people?

When they finally parked, having circled the same three corner bodegas and iron-gated kindergarten academies, passing three times the same lovely black flash of the Hudson, they rummaged for winter wear before they got out of the car. The temperature had plunged. Ice formed on the windshield. "I think I might have a hat for you," she said. In the back of the car, one of the backpacks that she'd taken from her dorm at Hartwell was stuffed full of her old school uniforms and textbooks. They pulled the bag from the backseat to the front. The stereo played low. A street sweeper passed.

He unzipped the top. Then he made a small, almost imperceptibly exhausted noise. "Oh God, Lydia," he said.

He held the blue box containing the small weathervane. Beneath the streetlight, the chips and dents on it were clear. The patina on it looked worn and green and smudged with dirt. She had swiped it from the house last month, on her visit home, for no other reason than because at that moment Lydia was sure that it was doomed for the trash, just like everything else in the house, everything that at one point had ever meant something. She had watched her grandmother that night at home. The catatonic misery of disposal. This was the reality of widowhood: she went room to room with a big trash bag. Her grandmother was junking her life.

"You took it," he said.

"I saved it," she said.

He turned it over in his hands. She had admired it perhaps for the same reason that her grandmother had kept it all this time on the mantel downstairs. It always seemed important to remember that men rendered liberty as a woman.

"She's been looking for this," her father told her.

She took it from him. "I found it at the house last month," she said. "She was going to throw it away." She saw his face. She winced.

"You came home and you didn't let me know," he said.

On the underside of the statue she could see where it had snapped off the roof. She ran her hand along the jagged fissure. "I'm guessing you're not happy about me coming home and not telling you."

He nodded.

"I should have called you," she said.

"It's okay," he said.

"You missed me," she said. "I know."

"I got pretty used to having you around," he said.

She bowed her head.

"We were buddies," he said. "Right?"

She looked up at him. It had so often been just the two of them, him and her, she and he.

"I figured I had at least another few years before you began to openly ignore me."

"Shitty thing to do, I know," she said.

He shrugged. "Sad thing."

"Does it help to say that I didn't really think about it?"

He started to laugh. "That you didn't think about me?" he said. "Oh, yes. That makes it so much better."

"Is there something I can say that doesn't make me sound like an awful person?"

He thought about it. "You could say that you just wanted your mother," he said. "That's never not an acceptable thing to say."

She thought about it. "Are you sure?"

They got out of the car. The neighborhood was quiet. She heard her footsteps on the sidewalk. He fell behind her, looking around. She stopped. He was not certain which building was which. She could tell. He was lost. The facades had been changed or washed or painted over. Overhead clouds obscured the moon. Ferries in the water blew their horns beneath the George Washington Bridge.

When her father finally oriented himself, they stood on the curb in front of the building where she had been a baby, and she reached out to take her father's hand. Lights were on in every window. Tree roots bulged the sidewalk. This isn't it, he said. He looked disappointed. This can't be it. So shitty, so dirty, so trash-strewn, so poorly maintained. They had taken her here, home from the hospital, on her second day on earth, and her father had carried her up into the apartment. They had gone up, she'd been told, so incredibly slowly, step by step by step, afraid she might break.

While her father walked up the block, she crossed the street and sat on a bare stoop and took out Charlie's phone. The screen had his fingerprints on it. Her immediate instinct was self-preservation. Were there any more pictures of her? Could he continue to torment her? She had hoped this part would be easy. She would merely, just easily delete everything. Photo after photo would vanish. All of them. Her body, his bed, her shame, the last weeks—all of it would vanish. But it didn't work like this. Maybe he had already deleted everything himself. Maybe she was looking in the wrong place. She flipped aimlessly, searching for something, anything, to delete, until, finally, she landed on a note with her name in it.

Thoughts on Lydia

She looked, scrolled. He had written nothing. He had, apparently, no thoughts on her at all.

She found this, for whatever reason, hysterically funny. Her laughter rebounded across the empty street.

"Are you okay?" her father asked.

Behind him, at the end of the street, beyond the tree line, across the river and past the boats, lights glinted on the shore in Jersey. He came running.

# Part
# IV

# 34.

The afternoon before Lydia's suspension ended, Henrietta took her for lunch in downtown Boston. They left in the early afternoon, taking the Green Line trolley from downtown Aveline. She would have preferred to take Lydia to a proper meal, she told her on the train as it wended aboveground through the snowy fields and the frozen city reservoir, but proper meals necessitated actual money belonging to an actual bank account that she hadn't overdrawn. Which was why they had come here.

It was a Monday in mid-February and the streets were quiet and mostly empty. They emerged near the Christian Science Plaza, the ledge of the reflecting pool flush with pigeons and skateboarders, the fountain water frozen over. She took Lydia's hand as they got closer. From here it was difficult to tell that anything had changed. She had known all along that this was not the case, of course. Jerry Stern had told her. He sent along updates every week, at first. They had taken down the sign, he would tell her. Or they removed the awning, the door, the flower boxes. You know the back steps where the cooks smoked cigarettes? That was gone. Or do you remember the big sugar maple and how the roots bulged the sidewalk out front? They

dredged the whole goddamned block. She had to tell him to
stop updating her. She didn't want to know.

Cities changed. She knew this. It was the old story. Eventually everything gets knocked down. The Penn Station of her
youth, gone. Ebbets Field, gone. The back alley of the restaurant in Manhattan where Harold had taken her on that first
date—Honey's on Fifth—it, too, was gone. She had resolved
to remain unaffected by this, if only because she considered
the alternative to be juvenile. Others cared. Others wept when
houses were razed. Others wrote letters to the local architec-
tural boards, the city zoning commissions; other people stood
out in the rain protesting the demolition of something particularly crucial or holy or historically important. She, on the
other hand, believed it to be progress. Athens burns, Athens is
rebuilt. One day Honey's on Fifth serves a particularly divine
*escargots à la bourguignonne* that contributes in some small
way to you falling in love with your husband, and then, a
decade later, it is transformed into a rather bland condominium tower, indistinguishable from the hundreds of other
bland condominium towers in Manhattan. Whom did it benefit to be the madwoman standing out front on the sidewalk,
informing passersby about what used to be? *My mother cheered
Jackie Robinson here!* Or: *My husband kissed me here for the
first time! Right here! In that alley where the rats are scurry-
ing!* She could remember standing outside Penn Station the
day the demolition cars were unloaded onto the street. If
that magnificent building could be demolished, then anything
could. She and her mother and her aunt Essie went uptown
to 34th Street that day, specifically to see all the machines
gathering on 8th Avenue—the bulldozers, the front-end loaders. Her mother and her aunt both worried that the city's
willingness to kill such a beautiful building was an indication
that the country was doomed. Her mother and her aunt stood

out on the sidewalk with some degree of glib satisfaction on their faces—satisfaction because their anxieties had been confirmed. They were women who had worried every day of their lives—worried about their children, about their poverty, about whether or not they were actually and sufficiently American. They were women inured to disappointment, to hot factory floors, to misery, to all the countless stories their friends told them of their families being murdered, of generations lost. Henrietta was spared all of this. She was wholly American, born the year after the Fascists lost. If she was inured to anything, she was inured to bliss and peace and the swell of people on the uptown 6 train. She was nineteen that October, a college sophomore, reading Hegel and Martin Buber and gathering at night at the Judson Church to organize about the rights of women and black people and underpaid workers and destitute children. What was so important about a building, anyway? Buildings go up and buildings come down, do they not?

So it should not have surprised her to see this.

The Feast was a taqueria now. *Boston Taco.* A terrifically large neon sign blinked in a rhythm, first the letters going *T-A-C-O-S,* and then the words *Fast, Good, Eat.* Henrietta stopped a block away. Lydia, sensing her apprehension or her queasiness or maybe just the shock of feeling the loss all over again, squeezed her hand tightly. A long line drifted out the front door. Nothing remained. The new owners had gutted the front face, exchanging the pair of small windows on the front wall for a single clean sheet of glass. These same small windows on whose sills diners who had needed to wait outside for a table often rested their glasses of wine on summer nights. The lantern lights mounted to the brick wall were gone, as were the bricks.

"Should we go in?" Lydia asked.

Henrietta stood frozen across the street. Was it better this way? To see no trace of it left? To see such a terrific crowd here when for so long there had been nothing, nobody, just the empty pavement, the blank sidewalk?

"I think we should go in," Lydia said, crossing Huntington and all but dragging Henrietta along with her.

"Why?" Henrietta asked.

"So we can eat food," said Lydia.

Standing here on the block like this reminded Henrietta of opening night, when the crowd was equally large and she had come carrying Oona. She started to say this aloud but stopped.

"What is it?" Lydia asked.

She waved the thought away. "It's nothing you haven't heard, probably," Henrietta said.

Once they were inside, she saw that the entirety of the dining room had been rearranged so that the cooks and the dishwashers and the diners were all in the same room. Surely this was a matter of economics. Doing away with Harold's kitchen, his pantry, his pastry section, allowed for more tables, more people, more money. But this arrangement, with the cooks here and the customers in a line watching while a man with a cleaver split so many dozen chicken breasts, disallowed the romance and the art of food, disallowed the hungry impatience of waiting for the kitchen door to fly open and reveal a man balancing a tray of perfectly braised osso buco. This was something, she was sure, that nobody cared about. Everything was clean and gleaming white.

Lydia took a seat by the window.

"This is nice," Henrietta said.

"Is this nice?" Lydia asked, looking around. "It's sterile. Everything is blank and white. It's like eating in a laboratory."

"I meant being here with you," Henrietta said. "Not the restaurant."

Lydia allowed a shy smile. "Right."

The conversation was not easy. They had been together most

of the morning and this was the extent of it. Henrietta had not done this enough. Been in a restaurant with just her grand-daughter. Traveled on a train with her. In the beginning it was the kind of thing she had imagined would happen more. Decent grandmotherhood, she had always suspected, depended on be-ing able to do this well—to dote, to dispense wisdom, to spoil an unduly precocious young person with gifts and irreverent hu-mor and perhaps an illicit afternoon glass of white wine. Had she written down her goals for being a grandmother, this kind of thing would have been part of her hopes.

"Did Grandpa even like tacos?" Lydia asked.

"I don't know, actually," Henrietta said, which felt like a ter-rible thing not to know.

"Do you recognize anything about the place?"

She looked around. They were crammed tight beside the next table. This was a difference. The lack of breathing room, the absence of privacy. Stark high-contrast photography hung on the walls showing happy-looking pigs and sustainable-seeming fields of corn. She had met Spencer for the first time in this exact spot. She had come here the night *The Inseparables* was published, sat probably in this same spot. They had cel-ebrated Oona's sixteenth birthday here, Harold's fortieth, fiftieth, sixtieth.

"What about you?" she asked Lydia. "Do you remember anything about this?"

Lydia thought about it. She had been a girl when it closed. "I remember butter," Lydia said. "A tremendous amount of butter."

This made Henrietta happy. "If that's all you remember, then you really do remember it."

From here tiers of scaffolding obstructed the front face of Symphony Hall. In the beginning they served all the best musi-cians, the conductors, the most prestigious visitors. Harold once curried enough favor to have a cellist take them around that first season. The orchestra was in rehearsals. Henrietta dressed up for the occasion. This was Harold's way to get her to see that there was culture here. Those first few years he worried that she would pack up and go back to New York. She got to sit on the edge of the stage while Beethoven played. Harold wore a big grin. They were new parents. She carried Oona against her chest, she remembered. But maybe this was an inaccurate memory. It could have been a different year. A different season. Maybe Oona had run around the stage. Maybe Oona was older then. Henrietta resisted these thoughts. Time goes. Memory changes. Everything shifts.

"The only thing that's really the same is the view," Henrietta said finally. "That, at least, is the same."

Lydia looked to see. The busy wide avenue crowded with midday traffic. The noise. The columns on the Christian Science church. The gray sky. The birds. The bare trees.

"I only went to dinner with my grandmother one time," Henrietta said.

"Was it as nice as this?" Lydia asked, laughing as a man bumped into her, spilling a splash of diet cola onto the table.

"I remember her saying, 'Life is tough. A bird could come through the window right this instant and impale you.'"

Lydia squirmed. "Yikes."

"She was a very sweet woman nonetheless."

"Seems that way."

"My grandmother didn't speak much English. She was giving me advice, I think."

"Advice on what, exactly?"

"I don't remember. Birds? Windows?"

Lydia swept a loose bothersome strand of hair away from her face. She had become graceful. Maybe last month it had happened. This small motion was evidence. A particular elongation of her fingers as they glanced at her hair. An ability to passively inhabit more than one place at one time: the past and the future, boarding school and a taqueria, the Internet and also the present real moment.

"If your grandmother didn't speak English, then what did you speak about?"

"Nothing important that I can remember," Henrietta said.

"I don't believe that. Didn't she live in the apartment down the hall from you? You never talked?"

Henrietta nodded. "Sometimes she would worry in front of me. About all sorts of things. Food. Death. Nuclear conflict."

"In English?"

"You can talk about worrying without using words." She made the shape of a mushroom cloud with her hands. "Especially nuclear war."

Traffic crawled slowly outside. A car pulled into the empty space by the front window. It was the exact model and color of Oona's car. Henrietta watched Lydia's eyes open with a tiny glimmer of optimism. This never leaves. The hope for your mother. The car parked. It was not Oona.

"Don't look so disappointed," said Henrietta. "I'm not a monster."

"It's just that we've never done this before. It's not personal. I just don't know what to talk about."

"We can talk about anything."

Lydia folded her hands in her lap. Her deep impatient breathing was the most awful sound.

"Except death and money and Israel and the weather," said Henrietta, "we can talk about anything."

"If those are your subjects to avoid, then mine are pornography, humiliation, men, technology."

Henrietta smiled.

"What does that leave for us, then?" Lydia asked.

"Paris. Jazz. Swimming. Chocolate. The good things."

Lydia put her hands flat on the table, every one of her finger-nails jagged with bite marks. Maybe Henrietta was wrong about her granddaughter's impending grace and elegance. But here at least was something Henrietta's grandmother would have seized on, three generations between them: these half-moons of dried blood on Lydia's fingertips. Worry!

Lydia slipped the familiar pink book onto the place mat.

"Or that," Henrietta said, moaning, pointing, using a napkin to push the book away and back onto Lydia's lap. "I forgot to add that to my list."

"Too late," Lydia said. "I read all of it."

"Your poor brain."

"I read every word and every caption on every diagram."

"Did you feel your intelligence and good taste dissipating with every passing page?"

"I have some notes," Lydia said.

"Oh, *you're* going to critique me, too!"

"First, compared to the Internet this is a children's book."

"Oh, it seems tame to you?"

"Ridiculously tame," Lydia said.

"I'm passé now. Is that it?"

"Second, I don't get why you're still so ashamed of it. You shouldn't be."

Behind Henrietta meat sizzled on a griddle. "That's nice of you to say, Lydia."

"I'm being serious. What can we do to make you feel better about this?"

"More than once I've tried burning a few copies," Henrietta said. "It doesn't completely alleviate the suffering. But it helps. We could go burn this one outside. There's a place behind the building where Harold and I used to roast meat. Maybe we can ask them to put it on the grill behind us."

Lydia was unmoved. "The fact is that if you'd published this thing under your husband's name, nobody would have paid attention. Another book about another man putting his dick in another woman. Who could be bothered to care about that?"

Henrietta regarded her. The sure smile. The casual easy command of a whole orbit of sexual politics and social woe. Who was to say whether this was actually something Lydia knew about, something perhaps accrued over six months in southern Vermont among the filthy and the filthy rich, or whether every fifteen-year-old girl, having been cyberogled or harassed on the catwalk of the local shopping mall, could so swiftly diagnose her book the way Lydia just had?

"That was the big mistake," Lydia went on. "Then you could have had your characters fucking twice as many people in hot-air balloons. It wouldn't have bothered anyone, or violated any inherited social taboos."

"Listen to you," Henrietta said.

"What?" Lydia said defensively.

"Clearly Hartwell has done wonders for your critical acumen."

Lydia shrugged. "I was the stupidest person there."

"I can't see how that was possible."

"Aside from the politicians' kids, who were practically illiterate." She put her hand out in front of her and pantomimed a ladder. "Senators' kids were at the bottom. Then there was me."

"I hope you decide to go back," Henrietta said.

"Of all people, I'd expect you to have the opposite opinion," Lydia said.

She had yet to decide whether or not to go back. At home, Henrietta knew, Lydia had her things packed for Hartwell, her navy uniform laundered and pressed, her course work completed. But she had also made inquiries about going back to the school in her town, the regular school where they taught regular math and literature. Henrietta saw it both ways. Why return to a place full of boys who had anonymously harassed her, and with an administration that had reacted so tepidly? But why give them the satisfaction, and the victory, of allowing that harassment to keep her away?

"You have to move forward," Henrietta said. "That's my opinion."

"I've considered it," Lydia said. "Shame is a choice. Isn't that what you said?"

"Did I say that?"

"You did."

"It's not as unrealistic as it sounds."

"I've also considered hiding out. Getting full-body plastic surgery. Moving to Brazil. Living on the beach. That seems potentially rewarding."

Henrietta pointed to the book. "I looked into that once, too."

They were quiet awhile. The line out the door grew longer, wrapping itself down the block. For the briefest instant, it was easy to forget that she had ever been in this room before. Buildings go up and buildings come down. Maybe this was a good thing.

Lydia put her purse on the table. "I almost forgot," she said. They had already negotiated the handoff of the weather-vane. Spencer had called, and then Oona had called, and finally Lydia had done so as well, which was, as far as Henrietta could remember, the first time Lydia had ever called her on the telephone. In a way, this was the real reason they were having lunch—so that Lydia could hand it over, which she did, with a chastened grin. Henrietta wanted to take a moment to savor having it again, but, holding it in her hands finally, she wasn't sure whether the money to be garnered from selling it would be worth all of the past few days. She wanted to say to Lydia, *Do you know how much this is worth?*, but she knew that a fifteen-year-old had no concept of money, and that Lydia would very likely assume that she meant emotional worth or psychic worth or anything apart from what some person in an auction house might pay for this. She held it in her hands for a moment and then quickly put it away in her bag on the seat beside her.

Light glimmered on Lydia's forehead. Henrietta took her granddaughter's hands, which were cold and soft.

"We have done this before, you know," Henrietta said. "You were just very young."

"That doesn't count."

"It was you. And it was me. We actually were together. On earth. Alone. At the same moment. I think that counts."

Lydia leaned forward. "When was this?"

"The day after you were born."

"Oh, that definitely does not count!"

"It most certainly does count."

Lydia shook her head.

"I came down to New York to your parents' apartment. You've probably heard them talking about it. I'm sure they make it sound like the Ritz. But it was the most cramped, awful place. They'd filled it with all these cookbooks. It was always so dusty. Your mother had been telling me before you were born, *Don't come, I can manage.* Or, *Don't come, I need time to be with my husband and my new baby and adjust.*"

"Sounds like her."

"The closer you got the more colorful she got. *If you dare show up I'll get a warrant served on you.* Delightful things. She was so charming when she was young. So this is why I wasn't there when you were born. I wanted to be there in the hospital with your mom. But Harold and I just walked all around the farm that whole morning. We looked like maniacs, I'm sure. Regardless, the first night, four in the morning, your mother calls.

This is the first night you're alive. I sit up in bed. We think that you're dead. Well, not we. *I* think you're dead. That's where my mind tends to go when it worries."

"Death?"

"Yes. Death."

"That's productive."

"It keeps me sharp, I think," Henrietta said. "Anyway, your mother calls from her apartment, breathing heavy, clearly in a panic, having realized, I'm sure, that you were not a dog."

"A dog?"

"You see, they had looked after a friend's dog a few weeks before you were born, thinking that it was a practice human. And she was convinced that because they'd kept the dog alive they could keep you alive, too."

"So you came," Lydia said.

"I show up right away. Your mother is sleepless. Your father is sleepless. I put them both to bed. Like they're children themselves. I tucked your mother in. Kissed her on the forehead. Then it's you and me."

Lydia smiled. "Basically a party."

"This goes on for a week. I would take over when your mom and dad needed to sleep. That whole time, though, my mother is calling. She wants to see you. She wants me to bring you down to the old building. She refuses to go that far uptown because the walk to Riverside Drive from the subway at 86th is too far. The walk, my mother claims, will actually kill her. I didn't want to wake your parents up. So one day I take a chance while they're asleep, grab some diapers and breast milk, and take you out."

"This is not a true story."

"You're practically a hundred and fifty hours old."

"This seems so unlikely."

"I swear this is true."

"If it is, if you're not lying, I bet she adored you for this."

"I show up downtown. My mother's weeping, holding you up like you're an offering to the gods. You know: two hands, above her head, right up to the heavens. *Another generation! Life! We've survived!* Soon the whole place is filled with my family. My uncles and my aunts. My cousins. The tiny kitchen is packed. My mother is making everyone terrible wine spritzers. Someone brought in sandwiches. It's eleven in the morning. We're drunk. Aside from some minor crying, you're the happiest little thing. More people come over. I have family upstairs on the fifth floor. They come down. I have family in the building next door, they come over. My aunt Essie, she's holding you, kissing your little head, rubbing your tiny feet, talking gibberish to you in Yiddish. Everyone wants to hold you. My cousins Ruthie and Seymour and Morton. Everyone's gawking at you, saying you look like so-and-so, some great-uncle dead for a hundred years. Or everyone thinks you look like some ancient aunt murdered centuries ago by some marauding gang on horseback. Oh, it was very special and wonderful."

"And then my mother woke up and freaked out that you exposed her one-week-old child to all these old-world germs?"

"Oh no," Henrietta said. "I eventually took you back uptown. I hired the two of us a very fancy town car. We were up and back in ninety minutes. You sat on my lap. I hugged you tight to me. It was my old route to high school, actually. It was nice to be back in the city. I had missed it. You were very good. And by 'good' I mean you were asleep. And we came back and your parents were still out. They never knew about it."

"Really?"

"I never told them."

"Oh, I'm not good with secrets," said Lydia. "Everything gets out once I get ahold of it."

"You should know it, though. Your family. You should know that they knew you."

"That they drank wine spritzers over my infant body and held me up to the heavens as an offering?"

Henrietta smiled. "They're all dead, those people. Every person in that kitchen but me."

"Oh good, a nice story with a happy ending."

"I'm almost positive that you never saw any of them ever again. Your mother never liked them. They were old and she thought they were mean people. Petty, mean people full of outmoded ideas and ugliness. Which is true to a certain extent. She worried, I think, that she had those people in her. Their ugliness. And she worried that you'd have it, too. As if these things were communicable. She never understood that they were people who lived their whole life in these tiny rooms that were too hot and too cold and too crowded. That they had no money. They lived their whole life in the neighborhood, never got out. They were very rough people. Happy people, but rough. But they met you—you should know. All of them. Your family. They picked you up and kissed you and it was wonderful watching them passing you around, every one of them taking pictures. Your little baby face was on all of their refrigerator doors."

Lydia leaned forward wordlessly. The crowd in the restaurant had grown so large that it had become difficult to hear. For Henrietta, it was an old memory of what it was like to have this place so full of life. The sign on the front window pulsed. *T-A-C-O-S. Fast, Good, Eat.* Neon off, neon on, oil-slick, making prisms in the puddles outside. The window had fogged. Henrietta smiled at her granddaughter.

"What else can you tell me?" Lydia said. "What other important things do I need to know?"

"Life is tough," Henrietta said. "A bird could come through the window right this instant and impale you."

# 35.

On the first of March, Henrietta surrendered the keys to her house in a lawyer's office forty stories above Boston. She made the exchange in a conference room with a view of the whitecaps on Boston Harbor. The attorney who took the keys and approved the final stack of papers was sipping heartily on a diet soda, and for weeks afterward Henrietta would associate the loss of her house with that awful but appropriate sucking noise that a straw makes when there's nothing left in the can.

Afterward, she went back to the house that Oona had rented for the two of them. It was a small place, painted white, with a fenced-in yard where she kept Harold's rooster. It was close to the old house, close enough that she could walk there without much difficulty, and close enough that when the construction crews were taking it down, months afterward, in the dead heat of summer, she could hear the thrumming of the engines on the front loaders as they passed by on the way to tear apart her roof. For weeks afterward, before the new buildings went up and when the meadow was full of goldenrod, she would walk up to the top of the hill to see the view that she'd had from her kitchen window.

This was where she finally opened Harold's suitcase, in the

middle of July, having pulled it behind her on the mile walk from the house, through the woods and up the hill. It was late and near dusk. The lights were on in town. Behind her, where the house had stood, there was new grass. Fruit hung in the trees. A year from now there would be an entirely new neighborhood here, dozens of homes, everything different, everything changed. But at that moment she was alone.

There was a story she remembered reading once about the men who opened Tutankhamen's tomb. Before Howard Carter's men broke the rope-tied seal on the doors to the burial chamber in the Valley of the Kings, it had been closed for three thousand years. As the story went, immediately after they lifted the lid on the gold coffin, Carter's men saw that a garland of flowers lay wrapped around the neck of the boy king. Olive leaves and blue cornflowers and poppies, still colorful and intact. For a moment they all stood over it—the gold box, the tiny wrapped body, and this ornate string of flowers placed around his neck, maybe by his mother. When Carter finally reached to touch the flowers, they disintegrated into dust in his hands.

She thought of this when she opened Harold's suitcase. Because it smelled of him. Not of his cologne, which she had sprayed everywhere these last months, or his aftershave, which she had also, in a fit of olfactory mawkishness, splashed on her cheeks occasionally this last year, but of whatever it was that had made him. It took her a moment to register this. She stayed out on the hill and in the high grass until the sun set. Oona was mostly right. Inside was the clothing for the trip they did not take. And the books about Spain they did not read. And the tickets for the flight they did not take. Then, at the bottom, she found the note. If she was being honest, she'd admit that this was what she wanted all this time. A small white envelope, sealed shut. *To you*, it said, *from me*.

When she smelled him, she immediately shut the suitcase.

Surely some essence of him remained in this small, cheap thing, and it was getting out. She hugged it close to her, and then, to herself, out loud, she said, *This is just a suitcase I am hugging. Nothing more.*

A minute passed. The sound of the river grew loud. She took everything out then, piece by piece, and stacked it beside her on the grass, all his clothing, the books, the tickets, everything in two equal stacks. A gust came across the valley, and she left the suitcase open and empty and let the air come and rush in and clean it out.

Before she got up to go, she turned to see it again. The flat earth. The hills. All the good acres and the wind in the trees.

Remember this.

# Acknowledgments

For his wisdom and friendship and for his general constant excellence, I remain continually indebted to PJ Mark, who helped with this book in so many thousands of ways, and whose good humor and belief made it all possible. I owe a great deal to Stephanie Koven for her advice, for her encouragement, and for being such a great reader. Thank you to Marya Spence for seeing what this book was before I did. Thank you to Reagan Arthur for your patience and insight and for making this book better. Thank you to Laura Tisdel for your help pushing me across the finish line. To everyone at Little, Brown who helped in ways big and small: thank you. Thank you to Megan Mayhew Bergman for your friendship and for reading this book when it needed reading. And thank you to Nell Beram and Karen Landry for catching everything I missed.

And to my wife, who is the most brilliant person I know, and who makes everything so much better: I love you.

# *About the Author*

Stuart Nadler is the recipient of a 5 Under 35 award from the National Book Foundation and a graduate of the Iowa Writers' Workshop. He is the author of the novel *Wise Men* and the story collection *The Book of Life*.

# *The Inseparables*
## Questions and Topics for Discussion

1. A major theme in *The Inseparables* is the necessity of figuring things out on your own despite the best efforts of parents (and others) to offer advice. In what ways do Oona and Lydia learn from the mistakes of their parents? In what ways do they make the same mistakes all over again?

2. In our increasingly digital age, as we put more and more of our lives online, is anything truly private? In what ways do Henrietta and Lydia fight against the idea that there is no longer any privacy?

3. Why is Henrietta so embarrassed by her novel *The Inseparables*? Is it the book's graphic content, its commercial appeal, its conflict with Henrietta's feminist principles, or something else entirely that makes her reluctant to embrace a new edition? How would you feel in her place? Have you ever felt haunted by your past in a similar way?

4. Could Lydia gain any insights into her own situation by reading her grandmother's book? What specifically could *The Inseparables* teach her?

5.  Do you think there's anything that Oona and Spencer should have done differently as parents, knowing what they know now?

6.  As Henrietta prepares to sell the house she shared with her husband for years, she uncovers secrets about the man she loved and thought she knew better than anyone. Are unexpected revelations more painful or less painful when discovered after a loved one has died? Does Henrietta view these secrets differently because she knows she can't ask her husband for answers?

7.  *The Inseparables* features several romantic relationships in states of disarray. What's the most stable, or successful, romantic relationship portrayed in the book? What is it about that bond that you think allows it to endure?

8.  Do you think Oona is still in love with Spencer?

9.  In what ways do the mother-daughter relationships on display in *The Inseparables* remind you of your bond with your mother or your own children? How is the mother-daughter relationship contrasted with the father-daughter relationship over the course of the book?

10. How does the title of Henrietta's book inform the novel as a whole? What does it mean that both Henrietta's book and the book in which Henrietta is a character share a title?